The Alphabet Sisters

Monica McInerney grew up in a family of seven children in the Clare Valley wine region of South Australia. She has worked in children's television, arts marketing, the music industry, public relations and book publishing and lived all around Australia and in Ireland and England. She is the author of seven novels which were international bestsellers and have been published in translation in Europe. Her most recent novel, *Those Faraday Girls*, is published in spring 2008. She now lives in Dublin with her husband.

For more information please visit
www.monicamcinerney.com

Also by Monica McInerney

A Taste for It
Upside Down Inside Out
Spin the Bottle
Family Baggage
Odd One Out
Those Faraday Girls

The Alphabet Sisters

MONICA McINERNEY

PAN BOOKS

First published 2004 by Penguin Australia

This edition published 2008 by Pan Books
an imprint of Pan Macmillan Ltd
Pan Macmillan, 20 New Wharf Road, London N1 9RR
Basingstoke and Oxford
Associated companies throughout the world
www.panmacmillan.com

ISBN 978-0-330-46383-6

3 5 7 9 8 6 4 2

A CIP catalogue record for this book is available from
the British Library.

Printed and bound in the UK by
CPI Mackays, Chatham ME5 8TD

Visit **www.panmacmillan.com** to read more about all our books
and to buy them. You will also find features, author interviews and
news of any author events, and you can sign up for e-newsletters
so that you're always first to hear about our new releases.

To the Rum Sisters:
Ruby, Ulli and Mikaella

Acknowledgements

My thanks and love to my mum Mary, my own slightly alphabetical sisters Lea, Marie and Maura and my brothers Paul, Stephen and Rob for helping from afar with geographical details, waitressing tales, parenting tips and medical facts. My love and thanks also to my two Irish families, the Drislanes and the Dolans.

Thanks to Max and Jean Fatchen in South Australia for their recollections of General MacArthur and so much more besides; to Marea Fox and Andrew Storey in Queensland for their motel stories; and to my friends in the Clare Valley, especially Greg Cooley, Val Tilbrook, Tricia Jones and all at the Clare Library. Thanks also to Eveleen Coyle, Fiona Gillies, Nid Sangeengong, Sabine Brasseler and Michael Boyny.

Thanks to my agents, Jonathan Lloyd at Curtis Brown in London and Fiona Inglis of Curtis Brown Australia. My big thanks too, to my three publishers – everyone at Penguin Books Australia, especially Clare Forster, Ali Watts, Kirsten Abbott and Cathy Larsen; Imogen Taylor and all her team in Pan Macmillan in London; and Alison Walsh and all at Tivoli/Gill & Macmillan in Ireland.

Finally, and most of all, my love and thanks to my husband John.

CHAPTER ONE

London, England

'YOUR SISTER is married to your ex-fiancé?' Jessica's voice rose to such a pitch Bett Quinlan half expected the light bulbs to explode. 'We've worked together for nearly two years and you tell me this now?'

Bett knew right then she had made a big mistake. 'It didn't ever really come up until now.'

'Something like that doesn't need to come up. That's something you tell people within minutes of meeting. "Hi, my name's Bett, short for Elizabeth. I work as a journalist in a record company and my sister is married to my ex-husband."'

'Ex-fiancé,' Bett corrected. She tried to backtrack. 'Look, forget I mentioned it. I'm fine about it. She's fine about it. He's fine about it. It's not a big deal.' Liar, liar.

'Of course it's a big deal. It's a huge deal. And they'll both be at your grandmother's party? No wonder you're feeling sick about it.'

'I'm not feeling sick about it. I said I was a bit nervous about going home for it, not sick.'

'Tomato, tomato. Oh, Bett, you poor thing. Which sister was it? The older one or the younger one?'

'The younger one. Carrie.' Bett felt like the words were being squeezed out of her.

'And what happened? Were they having an affair behind your back? You came home from work early one day and caught them at it in your marital – sorry, engagement – bed?'

'No, it wasn't like that.' Bett stood up. She'd definitely made a mistake. That afternoon at work she'd decided to invite her friend and colleague Jessica back for dinner to tell her the whole story. She'd hoped it would help make this trip back to Australia easier. Prepare her for people's reactions again, like a dress rehearsal. But it wasn't helping at all. It was excruciating. She ran her fingers through her dark curls, trying to take back control of the situation. 'Can I get you a coffee? Another glass of wine?'

'No thanks. Don't change the subject, either. So did you go to the wedding?'

'Would you prefer tea?'

Jessica laughed good-naturedly. 'Come on, Bett. You brought it up in the first place. Think of it as therapy. It can't have been good for you to go around with a secret like this bottled up inside you. Did you go to the wedding?'

Bett sat down again. 'I didn't, no.'

'Well, no, of course you didn't. It would have been too humiliating, I suppose.'

She blinked at Jessica's bluntness.

'Did your sister use the same wedding invitations? Just cross out your name and put hers instead?'

'That's not very funny.'

Jessica gave a sheepish smile. 'Sorry, couldn't resist. So who was the bridesmaid? Your older sister? Anna?'

'No, she wasn't there either.'

Jessica frowned. 'None of her sisters were there? What? Did it cause some huge fight between all three of you?'

In a nutshell, yes. 'It was a bit like that.'

'Really? You haven't spoken to either of your sisters since the wedding?'

'No.' Bett shifted uncomfortably in her seat. 'Or seen them.' Not since the weekend of the Big Fight. Which had followed the Friday of the Revelations. Which had followed the Weeks of the Suspicions. 'Not for three years.'

'Your grandmother's party will be the first time you've seen your sisters in *three* years?' At Bett's nod, Jessica gave a long, low whistle. 'This is more complicated than I thought. No wonder you went so weird when that fax from your grandmother arrived.'

'I didn't go weird.'

'Yes, you did. Have you got any photos of your sister and your fiancé together?'

'Why? Don't you believe me?'

'Of course I do. I just need to get the whole picture of it in my head, so I can give you all the advice you need.'

'I'd rather you didn't –'

'Please, Bett. You know how much I love looking at photos.'

That much was true. Jessica was the only person Bett had ever met who genuinely enjoyed looking at other people's holiday photos. She wouldn't just flick through a packet of snaps either, but would inspect each one, asking about the subject, the setting, the film speed used.

Jessica was being her most persuasive. 'I'm sure it will help you. This way I'll know exactly who you're talking about.'

'Thanks, anyway, but –'

'Bett, come on. You've told me half of it. I may as well see the rest.'

'Look, I –'

'Please-please-please . . .'

Bett gave in, picking up the small photo album lying on top of the bookcase in the corner of the room. At least it would take Jessica only a few minutes to get through them. She had left South Australia in such a hurry three years earlier that she hadn't taken any of her photos with her. The only ones in her album were those her parents and Lola had sent with their letters.

As Jessica gleefully started turning the pages, Bett retreated to the tiny kitchen with the dirty dishes, feeling sick and steamrolled. Thirty-two years old and she still hadn't learnt how to stand up for herself. For a fleeting moment she wondered how her sisters would have reacted in the same situation. Anna would have given Jessica a haughty stare and chilled her into silence. Carrie would have tossed her blonde head and told her laughingly and charmingly to mind her own business. But not Bett. No, she'd just felt embarrassed about having said too much and then handed the photo album over anyway. She decided to blame the wine they'd had that night for this sudden need to show and tell all. Nine parts alcohol, one part truth serum.

She came back into the living room and picked up a music magazine, trying to pretend she wasn't watching Jessica's every reaction as she pored over each photo. For a while the only sound was pages turning, interrupted by Jessica asking the occasional question.

'Is that your mum and dad?'

Bett glanced at it. A photo of her parents, arm in arm in front of the main motel building, wearing matching Santa hats, squinting into the sunshine. They'd sent it in their Christmas card the previous year. 'That's right.'

Jessica read the sign behind them. 'The Valley View Motel. Is that where you grew up?'

'We moved around a lot when we were younger, but that's where they are now.'

Jessica nodded and turned the page. 'And this is Lola? The old lady wearing too much makeup?'

Bett didn't even have to look at the photo. 'That's her.'

'Would you look at those eyebrows! They're like caterpillars on a trampoline. She was your nanny, did you tell me?'

'Sort of.' Nanny always seemed too mild a word to describe Lola. She'd certainly minded them as children. With their parents so occupied running the motels, it was Lola, their father's mother, who had practically brought up Bett and her two sisters – but she was more a combination of etiquette teacher, boot-camp mistress and musical director than nanny.

'Is she wearing fancy dress in this next photo?'

Bett glanced over. It was a picture of Lola beside her seventy-ninth birthday cake, nearly twelve months earlier. She was wearing a gaudily patterned kaftan, dangling earrings and several beaded necklaces. Nothing too out of the ordinary. 'No, that's just her.'

Jessica kept flicking the pages, and then stopped suddenly. Bett tensed, knowing she had reached Carrie and Matthew's wedding photo. Bett had wanted to throw it away the day she received it, but had stopped herself. She hadn't wanted her grandmother to be right. It was Lola who had sent the photo to her, enclosing a brief note: 'You'll probably get all dramatic and rip this up but I knew you'd want to see it.'

'This is them?' Jessica asked.

'That's them.'

Jessica studied it closely. 'Carrie's very pretty, isn't she? And he's a bit of a looker too, your Matthew. Nice perm.'

At least Jessica hadn't said what people usually said when they remarked how pretty Carrie was: 'You don't look at all alike, do you?' As for her other remark . . .

'He's not my Matthew. And it wasn't a perm. He's got naturally wavy hair.'

Jessica grinned. 'Just seeing if you defended him.' She turned the page and gave a loud hoot of laughter. 'Now we're talking. I've been dying to see proof of the Alphabet Sisters. Look at you with that mad head of curls.'

Bett tugged self-consciously at that same head of curls, now at least slightly less mad. Lola had sent her that photo, too. It had arrived with just a scrawled note, subtle as ever. 'Remember the good times with your sisters as well.' It had been taken at a country show in outback South Australia more than twenty years previously, at one of the Alphabet Sisters' earliest singing performances. Anna had been thirteen, Bett eleven, and Carrie eight. Bett could even remember the songs: 'Song Sung Blue', 'Swing Low, Sweet Chariot' and a David Cassidy pop song. Just minutes after the photo had been taken, a fly had buzzed its way straight into Anna's mouth. Her shocked expression and sudden squawk had made Bett and Carrie laugh so much both of them had fallen off the small stage, a wide plank of wood balanced on eight milk crates. The memory could still make Bett laugh.

Jessica was inspecting it very closely. 'You were a bit of a porker back then, weren't you?'

The smile disappeared. 'Well, that was nicely put, Jess, thanks.'

Jessica was unabashed. 'I always believe in calling a spade a spade. And you were a plump little thing. Look at that little belly and those rosy-red cheeks.'

Bett didn't need to look. That little belly and those rosy-red cheeks had never gone too far away. She was about to ask Jessica if she still thought she was a porker – she had gone up and down in weight so many times she hardly knew what size she was – but Jessica was too occupied with the photo. She was taking in every detail, the flicked fringes, the matching dresses, the bad make-up – all Lola's handiwork.

She glanced up at Bett. 'Not exactly the Corrs, were you?'

Bett laughed despite herself. 'I bet they didn't look that good when they were teenagers either.'

'I bet they did. Have you ever wondered if there's a fourth Corr sister, a hideously ugly one they keep locked away?' Jessica looked at the photo again. 'You're not very alike, are you? Even apart from the appalling eye makeup and the different hair colours. Unless they're wigs?'

'No, all our own work, I'm afraid.' Anna had straight black hair, Bett's was dark brown and Carrie's dark blonde. She presumed her sisters' hair colours hadn't changed in three years. She'd find out soon enough. In less than two weeks, in fact. Her stomach gave a lurch.

The fax from Lola in South Australia had arrived at Bett's work out of the blue, just the one line. If Bett didn't come home for her eightieth birthday party, she would never talk to her again.

Bett had rung her immediately. 'Lola, don't do this to me, please,' she'd said, straight to the point as soon as her grandmother answered. 'You know what it'll be like.'

'Elizabeth Quinlan, stop being such a baby. You're scared of seeing your sisters. So what? I'm nearly eighty and I've got a lot more to be scared of than you have. I could die any moment. Now, hang up, book your ticket and get here as soon as you can. I've got something I want you to do.'

Lola had obviously taken her extra-strength bossy tablets that day. 'I can't drop everything just like that, Lola. I've got a life here now.'

'And you've got a grandmother in Australia who has missed you very, very badly and wants to see you again.' Her voice had softened. 'Please, Bett. Come home. For me.'

Bett had thought about it for two days, veering between excitement and dread at the idea. One image had kept coming to her. Lola, standing in front of the motel, beaming at her, waiting to give her a hug. In the end Bett had compromised. Yes, she would come back for the party, but it would be a lightning trip. She'd arrive in South Australia the day of the party and then leave as soon as possible afterwards.

Lola hadn't been at all pleased. 'But I need you here for longer than that.'

'I can't, Lola. I've got a life here,' she'd repeated firmly. It had been a strange sensation. She wasn't used to standing up to her grandmother either.

Beside her, Jessica was going through the album again. 'It's a tricky one, that's for sure. No wonder you're so nervous. Your first meeting with your sisters and the happy couple in three years, all of you in the same motel, not to mention the added tension of a party . . .'

Bett nodded, waiting for her friend's sound advice, the helpful comments.

Jessica shut the album with a snap. 'I'd say it's going to be ferocious.'

Sydney, Australia

Anna Quinlan knew that outside the sun was shining. That less than a kilometre away the waters of Sydney Harbour were probably glinting in the sun, to a soundtrack of ferry horns, gull cries and tourist-guide commentaries.

But it could have been the Sahara Desert outside. She'd been trapped inside this coffin of a recording studio for three hours now, trying to get the voice exactly right for a new range of kitchen sponges. She'd decided the client was not just from hell, but from somewhere much deeper, hotter and even more unpleasant.

She peered through the glass of the studio window again, counting to ten as she caught sight of him. He looked like a suit-wearing spotty child who surely couldn't have driven himself to the studio today. He didn't seem old enough. She snapped back to attention as Bob, the producer/technician, pressed the button on the intercom so his voice came into her headphones.

'Anna, Henry feels you are really getting there, but he wonders whether you could combine the laugh in your voice from that first take with the kind of bubbling tone you did on the one before that last one, and add a little more lightness to the whole thing.'

Henry leaned forward, speaking into the microphone as though he was an MC at a football-club presentation night. 'Yes, loved that bubbly sound, Anna. Just perfect for our demographic. You don't mind, do you?'

Mind? Mind that she had spent three hours saying one sentence in dozens of different voices? Mind that the preschooler in the suit had tried to describe the mindset of a kitchen sponge – a kitchen sponge! – to her? 'It's determined, it's energetic, it's fun . . .'

No, it's not, Henry, she'd thought. It's a three-inch square of detergent-soaked sponge with a scouring pad on one side that you do dishes with. It isn't Russell Crowe.

She bit her tongue. Whatever you do, Anna, don't let them see you're upset. Keep cool, keep smiling, keep up the front.

She'd learned that lesson after years of unsuccessful auditions for parts. No one wanted a moody actress. It was much better to be tagged as a thorough professional, even if it was sometimes mistaken for haughtiness. And at least Henry had definitely decided that the sponge was female. Today's booking had been set up, cancelled, then set up again while Henry, his advertising agency and his market-research team argued over the best gender for their new sponge.

Anna looked at Bob for help. He was just chewing, as normal, and hitching up his trousers, unfazed, also as normal. She knew he didn't care how long the client took. He charged an hourly rate.

Some of her frustration must have shown on her face. Bob took pity on her. He spoke again, surreptitiously inclining his head towards the client. 'Anna, perhaps it would help if you visualised yourself in the sink, getting psyched up to help your housewife – sorry, homemaker – clear all those dirty dishes. And there's one particularly greasy pot that's going to need special energy, but you know it will be worth it to scrub like mad until every spot is gone.' Another barely noticeable nod at the client. 'Whenever you're ready. Tape's running.'

It worked a treat. Staring through the glass, seeing her sharp bobbed hair and immaculate makeup reflected back at her, Anna imagined Henry evolving into a dirty, grease-spattered saucepan. She imagined herself as the sponge, leaping out of nowhere and scouring his face until every spot and blackhead had disappeared, shouting all the while in a voice that was a combination of Mary Poppins and kamikaze pilot. She leaned towards the microphone. 'Let me at it! I'm the clean machine!'

Henry's pimply face broke into a huge smile. 'That's it. Perfect. Thanks, Anna.'

She had just leaned down to her bag when his voice came in again. 'But would you be able to do it one more time? I think it needs just a touch more softness, to convey the moisturiser we've included in the washing-up liquid.'

An hour later Anna was driving out of the studio carpark. The voice of the sponge was now lodged in her head and she knew from experience it would stay there for the next few days or until a new character's voice took its place. Last month her internal voice, her mind voice, had varied between a kitten stuck up a tree (for a cat food commercial), a warm-hearted nurse in an old folks' home (health insurance) and a cake waiting to be iced. That had taken three hours to get right too, before Bob stepped in once again with her motivation. 'Imagine you're the cake, Anna, okay? You're scared. You don't know which brand of icing you're about to be iced with but you sure as hell want it to be high quality. So we need a combination of fear and anticipation and . . .'

Her seven-year-old daughter, Ellen, loved it, of course. She treated Anna's repertoire of voices like a human jukebox. Lying sleepily in bed listening to a goodnight story, she'd pick and choose the voices. 'Mum, can you read this one like the Zoomer Broom?' The Zoomer Broom featured in an animated TV commercial where the ordinary household broom metamorphosed into something Harry Potter could have used for Quidditch, babbling nonsensically all the while. Ellen's other favourite was the ocean pie, a gurgly underwater voice.

Anna parked on the street across from the hospital, ten minutes late. Hurrying towards the lift, she composed her face, already hearing the disapproving tones from her neighbour, who had grudgingly agreed to collect Ellen after school and bring her here to the clinic for her latest appointment. The lift door opened and Anna spied her little daughter in the distance, standing up on a chair near the nurses' station, chatting to one of the staff. In the dozens of hospital visits since Ellen's accident, she had got to know all the nurses very well. Anna tensed, as she always did when she remembered the trauma of those first months. She decided it was time Ellen had a good spoiling: she'd give her whatever she wanted for dinner, let her watch whatever video she wanted, and then read her all the stories she wanted, as well.

By nine o'clock Anna's patience was wearing a little thin. Ellen had been alternately tearful and cranky all evening, insisting on pizza, then not eating any of it, and not settling on any one video but wanting to watch specific scenes out of five different ones. Anna had finally had enough, speaking more crossly than she intended, which set off the tears again. She then read two extra stories, purely out of guilt, hardly finding the energy for the different voices.

Ellen still wouldn't settle, hopping in and out of bed. She stood in the doorway of the living room now, tears on her face. 'Is Dad home yet?'

Anna kept her voice mild with effort. 'No, darling, he's not.'

'Where is he?'

'At work, I think.' She thought. She didn't have a clue where Glenn was. He didn't ring and tell her any more if he was going to be late, or if he was going to be home at all, in fact.

'Can you read me another story, then?'

'Sweetheart, you've had enough stories. It's time to sleep.'

'I can't sleep. I'm scared again. I keep remembering.'

The doctor's voice came into Anna's mind. 'There will be some post-traumatic stress and recurring fear, but it's important you learn to listen without making too much of it. Children are children and very skilled at knowing which buttons to press.' So what was she supposed to do? Ignore Ellen's tears? Tell her to get over it? Of course she couldn't. She pulled herself up out of the deep sofa. 'All right, Ellie. You hop back into bed and pick another story. I'll be there in a moment.'

By the time Anna got to the bedroom, Ellen had changed her mind. 'Can I have a tape instead? Can I hear Really-Great-Gran's tape?'

'Again? You sure you don't want a story tape?'

Ellen lay back and shook her head. Her dark hair fanned out on the pillow.

The tape had arrived from Lola more than two years earlier, with a note to Anna attached. 'This is for you to play to Ellen. I'm still having no part of this nonsense between you and your sisters but I'm not losing a great-granddaughter because of it. Please play her this tape so I'm not a shock each time she meets me.'

Anna put the tape in, then lay on the bed beside Ellen, stroking her hair back from her face as Lola's voice filled the room. Her still strongly Irish-accented tones were clear and precise.

'Hello, Ellen. This is your great-grandmother speaking. Now, my little dote, I've been giving a lot of thought to what you should call me and I think I've come up with the best solution. Your scoundrel of a mother started calling me Lola when she was just a child and her two sisters followed suit, but you need a different name for me, I think. And not just Great-Grandmother. I'm much better than great. So, my darling, I would like you to call me Really-Great-Gran from now on. Okay?'

There was a pause on the tape.

'Are you listening, Ellen?' Lola asked.

'Yes,' Ellen answered sleepily beside Anna.

The voice on the tape continued. 'Good girl. And are you happy with that? Happy to call me Really-Great-Gran?'

'Yes, Really-Great-Gran,' Ellen answered in the pause. She knew this ritual off by heart.

'Good girl. Now, I'm going to tell you a few stories about your mother and your grandfather, but first I'm going to sing you one or two of my favourite songs. So settle back and relax.'

Relax? Anna bit her lip as Lola started warbling 'Don't Sit Under the Apple Tree' in her falsetto voice. The last thing Lola's voice would make you do is relax. She could clear a room in seconds. Ellen didn't seem to mind. Lola could have been singing a sweetly tuned nursery rhyme, the way Ellen was reacting. Her lids were getting heavier by the second, her lips mouthing the words along with her great-grandmother's slaughtered version. Anna smiled, remembering the song. It was one of the first ones Lola had taught Anna and her sisters. There'd been a row over who got to sing the high notes. Carrie had won, hadn't she? Or was it Bett? It certainly hadn't been her, cursed with as deep a singing voice as her speaking voice. She'd always sung the bass parts.

Lola reached a shrieking crescendo, then paused on the tape, as if expecting her performance to be followed by rapturous applause. 'One of my favourites, Ellen, and one of your mum and aunts' favourites too. As is this one. Are you comfortable? Sing along with me, darling.'

As Lola embarked on 'The Good Ship Lollipop' Anna glanced down. Ellen was fast asleep.

Back in the living room, Anna poured herself a glass of wine and pressed the TV remote control. She stared at the screen, trying to pick up the plot of the thriller, fighting the desolate feeling inside her that seemed to be rising closer to the surface each day. One phrase kept occurring to her. *I'm lonely.* Lonely. Yet she had friends in Sydney, didn't she? People she could meet for coffee? And hadn't there been joint friends, other couples who came over for dinner or who they met in restaurants occasionally? Not any more. They had all slipped away the past year or so, like extras in a film, Anna thought, silently stealing away and leaving the main action to unfold. She couldn't blame them. Who would want to be around to see how she and Glenn treated each other these days?

The TV program changed to advertisements and Anna noticed without pleasure that it was her voice coming out of the mouth of the animated mobile phone on the screen. She'd done that one two years ago now and here it was back again.

She put down the glass and rubbed her face with her hands. Who was she fooling? She didn't want to talk to Glenn or any Sydney friends or colleagues. She wanted to talk to her sisters again. She wanted Carrie to sympathise with her. She wanted Bett to cheer her up with some madly melodramatic account of how bad her day had been. She wanted to tell them both how awful things had become with Glenn, especially since Ellen's accident, but how wonderful Ellen herself had been, most of the time.

She could ring her mother or father at the motel, but she'd never really confided in either of them. It had always been too hard to get the timing right. They'd be either in the kitchen cooking for house guests, or out in the bar or doing the accounts, or any of the hundred things both of them always seemed to be doing. She could ring Lola, but lately those calls hadn't been having the calming effect they used to. For the first year or two after the big fight, Lola had been understanding, trying to see each of their points of view, as she always had.

Understanding had turned to exasperation. 'This is ludicrous. I'm ashamed of the three of you, carrying on like this.' She'd tried the frosty approach for a while. 'I'm not talking to any of you while you persist in this ridiculous carry-on.' But then Lola had missed their phone calls too. 'Just because I'm talking to you doesn't mean I've forgiven any of you.' But for the past six months there had been silence on the subject. Perhaps she'd realised, as Anna herself slowly had, that that was that. It had gone on too long now for things to change.

A scream on the TV made Anna jump. A young blonde detective was being chased down a dark street by two men in suits, her face in close-up, fear-stricken. 'Oh, shush, would you,' Anna said aloud. 'You're just acting, for God's sake.' She put the remote control on the shelf under the coffee table. As she did she noticed the mail in a pile, wrapped inside the free local newspaper. How long had that been there? She picked it up and checked the date – more than two weeks old. How many times had she asked Glenn not to leave the mail there? Is this what it had come to? Each of them deliberately doing the things they knew most annoyed the other?

She flicked through the bundle. Bills. Advertising material. A fundraising letter from Ellen's school. And a thick cream envelope. She turned it over, recognising the handwriting immediately. Puzzled, she tore it open. It was an invitation. She read it again. No, not an invitation. A summons.

Clare Valley, South Australia

Lola Quinlan turned her gaze away from the vineyards visible through the window of the Valley View Motel dining room and back to the table where her youngest granddaughter was sulkily folding serviettes. 'Did I tell you what happened in the charity shop this morning, Carrie? A young woman, around about your age, perhaps a bit older, came in and said, "Could I try on that dress in the window?" And I said, "Yes, of course, but I'd much rather you used the changing room."'

Carrie didn't smile or look up. 'You've been telling that one for years, Lola.'

'Good jokes never die, you know. What did the zero say to the eight? Nice belt.' She glanced at the elegant gold watch on her thin wrist and stood up. 'Time for *Days of Our Lives*. I'm not going to offer you any help because you're doing such a marvellous job of it yourself. And you know how important I think it is for you young people to see a job through from start to finish.'

Carrie ignored her, not looking up as her grandmother came closer.

'Carrie, are you ignoring me?'

The younger woman kept her head down.

'That's fine, but don't frown like that, darling. It's very bad for the skin. If you're going to sulk, at least do it with a smile on your face. Or try doing those exercises I showed you, the ones that firm your chin. See, like this.' Lola started grimacing, stretching her lips sideways, then into a tight pout; out, then in again. 'Twenty of those a day and it's like a gym workout for your face, so I read. A little alarming for any passers-by, but that's the price we pay for endless beauty, isn't it?'

Carrie started to smile.

'That's more like it,' Lola said. 'And I know what you're thinking and, yes, I am a wizened interfering old bag of bones and quite happy to be like that.' She leaned over and kissed her granddaughter on the top of the head. At five foot nine, her posture still excellent, Lola towered over Carrie. 'But I still love you, you know.'

'If you really loved me, you wouldn't have –'

'Yes, I would have.' Lola collected her handbag. 'Will you be staying on for dinner tonight? Thursday, schnitzel night.'

'No, I'll go home, I think.'

'How are those renovations going?'

Carrie and her husband had bought an old farmhouse several kilometres south of the Valley View Motel the year before. 'Fine. Slowly.'

Lola was watching her. 'And how is Matthew, Carrie?'

Carrie turned back to the serviettes. 'He's fine. Up to his eyes in sheep manure and vet magazines as usual. You know the sort of thing.'

'You're getting on all right, are you?'

'Yes, thanks.'

'Really?'

Lola was like a human sniffer dog, Carrie thought, still not looking up. Line up a row of people and she'd sniff out each of their problems instantly. Not this time, though, Carrie decided. The days of confiding in her grandmother were well and truly over. 'Really. It's a bed of roses, in fact.'

'Rubbish. No marriage is a bed of roses. That at least was one of the positive things about Edward dying so young. We might have missed out on the good times but we missed out on some of the bad, boring times as well.' Lola was amazed, as always, at how easily the lies about her husband tripped off her tongue. 'Tell me, do you ever get bored with Matthew, Carrie?'

'Tell me, do you ever think you're overstepping the mark with your questions, Lola?'

'Oh, good Lord, yes. But people are usually so shocked, they've answered me before they've had time to think twice. Do you know what I found out this morning? That Mrs Kennedy is stepping out with her son-in-law's father at the moment. Talk about keeping it in the family. Having a grand old time, she told me.'

Carrie felt a rush of combined affection and annoyance, her usual reaction to Lola's behaviour. 'That's the only reason you're still working in that charity shop, isn't it? It's nothing to do with helping the poor or keeping yourself busy.'

Lola made an elegant gesture with her hand. 'If people choose to tell me things, there's nothing I can do about it. I see it as my gift to society: helping people unburden themselves of their problems.'

'Digging the dirt on them, you mean.'

'I noticed you changed the subject, by the way. Don't think that's the end of it.'

'I don't know what you're talking about.'

'Oh, I think you do. Now, then, I must be off. I'm going to call on your mother in the kitchen and beg some afternoon tea. I really do have the perfect set-up for an old lady, don't I? A son and daughter-in-law with their own motel and restaurant and a granddaughter who is the sweetest in the world.' Lola gave Carrie another kiss, then swept out of the room, leaving a faint trace of expensive perfume behind her.

Alone in the dining room once again, Carrie worked quietly until she had folded the last of the serviettes. With a loud sigh, she leaned back in her chair. One hundred paper swans surrounded her. This time in two days the room would be transformed for a wedding reception, the paper swans swimming elegantly up and down the rows of long tables. She'd already strung up the fairy lights the bride had requested. She'd ordered the special candles from Adelaide and they were due to arrive any moment. The bridal arch had proved tricky for a week or so. It would all come together, though. She'd done it enough times to be sure of that.

She sat back and flicked at one of the paper swans with her finger. It toppled, falling against the swan beside it, which also toppled. Within moments a whole row of them had fallen, domino-style. She could have jumped up and stopped them but instead watched idly as the last dozen or so flipped and rolled onto the unswept floor.

She didn't care. At that moment she was sick of it all. She was sick of her job. She was sick of the motel. She was sick of the fact people made such a mess while they were eating that they needed serviettes in the first place. She was feeling especially sick about her grandmother wanting to throw a birthday party for herself and insisting that Bett and Anna attend.

'But why, Lola? Why now? It'll ruin everything,' Carrie had said that morning, hoping she wasn't giving too much away. 'All that tension.'

'I've given you all three years to sort it out and you haven't even got to the starting gate. So I'm taking charge once and for all. I've written to both of them as well. Insisted they come or else. So they will, I know.'

Carrie opened her mouth to protest but one of Lola's quelling looks had blasted her way and she shut it again.

Scooping up the paper swans now and ignoring the state of some of their wings, Carrie replayed the conversation yet again. If only Lola had turned eighty a few months ago. A year ago, even. But no, it had to be now. And she had to insist on throwing a party. A huge party.

'You wouldn't be happy with a nice family dinner, you and me and Mum and Dad?' Carrie had suggested hopefully.

'Of course not. I could die any day and I want to go out with a bang. And I want Anna and Bett to see the explosion. Besides, I've got something very important I want the three of you to do for me.'

'Important? What's wrong? Lola, you're not sick, are you?'

'Don't pry, Caroline. I said I want to talk to the three of you about it. Once I have the three of you in the same room together again.'

The three of them. The three of them who hadn't spoken to each other for years, let alone been in the same room. Or the same town. Or the same country even. And whose fault was it?

Hers.

Who did everyone blame?

Her.

But now it had all changed, hadn't it? The reason none of them had spoken to each other in that time no longer existed. Which would make this reunion of Lola's even more hideous and humiliating and horrible than it would normally have been.

Carrie took her anger out on the last of the paper swans, crumpling it up in her hand and then immediately feeling guilty. 'Sorry, swannie,' she said out loud, smoothing the serviette and readjusting the little paper beak. It now looked like it had been in a washing machine. She tucked it away in her pocket. The way her luck was going this one would end up on the bride's place-mat and she'd cause a scene. Carrie had already spent enough hours calming the young woman, as she'd fretted about everything from the number of prawns to be served in the prawn cocktails to the mathematical probabilities of it raining on her wedding day.

Carrie had wanted to snap at her more than once. 'You think the wedding day is stressful? Try getting through the marriage.'

She jumped as the bell at reception rang once, twice, a third time. Right now she'd had enough of guests, too – especially guests who rang the bell more than once. She walked out, plastering a smile onto her face, knowing it was just several teeth short of a grimace. At least she was exercising her facial muscles. Lola would be pleased.

'Good afternoon,' she said to the waiting couple, her voice sickly sweet. 'I'm very sorry to have kept you.'

CHAPTER TWO

A WEEK before her flight back to Australia, Bett walked into the record company's office in the centre of London, took off her raincoat, sat down and slowly, rhythmically, banged her head against the pile of papers on her desk.

'Great new move,' Jessica said, wandering over. 'Can't see it taking off in the clubs though.'

Bett looked up, her head still on the desk. 'You should have seen this one, Jess, heard the things he was saying.'

Sprawled on the sofa in the plush Kensington hotel room, the young pop singer had fixed Bett Quinlan with a sincere blue gaze and tossed his head so a lock of blond hair shimmered across his forehead. 'I want to grow with my music but stay close to my beginnings. Most of all, I want to keep it real.'

Bett had blinked twice at him and tapped her pen against her teeth. Keep it real? That could be tricky. With all the makeup and hair gel he was wearing it was already hard to tell where his body stopped and the cosmetics industry took over. As for staying close to his beginnings – he was barely out of his teens as it was. Any closer to his beginnings and he'd be back in a pram.

There'd been a long awkward silence before he finally shifted in

23

his seat and shot her another of his well-practised blue gazes. 'Well? Was that answer okay?'

Answer? She'd already forgotten the question. Her mind had been drifting to Lola's birthday party. Come on, Bett, concentrate. She gave herself a mental shake. 'Sorry, Grover.'

'Groover.'

'Pardon?'

'My name's Groover, not Grover.'

'Groover, sorry. Yes, that answer was great, thanks. Well-rehearsed. Well-delivered.' She ran her eye down the list of sample interview questions in the notebook in front of her, fighting an inclination to pick Groover up, tuck him under her arm and make a run for it. She could tell people he was her foster child. Her butler. Anything to get him out of the music industry before it had eaten him alive, pretty face, sweet singing voice and all.

'Where are our consciences, Jess?' Bett asked now in mock despair. 'We're sending young men to their deaths, armed with nothing but microphones.'

'Rubbish. We're sending them on their way to fame and fortune. Don't tell me you're getting all pure about music again. You child performers are all the same, pining after more innocent times, when all it took to put on a good show was a few matching outfits and a tinny backing track.'

'Yes, hilarious.' Jessica hadn't stopped teasing her about the Alphabet Sisters or the situation with her sisters since the night in Bett's flat. 'You're very cruel, you know. I thought you'd promised to leave me alone about all of that.' She should never have mentioned it to her.

'No, I promised to help toughen you up about all of that. Anyway, I can't leave you alone. I have to give you another assignment. Karl wants you to get onto it straight away.'

'He deigned to ring?' Since their boss had floated the record company on the stock market and become an instant millionaire he hadn't found it quite so necessary to come into work every day.

'Well, a quick call. Then he faxed. He's in Spain, I think. Or Portugal. He told me he wants to work you to the bone till you leave on Friday. Said he must have been off his head giving you that week off to go to your granny's party.'

'He was, actually.'

Jessica put the folder on the desk beside her. 'It's this new band from West London he's signed. He wants you to whip up a quick article for the instore mags.'

'But I can't write about them. I haven't seen them play live yet.'

'That's because they haven't played live yet. Probably never will play live. Don't even know if they can play live. Here, have a look.'

Bett took the biogs and photo. Five children in heavy eye makeup sneered at her. If they were hers she'd tell them to wash that muck off their faces and go and do their homework. 'What are they called?'

'Dogs from Hell. Except Karl calls them Puppies from Hammersmith.'

Five Go Mad in Mummy's Makeup, more like it, Bett thought. 'What on earth's Karl thinking this time?'

'He's hoping it'll revive punk. He bought the back catalogue of all these old punk bands and he wants to give them a kick-along.'

Bett looked at the photo again. 'So they're angry young musicians?'

'Oh, very angry,' Jessica laughed. 'They're furious. Cross as two sticks. Haven't stopped stamping their feet since we signed them.'

Bett turned the sample tape over, then rattled it, as if that would give her a taste of their music. The tape machine was broken and the CD player was currently propping up a bookshelf. 'What do they sound like?'

Jessica emitted a high-pitched screech, shook her head so her hair flew around, then sang in a guttural voice. '"Ravens in the night, kill the beast, anarchy rules", that kind of thing. Except on the first demo they sang an-Archie. As in the man's name. Isn't that sweet? They can't even read.'

Bett pretended to weep as she opened a new document on her computer screen. As she wrote she started speaking the words aloud in a dull monotone, silently saying goodbye to any final shred of journalistic credibility.

They're young, they're angry and they're here. London's newest music sensation, Dogs from Hell, has arrived with a bang and a wallop . . .

She stopped there, finding it hard to concentrate. More to the point, finding it hard to care about the sulky-faced brats who she knew had been chosen for their looks rather than any musical talent. She stared out the window instead, suddenly filled with gloom.

She'd been working in the press office of this small but very successful record company for two and a half years, writing media releases and puff pieces for record store magazines, as well as training their artists in interview techniques. At the start it had been a dream job, a combination of her love for music and for writing. But lately it had started to wear her down. She'd been feeling the same way about London, even though she had loved it when she first arrived. Little things seemed to be getting to her.

The night before she'd been working back late, coaching a new rap singer in radio interview techniques. It had been past nine o'clock when she left the studio, caught the tube home and started the fifteen-minute walk from the station to her basement flat, one of eight in a large three-storey Camden Town terrace house. She was tired, hungry and cold by the time her street was finally in sight. She was five steps from her door when she remembered taking her keys out of her bag that afternoon when she searched for her diary. Four steps away when she remembered seeing them on her desk and thinking 'don't forget those'. And two steps away when she realised she'd left them at work.

'In you go, then, love.' The locksmith had taken less than ten seconds to open her door. It had, however, taken him nearly two hours to arrive. Bett was frozen.

'Thanks,' she'd said, through icy-cold lips, handing over nearly fifty pounds. It was easy to see why he was so cheerful.

'Now, love, far be it from me to put myself out of a job, but have you thought about leaving a spare key with friends or family? In case this happens again?'

She'd nodded, smiled politely. She'd spent the time waiting for him thinking just that, before realising with a dull aching feeling that not only did she have no family here, but no friends close by either. Jessica lived on the other side of London. There were several other people, journalists and a band booker in one of the live music pubs, who she met occasionally for a drink, but she could hardly call them close friends. She couldn't really leave a key with them either.

She blinked now and dragged her attention back to the computer in front of her, trying to concentrate again. Cheer up, Bett, she told herself firmly. She gazed around the office, taking in all the band posters, the piles of CDs, the overflowing files of press clippings. Everything was peachy, wasn't it? She was living in the epicentre of the music industry, she had a great job, she'd never been happier.

Not only that, she was about to fly home to Australia, to see Lola and her parents for a week. And yes, all right, Anna and Glenn and Carrie and Matthew would be there, and yes, it would be awkward and uncomfortable, but she was a grown woman and she'd cope. And it would be great to see her niece, Ellen, again too, wouldn't it? Yes. Exactly. She shut her eyes tight, then opened them again, stared intently at the computer screen and started typing.

Lead singer Mutt Dagger says it's time that real music took over from the manufactured bands. 'Enough of this candy crap. People want truth and energy in their music and that's what we're giving them. This is us telling our stories with our music. And the difference is we're telling it as it is.'

Bett pressed save, then glanced down at the folder of plane tickets beside her coffee cup. She'd spent her lunch hour with her travel agent, running through all the flight details, paying the final instalment. It was only afterwards she noticed she'd conducted the entire conversation with a piece of spinach from her lunchtime salad on her front tooth, covering it so completely, in fact, it looked like she had lost a tooth, in pure witch fashion. On the way back to the office she'd had an overwhelming urge to ring her sister Anna in Sydney, to tell her about it and hear Anna's laughs. Except she didn't make those sorts of calls to her sisters any more, did she? Calls about disastrous days or wild nights, work trials or love lives or friends or recipes or hangovers or . . . anything.

The band combines a youthful energy with pure adrenalin, producing a raw, rocky sound, guitar-edged and bass-driven.

No, they don't, she thought. She typed quickly. *The band do what they're told by a middle-aged man who is living out his own musical fantasies and making a lot of money along the way out of kids reared on reality TV programs.*

She started to growl, a constant, satisfying kind of noise from the back of her throat.

Jessica peered over her own computer screen. 'Bett, are you okay?'

She stopped mid-growl to nod, then started it up again as she kept writing.

The band's drummer, Raven Deathmask, is a self-described anarchist and spotty-faced little tosshead who looks like he may still wear nappies.

Bett pressed delete and tried again.

The band's first album is a remarkable feat of hideous guitar squeals and nonsense lyrics about rebellion when the most any of the spoilt kids in this manufactured band have had to rebel against is –

Stop it, Bett. She pressed delete once more.

Dogs from Hell are a force to be reckoned with, combining youth, anger and bad haircuts –

Bett stopped writing altogether. A new, frightening thought had appeared in large letters in her head.

She didn't want to do this any more. It wasn't about music, it was about packaging. Karl had said as much to her a month ago, on one of his fleeting visits to the office. 'Just a licence to print money, Bett. Stop taking it so seriously. Pop singers, disposable music, remember?'

She looked out the window at the rain, the sky dark at four p.m. She thought of her flat. Small and cold, about as homely as a bus shelter. She thought of the Christmas just past. She had celebrated with Jessica and her family at their home in Suffolk, keeping her voice bright and cheery on the phone to her parents and Lola in South Australia. She'd felt miserable inside.

She pictured the travel agent earlier that day. 'It's such a long way to travel for seven days. You'll have only just recovered and you'll be on your way back. Are you sure you can't stay longer?'

Her words to Lola the day she'd received her fax flashed into her mind. What had she said? That she couldn't come back to Australia because she had a life here in London? What she had here wasn't a life. Not the sort of life she wanted any more, anyway.

The letters in her head were now in flashing neon. There were shadows and doubts underneath – what she would do for work and where she would live, not to mention the idea of her sisters – but she batted them away. She stared over at Jessica, amazed at what she was about to say, and even more amazed by how sure she felt about it. Do it, Bett, she thought. Quickly. Before you change your mind.

'Jessica, can you give me Karl's mobile number?'

The other woman glanced up from her computer. 'You're going to ring him? That's taking your life in your hands. Why would you want to do that?'

Do it, Bett. Be brave. Go home for good. Bett swallowed. 'I think I'm about to resign.'

In Sydney, Anna Quinlan was finishing her packing. She looked up as her daughter came into the room holding a framed photograph.

'Should I bring this, Mum?'

Anna took the photo. It was the two of them, taken twelve months previously, both smiling at the camera, Ellen's perfect six-year-old face upturned. 'Why do you want to take it, Ellie?'

'So I can show Really-Great-Gran what I used to look like. In case she's forgotten. In case she decides she doesn't like me like this either.'

'Ellie, Lola doesn't need to see that. She loves you whatever you look like.'

Ellen's voice became small. 'What if she calls me names, though? Like everyone else does?'

'Oh, Ellie, she won't. Don't think things like that.' Anna tried to keep her voice steady. How was she supposed to handle this? Ask Ellen to hold on a moment while she ran and checked the self-help books? It kept happening – just when Anna thought she had things running smoothly, out of the blue there'd be a question like this. Or a loud child's voice in the supermarket like yesterday.

'Mummy, what's wrong with that girl's face?'

'Shh, don't stare.'

Anna had at least had experience of that situation and knew the best thing to do. She had coolly answered the child. 'It's a scar. My daughter was attacked by a dog last year.' She was half tempted to carry a photo album with her. 'See,' she'd say at times like that, 'she was perfect when she was born. But then I foolishly took her to the park one afternoon and someone had a Rottweiler on the loose and the dog thought my little girl was a toy. And by the time I could drag her away from him his teeth had torn half her face.'

Anna smoothed back her daughter's hair. 'Ellie, your dad and I and your Really-Great-Gran and your gran and your grandpa love you no matter what you look like.'

'My aunties too?'

Anna's voice didn't change. 'Your aunties too. All of us, no matter what you look like, what you're wearing, how messy your hair is and how bad you smell, okay?'

That brought a glimmer of a smile. 'Even if I smell really bad and haven't brushed my hair for a year?'

'Two years even. Now, put that away and let's finish your proper packing.'

Ellen put her hands on her hips. 'I have finished. Can we run through our checklist?'

Our checklist? Anna had been hearing phrase after phrase of her own coming out of Ellen's mouth lately. She bit back another smile, not wanting Ellen to think she was laughing at her. Ellen had answered the phone ahead of the babysitter when Anna rang home several nights earlier. 'May I help you?' Ellen had said. They had spoken for a few minutes before Ellen had asked, in all seriousness, 'And were you ringing about anything in particular?' There was something about these pronouncements, and that solemn little voice and face of hers, that always went straight to Anna's core. She barely noticed Ellen's scar any more. She was aware of it – how could she not be? – but it didn't change the essence of Ellen. The body was . . . what was it? Her casing. The wrapping. Everything else was normal.

Except Glenn hadn't been able to see it that way. In his eyes, things had changed forever and it was all Anna's fault.

'I'm not the first man to feel like this, Anna. This happens to lots of marriages after a child trauma like this. I read it on the web.'

Her voice had grown icy. 'You've been researching reasons to back up why you're having an affair? Why you're walking out on us?'

'I'm not walking out on you.'

'Shall we look up the web for other ways to put it, then? Key "selfish" and "immature" into a search engine and see what websites turn up?'

'Anna, you're not making this easy.'

She had lost her temper then, hardly knowing what she was

saying. 'Glenn, I don't want to make it easy. I want to make it as excruciatingly hard for you as I can.'

Ellen had heard them fighting, Anna knew that. Ellen also knew Anna and Glenn were sleeping in separate rooms. And that her father wasn't home every night. Anna wanted to tell Ellen it wasn't her fault. He still loves you, Ellie, I know he does, she thought. It's me he doesn't love any more. It's me he blames.

Perhaps things would have been different if they'd been on steady ground before Ellen was attacked. But the foundations had been eroding for years, gaps and holes slowly appearing. Fights about his work taking up too much time. Snide remarks about her great acting career ending up in sound-recording booths. Even digs about her appearance. She'd put on a few kilos a year or two after they married, nothing too serious, so she'd thought. It had been nice to stop the endless weight watching and calorie counting that came hand in hand with a career as an actress. Until Glenn had brought home gym brochures, made pointed remarks about people letting themselves go.

'Me?' she'd said, good-humoured at first. 'Glenn, are you joking? All my clothes still fit, don't they?' Size ten at that. 'I thought you'd like to see me a bit more curvy.'

He hadn't smiled. 'I just want you to look your best.'

And that phrase had been the key, she'd discovered. He loved her, wanted her, when she looked her best. But not when her voice-over work increased and the travel between appointments lengthened and she started to get too tired to work out, wear full makeup, work constantly to keep her skin and hair in salon condition. 'Glenn, I'm a human being, not a mannequin. Would you stop going on at me all the time?'

Ellen's arrival had soothed things on one level. Glenn had shifted his attention onto her, showering his daughter with gifts and love, while he withdrew the same things from Anna. Their fights became less regular, the mood shifting from tension to indifference. They talked about Ellen, through Ellen, because of Ellen. He had been only mildly interested to hear about the fight between her and her sisters – he'd never met Matthew and had never got on with Bett or Carrie. His attention had turned to work, while she kept her days busy with Ellen and the voice-over jobs. Sometimes at night he'd be home in time to put Ellen to bed, have dinner with her, but often enough he would go out again afterwards. They were living separate lives under one roof, using guerilla tactics rather than open warfare.

Until the day in the park changed things for the worse. The long days in hospital were followed by nights of tension at home.

'How could you let this happen?'

'I was on the phone. I didn't see the dog coming.'

'You must have.'

'It's not my fault, Glenn. You think I wanted this to happen? That I wouldn't change everything, every single moment of my life, if I could make it not happen to her?'

The blame seeped into every one of their conversations.

Glenn turned further away from her, to his job – and to Julie. Anna was sure of the timing. The late nights working back with his PA had only started after Ellen had been attacked. Likewise, the weekends away at supposed conferences, business trips. She even discovered credit card bills for flowers she hadn't seen and dinners she hadn't eaten. Every corny step of it . . .

'Mum? The list?'

Anna focused back on Ellen. 'Ready when you are. Books?'

A nod from Ellen.

'Clothes? Teddies? Puzzles?'

More nods.

'Sounds good to me. You have enough for two weeks?'

Another solemn nod. 'Will I be able to help in the motel kitchen again? Even help to clean the rooms?'

She and Ellen had been back to the motel twice in the past three years, timing their two-week visits for when Carrie and Matthew were away on holiday. Ellen had enjoyed every minute, trailing behind Lola most of the time. 'Of course you can. Your grandmother would love a hand, I bet.'

'I really like it there.'

'Do you? Why?' Anna waited for her to say something about being in the country, being with her grandparents and Lola again.

'It's peaceful.'

'Peaceful?'

Ellen shuffled a little, wouldn't look at her. 'No one picks on me there.'

Anna's breath caught. A seven-year-old shouldn't be looking for peace. Shouldn't be looking forward to going to stay at her grandparents' because no one would be picking on her. But it was true, Anna knew that. Life in Sydney had been hard for Ellen since the attack. Yesterday's remark in the supermarket hadn't been the first. Her friends at school had changed towards her too, already at an age where appearance mattered. She crouched down and brushed her daughter's hair away from her face, looking straight into her eyes. 'Has it been that bad?'

There was a little pause, the smallest of nods and then Ellen started to cry, noiselessly. Anna took her into her arms and held her tight, feeling her daughter's body shuddering against hers. 'Ellie, it's all right, it's fine, it's all right,' she said over and over again. Ellen's tears didn't stop. As Anna rocked back and forth, soothing her, kissing the top of her head, another part of her mind switched into decision-making mode.

Could they stay on after Lola's birthday party? For a month or two? Longer, even? Since the attack Ellen had become fearful of everything, wetting the bed occasionally, nervous of school, of new people. But perhaps she wouldn't feel like that back in the motel, with family all around. There were good schools in the Valley these days. Could she even school Ellen herself? Of course, her work could be a problem. She doubted there'd be much demand for a voice-over artist in the Clare Valley. But perhaps she could rearrange her schedule, fly up to Sydney for a day or two a week. Or stop work altogether for a while, living off the money that Glenn, regularly, guiltily, was putting into her bank account. As for coping with seeing Carrie and Matthew every day, well, she'd face that when she had to.

Ellen's sobs had now turned into breathy gulps. Anna kissed her daughter's head again and held her tight for another moment, soothing her. 'It's all right, sweetheart. It'll be all right.'

Her voice against her mother's shoulder was muffled. 'I just get scared here sometimes.'

That was all Anna needed. She stood up, lifting Ellen onto her hip as if she was a toddler. 'I've got a good idea, then.' Holding her tight with one arm, she reached up into the wardrobe with the other and pulled out a bigger suitcase.

'Ellie, fill that one as well, will you? We might stay away a bit longer than two weeks.'

In the ladies' powder room of the Valley View Motel, Carrie Quinlan stood staring at her reflection in the full-length mirrors.

She cleared her throat. 'Bett and Anna, there's something you should know before you get here. Matthew and I have separated. And I'm not going to go into the reasons but, yes, I think it's for good.'

No, too apologetic. And maybe it would be better if she broke the news to them one by one. 'Anna, I want you to know something important. Matthew and I have decided to separate.'

Not bad. But then Anna would be the easiest to tell. Carrie took a breath. 'Bett, I don't want you to gloat but I've got some news for you.'

For a second it was as if both her sisters were standing in front of her. She pictured their reaction to her news and her temper flared. She glared at her own reflection and spoke in a fierce voice. 'Yes, I think it is for good. And no, it doesn't prove you right and it doesn't mean I shouldn't have married him in the first place. It just happened.'

She was interrupted by a knock at the door. 'Carrie?'

Carrie blushed, embarrassed. How long had her mother been outside? She didn't answer, stood stock still. She'd locked the door and put up the bright-yellow 'Sorry, I'm temporarily closed for cleaning!' sign, but it obviously hadn't been enough.

Another brisk knock. 'Carrie, did I hear you talking to yourself in there? Can you come and give me a hand moving these tables? We've got a group of Landcare people in tonight.'

Landcare-schmandcare. It was all right for them, talking to each other until the cows came home about soil levels and salinity. If only pH levels were all she had to worry about, instead of a marriage breakup, the imminent arrival of her sisters, Lola's ridiculous birthday party . . .

'Carrie?' The door handle rattled. 'Are you all right?'

Oh, perfectly all right. Couldn't be better. One final glare, a smoothing of her hair and she unlocked the door. 'Sorry, Mum. I'm coming.'

She stepped out just as her mother finished brushing specks of dust off the large banana plant by the front door. As petite as Carrie, Geraldine Quinlan was dressed in her usual trim skirt, crisp shirt and sensible shoes. Her hair was as no-nonsense as the rest of her – short, dark, neat.

She gave her daughter a speculative look. 'Is everything all right?'

'Everything's fine, Mum. Thanks.'

'Are you sure?' There was a little pause. 'You're not sick, are you? Feeling nauseous or anything . . .'

'No, it's not that.' Carrie said, colouring. Several months back, before the final big fight with Matthew, her mother had caught her reading pregnancy magazines at the reception desk. She hadn't said anything, but there had been a quick exchange of smiles.

Geraldine gave her a similar smile now. 'That's a shame.'

'Mmm,' Carrie said, trying to sound upbeat. If her mother only knew how nonexistent that possibility was these days. She gave a fake laugh. 'No, the only thing making me feel sick these days is the idea of Lola's birthday party.'

'You're not alone there.' Geraldine's lips tightened. 'It would have been nice to have been given some warning about it before she sent out all those invitations. I tried to explain to her that events like this need proper organisation, that neither you nor Jim and I can just drop everything. But of course that was like water off a duck's back.'

'I bet it was.' Carrie had actually been talking about the idea of Anna and Bett coming back making her feel sick, not the party itself. But Geraldine had never had any time for those sorts of conversations. She had been very firm about it from the start. 'You are grown women and it is up to the three of you to sort this out in your own good time.' Matthew's thoughts on her mother came to mind. 'That's just the way she is, Carrie. Anyway, you'd hate it if she was the fussy, nosy type of mother, you know that.'

She tuned back in, trying to look sympathetic as Geraldine outlined the latest episode of her silent war with Lola. It seemed she had caught Lola using the office computer to print up some sort of flyer. 'I've asked her not to do it, but she just ignores me. She goes through paper like nothing else, and never thinks to order more to replace it. I had to print out last week's menus on coloured paper, because she'd used all the white paper for a new batch of birthday invitations or some such thing.'

'She'd try the patience of a saint,' Carrie agreed, unconsciously echoing one of Lola's own Irish sayings. The difficulty was Carrie could see both sides. Lola could indeed be the most annoying, interfering, meddling old woman on the planet and Geraldine in turn was sometimes the most inflexible, single-minded, humourless woman in Australia, as Lola had once put it so succinctly. Carrie dragged out another fake laugh. 'Still, I suppose it's not every day she turns eighty.'

'No, thank God.' Geraldine glanced at her wristwatch, a functional one bought purely for timekeeping, not decorative purposes. 'So, can you come and help me move these tables? Your dad's not back from the wholesaler's yet, otherwise I'd ask him. I also want to go through the casual staff rosters with you. And I wouldn't mind your help with the new computer program, either, if you don't mind. I still can't make head nor tail of it.'

'Of course.' This was more like it. Back onto work matters, not the precarious rocky shores of emotions and feelings. Carrie felt much better as she followed her mother into the function room.

CHAPTER THREE

IN THE forecourt of the Valley View Motel one week later, Len the local butcher slammed the door of his delivery van. Short, plump and with a bald pink head, he often joked that he wasn't unlike one of his tasty homemade sausages himself.

'All set for old Mrs Quinlan's hooley tonight, Jim? Sure you don't want me to DJ again?' He started speaking in a bad American accent. '"You're listening to Len's Mobile Disco, spinning the hottest new tracks for young and old."'

Jim Quinlan remembered the last time Len had DJed at a motel function. He'd had to refund half the room booking fee when the twenty-one-year-old and her parents complained. Len had been unrepentant. 'Islands in the Stream' was a classic, a beautiful song, he'd insisted. Not seven times in one night, though. 'Not this time, Len. No thanks. You just come along as our guest and enjoy yourself.'

'It's going to be some party, by all accounts. The two older girls still coming home for it?'

'That's right.' Jim wondered, not for the first time, if his family's daily activities were actually being broadcast directly to television sets around the Valley. Fifteen years they'd been here and he was still amazed at how news travelled. He made a point of looking at his watch. 'They're due any minute, actually. So if you can give me the invoice . . .'

Len gave a throaty laugh. 'The Alphabet Sisters together again. What I'd give to be a fly on the wall at that first meeting.'

Jim kept his face expressionless. It seemed the entire population of the Valley was hoping to be a fly on the wall at this reunion of his three daughters. One spray of an extra-strong pesticide and a good percentage of them would be lying on the floor, legs wriggling. It was a comforting thought. 'Good to know my family's providing so much entertainment, Len. I would have thought you'd have plenty of other things to keep you busy.'

Len was unabashed. 'Girls will be girls, won't they, Jim? I know my two can be tearing each other's eyes out one moment, giggling over a bottle of wine the next. When we first had two daughters I was a bit upset, don't mind telling you that. I wanted boys, sons, to play footy with. Now, I love it. The dramas! No need to watch soapies with them around the place.'

Jim knew Len's daughters well. As gossipy as their father, what they didn't know about people they made up. Well, let them make up what they liked about Anna, Bett and Carrie. The gossip would blow over soon enough, once something else happened in the town to grab everyone's attention. He'd actually admitted to Geraldine he was glad Lola had done what she'd done, bringing the girls back together like this. They'd both felt a twinge of guilt that they hadn't thought of it themselves. But when did they get time to sort out things like that? And neither of them had ever wanted to be the interfering kind of parent.

The phone rang, the sound echoing across the forecourt. Jim knew Geraldine was at the reception desk and would answer it, but

Len didn't. He leaned over and took the invoice out of the butcher's hand himself. 'Better run, Len. See you tonight. And thanks for the meat.'

Geraldine winked over at her husband as he came in through the front door, rolling his eyes. Len drove them both up the wall, but his meat was first rate and he delivered to their door. Holding the phone against her ear with one hand, she took the invoice from Jim with the other, mouthed a thanks and kept talking, even as she carefully filed the piece of paper in the 'Bills to be paid' folder to the left of the computer. From the bar she heard the sound of Jim picking up the plastic bin of empty bottles, ready for a trip to the recycling depot.

She concentrated on keeping the warm, friendly tone to her voice. 'That's no problem at all, Mr Lawrence. And you're still happy with that room? Very good. Thank you very much.'

This Richard Lawrence in room two was turning out to be the perfect guest, she thought as she hung up. Extending his stay week by week, keeping to himself, and so polite. Such a charming English accent too. Geraldine was mildly curious what he was up to – some sort of writing project, she'd gathered, after seeing the computer and the piles of paper spread around his room when she delivered his breakfast or cleaned his room – but she wouldn't dream of asking him for any details about it. Not like some other people in this motel . . .

She made a note in the bookings register and then, using two fingers, carefully typed the same information into the computer on the desk beside her. Carrie had been very persuasive, insisting that it really was very efficient and of course Geraldine would be able to master it. One day, perhaps. She tentatively pressed save and gave a satisfied sigh, just as a blue station wagon pulled up outside.

A casually dressed man with dark hair leapt out of the driver's seat, reached into the back for a pile of newspapers, then took the steps, two at a time and came inside. 'Mrs Quinlan? Your copies of the *Valley Times*, hot off the press. Will I leave them here?'

'Yes, thank you.' He wasn't the usual newspaper delivery man, but he did look vaguely familiar. Then again, so did half the towns-people when you'd lived in a place this long. 'Where's Pat?'

'He had a bit of an accident last night.'

'Not again. Is he all right?'

'Nothing two weeks in a drying-out clinic won't fix.'

'Oh dear. He fell off the wagon again?'

'Not so much fell as took a great, voluntary leap, I think.'

'Who are you talking about?'

They both turned. Lola had come in behind them.

'Pat from the newspaper office,' Geraldine explained. 'The man who normally does the deliveries.'

Lola nodded, giving the new arrival a good close look. His hair was a bit long but she liked those laughter lines around his eyes. 'Well, you're certainly far better looking than poor old Pat. You've taken over from him permanently, have you? Can we look forward to seeing you here every week?'

The man laughed. 'No, I'm double-jobbing. I usually do the photographs, but we've divided up his round between us today.'

She peered at him. 'I know you, don't I?'

'I know you, too, I think. From the charity shop. Lola, isn't it?'

'Cheeky monkey. It's Mrs Quinlan to you.'

A hint of a smile again and a glance at both women. 'It's just there are two Mrs Quinlans here. I didn't want to confuse myself.'

Lola clapped her hands. 'Marvellous. A man with a bit of wit about him. Are you married?'

Geraldine interrupted, exasperation in her voice. 'Lola, would you leave the poor man alone? And would you both excuse me, I need to make a few calls before the girls get here.' Not just make a few calls, but also re-organise the walk-in freezer and brief her stand-in cook about tonight's dinner preparations. Sometimes Geraldine wondered if Lola had deliberately forgotten how much work was involved in running a motel, not to mention organising birthday parties at the drop of a hat . . .

'Of course, my dear.' Lola didn't go anywhere, staring at the man for a long moment, eyes narrowed. 'I have it now. It's Daniel Hilder, isn't it?'

'You've got a very good memory.'

She batted her eyelashes in an exaggerated way. 'I never forget a good-looking face. And I remember you taking those photos when we re-opened the charity shop a few years ago. Remember, all of us old ladies dressing up? It was like a Paris fashion shoot, wasn't it?'

Daniel's lip twitched. 'A bit like that.'

'Lola, please?' Geraldine stood with the phone and a pained expression.

'We're just leaving, aren't we, Daniel?' Lola took him by the arm and steered him outside. 'Now, what are you doing back in the Valley again? I'm sure someone told me you moved away.' Who was it had told her that? Her memory was so slow these days she was surprised people didn't hear creaking sounds coming out of her skull.

'I've been in Melbourne the past few years, but I came back six months ago. My mother's still living here.'

'You were in Melbourne?' Lola remembered then exactly who he was and why she knew his name. Her smile stretched even wider. 'Well, you're a good kind boy to come and see your mother and you're very welcome home. Tell me, would you be a good kind boy to me too? I need a little hand in my room with something. Your newspaper deliveries can wait a moment, surely?'

Daniel looked amused. 'Of course they can. Lead the way.'

Geraldine watched, shaking her head, as her mother-in-law led the man across the forecourt, talking all the while. There'd be a picture needing straightening that Lola supposedly couldn't reach, or a shower rose that was pointing the wrong way or some other imaginary task that would give her the opportunity to grill her poor victim.

God help him, Geraldine thought as she reached for the phone.

'There it is, there it is,' Ellen shrieked.

Anna glanced at her daughter, who had nearly clambered out of the car seat and on to the dashboard in her excitement. 'Where, Ellie? I can't see anything.'

'There, up on the hill.'

Anna pulled the hire car onto the side of the road and looked out the opposite window. She saw vineyards and gum trees, the foundations of a house, and two vans with Clare Valley Builders written on the side in large letters parked beside it. 'I can't see anything. Are you sure?'

Ellen was laughing now. 'Mum, you're looking the wrong way.'

Anna looked down at her feet. 'No, nothing here.' Then she looked up. 'No, nothing there either. Ellie, your eyesight must be much better than mine.'

'*Muuum*.' Ellie unbuckled her seatbelt and leaned over, placed a little hand on either side of Anna's face and turned it in the right direction. 'See, there.'

'It does look a bit familiar. What does that sign say?'

'It says The Valley View Motel. Vacna . . .' Ellen struggled with the word at first. 'Vacancies. Restaurant and Bar. Function room available. What's function?'

'Another word for a party.'

'Is that where Really-Great-Gran's birthday party will be tonight?'

'I think so.' Anna gazed at the motel. Built in the 1970s, it was a perfect example of the architecture of the time: a series of building blocks, placed clunk-clunk-clunk beside one another on the hillside just north of Clare, the largest town in the Clare Valley. There were fifteen guest rooms, one row of seven facing another row of eight, with the extra room the linen store. Linking the two lines of rooms was the small bar, a tiny reception area, a medium-sized restaurant and kitchen and a large function room. Anna had always thought the motel would make the perfect setting for a retro drama series, right down to the brown carpets, white plastic bathrooms, nylon curtains and orange bedspreads.

'Mum, come on.' Ellen was tugging at her arm. 'We're not going to park here, are we?'

'You're sure you're ready? Sure you want to go there?' Anna teased.

Ellen considered the question seriously. 'I am feeling a little bit shy. I haven't seen them for a long time, have I?'

Anna knew exactly how Ellen felt. She was nervous about seeing her sisters again too, she realised. Three years on she still felt caught in the middle – trying to make peace between Carrie and Bett, she'd managed beautifully to make things worse. 'Nothing to be frightened of here, Ellie, I promise you. They're your family, remember?'

Her cheery tone convinced Ellen, but it did nothing for herself. She wished she felt fresher, more ready for this. It had only been a two-hour flight from Sydney to Adelaide, and then the same length drive from the airport to here. She'd always liked the drive from Adelaide to Clare, too. The long straight highway through flat plains and wide yellow paddocks slowly giving way to the curving roads of the Valley, vineyards and tree-covered hills on either side. But she still felt drained. It must be the tension of coming home, she thought. Or the aftermath of emotion from that morning's spat with Glenn. He'd made a point of being there to say goodbye to Ellen.

'You know I'll cry myself to sleep every night while you're away,' he'd said, as he picked the little girl up in a hug. He was so broad it took nothing out of him. Ellen could have been two, not seven.

'Me too,' Ellen had giggled, as Glenn tickled her. She had thrown back her head, laughing, completely unself-conscious with him about her scar.

'And don't forget to do me lots of drawings. And to breathe in lots of that country air.' He had done some mock deep breaths, making Ellen laugh even more. 'And you won't forget you're my favourite daughter, will you?'

Ellen shook her head.

'And not only that,' Glenn continued. 'But the best daughter in –'

'The whole wide world!' Ellen had finished it for him, as she always did.

Anna had received no such attention. She and Glenn had spoken quickly, coldly to each other. She'd been deliberately vague about how long they might be away, knowing it would annoy him. He had reminded her of the possibility he'd need to go to Singapore for business, if the office expansion ended up going ahead. She had pretended she had forgotten all about it, and enjoyed the little dart of annoyance she knew that had sent through him. How had it got so bad? she'd wondered, even as she said goodbye in her most carefree voice. Ellen hadn't noticed a thing – she hoped. She had been too busy waving until her father was long out of sight.

Anna tried to block out those thoughts and smiled across at her daughter now. 'Ready, sweetheart?'

'I'm ready, sweetheart,' Ellen replied, grinning at her own cheekiness. 'But we can't go yet.'

'Why not?'

'You have to look at yourself in the mirror first. That's what you always do.'

Anna laughed. Indeed she did. 'You don't miss a trick, do you, Miss Ellen?' She ostentatiously checked her face in the rear-vision mirror, wrinkling her nose, squinting, baring her teeth, playing up to Ellen's laughs beside her, even as she quickly took the opportunity to dab away a tiny spot of mascara and reapply her lipstick. Then she took a deep breath and started the car.

In the flower shop in the middle of Clare, Carrie glanced at her watch. The young florist noticed.

'Carrie, if you're running late, I can drop these up to the motel for you later today. The party doesn't start until seven, does it?'

Carrie didn't mind if it took all day to prepare her order. She didn't mind if she had to live in the flower shop from this moment on. Anywhere was better than being at the motel waiting for Anna and Bett to arrive.

'Carrie? Do you want me to do that?'

Carrie took a seat beside the counter. 'No, I'm in no rush at all. Honestly, take as long as you like. In fact, why don't I go and get us both a cool drink?'

'The weather hasn't helped, of course. The past week or so it's been more than thirty degrees every day. People want to head for the sea not the countryside. Still, just as well we have a few empty rooms with you girls being home again.'

'Yes, isn't it?' Anna said, trying to keep up with her mother's update on the motel occupancy rate.

Anna and Ellen had walked through the reception area into the kitchen, surprising her mother who had been wrestling with something in the walk-in freezer. Geraldine looked immaculate as ever. Not unlike a 1950s housewife, Anna had always thought. There was a brief hug, then her mother turned to Ellen, bending down, giving her a quick hug and kiss too. 'And welcome to you too, Ellen.'

Anna watched, waiting for some reaction to the scar. It wasn't the first time her mother had seen it. She had come to Sydney after the accident happened, to lend a hand, much to Anna's surprise. But it was the first time she'd seen it in months.

'Well, aren't you both looking great. Ellen, you must have grown three feet since we saw you last.' Geraldine straightened up, put her hands on her hips and stepped back.

That was the physical contact over for the visit, Anna thought. She knew it wasn't her mother's fault she wasn't a tactile person, but it had been hard at times to be her affection-craving daughter. Anna showered Ellen with hugs and cuddles and caresses, more than the child wanted sometimes. Ellen pressed close against her now, still shy, her hair forming a curtain over the right side of her face.

Geraldine busied herself in the kitchen again, passing on news over her shoulder. Anna and her sisters had always laughed at their mother's conversational style. She had to be doing something while she asked questions or relayed information, be it mopping the floor or preparing meals for guests or sometimes, in shouts, over the noise of vacuum cleaners. She'd had the same approach to mothering, in fact – fitting it in around her other, more pressing tasks.

'Carrie will be back in a moment. She's gone into town to collect the last of the flower displays for the party. Bett's flying in today too, of course. Insisted on driving herself up from Adelaide. Lola is around somewhere. I'm surprised she didn't hear the car coming in. Your father had to make a quick trip to the bottle depot this morning but he said he'd be back as soon as he could –'

'He's here now, in fact.'

They both spun around at the sound of his voice. He'd come in through the back door. 'Hello, Anna, and aren't you looking beautiful?'

'Dad! Full of charm as usual,' she said, smiling at him.

'No, just telling the truth. You took after your mother, luckily,' he said with a wink in Geraldine's direction.

Anna was amazed to see her mother get soft-eyed at the praise. Honestly, what were the two of them like? She waited, and sure enough, her father dropped a kiss on her mother's head as he went past her.

'You should be glad your parents get on so well. Mine fought all the time. That's much harder to live with,' Glenn had said in their early days, when she'd tried to explain how excluded she and her sisters had sometimes felt. 'It's unusual, though, I'll give you that. Business partnerships and marriages don't tend to last.' But her parents had always loved working together, putting across a united front, making decisions together, a true partnership. Anna had childhood memories of lying in bed at night, hearing her parents come in from locking up the motel, listening to the murmurs of conversations as they talked over their day, planned for tomorrow.

That's what she'd wanted when she met Glenn. What she'd thought she had when she met Glenn.

Anna reached up to give her father a quick kiss on the cheek, followed by a warm, close hug. He was tall, like Lola and herself, but chubby, not thin, his square, open face red from too much sunshine. She watched intently again as he got down on his haunches to be at eye level with Ellen. She'd spoken to Lola from Sydney before they left, asked her to remind her mother and father to build Ellen up as much as possible.

'And welcome to you, Miss Ellen. And aren't you looking beautiful as well? All set for the party tonight?'

Ellen nodded shyly again, struck dumb by the attention and the new surroundings.

Jim tousled Ellen's hair. 'Good girl. It's great to have you both home again.'

Ellen stared at him. 'It's not really home. My home is in Sydney.'

Jim gave a roar of laughter. 'You can't call a big city like that home, darling. Home is where the heart is. Isn't that right, Geraldine?'

'That's right, Jim.'

'But isn't my heart in my body all the time?' Ellen asked Anna, looking confused. 'Not just when I'm at home?'

'Grandpa's teasing you, Ellie. Don't mind him.'

'Best advice I've heard all day,' an Irish voice behind them said. 'Hello, my darlings. The birthday girl is here.' It was Lola, dressed in a pants-suit made of pink flowing material. She was in full makeup, with a small pink rose pinned in her white hair.

'Lola! Happy birthday!' Anna found herself rushing to meet Lola as if she was a child again herself. Now she knew for sure she was home. Lola turned from her hug with Anna, then leaned down with melodramatic groans to Ellen's height, took her face between both hands, gazed at her for a long moment and then kissed her extravagantly on both cheeks. 'That scar is fading so quickly there must be a miracle at work.'

Anna relaxed. Trust Lola to mention it, to point it out and bring it into the open. Ellen didn't seem to mind, she noticed. She was nodding. 'It is going a bit, I think, Really-Great-Gran.'

Lola gave a shout of laughter and kissed Ellen again. 'You're still calling me Really-Great-Gran, you dear little pet.'

Ellen looked delighted with herself. 'I listen to that tape a lot.'

'You're a little girl with wonderful taste. I know it in my bones.' She stood up with another groan. 'Creaking and feeble as those bones might be. Enough of dilly-dallying with this riff-raff, my dear Ellen. It's time for a tour. And may I introduce your tour leader for the day. Myself, your Really-Great-Gran.'

Ellen beamed up at her. 'But can I call you Lola, now, Really-Great-Gran? Like Mum does? Now I'm here?'

'You can call me all the names under the sun, my little darling,' Lola had said, before sweeping out of the room with her.

Anna looked out the kitchen window now and saw Lola and Ellen walking by the back fence. On one side was bushland, gum trees and scrubby earth covered in dry bark and wiry grasses. The other side of the fence marked the start of the motel grounds, with a strip of bright-green lawn, flowers and bedding plants, all their father's work. It was an island of green amid the dry South Australian landscape. As she watched, a tubby white sheep trotted up behind Lola and Ellen. Her parents had bought it the year before, to help keep the grass down around the motel. Anna saw Ellen's reaction, a shriek and then a push against her great-grandmother, looking for a shield. As her hands clenched, Anna felt her mother's eyes on her and gave an embarrassed smile. 'It's that obvious, is it? I'm trying not to run out there. The doctor says I have to be careful not to make her any more anxious than she already is.'

'Sheep have fairly blunt teeth. She'll be safe enough.'

Surely her mother wasn't making light of it? 'It was terrifying for her, Mum. For all of us.'

'I know it was. I'm not laughing at you or her. I'm saying it as it is – she'll be all right with Bumper. Besides, Bumper is so besotted with Lola she only has to whisper a word and he behaves.'

The sheep was now on one side of Lola, Ellen on the other. Lola had a hand on each of their heads and was inclining her head towards one and then another. Introducing them again, Anna realised. Probably explaining the sheep's name once more. Bumper as in Bumper Baa. Lola's idea – she'd thought it was hilarious.

Lola's voice filtered in. 'Can you feel his lovely soft wool, Ellen? Sheep have lanolin in their wool, one of nature's very best moisturisers. If you ever meet a shearer, ask to shake his hand. You'll never feel softer skin in all your life. Now, let's go and say hello to the chickens as well. They're a bad-tempered bunch. We won't worry about shaking their claws today.'

Anna turned from the window, a smile on her face. At that moment the kitchen door opened and Carrie walked in, carrying a large bundle of long brown twigs.

Anna's stomach gave a leap and the smile froze. 'Carrie. Hello.'

Carrie stopped short. 'Hello, Anna.'

Anna swallowed, kept a smile on her face. 'You look well.' She did too. Small, pretty, she looked like a dainty forest creature. Anna was unreasonably disappointed. What had she expected? Carrie to have turned into a garden troll since they'd seen each other last?

'So do you.'

Anna accepted the compliment with a brief smile. So she would want to, all the money and effort she put into it – constant dieting, fake tans, manicures, pedicures, eyebrow shaping . . .

'Have you been here long?'

'About half an hour.'

'How was the trip?'

'Fine thanks.' Anna forged ahead. She was going to be polite, she was going to handle this if it killed her. 'All set for tonight?'

'Just about, thanks.'

Geraldine looked up from the oven. 'You would have been ready days ago if Lola hadn't kept changing her mind about the way she wanted the serviettes folded. Swans one minute, bishops' hats the next. What was it you ended up with, Carrie?'

'Fans,' Carrie said shortly.

Anna gave a genuine smile. As teenagers they had spent what felt like months learning how to fold different sorts of serviettes for various functions – bishops' hats for business meetings, fans for ladies' lunches and swans for weddings. The three of them could do it in their sleep. Once upon a time Anna would have reminisced about those days, gone straight over, taken the foliage from Carrie, chatted easily and dragged her out to say hello to Ellen. Now they were standing like two store dummies, stiff and awkward, making equally stiff and awkward conversation. She tried again. 'Do you need any help?'

Carrie paused for a few moments too long. 'No thanks. Everything's under control.' She glanced around. 'Where's Ellen?'

'Lola's showing her around.'

'And Glenn?'

'He couldn't make it. Work.'

'Oh.'

Say it, Anna, say it. 'And how's Matthew?'

'Fine. Good. Busy.'

The air grew tense and the silence stretched out.

Lola had seen Carrie's car arrive. She flung open the door with a flourish, talking loudly to Ellen, deliberately interrupting. 'And here we are back in the kitchen. Oh, and look who's here, your Auntie Carrie. Carrie, you remember Ellen, our beautiful Ellen?'

Carrie turned and after a flicker of something passed over her face – shock, surprise – so quickly that only Lola noticed it, she bent down to her niece, who had gone straight over to Anna. 'Hello, Ellen. It's great to see you again. Did you have a nice trip?'

The little girl nodded, her face pressed against Anna's side.

'She's gorgeous, isn't she?' Lola said proudly. She glanced around, judging the mood. It was like Iceland in here. Time for some defrosting. 'Carrie, don't tell me that pile of twigs over there is for my party, is it? Are we having a bonfire tonight?'

'They're for the flower displays,' Carrie said sulkily. 'You told me you wanted a bush theme.'

'Did I?' Lola asked. 'Good heavens. Was I drunk?'

At Adelaide airport at that moment, Bett was walking up to the car hire desk.

A young man in a badly fitting suit smiled at her. 'Can I help you, madam?'

She smiled back. Madam? How sweet of him. A more honest query would have been 'Can I help you, you bedraggled-looking weirdo?'

'I've booked a car, thanks,' she said, handing over the paper-work. As he started pressing keys on the computer, she saw her reflection in the mirror behind him and only just stopped herself from poking her tongue out at her own rumpled, baggy-eyed reflection. She looked like the beagle she'd seen sniffing at suitcases in the arrivals hall.

Was it too late to find a gym and lose a stone? she wondered. First impressions were going to be very important. She wished that Lola had called this party two years ago, when for five glorious months, after a long bout of flu and poverty, Bett had actually been skinny, a size 12, and change rooms were welcoming places, not temples of fear and doom. Anna had always had a comforting theory about women and body fat – that there was only so much fat in the world and what it did was redistribute itself around women all over the planet. When someone on a diet lost a few kilos, another poor unsuspecting woman in a country far away would discover to her astonishment that she had gained a few. Please, God, let Anna be wrinkled and plump and Carrie scruffy and taken to wearing nylon clothes that stick to her all over. With split ends. And adult-onset pimples. Bett turned side on, sucked in her stomach as hard as she could and nearly fell over in the process.

'Is everything all right, madam?'

'Fine. Just doing some after-flight exercises.'

He looked a little suspicious.

Standing sideways again, she wondered whether it would be possible to buy a pair of those super-control tights somewhere nearby. Mind you, her only experience with a pair had been disastrous. When she finally pulled the things on, it was as if they had dragged every spare bit of flesh up with them. She'd been left with slimmish thighs, certainly, but also with the most extraordinary roll of fat over the top of them, as if she'd been stuck in a lifebuoy.

'Madam?'

The young man was now looking concerned. 'Your keys, madam. Car number fifteen.'

Pulling her case behind her, she stopped at the airport door, struck by the high temperature now she was outside the airconditioned building. It felt like someone had opened an enormous oven nearby, sending out a hot, dry rush of heat. A woman in the arrivals hall had been full of the news that it had been one of the hottest summers in years, nine days straight of temperatures in the high thirties. Bett looked around for a phone box and spied one in the carpark. She'd promised Lola she'd call and let her know she was on her way. It had been her choice to hire a car, drive up herself, arrive independently. The phone box was no cooler, the receiver hot to touch. She stared at the phone for a moment, doing the deep breathing that all the books recommended, calming herself down. Of course she could handle this. Hadn't she been out in the world for the past three years, surviving in Melbourne, Dublin and London? Making a career for herself? Be strong, Bett. Be brave, Bett. Ring and tell them you're in Adelaide and you'll be up in a few hours.

She dialled. A cross-sounding voice answered. 'Valley View Motel.'

It was Carrie. Bett hung up immediately.

'Hello? Hello?' Carrie waited a moment, then hung up. People were so rude. At least the ringing phone had got her out of the kitchen, though, before she exploded at her grandmother in front of everyone. Did Lola have any idea how hard it had been for the florist to find all those twigs?

She waited a moment to see if the caller rang back, but the phone stayed quiet. It had probably been another one of Lola's mad friends ringing up to RSVP at the last minute.

'It's not just going to be a room full of old people reminiscing, is it, Lola?' Carrie had asked her several days before. 'There seem to be a lot of croaky old voices ringing up.'

'All human life will be represented, Carrie my dear. And there'll be some reminiscing, some entertainment, a little bit of this and a little bit of that.'

'A little bit of what?'

'It's a surprise.'

'Lola, please. You're the one who is supposed to get a surprise at your party, not us. What are you planning?'

'Carrie, how many times do I have to ask you to please treat me with adoration and respect. I'm not telling. All you have to do is set up the room exactly as I've outlined, follow the running order we have discussed and then leave the rest to me.'

'You're not going to tell me why Frank from the electrical hire shop was here yesterday, are you? Or what was in that big box I saw him carrying in?'

'No, I'm not.'

'Have you finished your table settings yet, then? Are you still expecting about sixty people?'

'More like seventy now, I think. All sorts of people have told me they'd love to come. Oh, and I also invited that quiet Englishman who's staying in room two. He said he'd be delighted to attend. Actually, I think he said he'd be charmed to attend. Have you spoken to him yet? He has the most beautiful manners.'

Right then Carrie didn't care if that Englishman was the most well-mannered man in history. Honestly, her grandmother drove her *crazy* sometimes. 'Lola, you have to tell me these things. That changes everything. All the catering arrangements, everything.'

'Only slightly. Really, Carrie, you have to learn to relax or you'll give yourself high blood pressure.'

'It is you and this party and this neverending guest list that will give me high blood pressure. What are we supposed to feed these extra people?'

'Oh, they won't mind if they have to share their meals.'

'I mind, though. If I'm trying to get more business into the motel, then every occasion like this is a chance to make an impression. And I won't make a good impression if people don't get enough to eat at a birthday party for one of the owners.'

'I'm not an owner any more. I'm just the matriarch these days.'

Carrie had given in and started to laugh. 'You're just a law unto yourself, that's what you are.'

It had been funny then but it wasn't funny now. Nothing was funny now. Carrie took her pulse, felt her heart beating. Yes, it was definitely fast. And no wonder, all the pressure she was under. She heard laughing and looked out in time to see Lola, Anna and Ellen head over to Anna's favourite room, number seven. She fought off a little feeling of hurt, picked up her car keys and scribbled a quick note to her mother. She was going back into town for a long, slow cup of coffee.

CHAPTER FOUR

'AT LAST, at last, at last.' Lola held Bett tight in another hug, then stepped back to look at her again, a wide smile on her face. She had been sitting waiting on a chair at the front of the motel for the past hour. 'You had me worried sick. I thought I'd have to start the party without you.'

Bett was surprised to find herself fighting tears. 'As if I'd let the birthday girl down.' Another hug. 'Let me look at you.' Bett took a step back, still holding Lola's hands. She'd felt bones under Lola's pink clothing. 'You've lost weight, Lola.'

Lola was looking at her just as closely. 'So have you. Not too much, thank God. I wouldn't know you without your curves.' She tucked a bit of hair behind Bett's ears. 'And your eyes are as beautiful as ever, your cheeks as rosy, and I like that colour in your hair. What's it called? Chestnut brown?'

'I don't know what it's called. It's my own colour.'

'Is there such a thing? Imagine that.'

Bett glanced around her. 'Are the –'

'Others here? No darling. I poisoned them all this morning. I decided it would make for a much more peaceful life if you and I had the place to ourselves.'

The sound of the front door opening halted any more questions. Bett looked up as her mother and father came out towards her. 'Bett! Welcome home!' She was enfolded in hugs from another two sets of arms.

An hour later, her head was spinning with news of the motel, of the Valley, of the party that night. There had been no sign of Anna or Carrie yet, and no mention of them. Her parents hadn't asked her too many questions about her life in London either. They knew some of it, of course, from her letters and phone calls, so it wasn't as if she had crawled in from the wilderness. But she had just got back from three years overseas. Shouldn't they have had more questions?

Lola was sitting on the sidelines, watching beady-eyed. Grasping a break in the conversation, she stood up with a groan loud enough to make them all look at her, then crossed to Bett and tucked her hand into her arm. 'Now, come on, Bett, I'll help you unpack. And while we do that, I want you to tell me every little thing you've been doing while you've been away.'

Lola was like a mind-reader sometimes. 'You know it all. It was in my letters.'

Lola steered her out of the kitchen. 'They were a tissue of lies. I know that and you know that. Come on, darling. You can tell me the truth now. By the way, I've organised room six for you, your favourite.'

Lola and the three girls had been sleeping in the motel rooms rather than the manager's quarters ever since the family first moved in, fifteen years before. It had been Lola's idea. She'd decided it was better to use the rooms during quiet times, rather than have them lie idle and unused, getting all musty.

As they walked out into the sunshine, Bett noticed quite a few rooms had a car parked in front of them. 'It's busy enough for this time of year.'

'Not bad, actually. Carrie has been working hard. Mostly one-nighters, though room two has been here for two weeks now. An English fellow. He's coming along tonight, actually. I called on him last week, had a very nice chat. He's researching a book or something fascinating like that. I'm dying to find out more about it.'

Bett kept her mouth shut. Many times in the past her mother had asked Lola not to call on the guests like that, but she was obviously still ignoring her. It would be a bit alarming, Bett supposed, to be booked into a motel room and have a heavily made-up old lady carrying a clinking gin and tonic appear at your door asking for your life story.

With a flourish, Lola produced the key to number six. 'Here you are, darling. All yours once again. I actually had to move a couple out that Carrie had accidentally booked in. I said there might be a problem with a nest of huntsman spiders and they seemed happy enough to move.'

'Move rooms or move motels?'

'Motels, now I think of it. Now, be sure to make yourself at home. If your luck holds and we don't get many guests, you might be able to stay put the whole time you're here. You do have neighbours, though.'

'Neighbours?'

The door to number seven beside them opened and Anna and Ellen came out. Bett's stomach flipped as she saw them for the first time in years. Anna looked as fresh and elegant as ever, immaculately made-up, wearing a white shift dress that showed off her toned, brown body. Ellen was in a pale-blue sundress, holding a straw hat. Bett stood up a little straighter, suddenly conscious of her own creased T-shirt and makeup-free face.

Lola coughed politely. 'Anna Quinlan, may I introduce your sister, Bett Quinlan. Bett Quinlan, this is Anna, your older sister.'

'Hello, Anna.'

'Hello, Bett.'

'And this is Ellen,' Lola continued. 'You remember Ellen.'

Bett looked down at the little girl, feeling Anna's eyes boring into her. Ellen was lovely, a mini version of Anna, with big eyes, straight dark hair and olive skin. Bett glanced at the scar on her cheek, keeping a big smile on her face. Lola had warned her Anna was extremely sensitive about people's reactions to Ellen's scar. She leaned down. 'Hello, Ellen.'

Ellen pressed close against Anna and wouldn't look up.

'Ellen, this is Bett, your auntie. My sister.'

Ellen still didn't look at her. Anna gave Bett a tight smile, a half shrug, as if to apologise.

Bett looked behind her, waiting for Glenn to emerge as well. Anna noticed.

'He's not here,' she said.

Bett felt the rush of colour into her face. Had Anna kept him away because of her? Because of the things she'd said about him? Oh, God. Talk about things getting off to a bad start. 'Look, he's –' Very welcome to be here, too, she'd been about to say.

'Very busy at work,' Anna said smoothly. 'He wasn't able to get away.'

Bett relaxed slightly. 'Oh. I see.'

Anna spoke again, her voice measured, in control. 'So how was your flight?'

'Fine. Long. But I had a night's stopover in Singapore, so I'm not too exhausted. And you? Did you drive down or fly?'

'We flew. Took the ten o'clock this morning.'

Lola stepped in, shaking her head. 'Well, it's a credit to the both of you. Three years' separation and look at the conversation you manage to strike up.'

'Lola, please.' Anna and Bett turned to her and spoke as one.

'Mum,' Ellen's voice was little more than a whisper, as she started pulling at her mother's hand.

Anna leaned down, stroking her daughter's hair from her face. 'You're hungry, I know. Come on, darling. We'll go and see what Grandma has for you. See you later, Bett.'

'Yes, see you, Anna. See you, Ellen.'

As they walked away towards the kitchen, Lola was half laughing, half sighing. 'You'll be the death of me. If that was the best you and Anna could do, then God knows what you'll do with Carrie. Lunge at her with a knife, probably.'

'Lola, sorry, but you have to stop all these cracks. This isn't some little tiff between us. This is big, serious stuff. Grown-up stuff.'

'Nonsense. It's been the world's most ridiculous feud. Over Matthew, of all people.'

'It wasn't just over Matthew. It was –'

'What?'

'All sorts of things,' Bett wasn't ready for this. She tried to find the words. 'Maybe we were unnaturally close all our lives, you know, with the three of us moving so much and the whole Alphabet Sisters thing.'

'So now you're blaming me?'

'Lola, of course I'm not blaming you. I loved the Alphabet Sisters, until –' She stopped short. Was that actually the truth? She grabbed her grandmother's arm. 'Can we please not talk about it right now? Just for a little while? Can you and I go inside and talk about normal things, like terrible gossip from the charity shop or the party tonight or –'

'In a moment.' Lola had heard the sound of a car coming up the driveway. 'Carrie has just arrived back and I want you to meet her. Now.'

'No.' To her own astonishment Bett leapt inside and shut the door of the room.

A second later it opened and Lola came in. 'What happened to you in London? Have you been regressing rather than aging? Don't tell me you were about to hide under the bed?' Bett had spent hours of her childhood under the bed. Looking for peace, she had insisted. Hiding from work, Lola had preferred to put it. 'I'm sure you weren't this cowardly before you went away.'

'I wasn't. And I wasn't this cowardly while I was away.'

'So you admit you're being cowardly now, wanting to hide under the bed? Did I tell you in any of my letters that your mother found some rope under one of the beds last year? Several metres of it, imagine. We had quite a discussion about what that might have been used for. I have to say I think your mother was shocked.'

Bett glared at her, trying not to laugh. 'You're the equivalent of that white noise that armies use to confound their enemies, aren't you? When they play noise at such a volume and for so long that the enemy gives in eventually.'

'Enemy? You're not my enemy. You're one of my dearest girls in the world. Now, come and meet another of my dearest girls. Her name's Carrie and she's your sister.'

At first there were fifty metres between them. Then forty. Thirty.

'Good afternoon, Carrie,' Lola called as they reached ten metres.

'Hello, Lola.'

'Carrie, may I introduce your sister?'

'Stop it, Lola,' Bett muttered. She forced herself to look directly at Carrie, taking in the blonde curls, the petite figure, dressed in jeans and T-shirt, an inch of flat brown belly showing, casual, stylish, neat. In her own mind she ballooned to Michelin Man proportions, her skirt and T-shirt turning super size, her cheeks expanding like balloons, getting redder and redder . . .

Lola interrupted her train of thought. 'But of course neither of you need any introductions. Say hello, girls.'

'Hello, Carrie.'

'Hello, Bett.'

'How was your flight?'

'Good thanks. Long.' She swallowed. 'How is –' she couldn't say Matthew's name. She tried again. 'How is work?'

A look of relief crossed Carrie's face, Bett was sure of it. Perhaps Carrie didn't want to talk about Matthew yet either. 'Fine. We're busy enough for this time of year.'

Lola was beaming between them, for all the world like a country matchmaker.

Then there seemed to be nothing else to say. 'I'd better finish getting ready for the party, then,' Carrie said briskly.

'Do you need any help?' Bett forced out the words.

'No.' Carrie answered too quickly.

'Are you sure about that, Carrie?' Lola's voice was firm.

'It's under control, thanks, Lola. See you, Bett.'

'See you, Carrie.' They stood silently as Carrie walked through the back door of the kitchen.

'Well, that went okay,' Bett said, once she was out of sight.

'Gloriously. Imagine that, all those years of rancour swept

away in one easy and honest conversation. I'm so proud of you.'

'Sarcasm is the lowest form of wit, Lola. You taught us that yourself,' Bett said, stung. She thought it had gone okay. Better than she'd expected, anyway.

'Well, it's a start, at least,' Lola said. 'Carrie probably does need help with the party, by the way, if you truly want to give her a hand.'

'Um, no. I might unpack, I think. Relax a little before the party. I've been very busy getting organised to come back.' A wave of tiredness and emotion hit her as they walked back to her motel room. 'Not that anyone in this family seems to care enough about my life to have actually asked what I've been doing in London the past few years.'

Lola surprised her with a loud burst of laughter and a kiss on her cheek. 'You definitely have regressed. You know you used to be the same at the end of some school days, especially if I dared to have something else I wanted to talk to you about. I promise we will talk about you, my dear Bettsie. We'll talk about you until we are both bored rigid or blue in the face, whichever event takes place first. But all in good time. Don't rush things, Bett. Let things happen slowly sometimes.'

Caught out, Bett grinned. 'You're a fine one to talk. The woman who's summoned us all home like this, forced it to a head.'

'I had to.' Lola decided there was no harm in dropping another hint. 'I need the three of you to do something for me.'

Bett stopped at the door to her room. This was the second time Lola had referred to something needing to be done for her. 'Lola, what is it? You're not sick or anything, are you? I mean, you look well.' As much as she could tell. Lola had gone overboard on the makeup that morning. There were smears of red blush like jam stains on each cheek.

'Right now, because you are here, I feel one hundred per cent. Patience, Bett. All will be revealed in good time. Now, come on. Let's get you unpacking and making yourself at home. Haven't I always said the devil makes work for idle hands?'

'No. Your favourite phrase was that one about too many cooks spoiling the broth. And not counting your chickens before they were hatched. And the one about water under the bridge.'

'I really am a font of wisdom. Now, you unpack while I watch.'

As she opened her case, Bett glanced at Lola. 'I thought Anna looked well. And Ellen is very sweet.'

'Anna doesn't look well. She looks exhausted. And unhappy. Something's wrong there. And Ellen is a bag of nerves as well. That scar is fading but not as quickly as it should be. The city air is no good for that child. Nor is that psychiatrist she sees every month. Have you ever heard anything more ridiculous in your life, making her go over and over the incident? The child has to move on, put it behind her, get on with life, not go back every four weeks and talk about her feelings. Now, have you had any thoughts about work yet?'

Bett laughed. 'Lola, I've just arrived.'

'It's just I had a fascinating conversation with Rebecca Carter last week. You remember Rebecca?'

'Of course.' She and Rebecca had worked side by side as reporters on the *Valley Times* for two years. Until the day Bett had left so suddenly.

'She's editor now, imagine. Filled with ideas, too. She was so interested to hear you were coming back home and looking for work locally.'

'But I'm not.'

'Of course you are. As we just said, the devil makes work for idle hands. You'll see her at the party and you can have a good talk about it with her then. So, show me what you're wearing tonight.'

Bett blinked, wondering which part of this conversation she could blame on jetlag and which part on Lola's conversational style.

'Bett? Your outfit?'

Bett took out the dress and held it against herself. She'd found it in a vintage shop in London. The style was sleeveless and simple, the fabric a rich red brocade, swirls of colour picked out with gold thread here and there.

'Beautiful. Try it on for me.'

Bett did as she was told.

Lola asked her to turn around, inspecting her from all sides. 'I think that back seam could do with taking in, to stop the skirt flaring so much. Would you like me to do it for you?'

Bett took it off and handed it over without argument. If she didn't agree, Lola was just as likely to come running after her at the party with a needle and thread.

'I'll drop it back in a little while. By the way, I don't think you're looking well either, despite what I said when you first arrived. You look like you need some fresh country air too.'

Bett glared for a moment, then a smile started on her face and a warm feeling started in her chest. 'You really are a nasty old crone, aren't you?'

'And getting worse every year.' She held her granddaughter tight against her for a moment. 'I really am very, very happy to see you.'

'I'm very, very happy to see you too. I've got something for you, by the way.'

'A present? How splendid.'

Bett reached down into her handbag, where she had been carrying the gift, not wanting to let it out of her sight. She had spent the last two weekends searching through the stalls at Camden market until she found what she wanted. She watched as Lola opened the blue velvet box. Inside was a pair of costume jewellery earrings and a matching necklace, made from extravagantly coloured glass beads of different sizes and shapes. Lola looked up, eyes wide. 'Bett, they're beautiful.'

'Do you like them?'

'I love them. Where did you get them?'

'In London. An old grey-haired woman in a rainbow cloak was hobbling along the road near the Houses of Parliament as I drove past one morning. As I got close she dissolved in a flash of silver smoke and there lying on the ground were these. So I picked them up and brought them home for you.'

Lola clapped her hands gleefully. It was one of her traditions – anything brought home from a market or charity shop had to be handed over with a story attached. 'You haven't forgotten the rules, have you? I adore them, thank you.' Bett was enveloped in another hug, and then spoken to sternly. 'Now, leave your unpacking for the time being, climb into bed there and have a quick nap. You've bags under your eyes big enough to take shopping.'

Bett did as she was told, peeping up at Lola from under the sheets, the white cotton pulled up to her nose. 'Thanks, Granny.'

'Don't you Granny me, you bold girl.' With that, Lola pulled the curtains, turned out the light and shut the door firmly behind her.

She'd been surprised at how quickly they'd taken to it. Anna's
voice had been distinctive even back then, deep and melodic.
Carrie's voice had matched her looks, sweet and instantly appealing. But it was Bett who shone musically, quickly displaying not
just an ear for harmonies but a real talent at the piano. Lola had
silently and belatedly blessed the elderly music teacher from her
own childhood, who had come to her house twice weekly and joylessly taught her scales, folk tunes and simple classical pieces. Lola
had passed it all on to Bett, with much more enthusiasm, she hoped.
The two of them had spent hours side by side on the wooden piano
stool, graduating quickly from simple tunes to lively duets. Bett
had soon started teaching herself to play more complicated songs.
When they'd moved to a new motel the following year, the first
thing they'd bought was a good-quality piano. It had been with
them ever since.

It wasn't the piano, though, but three dresses that had marked
the start of the Alphabet Sisters. Lola still couldn't think of the day
she brought home that first trio of dresses without laughing. Anna
had been twelve at the time, Bett ten, Carrie seven. The dresses had
been made for little girls of fifteen, thirteen and eleven, but Lola
folded and pinned each of them until they just about fitted. Then
she lined the three girls up, eyes shut, in front of the mirror in her
room and then told them to take a look.

Anna was appalled. Bett was horrified. Carrie was quite pleased.
The dresses were of green and red gingham, with tight bodices and
full skirts.

'We look like we should be in *Little House on the Prairie*,' Anna
said in a disgusted voice.

Bett was just as alarmed. 'We look like we should be in a dustbin.'

'I think we look nice,' Carrie said.

CHAPTER FIVE

LOLA WALKED two doors down and let herself into her own room.
Number four had always been her favourite, with its view over the
vineyard-covered hills. She liked number fifteen, too. It was the
most peaceful, when she was in that kind of mood. Number eleven
was the best one in high summer, she'd discovered, nice and cool,
and number eight was the best for the Christmas party season, with
its excellent view over the carpark and all the shenanigans that took
place there late at night.

She'd always enjoyed all the moving around, had never found it
at all unsettling. Of course, it helped that the décor in each room
was identical: brown carpet, pale cream walls, one double bed, one
single bed, a pastel print of a vineyard scene – from France, not the
Clare Valley, but the guests weren't to know that – a small table
and chairs, a wardrobe which contained not just tea- and coffee-
making facilities, but a bar fridge and a mini safe. There was even
a full-length mirror installed on the long single door. All a person
could need.

She went straight to her CD player and put on a Glenn Miller collection, a little louder than usual, then sat down and shut her eyes,
all the better to review things so far. She always played Glenn Miller

when she needed cheering up, and the sad truth was that's what she needed right now. Was it wrong to be feeling so disappointed? What had she expected, after all? That the girls would only have to glance at each other and all the troubles and cares of the past would melt away? That they would turn back into her little Alphabet Sisters again? It wasn't going to be as simple as that, it seemed. Not when the three of them had such stubborn, dramatic streaks. All her own fault, of course. She'd always encouraged it in them.

She still found it hard to believe this rift between the girls had lasted so long. And even harder to believe the whole row had been caused by Matthew, of all people.

'The three girls had a terrible cat fight over him, I believe,' Len the butcher, the town gossip, had said to her eagerly just after it had happened.

Lola remembered briskly suggesting he shouldn't believe everything he heard. A cat fight, indeed. But afterwards the term had quite appealed to her. Her granddaughters weren't unlike a trio of cats. Anna, the eldest, like a Siamese, all sleek and sophisticated. Carrie, the youngest, still in her kitten stage, even though she was nearly thirty. Sweet as can be one minute, hissing and spitting the next. As for Bett, her middle darling – Lola softened at the very thought of her. Bett reminded her of a lost stray sometimes, needing lots of affection and love but then repaying it in spades.

For weeks now she'd been thinking of nothing else but this reunion. She was sure the other ladies in the charity shop were sick of hearing about the three girls, and especially about their days as the Alphabet Sisters. At least Mrs Shaw, God bless her, always seemed interested.

'Was it a serious thing?' Mrs Shaw had asked. 'Like the Andrews Sisters? Proper tours and recording contracts and all of that?'

'Oh, good heavens, no,' Lola had answered. 'I starte[d] a way of keeping the three of them occupied, to tell you

It had been her idea to take on the role of minding the Jim and Geraldine got on with the running of the mo been concerned how little attention the girls were get their parents. Too many late nights and too much roamin unchecked hadn't been good for the three girls, she'd th wasn't that they were neglected, exactly, just more in n firmer hand.

The new arrangement had suited everyone very well f start. Lola's great affection for her granddaughters had tur a love so strong it had surprised even herself. She had been trying to find her feet in Australia when Jim was a child t never had the luxury to enjoy being a mother. They had close, and still were, but being a grandmother was comp' ferent to being a mother, she'd discovered. More carefree. Watching her granddaughters running around outside shine, or even hearing them call to each other in thei accents had once or twice even brought her to tears. were hastily wiped away. Anna, Bett and Carrie had settled here in Australia, she'd realised. Made all the early days worthwhile.

But Lola had also discovered that three stron gent little girls needed more than dolls and puz them stimulated. 'Music has charms to sooth a remembered reading. She'd hoped it would hav three near savages of granddaughters. She s Irish songs she'd known since she was a child on the old piano that took up a corner of motel they were living in at the time.

Anna reached behind her, trying to take her dress off. 'It's all right for you, Carrie. You do look nice. Lola, can you help me get this off?'

'No, not yet. And stop pulling at it like that. You won't be able to get out of them yourselves, darling. I had to pin the backs to make them fit.'

Bett was wriggling in her dress as though it was coated in itching powder. 'Lola, please.'

Carrie had been silent, happily admiring herself in the mirror.

'Who did they belong to?'

'I asked the lady in the charity shop, and it was quite some story. They apparently belonged to a famous trio of child conjurers called the Okey Dokey Gals, who toured the world with their pet camel and a small grey-faced cat, doing magic tricks and chores around the house for anyone who took their fancy.'

'So how did their dresses end up in a charity shop?' Bett challenged.

'It was a tragic story and one for another day. So what do you think of them?'

Anna was not happy. 'They'd suit the Pokey Yokey Gals better than the Okey Dokey Gals.'

'Or the Yukky Pukky Gals,' Bett added.

Anna again. 'They'd be perfect for a country and western singing group called the Yukky Pukky Gals, in fact.'

Lola was actually pleased. 'Do you really think you look like a singing act?'

Anna nodded. 'We look like those poor kids you see forced on to talent shows on the TV.'

Carrie brightened. 'I'd like to be on one of those shows.'

'Would you, Carrie?' Lola smiled, feeling like a fisherman slowly bringing in a catch. 'That's good. Because I've entered the three of you in a competition the local TV station is running. The winners get to perform at the agricultural show next month. All proceeds to charity. Just a little effort from each of you, with my guidance, and think of all the joy you will bring to the world. Charity begins at home, remember.'

Anna groaned. 'Lola, no way. I'd die of embarrassment. Who sings in public with their sisters?'

'There is a long and honourable tradition of family singing groups.'

The three girls looked at her.

'The Von Trapps. The Partridge Family. The Osmonds. The Jackson Five. And now there's –'

'The Quinlan Sisters,' Carrie called out.

Bett wasn't impressed. 'It's not very catchy.'

'Anna, Bett and Carrie?' Lola suggested.

Carrie pouted. 'Why am I always last?'

'Because you're the thickest,' Anna said. Carrie pinched her. 'Ow! Lola, Carrie pinched me.'

'Only because she got there before me. Carrie, you are always last because your two older sisters are preparing the way for you, in the way flower girls prepare the way for a beautiful bride.'

Anna and Bett rolled their eyes. Carrie looked happier.

Lola clapped her hands. 'I have it. Anna, Bett and Carrie, the ABC Girls. No, let's make it even catchier. Not the Andrews Sisters but the Alphabet Sisters. Perfect for TV.'

Lola laughed out loud now, alone in the motel room, as she remembered their first TV appearance. Over the years the girls had got used to singing on TV, but that first time they had been over-awed by the lights, the cables and the cameras, not to mention the excitable hostess. Their harmonies had disappeared, their carefully rehearsed hand movements had looked more like violent twitches and each of them had had the same panicked expressions in their eyes. The whole family – and several bemused guests – had watched it go to air on the TV in the motel bar the following week. The three girls had shrieked with embarrassment the whole way through. As Anna had said, they'd looked more like the Zombie Sisters than the Alphabet Sisters.

Lola felt a sudden welling of tears in her eyes, as the tension she'd been feeling for the past few weeks drained out of her. She'd been waiting and worrying for something to go wrong. For Anna to call and say she wasn't going to be able to make it. For Bett to say she had decided to stay in London. Lola had hardly been able to contain herself when Bett had rung to say she wasn't just coming home for the party, she was coming home for good.

Had her girls any idea at all how much she had missed them? she wondered. Not just their physical presence, but all the stories and jokes and even the rows that had shot back and forth between them all their lives, to Lola's great and constant entertainment. She wasn't fanciful enough to think that things would ever return to the glory days of the Alphabet Sisters. All the dressing up, and the attempts to get them to rehearse their songs, and those early morning drives to this show or that country TV station. And of course the fights over who got to sit in the front of the car beside her, or whose favourite song would be sung first, or which order they'd stand in. But for every fight there had been a funny moment – missed cues, out-of-tune singing, on-stage spats between them – even if Lola had to pretend to be cross with them, to try and keep some control at least. Some chance. As the past three years had shown, she had no control over them at all.

There had been a moment a year ago when she'd thought the feud was about to be over. The terrible time when Ellen was attacked by that dog. Bett and Carrie had been shocked when she'd told them and Lola knew for a fact that they had both contacted Anna in the days afterwards. Bett had written, and Carrie had rung and left a message with Glenn. But nothing more had come of it. Which was when she'd realised she was going to have to try another way . . .

Oh, if only this had all happened years ago, when her bones weren't as creaky, her mind faster, when she didn't feel so tired all the time. 'You are nearly eighty,' her doctor had said at the last visit, when Lola admitted she needed a long afternoon nap some days. 'Though you're in remarkably good nick, I'll give you that.'

'That'll be the gin,' Lola said. 'I'm preserving myself.'

'Good Irish blood, probably, and all that hard work over the years. How are those hips of yours?'

Lola had had both hips replaced five years previously. 'I feel like they've been mine forever.'

'Are you still doing those stretching exercises twice a day?'

Lola nodded. 'I'm so agile I could get a job in a Bangkok nightclub.'

The doctor had nearly choked. 'Lola, you get worse every visit and you know it. I can't give you any more advice. You already know what you have to do. Try to take things easy, don't get too stressed about anything, enjoy yourself. You deserve it.'

Of course she did. And she did try and take things easy, having her nap most afternoons, drinking eight glasses of water a day. Well, eight glasses of something every day. Surely there was plenty of water in tonic water? And on the days she didn't feel so good, there was always makeup. It helped that her skin was still in good condition. All those years of wearing inch-thick foundation, Anna

CHAPTER FIVE

LOLA WALKED two doors down and let herself into her own room. Number four had always been her favourite, with its view over the vineyard-covered hills. She liked number fifteen, too. It was the most peaceful, when she was in that kind of mood. Number eleven was the best one in high summer, she'd discovered, nice and cool, and number eight was the best for the Christmas party season, with its excellent view over the carpark and all the shenanigans that took place there late at night.

She'd always enjoyed all the moving around, had never found it at all unsettling. Of course, it helped that the décor in each room was identical: brown carpet, pale cream walls, one double bed, one single bed, a pastel print of a vineyard scene – from France, not the Clare Valley, but the guests weren't to know that – a small table and chairs, a wardrobe which contained not just tea- and coffee-making facilities, but a bar fridge and a mini safe. There was even a full-length mirror installed on the long single door. All a person could need.

She went straight to her CD player and put on a Glenn Miller collection, a little louder than usual, then sat down and shut her eyes, all the better to review things so far. She always played Glenn Miller when she needed cheering up, and the sad truth was that's what she needed right now. Was it wrong to be feeling so disappointed? What had she expected, after all? That the girls would only have to glance at each other and all the troubles and cares of the past would melt away? That they would turn back into her little Alphabet Sisters again? It wasn't going to be as simple as that, it seemed. Not when the three of them had such stubborn, dramatic streaks. All her own fault, of course. She'd always encouraged it in them.

She still found it hard to believe this rift between the girls had lasted so long. And even harder to believe the whole row had been caused by Matthew, of all people.

'The three girls had a terrible cat fight over him, I believe,' Len the butcher, the town gossip, had said to her eagerly just after it had happened.

Lola remembered briskly suggesting he shouldn't believe everything he heard. A cat fight, indeed. But afterwards the term had quite appealed to her. Her granddaughters weren't unlike a trio of cats. Anna, the eldest, like a Siamese, all sleek and sophisticated. Carrie, the youngest, still in her kitten stage, even though she was nearly thirty. Sweet as can be one minute, hissing and spitting the next. As for Bett, her middle darling – Lola softened at the very thought of her. Bett reminded her of a lost stray sometimes, needing lots of affection and love but then repaying it in spades.

For weeks now she'd been thinking of nothing else but this reunion. She was sure the other ladies in the charity shop were sick of hearing about the three girls, and especially about their days as the Alphabet Sisters. At least Mrs Shaw, God bless her, always seemed interested.

'Was it a serious thing?' Mrs Shaw had asked. 'Like the Andrews Sisters? Proper tours and recording contracts and all of that?'

'Oh, good heavens, no,' Lola had answered. 'I started it more as a way of keeping the three of them occupied, to tell you the truth.'

It had been her idea to take on the role of minding the girls while Jim and Geraldine got on with the running of the motels. She'd been concerned how little attention the girls were getting from their parents. Too many late nights and too much roaming around unchecked hadn't been good for the three girls, she'd thought. It wasn't that they were neglected, exactly, just more in need of a firmer hand.

The new arrangement had suited everyone very well from the start. Lola's great affection for her granddaughters had turned into a love so strong it had surprised even herself. She had been so busy trying to find her feet in Australia when Jim was a child that she'd never had the luxury to enjoy being a mother. They had been very close, and still were, but being a grandmother was completely different to being a mother, she'd discovered. More carefree, more fun. Watching her granddaughters running around outside in the sunshine, or even hearing them call to each other in their Australian accents had once or twice even brought her to tears, though they were hastily wiped away. Anna, Bett and Carrie had made her feel settled here in Australia, she'd realised. Made all the hardship of the early days worthwhile.

But Lola had also discovered that three strong-minded, intelligent little girls needed more than dolls and puzzle books to keep them stimulated. 'Music has charms to sooth a savage breast', she remembered reading. She'd hoped it would have the same effect on three near savages of granddaughters. She started teaching them Irish songs she'd known since she was a child, picking out the tunes on the old piano that took up a corner of the dining room in the motel they were living in at the time.

She'd been surprised at how quickly they'd taken to it. Anna's voice had been distinctive even back then, deep and melodic. Carrie's voice had matched her looks, sweet and instantly appealing. But it was Bett who shone musically, quickly displaying not just an ear for harmonies but a real talent at the piano. Lola had silently and belatedly blessed the elderly music teacher from her own childhood, who had come to her house twice weekly and joylessly taught her scales, folk tunes and simple classical pieces. Lola had passed it all on to Bett, with much more enthusiasm, she hoped. The two of them had spent hours side by side on the wooden piano stool, graduating quickly from simple tunes to lively duets. Bett had soon started teaching herself to play more complicated songs. When they'd moved to a new motel the following year, the first thing they'd bought was a good-quality piano. It had been with them ever since.

It wasn't the piano, though, but three dresses that had marked the start of the Alphabet Sisters. Lola still couldn't think of the day she brought home that first trio of dresses without laughing. Anna had been twelve at the time, Bett ten, Carrie seven. The dresses had been made for little girls of fifteen, thirteen and eleven, but Lola folded and pinned each of them until they just about fitted. Then she lined the three girls up, eyes shut, in front of the mirror in her bedroom and then told them to take a look.

Anna was appalled. Bett was horrified. Carrie was quite pleased. The dresses were of green and red gingham, with tight bodices and flared skirts.

'We look like we should be in *Little House on the Prairie*,' Anna said in a disgusted voice.

Bett was just as alarmed. 'We look like we should be in a dustbin.'

'I think we look nice,' Carrie said.

had said once. Her skin probably hadn't felt a ray of sunshine in sixty years of living in Australia. She picked up her perfume bottle, an expensive French brand, one of her few luxuries, and squirted a little on her wrists. What was that joke she'd overheard two schoolboys tell last week? 'Why do girls wear makeup and perfume?' 'Because they're ugly and they stink.'

Lola put a finger on each temple and gently massaged, thinking hard. Her birthday party was just hours away and she was certainly in no mood to have the girls edging around each other the whole time, the way they had been so far today. Anna was so rigid it was amazing she'd been able to walk at all. Bett was a bag of nerves. Carrie was sulking and stomping about. None of them was being anything like their usual lovely selves.

How much further could she push them? She had been treading on thin ice today already, she knew. There had been little flashes of anger from all three of them, when she had joked and tried to ease the tension between them on their first meeting. But it was so hard to be patient. Every day she was so conscious of time ticking away from her. The idea of turning eighty had hit her with a terrible shock and propelled her into making these plans, getting them back together. There was something so *old* about being eighty. She had never had such a sense of urgency, or such a feeling that she was living on borrowed time.

She looked over at the portable bookcase and writing desk in the corner of the room. Jim had made it especially for her, so she could wheel it from room to room and feel immediately at home. The folder containing her special project was tucked well out of the way on the third shelf. Should she take it out now? Get everything out into the open? Would they be angry with her? Or would they guess the whole purpose of it was to keep them together for as long as possible? Get them working closely together again? She didn't mind if they did guess. But no, it was too soon. Besides, she wanted to reveal it in a far more dramatic fashion, and in front of as large an audience as possible.

What could they work on together in the meantime? The food was prepared and the room was arranged, so there was nothing to be done there. Then she thought of the large pile of twigs Carrie would soon be putting into vases. Or not, perhaps . . . She picked up the phone and dialled the florist shop in town.

An hour later Lola was standing in the function room with ten newly emptied vases, eight bunches of freshly delivered flowers and three stony-faced granddaughters. Carrie had been summoned from the office, Anna from the kitchen, Bett out of her bed. Ellen had been dispatched to the kitchen to find ice-cream.

Lola gave them her most winning smile. 'I know I'm the very devil for changing my mind at the last minute, but seeing the three of you together again reminded me of those wonderful room decorations you used to do for me when you were little. Do you remember that one Christmas, when you strung up mistletoe and pine cones all over the motel for me?'

Bett stared at her blankly. Perhaps it was jetlag, but she couldn't remember ever doing Christmas decorations for Lola. It had always been Geraldine in charge of the decorations. They'd be hung up neatly exactly three weeks before Christmas, then folded away just as neatly exactly twelve days after Christmas.

'And I realised it would be the icing on my birthday cake to see your flower decorations at my party tonight,' Lola continued. She patted each of them on the cheek as though they were small passing animals. 'So will you get to work? And no hard feelings about the bush theme, Carrie? I'm sure we'll find a use for all those twigs.'

Half an hour later, eavesdropping from outside, Lola was forced to admit her plan hadn't worked. It was more dysfunction than function room in there. No laughing and joking together as they merrily arranged the flowers. No cheerful 'Doesn't the room look beautiful for the party?' conversation. No lively chitchat as they took the opportunity to catch up on each other's lives. Just several frosty exchanges.

'Please don't put that vase there, Anna,' she heard Carrie say in an overly polite voice.

'Why not? I think it looks good.'

'All the flowers are to go on the side tables.'

'But you'll hardly see them once you're sitting down.'

'I've given it a lot of thought over the past few weeks and decided that is the most practical place for them.' Carrie was now speaking in a steely tone.

Outside, Lola winced. The underlying message being that Anna had no right to just march in and do what she liked . . .

There was silence for a minute or two, then she heard Bett's voice. 'Are there any more vases?'

'I'll get them for you.' Carrie, her voice still stiff.

'That's all right. I can get them.'

'They're in the cupboard under the bar.'

'Yes, I know.'

Carrie's tone was sharp again. 'It's just you've been away for so long, I thought you might have forgotten.'

After Bett came back there'd been more silence, broken only by the sound of vases being moved and stalks being snipped. Lola wasn't quite sure what to try next. Should she go in and tell some of her jokes? She'd thought of a good one. What's brown and sticky? A stick. Perhaps not. She had a feeling it would take more than a joke to fix this.

She walked into the room. The flowers were beautiful. Much nicer than the twigs had been. 'Oh, well done, girls.' There was no response. She ambled over to the piano, lifted the lid and experimentally ran her fingers up and down, playing one or two chords.

'Do you remember this one, Anna?' she said loudly. She thumped out the beginning notes of 'Don't Sit Under the Apple Tree'.

Anna shook her head.

'Poor Anna. Your memory gone and you still so young. Bett, your turn. What about this?' She played a swirly introduction to 'Danny Boy'.

Bett glanced over. 'I can't place it, Lola, sorry.'

'Too much smog in London, darling. Your brain cells obviously need a shake-up. Carrie, what about you, my dear? What's this one?' She played the introduction to 'My Favourite Things' from *The Sound of Music*.

'I'm not sure,' Carrie said, not looking up.

Lola was shocked by a surge of anger. Enough was enough. She stood up and clapped her hands, once, twice, three times. 'Right, you little buggers.'

Three startled faces turned to her. Lola rarely swore and she even more rarely used Australian swear words. 'I want to speak to the three of you. Over here, now.'

She gave them a moment to get closer and then glared at them, genuinely cross. 'I know I should be more patient with you. I know you are probably jetlagged, Bett, and you must be tired too, Anna. But I'm sorry, I've been waiting three years for this, wanting this feud to be over every single day and I can't wait any longer to get it all sorted.' She pointed a long, varnished fingertip at her middle granddaughter. 'Bett Quinlan, tell me the truth. How do you feel right now?'

Bett coloured, transported straight back to being a ten-year-old. 'I really don't want to play this, Lola.'

'Play it, Bett. How do you feel right now?'

'Lola . . .'

It was a game she had played with them when they were children. Some trick she'd picked up at a drama class or from some TV documentary. Back then she'd had a magic wand that she would point at them. The truth stick, she called it. She said it saved time. Point and talk. How are you? What's wrong? How do you feel and why? They had to answer. Back then the answers had been simple. 'I'm cross because Mum told me off.' 'I'm sad because I didn't win the race today.' 'I'm mad because the other two got more ice-cream than me.'

Lola turned away from Bett. 'All right, then. Carrie, I'll start with you instead.'

Carrie was looking at her feet.

Lola kept pointing. 'Carrie, the quicker we do this, the quicker it is over and done with.'

A long pause and then a low voice. 'I'm cross because you keep changing your mind about the decorations and it's driving me mad.'

It wasn't what Lola had hoped to hear, but it was a start. 'The customer's always right, Carrie, remember. Anna, what about you?'

Anna glared at her. 'I'm furious because I am thirty-four years old and you are treating me like a child.'

'You're all behaving like children so I'm going to treat you like children. Thank you, Anna. Bett?'

Bett hesitated. 'I'm upset because I hate this.'

'Do you really?' Lola said a silent thanks. Now she was getting somewhere. Say it, Bett, she urged. Say how much you have hated fighting with your sisters. How much you've hated being away from them. 'What do you hate exactly?'

Bett lifted her head, a picture of defiant misery. 'You telling us off. And this truth stick business. I've always hated it.'

Lola put down the imaginary stick. It had been a last-ditch effort in any case. 'Very well. I'll try some straight talking instead. You see, I've always had the idea that you might have missed each other during the past three years. That perhaps there had been times when you'd wished you could call on each other. And then I had the even more obviously ridiculous idea that all it would take for you to become friends again was to get you together to talk about it.'

No response.

'No? Then it seems in my old age I am getting not just feeble of body but feeble of mind, and I have got it all wrong. Such a shame. However, as has always been my wont, I am going to try and make the best of a bad situation.' She glared at them. 'So, my little brat-faced princesses –'

Bett suddenly had to bite back a smile. Lola hadn't called them brat-faced princesses in years.

'Do you think it would be possible for the three of you to put this ridiculous fight – all right, not ridiculous, this extremely worthwhile and valid fight – behind you for a short time? Because, girls, the way of it is I want to enjoy my party and I certainly won't if I have to see your sulky faces all night long. Or all week long. And possibly beyond that. In fact, let's say definitely beyond that.'

She ignored their looks of surprise and clapped her hands again.

The three of them jumped. 'From now on, there is to be conversation between you, do you hear me? I want some smiles too. So I hereby lay down the law. There is to be no mention whatsoever of the events of three years ago. Do you understand?'

There was a flash of temper from Anna. 'Oh, sure, Lola. As if we aren't thinking about them.'

'You can think all you like. You can think of nothing else if you like. But while you are all living and working here, I want peace and conviviality between you.' She turned to Carrie. 'I know this will be hardest on you at the moment, Carrie, Matthew being your husband and all. But I'd like you to keep him away from here for the time being. Do you think you can manage that?'

Carrie swallowed hard. If Lola only knew how easy it was going to be. She nodded, not daring to speak.

'I think it's better if he doesn't come to the party tonight, either. Tell him I'm sorry, but that's the way it has to be. There'll be enough gossiping about you all without him being there as well and everyone watching and listening to see what happens. Besides, I want all the attention to be on me, not him.' She gave a broad grin.

Carrie looked at her feet again. She'd long ago banned Matthew from coming to the party.

'So there we have it. Now, get to work please. It won't be long before my guests come marching up the carpark and there's still plenty to be organised. Carrie, ask your sisters to help you. Bett and Anna, do what she says.' She was almost at the door when she remembered something else. 'One last thing.'

They turned to her as one, like a chorus line, waiting.

She gave them a beautiful smile. 'Thank you all for being here. You've made an old lady very happy.'

CHAPTER SIX

THE FUNCTION room was a mass of fairy lights. There were ten round tables, each set with white linen, sparkling glasses and gleaming cutlery. Irish music played quietly in the background, overlaid with conversations from the seventy guests, a mixture of older couples, teenagers, middle-aged women, several elderly men and even a baby in a carry-cot. There were candles and the vases of fresh flowers on the long side tables, with several bottles of wine already opened on each. Young waitresses in white shirts and black skirts were circulating with trays, collecting empty champagne glasses. Everything was in the room except the guest of honour herself.

At the door, Carrie glanced at her watch, then across the room at her oldest sister. She had stiffly asked for her help that afternoon, and just as stiffly Anna had agreed. 'Are you ready?' she mouthed.

'Ready,' Anna mouthed back.

Carrie signalled over to her other sister in the far corner by the speaker system. It had been just as hard asking Bett for help, but she'd had no choice. Lola's complicated running order for the early stages had made it impossible for Carrie to manage on her own. At Bett's nod, Carrie turned the room lights on and off and on again to get everyone's attention, then turned them off once more, leaving a spotlight over the main door. The room went quiet. Anna turned on the microphone and in her best public speaking voice – one she'd used to great effect in the children's cartoon *Hatty and the Headmistress* – made her speech: 'Please will you stand and welcome the belle of tonight's ball, the reason we're all here, the woman who is celebrating her eightieth birthday this very day – Lola Quinlan!'

Lola swept in to the sound of The Kinks' 'Lola'. She stood in the doorway for full dramatic effect, then gazed around the function room with pride and glee. The girls had done themselves and her proud. Waving majestically, she inclined her head as her friends and family started clapping, many of them laughing at her choice of music.

'You do realise it's a song about a transvestite?' Carrie had asked Lola the previous week.

'Is it?' Lola had said blithely, peering at Carrie over her glasses. 'Never mind. People will think I'm being ironic about my makeup.'

Bett watched now as Lola moved from table to table, greeting every guest in person, having a word here or a word there. She also watched people's reactions after Lola had moved on – a mixture of amazement, amusement and sometimes, outright laughter. It seemed Lola had the same effect on everyone who knew her, not just her granddaughters. It was an oddly comforting thought.

Across the room, Carrie glanced down at the running sheet in front of her. So far so good. Guests to be greeted in person at front door. Tick. Champagne to be circulated by waiting staff. Tick. In the past two days Lola had gone into a kind of white heat. 'What do you think about playing "I Do Like To Be Beside the Seaside" as the waitresses bring out the prawn cocktails?' 'Wouldn't one great big long table look better than ten round ones?' 'Do you think it's too late to ask everyone to come in costume, as pirates or gypsies or something dramatic like that?'

Carrie had finally put a stop to it. 'Lola, it's an old lady's birthday party, not a Broadway production.'

'Do you think it's like a Broadway production? Really? Which parts?'

It wasn't supposed to be a compliment, Carrie stopped herself from saying. 'I just think it might be best if you don't get too carried away. From what you've deigned to tell me, you already seem to have a lot of different activities throughout the night. People will want to talk to each other and eat their meals, remember. You need to let a bit of it happen of its own accord.'

To her surprise, Lola had agreed, taking the pen and swiping it through several items on the rundown. Probably just as well, Carrie thought – she hadn't been too sure the crowd would join in on a version of Stevie Wonder's 'Isn't She Lovely?', though Lola had been fairly confident. She had kept in two items, though – one dubbed S and the other SS.

'What do they stand for?' Carrie asked.

'Surprise and then Super Surprise.'

'I don't like surprises. Tell me.'

'You'll find out when you need to find out,' Lola had said grandly.

Which wouldn't be long now, Carrie thought with some relief. Dramatic entrance? Tick, she noted, as she watched Lola take her seat. It was all good experience, though. She'd probably be able to manage the inauguration ceremony for the President of the United States after this. It might even be simpler.

Two hours later it was ten minutes to Item Seven, the first of Lola's surprises. The starters and main courses had been served – prawn cocktails, followed by wiener schnitzels served with chips and salad. There had been three spot prizes, also Lola's idea. The lucky winners had received bottles of Lola's favourite gin. Dessert was to follow after the next set of speeches. There was a choice of fruit salad and ice-cream or homemade chocolate pudding which was in fact factory-made chocolate pudding with a slightly homemade chocolate sauce on top.

Carrie and Lola had argued about that as well. 'You can have any food you like, you know. Something special if you want.'

'I like your mother's menus. Plain, nourishing . . .'

Boring, Carrie didn't say out loud. The motel food had long been a sore point between Carrie and her mother. Geraldine had her favourites and had never seen any reason to change them. The starters were always either prawn cocktail or soup of the day – generally vegetable. The main courses were usually a choice of T-bone steak, ham steak and pineapple or wiener schnitzel, all served with chips and salad. The desserts didn't often change either: apple pie, chocolate pudding or fruit salad, all served with vanilla ice-cream. The coffee was defiantly instant, the tea made with teabags, not leaves. Geraldine billed it all on the menu as 'delicious homemade country-sized fare'. As the person who unpacked a good lot of it from the wholesaler, Carrie had argued about the term 'homemade' as well. She couldn't argue about the 'country-sized', though. The portions were always enormous.

Carrie caught Lola's eye across the function room. 'Ten minutes,' she mouthed, holding up both hands, fingers spread wide, for clarity. Lola nodded, sending her a beaming smile, before returning to her conversation with the neighbour on the table she was currently sitting at. She'd arranged the seating so there was a vacant seat at every table. 'That way I can move around all night, talk to everyone.' She'd explained her reasoning to Carrie at another one of their pre-party meetings. 'Don't you think it's silly to have me at a head table with your mother on one side and your father on the other? I can talk to them every day. I've always thought that's a ridiculous thing about weddings, actually – putting the bride and groom miles away, out of reach. They're going to spend the rest of their lives talking to each other, being beside one another, aren't they, Carrie?' She hadn't noticed Carrie's expression. 'I'm going to share myself around all night long. And I'd love it if you girls would do the same thing, take up my chairs when I'm not there. Just like those people do during the Academy Awards presentations. Have you heard about them, Carrie? Imagine doing that for a job, slipping in and taking a famous person's chair every time they nip out to the lavatory or for a cigarette. Or perhaps they go out for some drugs, would that be it?'

Carrie had stared at her for a moment, prayed for patience and then returned to the running order in front of them.

The table-swapping seemed to be working well, though. Anna and Ellen had already moved to a table on the opposite side of the room. She could see them both, Anna, with Ellen on her knee, talking to the lady from the chemist shop. Anna looked very glamorous, Carrie thought, in an elegant midnight-blue dress set off with a dramatic pair of earrings that were more art than jewellery. Ellen was all in pink, with a sweet matching hat.

On the other side of the room she could see Bett, laughing at something the local parish priest was saying. She was wearing a vintage dress for the party. Stunning material, Carrie admitted, but she knew in her heart that her own outfit was the most eye-catching. It was a deceptively simple long gold dress, with a matching gold silk wrap. She'd woven little silk flowers through her hair and taken a long time over her makeup, too.

'You look like a model,' Len from the butcher shop had said admiringly when he'd arrived with his wife. Then he'd fixed her with a beady eye. 'Matthew not here yet?'

She'd told the almost-truth. 'He's away up north on a sheep station, for the final part of his vet's training. Fantastic experience. It's just a shame it's so remote. Lola understood, of course.' She stared right at Len, daring him to ask her any more. He hadn't, but she could tell by his eagerness to get away he was dying to pass the news around to everyone in the room. Good, it would save her having to do it.

Looking at Bett again, Carrie noticed she had lost a bit of weight while she'd been in London, but she was still – well, not chubby any more, but certainly not thin. Guiltily, Carrie realised she was relieved. She'd been worried Bett would arrive back from London model-stick thin. She had a feeling Matthew preferred slender girls. She'd asked him one night as they were going to bed, in the early days, when she'd gone through a period of guilt and uncertainty. Before they had declared a blanket ban on talking about Bett.

'Matthew, did you think Bett had a better body than me?'

He'd seemed uncomfortable. 'Carrie, we promised we wouldn't talk about it.'

'But did you?'

'Carrie, I'm not answering that question.'

She'd been cross with him then, and decided to show it. 'Then you must have,' she'd said sulkily. 'Well, you should go back to her then, shouldn't you?' She had glanced up at him under her lashes. He hadn't been sure whether she was joking or not, she knew that. She had stood up, walked across the bedroom in her underwear – her extremely lacy and sexy underwear. She had discovered early on that Matthew liked sexy underwear. At the door she'd stood and relished the look on his face as he took in her body. 'I'll ring Bett, will I? See if she'll come back to you?'

Matthew was lying on the bed. 'Come here, Carrie.'

'Why?'

'You know why.'

'What will you do if I do come over?' From the look in his eye, she had a very good idea exactly what he had in mind. She'd come closer. He'd put out his hand. She'd leaned back, just out of reach.

'Don't tease me.' His voice had been husky and she'd relented, leaning forward . . . She shook the memory away. There was a time and a place for sexual fantasies and her grandmother's eightieth birthday probably wasn't it.

What would Matthew be doing now? She tried to picture him on the sheep station, two hundred kilometres away. The job offer had come out of the blue six months earlier, a perfect practical application of all he'd been learning in his latest course in veterinary farm management.

'How was today?' she'd asked in the early days, when things were still okay between them.

'Another sheep learning curve,' he'd replied.

'And the lecturer?'

'Baa-baric. He kept trying to ram all the facts home. He asked me what was wrong and then got cross when I said mutton much.'

Carrie had tried to keep a straight face. 'Have you finished?'

Matthew had just laughed at her. 'For the moment.'

'I hope that's the truth. You know I hate it when you try and pull the wool over my eyes.'

They had been good together, Carrie kept telling herself. They'd had lots of fun. They'd talked about everything. The first six months had been the most difficult, putting up with the whispers and gossip in the town, but cocooned in their belief that what had happened was bigger than both of them, had been beyond their control, they'd brazened it out. And then one of the Richards girls had a baby at the age of sixteen and the sports teacher ran off with one of the prefects at the school and there was a spate of burglaries in the Valley and everyone had plenty of things to talk about other than them.

Carrie started to feel sad and then anger took over. Had he any idea at all how hard it had been for her the past few years? And how hard it was for her tonight, facing everyone, knowing people would be talking about them? Especially knowing Bett and Anna would be watching her every move?

She was tempted for a moment to phone him, but stopped herself. She already knew what would happen. They'd just have another fight, and more likely than not she would find herself crying at the end of it. And tonight of all nights she didn't want to have blotchy skin and puffy eyes.

But she suddenly wished Matthew was there right now. That she could go across to him, whisper something funny or sexy in his ear, make it all right again that way, the way they used to do. Had done for months, until . . . She realised she was staring over at Bett when her sister caught her eye. She flushed and looked away.

Bett looked away too, embarrassed to have been caught staring at Carrie. There was no doubt about it, her younger sister looked stunning tonight. She had been proud of her own outfit, until she put it on and saw herself beside Carrie and Anna. The whole family had been summoned to Lola's room for one quick drink together before the party – a little pep talk, Lola had called it. Her father made a toast. 'We'll do this again publicly but for now, cheers to you, Lola, a wonderful mother, mother-in-law, grandmother and great-grandmother.'

'To our happy family, reunited again,' Lola had toasted in return. 'Jim, did you bring your camera? I'd love a shot of us all. And one with the three girls together again at last.'

Her father unfortunately had left his camera in the function room. 'We'll have to take that one later on,' he'd said. Bett had been relieved. She and Anna and Carrie had hardly exchanged a word with one another since the flower arranging that afternoon, let alone stood close enough to get a cheery arm-in-arm shot.

Lola had called Bett back as they were all leaving her room. 'You look marvellous, darling. Those last adjustments were just what that dress needed.'

In her room Bett had thought the now mended dress did look good, the vintage brocade such an unusual design, the colours picked up in her favourite high-heeled shoes. But one glance at Anna and Carrie and her spirits had plummeted again. 'Do you think?'

'Darling, you are my Bett, and I say you look wonderful. And you do. Some people might prefer the way Anna looks, all cool and elegant. And Carrie is a pretty young thing and she knows it and wears it well. Those are the facts. The third and final fact is that you look beautiful too. The colours are glorious and your hair is shining. I just want that glint back in your eyes that I haven't seen since you got here.'

'Sorry, Lola. Sorry to be so stupid on your birthday.'

'That's my girl.' She had pinched her cheek. 'Now, your turn to shower me with compliments. Do I look a picture? The truth now, mind.'

Bett had taken in Lola's outfit in all its glory. She was wearing a long purple taffeta skirt, a gold shimmering tunic, at least five necklaces, including her new one from Bett, and surprisingly tasteful makeup. A little too much rouge, perhaps – Bett was tempted to wipe it off then stopped herself. It would be more of a surprise to the guests if Lola arrived without her rouge, surely. 'You look sensational. Like you belong in Hollywood.'

'The very words I wanted to hear. Thank you, darling. Now go and have a good time. And by the way, you're sitting next to the Englishman from room two. Did I tell you he was a journalist too? Imagine that. You'll have lots in common to talk about.'

Bett had groaned, not in the mood for matchmaking. 'Lola, what have you done?'

'Whatever I like. It's my birthday, remember.'

Sure enough, when Bett got to her table there was a man sitting next to her. He was perhaps ten years older than her, lean, solemn-faced, wearing glasses. He was dressed in a casual suit. He smiled at her, a surprising, beautiful smile that completely lit up his face. 'Quite a party,' he said.

Bett smiled back. 'She's quite a woman.'

'Have you known her long?'

'All my life. She's my grandmother.' She held out her hand. 'I'm Elizabeth Quinlan, known as Bett.'

'Richard Lawrence.' They shook hands.

'You're English? Is that a London accent?'

'It is, yes.'

'I'm just back from there. Only this morning in fact.'

'All that way for a party? You are a social creature.'

Bett laughed. She noticed then he had very sparkly eyes behind his glasses. 'I didn't have a choice, believe me. And you're on holiday here, are you?'

'Well, a working holiday I supp –'

A slap on her back nearly sent Bett flying into the table. 'Bett Quinlan, great to see you again, love. Are you going to be back working on that newspaper?'

Her other neighbour had arrived, a man who had done the landscaping around the motel and knew the family well. He'd immediately launched into a conversation that hadn't let up through the first course. Out of the corner of her eye Bett had noticed Richard Lawrence being interrogated by his other neighbour, one of the local councillors. She heard snatches, something about doing research for a writing project. She'd been about to ask him more about it when Lola had wafted past her and whispered that it was time to move tables. 'Circulate, darling, circulate.'

Bett found the move between tables very difficult. Not quite as difficult as the walk into the function room in the first place, though. She had been intensely aware of people looking at her and talking about her. She'd kept a big smile on her face, greeting lots of old faces, friends of Lola's or people she knew from her years on the local newspaper, brightly answering their questions. Yes, she was finally back from London. No, the jetlag wasn't too bad. That stopover in Singapore had made all the difference. Yes, home for good, but she'd probably be heading off to Sydney or Melbourne fairly soon. Yes, it was great to see all the family again, not to mention a blue sky, ha ha ha.

No one had mentioned Matthew's name, or the circumstances of her leaving, not to her face anyway. No one except Len the butcher, of course. It seemed he hadn't changed his ways. She'd barely walked past after saying hello to him and his wife when she'd heard his remark, in a loud whisper that managed to carry beautifully around the room. 'That's the one I was telling you about. Her fiancé left her and ran off with the younger one. No, not the one with the child, the pretty one over there with the blonde hair.' Bett had resolutely kept moving, praying the low light hid her red cheeks.

By the time the main course had been served, she was feeling much better. The three glasses of local shiraz were helping things along beautifully too. She'd found herself sitting beside the local parish priest, who had surprised her with his rapid-fire joke delivery. She hadn't laughed so much in ages. To make things even more pleasant, one of her favourite dishes had been on offer for main course – lovely crispy wiener schnitzel, served with a pile of fat chips and salad. She knew it was deeply unfashionable to like such standard motel dining-room food, but she'd always loved her mother's cooking. Her all-time favourite was the chocolate pudding, all crunchy on the outside and molten on the inside, served with cream and ice-cream. She'd never found any reason to join in with Anna and Carrie over the years when they had tried to get Geraldine to update the menus, to offer more light and healthy options.

Bett knew full well that it was her love of her mother's kind of cooking – hearty, deep-fried, large servings – that was to blame for her constant battle with her weight. Lola had made it abundantly clear one afternoon, too, when Bett had gone to her in tears.

'It's not fair. How come Anna and Carrie got to be skinny and I didn't?'

'Anna and Carrie are skinny because they exercise a lot and they both eat like birds, Bett,' Lola had said bluntly.

'I eat like a bird too,' she'd said gloomily, knowing Lola was right. The only problem was her bird was a vulture.

She decided now to try and be disciplined and reluctantly left the last of her chips on her plate. A minute on the lips, a lifetime on the hips, she had once tried chanting. Unfortunately she'd quickly reworded it. A minute on the lips, even nicer served with chips. As she tried to ignore the chip's siren song, she felt a tap on her arm.

'Bett, have you heard the one about the horse who goes into the bar?'

'No, I haven't, Father, but I'd love to,' she said, turning to him with a smile. As she did she noticed one of the waitresses heading towards their table to pick up the plates. Oh, to hell with it. She was on holiday, wasn't she? As the priest began his joke, she picked up the last chip and popped it in her mouth.

Three tables away, Anna smiled up at the young waitress as she collected her plate. 'Thanks very much. That was delicious.'

The girl frowned. 'Why didn't you eat any of it, then? It looks like you hardly touched it.'

Anna tried not to laugh. 'I'm just not very hungry,' she said politely. She knew from experience that her mother would have called on her pool of casual waitresses for tonight – local schoolgirls, young mothers, anyone needing a bit of part-time work.

The girl looked a little uncertain. 'Will I bother bringing you a dessert then, if you're not very hungry?'

'Just a small one would be great, thanks,' she said. 'And one for my daughter. She'll be back in a moment.' Lola had come over and swept Ellen away a few minutes before. 'I want to show her off,' she'd said brightly. Ellen had happily gone off with her.

Anna tried not to react as the waitress dropped a knife onto the floor, narrowly missing her foot. She picked it up and handed it over with a smile. 'Don't worry. You're doing a great job.' Poor kid. She – and Bett and Carrie too – knew only too well what it was like to work part-time as a waitress. They'd spent their teenage years ferrying meals into the motel dining rooms. Their mother's unchanging menu items had at least meant easy serving, with no complicated sauces or cooking methods to explain. All they'd had to do was get the right meals to the right people at each table in the dining room. They'd worked out their own method of identifying each diner, scribbling one- or two-word snapshots of people in their order books. It had worked well until one evening Bett had inadvertently left her notebook on the table. When she'd come out to collect their dishes it had been to find the six people passing it around trying to work out which of them was which, from a choice of Big Nose, Ugly, Baldie, Flashy (the woman had been wearing lots of rings), Creepy Beard or Clownface. Anna remembered Bett being so mortified she'd run out of the dining room and not returned for the rest of the night.

Alone at her table for a moment, Anna looked around the room. Lola, hand in hand with Ellen, was moving regally from table to table. Her parents were standing nearby, chatting to another couple. Her father's arm was casually resting on her mother's back. Bett was still sitting two tables away, laughing at something the man beside her was saying. A possible suitor? Anna caught herself thinking. Then the man moved and Anna saw he was wearing a priest's collar. Perhaps not. Anna had wondered if Bett would arrive home with an English boyfriend. She'd casually asked Lola once whether Bett had mentioned any men in her life in any of her letters.

'Not a sinner,' Lola had said bluntly. She'd always been more than happy to keep each of them informed about the others' lives. 'I just wish she would meet someone over there. It would solve a lot of problems.'

Anna finally spotted Carrie, too, shining in her golden dress on the other side of the room. Her sister had become very skilled at running events like this, it seemed. Everything was running so smoothly, the staff checking with her constantly, looking at her with respect. Not surprising, really. Carrie had always had that confidence with people, the ability to charm them so effortlessly.

'Hello, love. Are you enjoying yourself?'

Anna turned and smiled up at her father. 'Dad, hello. Sit down.' She patted the chair beside her. 'It's a great night, isn't it? Carrie's done a very good job.'

'She has. She's doing wonders around the place, in fact. She'll have your mother and me out of a job before we know it. We'll wake up one day and she and Matthew will have taken over while we were sleeping.'

It was funny to see how naturally her father referred to Carrie and Matthew as a couple. She shouldn't have been surprised, she supposed. He'd had three years to get used to them both. 'It's all that good training you gave us as kids. Actually, I was just sitting here reminiscing about our waitressing days. That time Bett left her notebook on the table. Do you remember?'

Jim threw back his head and laughed. 'The times I've told that story. What was it again?' He reeled off the six insulting names, word perfect. 'And that time Carrie put those film people in their place. Do you remember that? When we first moved here?'

Anna laughed too, remembering it well. A film company had booked in to stay and over dinner in the public dining room openly started smoking joints. They'd become more and more obnoxious, ordering fifteen-year-old Carrie, their waitress for the night, around like a servant, complaining that there wasn't the rare brandy they wanted or the scotch they preferred. As Carrie had leaned over to change their ashtrays, one of the men had given her a pat on the bottom. 'These are just herbal cigarettes, love. Nothing to worry about.' Then he'd winked. 'Let me know if you'd like to try one.'

Without missing a beat, Carrie had removed his hand from her bottom and smiled sweetly. 'And do you see those two men over there in the bar?' She had pointed through the door at the local postmaster and the railway stationmaster, enjoying a beer together. 'They're from the drugs squad in Adelaide. Let me know if you'd like to meet them, won't you?'

Anna laughed. Not only had the film people put out their joints there and then, but they'd left Carrie a thirty dollar tip.

'Do you remember how furious Bett was?' Jim continued. 'She came marching into me in the bar. "How come Carrie always gets the tips? I'm going to start wearing a blonde wig when I'm waitressing from now on."'

Anna had forgotten that part of it. She gave a wry smile. 'So good that we've put all that fighting behind us now, isn't it, Dad?'

'I'm just glad to have you all home again,' he said simply. 'We missed you, you know. You and Bett. It's a shame it took so long.'

It was the most her father had said about it in a long time. 'It's good to be back.'

'Hi, Grandpa.' Ellen popped her head in between the two of them and then climbed onto her grandfather's lap. 'Can you do that trick where you take the coin from your ear and then put it in my ear?'

'That's not a trick, Ellie. I really do keep coins in my ear. It's much safer than the banks.'

'*Grandpa*,' Ellen said, shooting Anna a glance. 'He's joking, Mum, isn't he?'

'Oh no, Ellen. Your grandpa has a fortune in his ears.'

'Show me, Grandpa?'

He checked his watch, then touched the end of Ellen's nose. 'A little later, sweetheart. I just have to make a quick announcement about the birthday girl, but I'll be back as soon as I can.' He stood up and made a show of straightening his tie, smoothing back his hair. 'My moment of fame has come at last.'

Ellen watched him go, then turned to Anna. 'Mum, Grandpa is Lola's son, isn't he?'

'That's right.'

'They're both a little bit mad, aren't they?'

Anna burst out laughing. 'Yes, Ellie, they are.'

Bett said goodbye to the priest and moved back to her original table, carrying her fourth glass of red wine. She'd hardly have believed it possible, but she was almost enjoying herself. It seemed she just needed to keep herself mildly drunk and surrounded by a crowd at all times and she would get on just fine back here. She smiled at Richard the Englishman as she sat down beside him. 'You're enjoying yourself, I hope? All this Australian country hospitality not too much for you?'

'Good lord, no,' he said. 'In fact, I've been invited to join two local cricket teams.'

'You didn't accept, I hope. You know they only want another excuse to laugh at an English cricketer.'

'I had a funny feeling about that, actually.'

Bett laughed. 'Well, just make sure you think long and hard before you accept any offers.'

He picked up a bottle of wine and went to fill her glass. 'May I?' he asked. She accepted, impressed by his good manners.

Richard raised his voice over the sound of the Irish folk tunes. 'Lola told me all four generations of her family would be here tonight. Is that right? She seemed very happy about it.'

'That's right,' Bett said, hoping he wasn't about to ask her to introduce him to everyone. She didn't want to point out Anna and Ellen, or Carrie, she realised. She didn't want him comparing her to the other two, finding herself left on the sidelines once again. She was enjoying him too much herself. She was guiltily pleased when she noticed her father had started making his way to the microphone to introduce Lola's speech. 'Excuse me,' she said to Richard. He nodded and turned towards the front of the room too.

She wriggled around to get a better view of her father and then nearly leapt out of her seat as a sharp pain ricocheted through her right thigh. She moved and another sharp pain shot into her bottom. Bloody hell, had she sat on a spider? She lifted up her bottom an inch, lowered it and nearly shot out of her seat as the pain struck again.

Behind her, Richard noticed her jump. 'Bett, are you all right?'

'Something keeps biting me.'

'Good heavens. I promise you it's not me.'

That made her grin. 'I didn't think it was you. Don't mind me.' She couldn't get up now, make a scene, not during Lola's big moment.

Her father was now making his introduction. 'Once again, I give you my mother and the birthday girl herself, Lola Quinlan.'

The lights came on and in the front of the room was Lola, pulling back a curtain to reveal a large white screen. The guests shifted expectantly. Bett gingerly turned her seat around to make sure she had a full view, not moving her bottom, just the chair, trying to keep the insect or spider or whatever creature it was pinned underneath her bottom.

Lola waited until she had every last person's attention. 'Thank you, my darling Jim. Before I move on to the next important event of the night, I'd like to properly introduce my family to you all.

I'd invite them all up here beside me, but then you'd be looking at them not me.' There was a ripple of laughter. Lola pointed them all out, one by one. 'My son, Jim, and his wife, Geraldine, who have been so good and kind to me over the years, even when I was driving them mad.'

'Never,' Jim called across. Geraldine smiled stiffly.

'And my granddaughters. Anna, put your hand up, darling, would you? Anna's home from her successful acting life in Sydney for a little while with her daughter, my dear great-granddaughter, Ellen, who has just turned seven and is adorable.' Bett noticed Ellen was pressed against Anna, her hair hiding her scar.

'And at the table next to Anna and Ellen is my middle granddaughter, Elizabeth, known of course as Bett . . .' Bett self-conciously raised her hand as Lola continued, 'who has left behind her extremely glamorous life in London to come home and spend time with me.'

She turned and gestured towards Carrie, who was standing by the door. 'And of course my dear Carrie, there in the golden dress with the golden hair, who not only keeps me young on a daily basis, but has pulled out all the stops for tonight. Thank you, Carrie darling.'

Lola waited for the applause to come to an end before she spoke again. 'When we were first planning this evening's entertainment, I learned that a tradition these days is to have a little slideshow ready to surprise the guest of honour. Carrie suggested it and I turned her down immediately, not wanting to be embarrassed by photos of myself that I thought had long disappeared. But then I thought about it some more, and I decided, yes, perhaps it would be good, especially if I got to choose the slides, rather than have any naughty surprises.

'So I went ahead and prepared a little slide show of some of my favourite moments and I'd like to share them with you. Please, get yourselves a drink and then we'll get started.'

Uh oh, here we go, thought Bett. Anna was sitting at the table behind her, the two of them virtually back to back. She felt a tap on her shoulder and turned.

'Did you know anything about this?' Anna whispered.

Bett shook her head, surprised Anna was asking her. They both glanced over at Carrie. By the look on her face, this was a surprise to her as well.

Lola clapped her hands. 'Attention please, everyone. Anna, Bett, stop whispering over there.' She waved over at them. 'My darlings have come home especially for this, you know. So good at my age to have all the family around me again.'

In the quiet moment that followed before the slides began, two voices were clearly audible.

'Is the youngest one's husband here? The bloke that caused all the trouble?'

'No, he's been banned, I'd say.' Len the butcher's voice was easily recognisable. 'Shame, really. I was hoping to see another cat fight over him tonight.' He gave a loud laugh.

Bett stiffened. Bloody Len and his big mouth. She wished he'd go and choke on one of his own chops. From the corner of her eye she saw Anna spin around to spot the speaker. She didn't dare look in Carrie's direction. To her relief, the lights suddenly went down, the screen flickered into life and Lola's voice came over the speakers, her Irish accent strong and clear. 'Please forgive my indulgence as I reminisce a little about the past eighty years.'

A lilting Irish song started playing as slide after slide came up on the screen, with captions of the year and the place underneath. There was Lola as a child beside an enormous oak tree in front of her big family house in Ireland, standing with her parents behind her, the only child. As a young woman at a gala party, in Dublin. On her wedding day, Edward serious-faced, Lola almost a child bride. A photograph of them on the boat to Australia in the late 1930s, then several of Lola with a baby Jim on their own; by a beach; in the gateway of the Botanic Gardens in Melbourne; among a group of women, all with young children.

Bett was fascinated. She hadn't realised Lola had those photographs from Ireland, or so many from her early days in Australia. Lola had rarely spoken about those days in any detail. The memories must have been too painful for her, the three girls had decided. Bett heard whispers at the tables around her. 'She was widowed very young, wasn't she?' 'Tragic, wasn't it? Her with a young son, too.' 'Did she marry again?'

Something about the photo of Lola's house in Ireland struck a chord with Bett. She had visited it on behalf of Lola when she was living over there, taken photos of it and tried – but failed – to find anyone who remembered Lola and her family from years before. She'd like to have looked more closely at the photo but it had flashed past too quickly. She'd have to ask Lola about it another time.

The next slides were of Lola and Jim in the different guesthouses and motels they had gone on to manage all around Australia. They had moved dozens of times over the early years, from city motels to country motels, motels in farmland and motels by the sea. Geraldine and then the three girls started appearing on screen. There was a wonderful photo of Lola in her mid-fifties on holiday in Tasmania, on a beach with wind whipping through her hair, looking like a film star. Another of her in her late sixties, behind the counter of the charity shop here in the Valley, the year she had announced herself officially retired from motel work. One from her seventieth birth-day party in the middle of the vineyard in front of the motel on a glorious summer day, like today. The day that she had signed over all the ownership to Jim and Geraldine. Bett remembered it clearly. Lola hadn't listened to any arguments. 'I don't want money for it. It's yours to do what you like with, as long as there's always a room and a ready supply of gin for me.'

Bett relaxed as the screen went white again. Thank God Lola hadn't included any slides of the Alphabet Sisters. She knew there were dozens of hideously embarrassing photographs from their various performances all over the country, none of which Bett ever wanted to see again. Lola usually pulled them out at any occasion. Who'd have thought she'd have respected their privacy like that tonight?

Lola's voice sounded out over the room again. 'It's been a long and eventful life, and one of the most special parts of it has been not just the joy of having three granddaughters but having three immensely talented, performing granddaughters. So I'd also like to take this opportunity to share with you some of the finest moments from their years performing as the Alphabet Sisters. Music please, maestro.'

The room filled with the sound of Perry Como singing 'The Alphabet Song'. Bett covered her face with her hands as one photo after the other of the Alphabet Sisters in an array of outfits flashed up onto the screen. There they were in the gingham dresses they'd worn for their first performance on the TV talent competition. In the matching yellow satin dresses with flared skirts. In the pink and blue skirt and shirt ensembles. The bright-green taffeta party dresses . . .

Bett made a gap in one hand and peered through, hearing the

laughter around her. It was getting worse. Why had they reached their performing peak when puff-ball skirts, fluffy hair and fluorescent colours had seemed fashionable? As Perry continued crooning in the background, working his way through the alphabet one more time, on screen the three of them moved from childhood to teenage years. It was like time-lapse photography. Bett watched herself get plumper and plumper with each passing year. There was open and loud laughter all round now. People were laughing at her or the outfits or their makeup. She covered her face, praying for the song to finish, praying for an electrical fault, an earthquake . . .

At their table Anna and Ellen were in gales of laughter. Over dinner, Ellen had been solemnly informing the lady sitting next to her that her mother and aunties had once been famous singers. Behind her, Anna had been vigorously shaking her head, smilingly denying everything. Five seconds of these slides had been the proof. There they were, squinting into the sun, standing on makeshift stages on the backs of semi-trailers, or in country halls, surrounded by balloons and crêpe-paper decorations. Another of the three of them caught mid-dance movement, looking about as elegant as scarecrows. And the dresses! They were even worse than Anna remembered.

On her lap, Ellen was in fits of giggles. 'I hope you're not laughing at me?' Anna said mock sternly.

'You all look so silly,' Ellen whispered back. 'And look at Auntie Bett's hair.'

Oh, poor Bett, Anna thought, as another slide flashed up showing Bett with her mouth caught wide open in mid-song, her mad brown curls dancing around her head. Beside her Carrie was a demure golden-haired angel. Anna judged herself critically. Her hair had been as dark and straight, her posture as excellent then as it was now. She leaned down to her daughter again and spoke in a whisper. 'We actually couldn't sing very well either. But don't tell Lola. She thought we were gorgeous.'

By the door, Carrie was enjoying every moment of the surprise slide show. She'd been taken aback at first, but was now revelling in the memories. She had loved every moment of the Alphabet Sisters. The dressing up, the singing, the applause . . . and she'd never minded any of the dresses they'd had to wear. She'd certainly never carried on about them the way Bett and Anna had, in any case.

She found herself wishing again that Matthew was there, to see this as well. He had loved hearing the stories of the Alphabet Sisters. There'd been a few awkward moments in their early days, when she had been telling him stories, wondering if he had already heard them from Bett. He had taken her hand and kissed it one night, when she'd confessed her worry. 'Carrie, Bett and I didn't talk the way you and I talk. Now, please, keep going – you were in the car with Lola on your way to a concert one day and what happened?' She bit her lip as the slides kept coming, seeing the younger, happier version of herself smiling up on the screen. Perhaps if things got better between Matthew and herself again – one day – she could show these slides to him herself . . .

The lights finally came on again, and Lola moved back in front of the screen. Was she truly wiping away a tear, Bett wondered, or was it all for show? The laughter and chat in the room quietened as all eyes turned to Lola again.

'Some wonderful memories there for me, as I'm sure you'd agree. The days working with my little Alphabet Sisters were among the happiest of my life, and ones that I had thought, sadly but inevitably, had come to an end.'

And not a moment too soon, Bett thought, the tension draining out of her. Lola's next words had her sitting upright again.

'Then something wonderful happened. My darling granddaughters agreed to the most wonderful birthday present a grandmother could ask for. I would like to share it with you all tonight.'

Oh no, Bett thought. Surely she wasn't going to talk publicly about the rift? Please don't say she was about to produce Matthew out of nowhere, stage a tearful Oprah Winfrey-style reunion between them all? She glanced at Anna, and at Carrie. Did they have any idea about this wonderful birthday present? It didn't look like it. Anna shot her a questioning glance. Bett shook her head, signalled that she had no idea either.

At the side of the room, Carrie was glancing down at the running order. She seemed just as puzzled. Bett turned around. At the back of the room Frank from the electrical shop had moved back by the slide projector and was as alert as a gun dog, waiting for Lola's signals.

The room lights went out once again, leaving a spotlight on Lola. When had she rehearsed all this? Bett wondered.

Her grandmother's voice was assured. 'For the past ten years, I have been working on what I regard as my life's project. Apart from my son and granddaughters and great-granddaughter, of course. And I have this man to thank.'

The spotlight went out. On the screen behind her was a large photo of a man in uniform.

'The American General, Douglas MacArthur,' Lola said, now pacing in front of the screen as though she was a university lecturer. 'One of the heroes of World War II, famous for a wartime speech that galvanised hearts and minds all over the free world. Yes, indeed. "I shall return," General MacArthur promised, not just to his men in the Philippines but to all the Allied forces. It became the war cry of the Pacific campaign.'

Two older people near Bett nodded and whispered to each other. They obviously remembered it, even if it was news to her.

Another slide came up. General MacArthur standing on a platform at a small railway station, his elegantly dressed wife beside him, their small son between them.

Lola's voice filled the room. 'And where did he say those momentous words? In London? No. In Washington? No. Perhaps even in Sydney? No. General MacArthur said those words on the twentieth of March 1942 on the platform of the Terowie Railway Station. Yes, the little town of Terowie, South Australia, just sixty miles from here, as he travelled by train from Alice Springs to Adelaide. What an event for that tiny place, I've always thought, with the war and worries swirling all around them. It touched me deeply. Some years ago I started imagining and thinking and putting down ideas, and before I knew what was happening my thoughts had become a short story, which became a longer story, which became a musical. Yes, I, Lola Quinlan, in the twilight of my years, found that I had written a musical.'

Lola took a big, dramatic breath and paused. 'For many months it languished in my bottom drawer. Until I shyly showed it to my three granddaughters, as we reminisced about the wonderful days of the Alphabet Sisters –'

Bett shot Anna a glance. Anna looked over at Carrie. They'd done no such thing.

'And, to my great joy, they offered there and then not just to perform it for me here at the motel, but to mount a fully staged, complete musical in the Valley for everyone to enjoy, with all proceeds going to the Valley Ambulance Fund.'

The party-goers started clapping, some of them a little uncertainly. Lola reached into a bag beside her and pulled out a bundle of leaflets. She started moving from table to table, handing out a small sheet of paper to everyone in the room. She reached Bett and handed her one with a big smile. Bett scanned it.

Many Happy Returns

A Musical for all the Family

Written by Lola Quinlan

To be performed by

The Alphabet Sisters

and the people of the Clare Valley

Clare Town Hall, March 20

Bookings Valley View Motel

All proceeds to the Buy a New Ambulance Fund

She had to grab her grandmother's arm as she started to move away. 'Lola, wait! What in God's name is all this about?'

Lola lowered her voice. 'Darling, don't blaspheme in public, especially on my birthday.'

'I'm serious.'

She patted Bett on the head. 'In a moment, darling.' She glided off.

Carrie came up to her next, looking put out. 'Is this a joke, Lola? Because it's not very funny.'

Lola was unperturbed. 'Is the musical a joke? Well, it certainly has some hilarious moments, but it has a serious side to it as well.' She sailed past her too.

Anna came up behind her and helped herself to a leaflet, a smile fixed on her face. 'You've put us in an embarrassing situation tonight, Lola.'

'Really? I thought you all looked very nice.'

'You know we can't do this. You should at least have asked us.'

'But you might have said no.'

'Of course we'd have said no. Lola, the three of us might not be here next month to take you to lunch, let alone stage your musical.'

A well-dressed woman bustled up beside them, taking a leaflet from Lola's hand. 'A tremendous idea, Lola, and aren't you girls great to do something like this for your grandmother. I love her stories about the Alphabet Sisters. It'll be a pleasure to see you all in action.'

'That's the doctor's mother,' Lola whispered as the woman moved off again.

'I don't care if she's Andrew Lloyd Webber's mother. Lola, you have to call this off.'

'But they all look so interested.'

Anna glanced around. The people in the room did appear interested, with just about everyone reading the information. On the other side of the room she saw Bett at her table, with two of the waitresses standing beside her. It looked like they were giving her their contact details. In the other corner Carrie was also surrounded by a small group of people, answering their questions as well.

A petite woman came over to Lola and Anna, clutching the leaf-let. 'Will you be holding open auditions, Lola? My son is keen to get into drama school next year and the experience would be great for him.'

'Drama school!' Lola repeated. 'Isn't that marvellous. We'll be put-ting an ad in the *Valley Times* about the auditions, won't we, Anna?'

Anna recovered, finding a confident smile somewhere. 'We haven't talked through all the details yet, Lola, have we? Still a few grey areas to discuss.'

'Oh, nothing we can't sort out, though.'

'No, I hope not.' Anna's smile was very wide and very fake.

Across the room, as the waitresses moved away, Bett picked up the leaflet, reading the details again.

Richard Lawrence was watching her closely. He looked amused. 'Pardon me for enquiring, but are you slightly surprised about this?'

Her head shot up. Slightly? Overwhelmingly. And there was no way she was going to do it, either. But that wasn't something to admit to a complete stranger. She gave a light laugh. 'Oh, that's Lola for you. Always springing little surprises on us. She really is something else.' She moved back in her chair and yelped out loud as the worst pain yet shot into her bottom.

He looked concerned. 'Not another bite? Would you like me to look?'

'No!' She nearly shouted the word. 'I mean, no, thank you, any-way. Excuse me, will you?'

She moved through the room, dodging the waitresses carrying the trays of desserts. She practically ran into the ladies, which was blessedly empty, and started to unzip her dress. As she did so there was a tearing sound.

'Oh shit,' she said loudly. She locked herself into a cubicle and took the dress off completely. She heard another little ripping sound as the old material tore even more. What had the spiders done, eaten the skirt?

Something glistened in the seam of the material. She looked closely. They weren't spider eyes, but a whole row of silver pins. She picked one out. And not pins either. They were industrial-sized staples, their ends as sharp as needles. She groaned. Why had she trusted Lola to sew that seam? She'd thought it was strange how quickly she'd done the job that afternoon, but had been too jetlagged to comment. Now look at the mess she was in. She couldn't put the ripped dress on again, unless she wanted to treat the entire gathering to the lovely sight of her large black-undie-clad bum. And she couldn't run down to her room in her camisole, tights and shoes. Shit, shit, shit. She heard someone come in and tensed. She peered under the door. Please let it be her mother, or Anna or anyone but . . .

She recognised the gold strappy sandals. It was Carrie.

She couldn't ask her. She'd rather be here all night than ask Carrie for help.

Then the reality hit her. She could well be in here all night if she didn't ask Carrie. She had to get out there again. They'd be singing 'Happy Birthday' any minute.

'Carrie?' Her voice was small. 'Carrie?' A bit louder.

'Bett?' She sounded surprised. 'What's the matter? Are you sick?'

'I'm fine. It's just, I've, uhm, ripped my dress.'

'Just now? In there?'

'No, before I got in here. Lola mended it for me but she seems to have used a stapler rather than needle and thread.' Please don't laugh at me, she prayed.

'Come out, let me see.'

To Bett's relief, Carrie wasn't triumphant or sneering. She had a quick look. 'Oh, hell. I thought she'd stopped doing that. She just loves that stapler. It's a special upholsterer's one she got at the charity shop. I caught her stapling the curtains in her room last year. She said it was much quicker than sewing.'

'I thought a spider had bitten me, that I'd sat on a whole nest of them.'

Carrie grinned, then sobered again as the door opened and an elderly woman came in, smiled at them and went into one of the cubicles. Bett had managed to put the dress in front of her just in time. She climbed into it now, rip and all, before the woman came out.

'The staples are still in there,' Carrie whispered.

Bett whipped it off again and the two of them worked to pick them out. There were more than twenty.

Carrie shielded her as she clambered back into the dress again. As the toilet flushed, Bett turned and kept her back close to the wall.

The woman smiled at them as she washed her hands and pulled out a piece of paper towel. 'You're two of the granddaughters, aren't you?'

'That's right,' they said politely.

'You're wonderful to do that musical for your grandmother. We'll definitely be booking tickets. And all for such a good cause. The Valley could do with a whole fleet of new ambulances.'

They both smiled and nodded as the woman left the room.

'Did you know anything about this musical?' Bett asked, checking first the door was completely shut.

'Not a word. Had she said anything to you, in any of her letters?'

So Carrie had known that Lola wrote regularly to Bett. She

shook her head. 'It's ridiculous of course. There's no way we can do it.'

'Of course we can't. I don't know what she was thinking.'

There was silence for a moment and then a loud blast of music came from outside. Carrie started. 'I'd better get out there. It's the last spot prize before we sing "Happy Birthday". Look, what about this?' She took off the gold wrap from her shoulders and in a deft movement tied it around Bett's waist.

Bett sucked in her stomach, thrown by Carrie's closeness and waiting for a comment about her having put on weight. It didn't come. Instead, Carrie twisted the fabric, tucked it here and there and then tied a loose knot in the side, so the shimmering material fell in folds. 'I think it'll work. What do you think?'

Bett stepped back and looked in the full-length mirror. She wasn't sure what Carrie had done, but the effect was great. The gold wrap folded over the brocade as though it was meant to be there, adding a layer of texture to the whole outfit. 'It looks like a designer did it.'

'I saw it in *Vogue* actually. Multi-layering or something, I think it's called. Does it feel secure?'

Bett felt it. 'Yes.'

Lola's voice was clearly heard over the speakers, ordering everyone to sit down as the cake was about to arrive.

Carrie glanced at her watch. 'She's right on schedule. I'd better go.'

'Thanks a lot, Carrie.'

'You're welcome, Bett.'

It was the longest conversation they'd had in three years.

CHAPTER SEVEN

THE MAGPIES were calling into the sharp blue sky. Bumper the sheep was giving plaintive little bleats. The glass bottles were rattling as Jim Quinlan carried the first of the crates out to the bottle bank behind the kitchen. Car engines revved as guests prepared to leave the motel.

In bed in room number six, Bett groaned at all the noise. Couldn't they keep it down out there? Her poor brain was already suffering noise overload, crammed with snatches of conversation and flashes of memories from the party. What time had she gone to bed? Three or four? She peered at her bedside clock. Nine thirty. Whose bright idea had it been to have this emergency meeting about the musical at ten? And whose bright idea had it been to finish the evening with cocktails? Hers on both counts, she realised.

She leaned over, picking up the leaflet Lola had presented to her last night. She'd tried to look at it when she got back to her room, but her eyes were unable to focus, her head swirling with jetlag, too much alcohol and too many conversations. She glanced at it again now. *Many Happy Returns*. A musical for all the family. To be performed by the Alphabet Sisters and the people of the Clare Valley. Oh no it wouldn't be.

The night before, Lola had collared her on the dance floor in between the Siege of Ennis and the Walls of Limerick. 'Isn't that Carrie's wrap? What a nice touch. You're getting on so well already, then?'

Bett didn't take the bait. 'We still can't do it, Lola.'

'Can't do the musical? Of course you can. You have to have more confidence in your own abilities, Bett. I've been telling you that for years.'

'It's not about confidence, it's about . . .'

Lola smiled. 'Yes?'

Bett told the truth. 'It's about not being asked, about being presumed upon, about wondering whether any of us actually wanted to do this.'

'But I thought you would love to do it. I've been working on it for ten years.'

'Lola, you haven't. I've been gone a few years, I know, but I've never heard a squeak out of you about it.'

'I first read the article about General MacArthur ten years ago. You're just nitpicking. So will you do it or not?'

'It's not up to me. It's up to Anna and Carrie too.'

'So if they agree, you will too?'

'Lola, stop this.'

'Bett, I'm ashamed of you. Telling an old woman off on her birthday. We'll discuss it in full tomorrow when I give you the script.'

'You actually have written a script?'

'Of course. What did you think I'd done, scribbled a few notes on the back of a shopping list?'

Bett remembered an Alphabet Sisters performance that hadn't been too far from that. She'd been about to remind Lola when her grandmother glided off, cornering another man for a dance.

The party had continued for several more hours, with the DJ playing a mixture of Irish jigs, fifties dance tracks and old-style tunes. Bett had two waltzes with Richard. As they turned around the floor the second time, she noticed him laughing at something over her shoulder.

She turned in time to see Lola lift up her skirt and give a little high kick. Oh, no. Please don't let her do her *La Cage Aux Folles* impersonation here tonight. She had done it at one of the school concerts and, to Bett's eternal shame, three of her male classmates had caught sight of Lola's voluminous knickers and told the rest of the class about them. She'd been tormented by them for days: 'Does flashing your undies like that run in the family, Bett?'

'Is your grandmother always as entertaining as this?' Richard asked.

She shook her head. 'She's quite low-key tonight, actually. A little subdued. I must ask her if she's feeling okay.'

He laughed. 'I enjoyed all those photos of you and your sisters in your performing days, too. It looked like lots of fun. Certainly put my childhood days as a boy scout to shame.'

Bett just smiled. Lots of fun? In the early years, perhaps.

'You weren't tempted to do a surprise performance for Lola tonight?' he asked as they waltzed past Lola once again. 'Spring out of a birthday cake?'

'No. We broke up too many years ago for something like that.'

Another twirl. 'And why was that? You didn't want to make a career of it?'

She gave the answer she always did. Not true, but true enough. 'We were getting a bit old to be wearing matching dresses.'

Lola came up to them both. 'You're getting on. Good, good. I was sure you would. Bett's a journalist too, Richard. Did I tell you?'

'You did, Lola.'

'Richard is here researching a book, aren't you, Richard?'

'Really? What's it about?' Bett was glad to change the subject.

Lola waved her question away. 'Oh, plenty of time to hear about that tomorrow. Come on, Dicky, come and dance with me again.' And off they had gone.

Bett had also danced with her father. He had noticed her sitting at a table to the side of the dance floor and come over, bowed gallantly and asked her in extremely polite language if she would be so kind as to give him the next dance.

'If you put it so nicely,' she'd said, laughing as she took his hand. They walked out to the dance floor as the old-fashioned waltz music started up. It had taken only moments for her to match her steps to his. Jim had taught all of his daughters to waltz properly, as Lola had taught him as a boy. As children, they'd loved to crowd in on him in the motel bar after school, and, if it was quiet, take turns Foot-Dancing with him – standing on his feet and being waltzed around the room to the tune of whatever was on the radio or TV at the time.

'You're still mister twinkle-toes himself, I see,' she smiled up at him as they moved down one side of the dance floor.

'It helps when I have such a beautiful and graceful young woman to dance with,' he said.

'Charmer.'

'No, it's true, Bett. You were always the lightest on your feet.'

'Was I?'

'Yes, really. And I have to say you look a picture tonight. You've lost weight, haven't you?'

'A little,' she said, fighting a smile. Her dad had always said that to her over the years, no matter what size she was, bigger or smaller.

'Well, whatever you've done, you look great. The three of you do.'

They were silent for a few turns of the floor, then her father squeezed her hand. 'I was saying to Anna earlier, and I want to say it again to you now, we're very happy you're all home again.'

By 'we' Bett knew he meant he and Geraldine. Their father had often been the spokesman for the pair of them. 'I am too.' And she meant it, she realised.

'And you're not going to rush off again, are you? We get to have you back for a little while?'

'I don't know yet.'

'Well, there's a room here for you as long as you want it. And a job if you need it. You know that, don't you?'

She'd squeezed his hand then. 'Thanks, Dad.'

Bett turned over in bed again. The slide show came to mind, and with it a niggling thought that had occurred to her during the party. Something about one of the photos had surprised her, but between the debacle with the dress and then the rest of the party, she hadn't given it proper thought. And now her poor brain was so drenched in alcohol it wouldn't come back to her. Was it one of the Alphabet Sisters photos? Or one of Lola's? Oh, it hurt to even think . . .

She lay there hugging her pillow. Another party memory returned. Rebecca, her fellow reporter on the paper three years ago, had arrived late. Bett had noticed in a moment that she hadn't changed at all. She was tall, willowy, her hair in a stylish blonde ponytail. She'd headed straight for Bett, hugged her, poured them both a glass of wine, then made an offer, blunt as ever. 'The woman who took over from you is about to explode with a baby and I need a part-time reporter to cover for her maternity leave. The job's yours if you're interested.'

Bett had needed to shout over the noise of the music. 'I'm only home for a week or two. I'll probably be going on to Melbourne or Sydney.'

'Lola said you'd be staying here, though. Surely you've been yearning for the simple country lifestyle? Come on, Bett. Think about it.'

They'd talked about it over another glass of wine and a cocktail or two. It had started to sound so tempting. Not having to worry about moving yet. Not having to start job-hunting . . . But had she agreed to take the job or not? She really couldn't remember. Turning the pillow over to the cool side, Bett shut her eyes and gave another long, low groan.

Anna was first to arrive in the dining room. She'd left Ellen in the kitchen with Geraldine, helping to clear the guests' breakfast trays. Her mother and father had been up for hours. The function room was already back in order, the decorations tidied away, the last tray of plates and glasses going through the industrial dishwasher. Geraldine had waved away any offers of help, preferring to do it her way. Anna had been secretly relieved.

She took a seat at the window, looking out over the valley. When they first moved into the motel, the hills around them had been bare. Bit by bit the town of Clare was getting closer, houses being built on one side and across the road, a car showroom under construction to the left. The view was still beautiful, though, especially in the morning sunlight. The curving rows of grapevines across the road were a lush, glowing green against the dark soil.

'Morning.' It was Carrie.

'Morning.'

Carrie poured a coffee and took a seat at another table. 'Huge night, wasn't it?'

'A huge announcement, you mean.'

'It's ridiculous, of course.'

'Of course.'

'You did a great job organising the party, though. It all went so smoothly.'

Carrie coloured suddenly. 'Thanks.'

Anna decided to ask the question she'd been wanting to since she arrived. 'Before Lola gets here and catches me, I have to ask you something. Was Matthew okay about not coming last night?'

'He was fine. He understood,' Carrie said briskly. 'He's working up north at the moment, anyway. On a sheep station. It saved him a long trip.'

'Oh. Good.' Anna waited, but it seemed Carrie had nothing more to say about him. All right then, she wouldn't talk about him any more either. They stared out the window.

'Morning.' They turned. It was Bett, hair bedraggled, mascara around her eyes, wearing what was either a baggy pair of pyjamas or a particularly strange tracksuit. 'Has it been called off yet?'

'Any minute now,' Anna said.

The three of them sat silently, then the door opened again. Richard Lawrence stood there. 'Good morning. Am I too late for breakfast? I'm afraid I forgot to put my order out last night.'

Carrie stood up. 'It doesn't matter. I'll get something for you. Do you need our sore-head special or the puritan's delight?'

Bett translated, guessing he was probably as hungover as she was. The last time she'd seen him he was enthusiastically joining a conga line around the room. 'She means bacon and eggs for the full hangover cure or a smug continental breakfast.' She caught Carrie's surprised look. Of course she remembered the terms they gave the breakfasts. She noticed Anna was waiting to be introduced. 'Oh, sorry. I thought you two would have met last night. Richard, this is the oldest of us, Anna Quinlan, actress, and mother of one. Anna, this is Richard Lawrence from London. He's a journalist staying here at the motel while he researches a book he's writing.' Once again, she felt Carrie's eyes on her. Was she surprised Bett had learnt so much about him?

'Hello, Anna.' Richard gave her his lovely smile. 'I must say I'm thinking of throwing all that research away in exchange for another audience with your grandmother. Much more material there, I think.'

'Good. You can do the musical instead of us while you're at it,' Anna said.

He seemed surprised. 'You're not going to do it?'

'Of course they're going to do it.' Lola swept in behind him, dressed in a turquoise kaftan top over white trousers, in full makeup and jewellery. 'Dicky, dear, how are you? Marvellous dances we shared last night. You've a fine pair of hips on you. Snake hips, I'd have called you in my younger days.'

Bett was too hungover to protest at Lola's boldness for once. Her grandmother could have come in juggling puppies and wearing a sequinned bikini this morning for all she cared. She just wanted to go back to bed.

Carrie took Richard into the kitchen and handed him over to her mother, then came back and shut the door. 'So then, Lola, what's the best way to call this whole thing off?'

'Call it off? Why would we want to do that? I thought we agreed last night we'd do it?'

'No, we didn't,' Anna said.

'We can't do it, Lola,' Bett said.

'Why not?'

'Because we won't be here to do it,' Anna said patiently.

'You won't? Where will you be?'

'Well, Ellen and I are going back to Sydney, of course.' This definitely wasn't the moment to mention she'd been thinking about staying on for a month or two.

'Why?'

'Because it's where we live. Where I work. Where Ellen goes to school.'

Lola noticed Glenn wasn't mentioned. 'So? Live here for a while. It will do you both good. There are some fine schools here too.' She turned her attention to Carrie. 'What about you, Caroline? I'd have thought you'd leap at this. A chance to get back on the stage.'

'I'm very busy with the motel,' she said quickly.

'Bett, what about you? Didn't you tell me in one of your letters how much you've missed playing the piano? And you're staying here in the Valley, aren't you?'

Bett's head was throbbing now. 'I don't know for sure.'

'What about the job Rebecca offered you at the newspaper?'

'How do you know about that?'

'I told you. I had a word with her in the street last week. And I saw her talking to you last night.'

'Shall we just get a town crier to shout out everyone's secrets and be done with it?' Bett said crossly.

Lola wondered if her judgement was failing. She'd thought they'd leap at it. This called for plan B. 'Very well then. There's something else I need to tell you. The other reason I brought you all back here.'

Three heads shot up. They'd been waiting for this.

Lola paused dramatically. 'I was at the doctor's last week. She's worried about me.' She was too. Worried that Lola was drinking too much. She'd promised her she'd cut back after the party. And perhaps she would.

'Worried about what?' Bett asked the question for all of them.

She had their attention. Good. Now, use it. 'The fact that I am a very elderly lady and that my time on this earth is fast running out.'

'Your doctor actually said that to you?' Carrie exclaimed.

'She didn't put it exactly like that. But all I'm saying is who knows how long I might be here?' That was true enough, she thought – who knew how long any of them would be around? 'And it would mean so much to me if the three of you staged the musical,' Lola continued in her most cajoling voice. 'Anna, the local schools are very good, you know. There's even a choice of denominations, though I don't know what you believe these days. And, Bett, Rebecca tells me the job she's offering is part-time and for six months, which would suit you well, too. Plenty of time for rehearsals. And you, Carrie, well, of course we'll all lend a hand with the motel. But surely you'll be able to make time to learn your lines for the lead role.'

'The lead?'

Lola gave a light laugh. 'I keep forgetting you haven't actually read the script. Yes, I'd thought of you for the lead, Carrie. You as musical director, Bett, unless you would like to get up on stage again? No, I thought not. And, Anna, I actually saw you as the director of the entire production. We'd change the billing, to read "Written by Lola Quinlan, Directed by Anna Quinlan, Music by Bett Quinlan, Starring Carrie Quinlan". Oh, I can see the programs now.' A calculated pause followed, before she lowered her voice. 'Of course, once you've all read it you might have your own ideas.'

Bett knew at that moment how sheep felt when they were being nosed into a pen by a collie.

'So you have actually finished it?' Anna was still suspicious.

'Indeed I have,' Lola said proudly. 'I have had to resist some extra special finishing touches, but I do believe it is nearly there. About two hours with an interval. Seven main characters, a chorus, lots of minor characters. You'd be able to involve half the Valley if you wanted. There are even one or two parts for children. I was thinking of Ellen if you think she is up to it. And I've even written in a cameo for the Alphabet Sisters. Imagine. That was sheer indulgence on my part. You might decide to take that out.'

'We haven't decided anything.' Anna spoke for them all.

'Of course you haven't. You have to read it first.' Lola reached into the bag beside her. 'So here you are, your reading copies, hot off the press. Mind you, by the looks of the three of you, you might want to wait until those hangovers have passed. Why you insist on mixing the grape and the grain I don't know. Wine one minute, spirits the next. Yes, Bett, I saw you with those cocktails at the end of the night. I stuck to gin and tonics all evening so my system knew exactly what to expect and here I am right as rain.' She finished handing out the folders. 'So, now I'm off back to my room to write some thankyou cards.' She was off back for a sleep, actually. She was extremely hungover. 'So will we meet here tonight to see what you think?'

The scripts were nearly an inch thick. 'Tonight?' Anna squeaked, in nothing like her usual modulated tone. 'It'll take longer than that to read it, let alone to make decisions about it.'

'It's not as if we can drop everything, Lola. I've got a motel to run, remember,' Carrie added.

Bett said nothing. She just wanted someone to carry her to her bed.

'Very well, then,' Lola said. 'Shall we say tomorrow afternoon? Excellent. You can prepare all your questions and then we'll meet again. Splendid.'

Richard walked in from the kitchen at that moment, carrying a plate of bacon and eggs and a large mug of coffee.

Lola smiled at him. 'Ah, Dicky, all sorted then? Good. Enjoy your breakfast, won't you?'

'I will. And did you enjoy your meeting?'

Lola gave a happy sigh. 'It was marvellous.'

Later that day, after a long refreshing sleep, Lola made her way to the kitchen. Lunch had been served some hours before and the preparations for dinner were still to be done. It was Lola's favourite time in the motel. The large silver table in the middle of the kitchen was cleared and shining. The air was still filled with cooking smells. Geraldine was in the office sorting accounts. Carrie had gone home for the afternoon to make a start on reading the script. Anna and Ellen had gone for a picnic. Bett was in her room. Lola helped herself to a cup of tea and the remains of last night's chocolate pudding dessert. She had just opened the newspaper to the crossword when her son walked in.

'You look well set up. Geraldine not here?'

Lola made a show of looking under her cup and saucer. 'I can't see her, no.'

Jim grinned. 'I never learn, do I? Ask an obvious question –'

'Get a clever answer. How are you, Jimmy? Sit down here and talk to your old mother.'

They rarely had the opportunity, but Lola loved these moments, looking at her fine strong son, enjoying the energy that buzzed off him. So hard to think this nearly sixty-year-old man was the same little fellow who had traipsed from motel to motel with her in those early days. It had never been a bother to him. Sunny-natured he was, through some stroke of luck. God knows his father had been anything but sunny-natured.

Jim made himself a cup of tea. 'Can I get you anything else, Lola? More tea? More pudding?'

'I've had exactly as much as I want, down to the last crumb, darling, thank you. I want to hear you talk, that's what I want.'

They took a sip of tea. 'The girls seem to be getting on fine,' Jim said.

'Do you think?' Lola smiled.

'Well, I thought there might have been a bit of unpleasantness, on account of the situation with Matthew and all, but so far so good.'

'So far so splendid,' Lola agreed.

'If we could just get the three of them back cleaning and waitressing, it'd be like old times, wouldn't it? Do you remember those nights, when you were first training the girls? You had them all balancing books on their heads and carrying trays of glasses. We must have gone through a dozen that first night.'

'Their postures are excellent, though, Jim. You have to admit that.'

'It was great novelty value, too, having the three of them waitressing. Especially when you'd get them to sing at the end of the shift. I never saw anything like those tips in all my years in motels.'

'It is years now, isn't it? But you've never regretted going into the motel business with me, have you? Resented all that moving around?'

'Of course I have. Bringing me up like a gypsy. My entire childhood spent in kitchens and bars, never knowing how long I'd call one place home.'

Lola leaned back and smiled. She always enjoyed it when Jim teased her like this. 'That's right. And don't forget you were chained to the sink since you were barely able to walk.'

'Exactly. Rinsing glasses, washing pots and pans. Do you know I was the only boy in any of my schools who had dishpan hands?'

'And don't forget I always used to drag you out of those schools, just as you started to make friends.'

'Not to mention ruining any chance I had of being a professional footy player. Remember that time we moved motels three weeks before the grand final?'

'I'd forgotten that. Probably the best thing for you. You'd be a mass of broken bones and bruises if you'd gone on with the sport.'

'The move after that was the best one we ever made, of course.'

'Was it? Why?'

Jim laughed. 'It was where I met Geraldine.'

'Of course.' Geraldine had been working in the kitchen of that next motel, training as a cook. When Lola and Jim had moved on again, two years later, Geraldine had come with them, as his wife, and already pregnant with Anna.

Lola often wondered if Jim had ever noticed that she and Geraldine couldn't bear one another. Oh, they were both polite on the surface – with all of them living in such close proximity, there had to be good manners. But it had still been difficult. In the early days, Lola had seriously considered moving to another motel, leaving Geraldine and Jim to their own devices. But then the girls had come along and Lola had quite simply fallen in love with them. Since then she'd made a pact with herself to keep things fine between her and Geraldine. Jim was devoted to her, but Lola still couldn't see why. She was too much of a cold fish, in Lola's opinion. Buttoned-up. More interested in Jim and the motel than her daughters. It always hurt Lola to see the three girls trying to get Geraldine's attention and usually failing. It had been another reason for her to shower them with attention. If she had needed any more reasons.

Lola reached into her bag, took out a folder and passed it to her son.

'For me?'

'For you. For you and Geraldine, in fact.'

'What is it?'

'Have a look and tell me what you see.'

'Tickets.' He opened them. 'First-class train tickets.' There were two sets, one for a two-night trip on the legendary *Ghan* from Adelaide through the desert centre of Australia to Darwin. The other for the *Indian Pacific*, a four-day journey from Sydney across the Nullarbor Plain to Perth. In another folder were plane tickets for their connecting flights. He glanced through them too. 'All in the name of Jim and Geraldine Quinlan.'

Lola loved these sorts of moments. 'And now look at the dates.'

'Departing from Adelaide next week? And not coming back for a month? Lola, we can't take these.'

'Of course you can. I insist.' She held up her hand to quell his protest. 'I'll run the place while you're away. And don't tell me I can't because I was doing it long before you even had a notion. And I've got the girls to help me now, as you so rightly pointed out. I've been in touch with Geraldine's stand-by cook and she said she'd love the work. Carrie already knows this place backwards. Bett is a terrific cleaner once she sets her mind to it. And so is Anna, as long as you give her ten pairs of gloves. Ellen could help, too. And all three of them are very good waitresses. I'll take care of all the rosters myself.'

'Have you asked the girls about this? No, don't answer that one. And presumably you're going to tell me these tickets are non-refundable and that if we don't take them now and do as you say you'll never talk to me again?'

Lola nodded happily.

'And you've got the rest of your argument all worked out too, I suppose. That we haven't had a holiday in years and this is the best chance to do it.'

'That's right.'

Jim was grinning. 'So I'd better go straight to Geraldine and tell her to start packing, is that it?'

'In a nutshell. Come here, darling.' She reached up and gave him a big kiss on the forehead. 'Thank you, Jimmy. You always were such an obedient boy.'

CHAPTER EIGHT

IN HER room the next day, Bett stopped midway through unpacking the last items from her suitcase. She'd checked the bookings register and it looked like she'd have this room for the next few nights at least. That had always been the drawback of sleeping in the motel rooms, having to pack up quickly and do a hasty but thorough cleaning job when real guests turned up. As teenagers, the three of them had got it down to a fine art. Carrie held the record, having once moved all her belongings, remade the bed and cleaned, polished and vacuumed a room in the time it had taken the guests to walk from the reception desk to their car and drive around to the parking space in front of the room.

When they were in their mid-teens, their father had presented each of them with a large box on wheels. The boxes were perfect for storing or transporting their clothes, pictures, vases, posters – all the things they liked to bring into the rooms to make them their own. Even better, they looked official enough when they were being wheeled in and out of rooms. Their boxes of tricks, he called them. Lola had called them their personality boxes, after seeing them lined up side by side one afternoon, when they'd hurriedly needed to move out of their rooms. Anna's had been full of makeup samples, a small gold-framed mirror, a theatre magazine, a book of tips on stagecraft and a length of fake fur that she had taken to wearing dramatically wrapped around her shoulders. Bett's box of tricks had held a smaller box crammed with music cassettes, a portable tape player, a bundle of imported pop magazines, sheet music for the piano, empty chip packets and books. Carrie, animal-mad at the time, had stored her two cloth mice toys, a book of horse tales and three packets of plastic farmyard animals.

Bett had to force the wardrobe door shut. There was only just enough room for the shirts, skirts and dresses she had brought on the plane with her. The rest of her things were coming by ship. She'd slowly put together a whole new wardrobe over the past three years, having taken hardly any of her belongings when she'd left the Valley in such a hurry. She remembered ringing Lola from Melbourne a few weeks after the big fight and apologising for leaving so much behind. 'Mum told me you'd packed up all my things. Thanks, Lola. You've gone to so much trouble for me.'

'No I haven't.'

'But she said you'd packed up all my things and stored them.'

'I did. But I didn't go to any trouble. I just flung everything into lots of boxes and taped them shut. You'll have your work cut out whenever you decide to come back.'

It had turned out to be a good thing, in a way. Being forced to start from scratch, on a very small budget, most of her clothes had been picked up at vintage shops and second-hand clothing stores around Dublin and London. The high-street shops had never been any good for her, stocked with clothes made for women with far smaller and more willowy bodies than she possessed. And vintage clothes had their own appeal, or so she'd convinced herself. She'd smiled at the irony. After years of protesting about being forced to wear vintage clothes as the Alphabet Sisters costumes, she'd voluntarily started going out and buying them for herself.

A noise at the open door interrupted her thoughts. It hadn't quite been a knock, more of a soft shuffle against the wood. She turned in time to see Ellen duck out of sight.

'Hi, Ellie,' she called, in a bright cheery voice.

There was no reaction from Ellen. 'Hi, Ellie. You can come in if you like,' Bett said again, in a more normal voice.

The little girl came in, sidling against the cupboard.

Bett smiled at her. 'How are you?'

'Good.' The voice was very soft.

'Have you been helping Grandpa with the bottles?' She'd seen the two of them pushing the trolley that morning, her father giving Ellen little rides back and forth.

A nod.

'And did you have a good time at Lola's party?'

Another nod.

Bett wasn't sure what to talk to Ellen about. It had been years since she'd had anything to do with a child. And she didn't really know Ellen any more, did she? There was a big difference between a four-year-old and a seven-year-old girl. Especially one who had been through what Ellen had been through. Bett had a flash of how Lola used to talk to them – as if they were her co-conspirators, her equals. Could she talk to Ellen about her weight-loss and lack-of-boyfriend troubles? No, not much common ground there. They could talk about children's TV programs, perhaps, except Bett hadn't seen any in years.

Ellen was fiddling with the bottle of sunscreen Bett had left on the cupboard. She was feeling just as shy, Bett realised. Oh, the sweet thing. 'Come and sit here beside me, Ellie, and let's have a chat.' She left her unpacking and sat down on the floor, patting the carpet beside her.

Ellen hesitated. 'On the floor?

Isn't that what children did? Sit on floors? 'That's right. Would you rather a cushion? I didn't realise you were from a royal family.' She bit her lip. Keep your sarcasm to yourself, Bett. She is a child.

To her surprise, Ellen smiled. 'If I was royal, it would have to be a velvet cushion, wouldn't it?'

'With tassels,' Bett agreed solemnly.

'What's a tassel?'

'A sort of – um, a sort of ponytail of thread attached to the edge, like a decoration.'

'Yes, I'd have tassels. And a waiter standing there with a silver tray and some drinks.'

This was more like it. 'And what sort of drinks would we have? You mean we, don't you? You are planning on sharing?'

'Perhaps.' The little smile again. 'It would be chocolate milk for me and for you . . .'

Bett waited.

'Beer.'

'Not champagne?'

A shake of the head. 'Beer.'

Bett pulled a face. 'And after we've had our drinks, what will we do?'

'Play in the castle.'

'On our own? Or have we got pets?' Oh, bloody hell. Now what had she done by bringing up animals?

'No dogs. I'm scared of big dogs now.'

I bet you are, Bett thought, glancing quickly at the scar again. She was surprised Ellen had even mentioned dogs. She couldn't help herself blurting out a question. 'Do you remember much about it, Ellen?'

A little nod.

Should she be asking this? 'You must have been very brave, afterwards. It must have been very scary.'

The little girl wasn't looking at her now. She was concentrating on her feet. She shrugged.

'And you're so much better now, aren't you?' Bett said, feeling like a car hurriedly reversing out of a one-way street. Back to the game, quick. 'So we won't have a dog. Will we have a cat, then?'

'No, a sheep. Like Bumper.'

Good. They were back on track. 'What a great idea.'

A voice from outside interrupted them. 'Bett? Are you there? Is Ellen with you? I need some help.'

Bett had never been so glad to hear her mother's voice calling. 'Come on, sweetheart. It sounds like you've got potatoes to peel.'

Geraldine appeared at the door. 'There you are, Ellen. Come in and help taste some of tonight's desserts, would you? I can't tell if they're ready.'

Ellen skipped off cheerfully. Bett put away her empty suitcase and checked the time. Nearly three o'clock. She'd better hurry. Time for their first production meeting, as Lola was calling it. A get-out-of-this-if-we-can meeting, Bett was calling it. She peered into the kitchen as she went past. Geraldine was back at the stove, Jim at the table with Ellen on his knee, bowls of chocolate pudding in front of them. They were poring over a map of Australia and a pile of travel brochures.

Bett had been taken aback at the news of her parents' holiday. 'Don't take it personally now, Bett,' Lola had said to her that morning. 'They're not in a hurry to get away from you. It's a practical decision. Your poor parents haven't been away properly in years, and casual staff are so expensive. With the three of you home to lend a hand this is the perfect opportunity for them to get away.'

'But we've all just got here.'

'And you'll see plenty of them when they get back.' She had pulled Bett close, planted a big kiss on her forehead, then lowered her voice. 'I've actually done it deliberately, so I can have you all to myself. You know I never liked sharing you girls with your parents.'

Anna, Carrie and Lola were already in the function room when she arrived. Anna was explaining to Lola that it might be better if she left them alone for a little while. 'We want to talk about it on our own first, Lola. You know, in case –'

'You hurt my feelings?' At Anna's guilty nod, Lola laughed. 'I'm eighty, darling. I've no feelings left to hurt. No, talk away amongst yourselves and I'll look forward to hearing what you've got to say.' She gave them a cheery wave, then moved through the front door, around the side of the motel to the back of the function room. She'd been in earlier and opened all the windows, knowing their voices would float out. She'd even taken a chair out there. Silly things, as if she was going to let them talk about her musical without her hearing.

The sisters pulled their chairs around a table in the centre of the room, the scripts and a plunger of coffee in front of them. Bett shot both of them a look. Anna was as sleekly turned out as ever – designer clothes, dramatic silver jewellery, all thin lines and sharp hair. Carrie looked like she was on her way to film a shampoo ad, bouncy blonde hair and trim body, in hipster jeans and tight-fitting T-shirt. Bett tucked her unruly hair behind her ears, tugged at her waisted jeans and fortunately not tight-fitting T-shirt.

'So,' Anna said, taking charge. The mood was tense. 'Have you both read it?'

Carrie and Bett nodded.

'And what did you think?'

Neither Bett nor Carrie spoke, both looking down at their scripts. Anna waited a moment. Still nothing. Then she leaned forward and spoke, her voice very low and very firm. 'When I was at acting school, there were sometimes things I had to do that I didn't like. Pretend to be a dog. Stand in a chorus line when I'd rather have been the lead. It happens at work still. I have to take on some jobs I'd rather not because that's just the way it is. Sometimes you have to do things you would rather not, either to please other people or because they need to be done.'

Bett tried not to react. She'd always hated it when Anna lectured them like this.

Carrie felt like rolling her eyes. Who did Anna think she was? Their mother?

'Now, I don't know whether Lola spent ten years or ten minutes on this, but I think we owe it to her at least to talk properly about it. You both know as well as I do how good she was to us. Right now putting on a musical is the last thing I want to do, to be perfectly honest. But the way I see it is, the sooner we at least talk about it, and decide whether we do it or not, the sooner it's over.'

Bett stared at her script some more. The worst thing about Anna was that apart from being so bossy she was also so often completely and maddeningly right.

'I'm not asking you to do it for me,' Anna continued. 'I'm asking you to do it for Lola. It would make her very happy.'

Carrie looked up then. 'It's easy for you to say. She's been driving me and Mum bananas the past few months.'

'She's been driving Mum bananas for more than thirty years, Carrie, and you know it. And as for you – just think of it as good practice for when you and Matthew have children. If you can handle Lola, you'll be able to handle any naughty child.' She ignored Carrie's intake of breath and poured herself some more coffee.

Outside, Lola was weighing up whether to be hurt by anything she'd heard. After a moment's reflection, she decided not to be. Nothing there she hadn't known, anyway.

Anna took a sip of coffee before tapping the script in a business-like manner. 'So then, shall we start again? What did you both think of it?'

Recalling several of the scenes, Bett suddenly found herself trying not to laugh. 'It was certainly different,' she offered. She noticed quick answering grins from Carrie and Anna, before their shutters came down again. Different – the word used in the Valley for anything a bit challenging or out of the ordinary, a polite way of saying appalling. 'I like your dress, Anna. It's different.' 'You've had a new hair cut, Bett. Gee, it's different.'

'Let me rephrase that,' Bett said. 'I think it's the maddest piece of musical theatre I have ever read in my life.'

Anna's lip twitched. 'I'd agree with that. Carrie?'

Carrie still looked a little sulky. 'If you ask me it's like she took all her favourite pieces from all her favourite musicals, flung them into a blender with a few lines of dialogue and this is what came out.'

By the window, Lola smiled serenely. Good girl, Carrie. That was exactly what she had done.

Bett turned to Anna. 'Could you actually work out what was going on?'

'I think so. It's set in Terowie, at wartime, where the townspeople –'

'Or the villagers, as she calls them,' Carrie interrupted.

'The villagers get wind that General Douglas MacArthur is coming through on a train –'

Cue three verses of 'Chattanooga Choo Choo', Bett recalled.

'And a big row breaks out between two rivals in the local Country Women's Association over who will organise the welcoming party at the railway station. Which develops into a full-scale row – amazingly like the fight scene from *West Side Story*. And of course the son of one rival and the daughter of the other are secretly in love.'

'And just happen to be called Romeo and Juliet, those two common names in 1940s Australia,' Carrie said.

Lola bristled. They might well have been common names in Terowie. How were the girls to know? She listened closely as Anna, Bett and Carrie took it in turns relating the story. They might have been laughing at her musical, but at least it meant they were talking about something.

'But then Juliet starts falling for the young American GI who is organising MacArthur's visit. And Romeo gets jealous and they split up.'

'So the GI starts feeling guilty for wreaking all this havoc on a small town and confesses as much to the lad-about-town who's been watching all the antics from afar.'

'Who happens to be the nephew of a train driver and has the bright idea to get the GI himself to dress up as General MacArthur and arrive at the platform one day early. So the CWA women scurry around and prepare his welcoming party.'

'And then they pretend that for security reasons he'll have to do it all over again, so they bring the train through again the next day, except this time of course it's the real MacArthur.'

'And the other group gets to serve their morning tea and do the welcoming party, too, and that's when General MacArthur delivers his big "I shall return" speech.'

'And the GI and the cheeky lad-about-town laugh to themselves about the fact he has already returned.'

Ingenious, Lola thought proudly.

Anna leaned back elegantly in her chair. 'And they all live happily ever after, including the couple. Cue "Happy Talk" from *South Pacific*.'

'Has Lola actually made up all the General MacArthur business?' Bett asked.

'No, it's true,' Carrie said. 'I checked on the Internet this morning. He did stop in Terowie and that is where he made that famous speech. But I don't think any of that other stuff happened, especially the war scenes in the beginning.'

'No, I'd hardly imagine Mrs MacArthur singing "My Favourite Things" to her scared little son in that first scene, when they're flying in from the Philippines,' Anna said.

'And I don't reckon the Terowie villagers came out every day, gazed at their cornfields and sang "Oh What a Beautiful Morning",' Bett added, fighting another smile.

'At least she didn't have the CWA catering women singing that "MacArthur Park" song.' Anna was actually laughing now. 'I was sure I could see it coming. A chorus row of women upset because their cakes had been left out in the rain.'

Outside, Lola wasn't laughing. She had written a scene just like that. She'd only taken it out because she wasn't sure if they would be able to manage rain special effects at the Clare Town Hall.

'There were some good bits, though, didn't you think?' Carrie said. 'I loved the scene where the couple are dancing around the local football oval, singing "I Am Sixteen Going on Seventeen".'

Anna raised an eyebrow. 'You mean the scene that is a direct lift from *The Sound of Music*?'

'Well, that was always my favourite scene in the film, too,' Carrie said defensively. 'And I also liked that scene the night of the first MacArthur's visit, when the lead actress sings "I Could Have Danced All Night" from *My Fair Lady*.'

Bett knew that song well. It had been Carrie's most popular solo moment in the Alphabet Sisters days.

'But I don't think it works when the next day she sings "I Like To Be in America",' Anna said. 'Not when she's been going on about how much she loves the Australian countryside and that man, Romeo, or whatever his name is.'

'But that's the whole thing,' Carrie said passionately. 'She thinks she loves Romeo, but now her head has been turned by MacArthur and his GI and all the drama and talk of America. She's torn between her simple life in the country and the pursuit of her dreams.'

Anna stared at her. 'You've really lived this, Carrie, haven't you?'

'Well, I can see what Lola's trying to say,' Carrie said blushing. 'And I think that song is perfect there.'

That song which just happened to be Carrie's second-favourite song from the Alphabet Sisters days, Bett thought. She'd just realised what Lola had done.

Anna's tone was now extremely businesslike. 'And what did you both think of the Alphabet Sisters cameo in the second act?'

Bett's smile disappeared. 'I crossed it out.' She didn't look at Carrie.

'I did too,' Carrie said, not looking at Bett either.

Anna felt the tension in the room increase. She glanced between the two of them. 'Fine. I'll cross it out too.' She patted her script.

'Here's what I think. It's completely mad, of course, and it needs a bit of work, but it could be done. That's if Lola is actually serious about it.'

Lola popped her head up over the window ledge. 'I'm quite serious.'

They all jumped. Anna frowned. 'Lola, this is supposed to be a private meeting.'

'Don't be ridiculous. You must have known I'd be eavesdropping outside. But you spoke too low for my poor old ears at the end there. What did you all think of it?'

'It's actually very good,' Anna said.

'Don't sound so surprised,' Lola said.

'I really enjoyed it,' Bett said.

'I knew you would.'

'There's definitely something in there for everybody,' Carrie said.

'That was my whole intention. So it could work?'

'Well, yes,' Anna said. 'But it's not like the Alphabet Sisters performances, Lola. It isn't just the three of us standing up singing a few tunes wearing matching dresses. It would need a hall for a start.'

'I've booked it.' She waved the flyer at them. 'For March twentieth. It's the anniversary of General MacArthur's visit. Perfect, don't you think?'

'That's so soon. What about sets? Costumes?'

'Len the butcher said he'd be happy to help. He's not a bad carpenter. I've been tucking bits and pieces away for costumes from the charity shop for the past few months. If you don't like them, we could hire some in Adelaide.'

'And what about a band?'

Lola gestured grandly at Bett. 'Who needs a band when we've

got Bett? You could use the piano here for rehearsals and we could move it to the town hall for the show. Though there are lots of talented musicians in the Valley if you wanted more than piano.'

Bett was going through the song list. Lola had looked after her too. She had chosen many of her favourites, ones with lots of bright piano music.

Anna was leafing through the script again. When she first left drama school in Sydney, she'd joined a musical theatre group that put on mini musicals for corporate functions. That was how she had met Glenn. He'd been organising the Real Estate Association Christmas party. She'd picked up all sorts of tricks and tips for staging a show on a budget – how to use one backdrop for lots of different scenes, and how to make rapid scene changes to keep the action moving. Lola's script was surprisingly good, but she could see where a little cutting here and there would help it . . .

Lola was now all eagerness and excitement. 'I thought you could put an ad in the paper calling for auditions. I've got some wording for it here, look.' She waved another bit of paper at them.

Bett wasn't convinced. 'It's still very tight time-wise.'

Anna took a diary out of her bag. 'Not if we got moving with the auditions, then started rehearsals twice a week. Carrie, would this room be available?'

'I'd have to check the bookings, but it's usually free on weeknights. And we haven't got any weddings for a couple of months. But hold on a moment. Are you all going to stay in the Valley? Here in the motel?' Carrie looked from Anna to Bett. This was moving too quickly for her. 'What about your work, Anna? And Glenn?'

Anna's face was expressionless. 'If we did decide to do the musical, I could juggle work. Go up to Sydney for two days a week. Ellen could come with me.' She didn't mention Glenn.

'No, Ellen couldn't, actually.' Lola gave a guilty smile. 'She'll be in school here. I spoke to the principal today. She's a friend of mine. She said they can certainly find a place for her.'

Carrie turned to her other sister, fighting a feeling of panic. It was one thing hiding Matthew's absence from her sisters for days, but for weeks? 'And you, Bett? What about your work?'

Lola stepped in again. 'She's accepted a part-time job at the *Valley Times*. Haven't you, Bett?'

Bett stared at Lola in amazement. She'd only phoned Rebecca that afternoon. She'd decided to accept the job first and worry later about living so close to Carrie and Matthew.

The mobile beside Anna started vibrating. She checked the number. 'Excuse me,' she said, walking outside to answer the call. 'Glenn?'

'Anna, hello. How are things? How's Ellen?'

'Fine. How are you?' So stiff, so awkward with each other.

'Fine, fine. Big news up here. The Singapore trip is on. I leave in two days.'

'I see. How long will you be away for?'

'Three weeks to begin with. But it's only eight hours' flight from Sydney. I'll be back and forth. I'll still ring Ellen every night, of course. In fact, I'm thinking about getting her a mobile.'

'A mobile? She's only seven years old, Glenn.'

'I like the idea of her having one anyway. To keep her safe.'

One more dig at her failure as a parent. Anna felt very tired, even as she realised he'd just helped her make the final decision. 'As it turns out, Glenn, that works out well. We're going to stay here in the Valley for a month or so.' She didn't tell him about the musical. He wouldn't have been interested.

His anger came down the phone line like a sonic wave. 'Just like that? Without discussing it with me? At least I told you the

Singapore trip was on the cards. What if I hadn't been going there? When was I going to get to see Ellen?'

She walked further away from the motel building, her voice low, the anger only just controlled. 'When would you want to see Ellen? In between nights at Julie's house? In between conferences? Work trips?'

'Anna, I love her. She's my daughter. You know I see her as much as I can. And just because I'm not with her every hour of the day doesn't mean I'm not thinking about her. What are you going to do about her schooling? Your work?'

Anna had to sit down on a bench, her chest tight with anger. 'I don't know yet. We're still sorting it out.' There was a long pause and then she had to ask. 'Is Julie going to Singapore?'

He tried to bluster through it. 'Well, she's my senior assistant and it's a big deal to set up a brand-new office. I couldn't be expected to do it on my own.'

'Is Julie going as your lover as well as your assistant, Glenn?' Anna's voice was smooth. He wouldn't have guessed for a moment that her stomach was churning, her hands were sweating. She wanted the truth.

'Julie's coming with me, yes.'

So it was still happening. 'Look, Glenn, I can't talk now. I'll ring you tomorrow.'

There was a pause, then he spoke again. 'Okay, then. Fine. So will you give Ellen my love?'

'I will. Goodbye.' She hung up and sat for a moment trying to quell the desire to throw up. She felt her heart. It was racing. Her skin was clammy. She shut her eyes for a moment, waited for her breathing to calm, and then stood up. She used all the years of drama school training to put a smile on her face as she walked back into the function room. 'That's all sorted. Glenn's got to go to Singapore for work for a while, so the timing couldn't have been better. We can definitely stay.'

Still outside, leaning in through the window, Lola noticed Bett was humming one of the songs under her breath. Carrie was mouthing some lines. Anna was the only one who seemed a little distracted. Perhaps she'd had to fight with Glenn to be able to stay on. He'd always been possessive. Still, they'd talk about it later. She gazed at her three granddaughters. 'So have you definitely made a decision? Will you do it?'

Anna looked at Bett, who looked at Carrie, who looked back at Anna. Then they all turned to Lola. 'We'll do it.'

CHAPTER NINE

IN THE function room a week later, Bett was practising songs on the piano for the following night's auditions.

Their parents had left for their holiday that morning. Lola, Anna, Bett, Carrie and Ellen had stood waving on the forecourt as the two of them had driven off, smiling and waving back. They'd all been thinking it, but it was Lola who said it out loud. Jim and Geraldine were like newlyweds off on their honeymoon.

'What's a honeymoon?' Ellen asked.

'A holiday for people who have just got married,' Anna answered.

'Did you and Dad have a honeymoon?'

'Yes, for two weeks.' They'd gone to an exclusive resort in Fiji. Glenn had confessed on the plane on the way over that he'd heard it was an excellent place for networking business contacts.

'Why didn't you take me?'

Anna ruffled her hair. 'You weren't born yet.'

Ellen turned to Carrie. 'Have you ever had a honeymoon, Auntie Carrie?'

Bett and Carrie both stiffened. 'I have, Ellen, yes.'

'And you, Auntie Bett?'

Before Bett had a chance to answer, Lola gave a very loud moan. They all spun towards her, alarmed. 'Lola, what's the matter? Are you all right?'

She moaned again. 'It's just my arthritis, I think. It comes and goes in this damp weather.'

It hadn't rained in weeks and Bett knew for a fact that Lola didn't suffer from arthritis. Short of screaming 'Quick! Change the subject!' at the top of her voice, her grandmother couldn't have been any more obvious. But it had worked. The five of them had walked back into the motel and even managed to have a peaceful enough meeting about the work rosters.

Bett was on reception duty that night. She'd already interrupted her piano playing twice to welcome guests and give out room keys. Carrie had been in the bar earlier, serving rounds of drinks to a small group of people. It was now dark in there. Bett assumed Carrie had closed it all up and gone home for the night. Anna had been in the kitchen when Bett had passed through earlier. She'd been preparing the guests' breakfast trays, reading through the ticked forms, distributing little boxes of cereal, portions of jam and sachets of sugar. Ellen had been beside her, standing on a chair. With her tongue visible between her lips, she'd been folding the red paper serviettes into passable fans.

Bett finished playing 'Oh What a Beautiful Morning' and picked up the sheet music for 'Chattanooga Choo Choo'. She loved the smoothness of the piano keys under her fingers, the familiar tunes filling the room around her, the feeling of being in charge of the music, adding elaborate notes here and there. She worked her way through each of the songs, memories of different Alphabet Sisters performances coming back to her – singing 'My Favourite Things' to an audience of five, two of them dogs, at an agricultural show in New South Wales. She remembered one hot, dry day in country Queensland, midway through their version of 'Boogie Woogie Bugle Boy', when the three of them had inexplicably got the giggles so badly that Bett and then Carrie had fallen off the stage. It had almost become their party trick.

She stopped playing, walked to the window and stared out into the carpark. Being back in the Valley again was sparking all sorts of memories. Not just about Matthew, and the terrible fight with Anna and Carrie, but everything that had happened afterwards as well. Her mind had been filled with thoughts of it all week.

The morning after the fight, she'd got up at dawn, packed one small bag, filled her car with petrol and started driving. From a roadside motel en route to Melbourne she'd phoned the *Valley Times* office and taken leave without pay until further notice. She'd called a friend from journalism college now based in Melbourne and explained what had happened. By nightfall, she was set up in her friend's spare room.

The next three months had passed in a kind of frenzy. With too much time on her hands, she'd started drinking too much, talking too much to cover the hurt and confusion. She had found some freelance work with city newspapers, started falling in and out of bars with a fluid, rowdy gang of reporters, sub-editors, photographers. She hadn't told anyone the real reason she was in Melbourne. She'd done her best to block it out of her mind and nearly succeeded.

Until the night in Carlton, seeing a band in a new club, she had bumped into an old work colleague from home. She'd been surprised to see him. 'I didn't realise you were in Melbourne.'

'I didn't know you were here either.'

She didn't know if he knew the circumstances of her leaving the

Valley, but she was strangely glad to see a familiar face. He bought her a drink, then another one. She hadn't eaten all day and ignored the light-headed feeling. The vodka fuelled her confidence, helped her pretend to be carefree, as they swapped stories of newspaper life, keeping it light, fun.

It got later, and the band finished playing. They went for another drink, on to a late-night bar together for more vodka and then she found herself back in his flat, alone with him. She had been talking all night and remembered getting upset, even crying a little about something. Had it been about Carrie and Matthew? The fight with Anna? All of that and more. He had taken her in his arms and given her a sympathetic hug and that's when the evening had changed. She was the one who'd changed it into a closer hug, a different sort of hug. She'd made it happen. Insisted on it. She wanted to kiss him, touch him in a way she'd never done with Matthew. She wanted to rid herself of memories of Matthew, to feel different, to behave in a way she'd never behaved. She wanted to cancel out any tears and vulnerability she'd shown him that evening, wanted to cover it over with sex, sweat, kissing, stroking, thrusts, arched backs and marking nails and biting mouths . . .

When she awoke the next morning, wild and reckless Bett was long gone, leaving ashamed and hungover Bett lying there naked beside him. She lifted his arm from her waist, moved away, trying not to make any noise. 'Don't wake up. Please don't wake up,' she prayed, edging out of the room, into the living room, gathering her clothes, bag and jacket, dressing, then slipping out quickly. She didn't leave a note. It was a big city. They never had to see each other again.

Back home she'd taken to her bed for the rest of the day. By nightfall she'd been desperate to talk to someone about it. Too shy to tell her flatmate, unable to ring her sisters, she'd called Lola and told her everything. As she sketched the story, moments kept coming back to her, making her nearly yelp aloud in embarrassment. Oh, God. Had she really cried in his arms? Another shudder as she remembered insisting on kissing him. Insisting on having sex with him. She'd felt it in her body all day, a warm kind of ache, between her legs, on her skin. Memories that would have been sensual, pleasant, if they hadn't made her want to howl in shame.

Lola had been non-judgemental. 'Perhaps it was better that it was someone you knew, not a complete stranger. Did you use contraception?'

'Yes. Yes, we did.'

'Do you want to see him again?'

'Of course I don't. How could I face him?' Then she'd started crying. 'I'm unhappy, Lola. That's not me. I don't do things like that. I don't know what's happening to me.'

'Bett, it was a one-night stand, not a mass murder. Keep it in perspective. Do you want to come back home?'

'I can't.'

'You can. You'd get used to seeing Carrie and Matthew together.'

'Lola, I don't want to see Carrie and Matthew together. I don't want everyone watching me to see how I react, people talking about me behind my back.'

'This is such a scandal people would be talking about it in front of your back, believe me. Darling, have you lost your sense of humour somewhere? Come on, it's a broken romance. Millions of people have those every day.'

'But I never wanted to be like millions of other people. And I'm sick of making a mess of things.' The words started tumbling out of her. 'I wanted to be fearless and do something wonderful and splendid and remarkable and I haven't and I don't think I ever will. I'm scared all the time, Lola.'

'Scared of what?'

'Of being embarrassed. Of making a fool of myself.'

'You'll have to be more specific. Everyone is scared of those things. You need to be clearer with me, darling.'

Bett only had to think for a moment. 'I'm scared of loads of things. Of being on my own.' Of sex, whether she did it properly or not. But she didn't want to tell Lola that. She thought of other things instead. 'I'm scared of seeing my body in mirrors in changing rooms in clothes shops, and snooty shop assistants making fun of me.' She managed to laugh. 'I'm scared of stupid things, too. Like eating oysters. Reverse parking. Aeroplanes. Mobile phones . . .'

'Is that all? I thought you were scared about serious things.'

'They're serious to me.'

'But you can overcome all of them. You know the saying, Bett. You have to face your fears.'

'Where do I start? Make a list? Tick them off?'

'Leave it with me. For now, get into your pyjamas, go to bed and have an early night. Don't have a drink. Be patient. And calm down.'

The first decree had arrived exactly three days later. Just a post-card, addressed to Bett, with one line in the centre.

Eat an oyster.

That's all it said. For a moment she thought it was a new marketing ploy, targeting people one by one. Then she recognised the handwriting. Lola's. She phoned her. 'What do you mean, eat an oyster?'

'You're scared of them. So face them. Go and eat one. Then write to me – don't phone me – and tell me how you got on.'

She did it. She hated it but she did it nevertheless. Her report to Lola was also sent on a postcard. *I went to a seafood restaurant last night with my flatmate Yvonne. She ordered oysters and I ate one. It was the most disgusting thing I have ever eaten, like swallowing a salty slug that has been lying in water in the sun and gone bad. It took three glasses of wine to get the taste out of my mouth.*

The reply came by return post. *Good, brave girl.*

For the next four weeks the one-line postcards arrived like clockwork. *Go to the theatre on your own. Go out to dinner on your own.* Each time, Bett took on the task, and wrote home to tell Lola exactly what had happened. A week later, another card would arrive. *Good, brave girl,* with another task set beside it.

Then a surprising one arrived.

Go and live overseas.

She phoned Lola immediately. 'That's a bit of a jump, isn't it? From oysters to overseas?'

'I've been leading up to it. I've been pushing you to go for years. The money is burning a hole in my pocket.'

Lola had given each of the girls a return airfare to the place of their choice for their twenty-fifth birthday. Anna had gone to America for an acting course. Glenn had followed her out and proposed to her as they took a horse and carriage ride around Central Park. 'Blech, so tacky,' Carrie had said. 'Bet he had the carriage-driver playing violin as well.' Carrie had headed off on a round-Asia trip, which then turned into a year away. But between study and work, Bett had never found time to leave Australia. 'I can't take it from you, Lola.'

'Don't give me that nonsense. Your sisters took it gladly and so should you. And I'll throw in some spending money as well. Let's call it the interest I've earned on the capital because you've taken so long to decide to take it.'

'You can't afford it either, Lola.'

'Darling, you haven't the faintest idea whether I am poor-house material or a very rich old lady, and I'm not going to tell you. Just take it and run. I was going to leave you this money in my will. I might as well give it to you now, so I can see how you spend it.'

'I can't.'

'Why not? Are you scared?'

Bett laughed. 'Yes, I am actually.'

'Of what? The flight? Moving to a new country?'

'All of that.'

'You know the best way to deal with that.'

And so it had happened. Bett finally agreed to accept the fare, and two weeks after that conversation found herself in Dublin.

It had been hard at first. She'd brought herself to Ireland, not a new improved fearless model. The first month she stayed in a youth hostel in the centre of Dublin. She'd been worried she would be the oldest person there and was surprised when no one cared what age she was. With an Irish passport courtesy of Lola, she set off looking for work in newspapers, before realising that was the old her. She had imaginary conversations with Lola. 'What do you like?' 'Music. Writing.' 'Can you combine the two?' She discovered she could, by getting a job behind the bar in one of Dublin's many music venues and writing the occasional review of the gigs for music newspapers, websites and magazines.

She found a flatshare on the North Circular Road, near the Phoenix Park, sharing a four-storey red-brick terraced house with young Irish students, Nigerians, Asians, Romanians, their friendship confined to nods and hellos on the steep steps leading up to the red-painted front door. She walked to work through the fruit markets, dodging delivery trucks, stepping over cabbages, kiwi fruit, sometimes even mangoes squashed onto cobblestones.

She started living a strange upside-down life, working in the night time, sleeping in the daytime, seeing as many as ten live bands a week in the venues she worked in. She made friends with other bar staff, the sound engineers, the woman who took the money at the door. Just as the late nights started to lose their appeal, a chance conversation with Karl over the bar while one of his early signings played to an empty room led to a move to London and the job in his record company. It had been exciting, leaving one new city for another. She'd felt brave, adventurous, free . . .

But then she had started to miss things, too. Being free meant being unconnected, untethered. Which was fine when she was happy. But not when things were uncertain, when out of the blue she would find herself longing for conversations with Anna – and even with Carrie. She discovered a horoscope website, and read their signs each day, trying to guess what might be happening in their lives. Walking through a department store one afternoon she smelt a familiar perfume and was overwhelmed by a feeling of missing Anna. She asked for a sample. For the rest of the day Bett felt oddly comforted that Anna was nearby.

There'd been only one communication between them in the three years, when Lola told her about Ellen being attacked. Bett had been shocked by the news. That same night she sent Anna a card, brief, to the point, telling her how sad she was to hear about Ellen. She heard nothing back. After that, there hadn't been another opportunity. Not until the excuse of the eightieth birthday party had arrived.

Images of Anna and Carrie came to mind now. Things weren't as she'd expected with them. Anna wasn't as snooty or as aloof as the imaginary Anna she had been carrying in her mind these years. And Carrie wasn't as smug or self-satisfied as she'd expected either. In fact, they both seemed . . . what? Bett wondered. Normal? Familiar? Even a little troubled?

The phone rang, making her jump. She ran out to the reception desk. 'Valley View Motel. Can I help you?'

'What are you doing, darling?' It was Lola.

'Looking over the songs,' Bett improvised. 'Where are you?'

'In my room. I could see you staring out the function-room window and I wondered if you needed any help.'

'No, I'm fine. I'm finished for today, I think. I know enough for the auditions tomorrow anyway.'

'Good girl. Come and talk to me, would you? And would you bring the outfit you're going to wear to work tomorrow and let me have a look at it?'

Bett laughed. 'Lola, that's very sweet of you but it's a part-time job, not my first day at school.'

'I know. But first impressions can count. You want to be feeling good when you go in there, meeting people you haven't seen for a few years.'

'I saw Rebecca last week.'

'Indulge me, darling.'

Ten minutes later she was in Lola's room, carrying the clothes she'd chosen to wear to the newspaper office in the morning. It was a vintage skirt, dark-red silk, which she planned to wear with a simple white shirt. Her shoes were good. Italian leather, stylish but still very comfortable.

Lola put her head to one side and looked for a moment like a bright-eyed bird. 'Just about exactly right, I think. You have learned something while you've been away. Earrings?'

Bett held up the pair she planned to wear. They were also dark red, made from old glass beads. She'd found them at a Dublin market stall.

'Very nice. More to the point, how do you feel in the whole outfit?'

'Good, I think.'

'That's more important. And remember you are Bett who is thirty-two, who has been living in Dublin and London, who has eaten an oyster and gone to the theatre on her own, among many other brave things. Remember all that tomorrow.'

Bett smiled. 'Why? Is someone planning on springing *This Is Your Life* on me?'

'I just want you to feel good about yourself, no matter what happens, no matter who you meet.'

Bett softened. Lola knew there would be people at the office from three years ago when the whole business with Carrie and Matthew had blown up. 'Why do you do it, Lola?'

'Do what?'

'Put up with us. All of us. How can you be bothered?'

'Because I love you. And because I love making you do as I tell you. So you'll keep the chin up tomorrow, no matter what? Promise me?'

'I promise you.'

Lola gave a contented sigh and lay back on her bed. 'I never thought I'd say it but one of the bonuses of being an elderly decrepit old bag of bones like I am is that no one pays any attention to the way you look. You're just some old woman, not some thin woman or fat woman or ugly woman or beautiful woman. You're just old.'

'And does that bother you?' Bett asked as she returned her skirt to the hanger. 'Do you miss things about being young?'

'Of course, but I can't change it. I am old. On my last legs, probably, the clock ticking away as we speak.'

'Stop that, you old ghoul.' Bett sat down beside Lola on the bed. It was always a treat to have her to herself. 'Do you ever think about it, though, Lola? Are you scared of dying?'

'Why? Are you about to try and kill me?'

'No, not tonight. I like you tonight. But do you think about it?'

'Of course I do. Most people do. That's why you have to try and fill up each day as much as you can, in case it's your last day.'

'But if you truly lived life like that, you'd never go to work, would you? Or wash dishes. Or sweep floors. Because you wouldn't want to spend your last day on earth doing boring things like that.'

'Exactly. Which is why I don't let a day go past without having a gin and tonic. No point rationing it out, in case the day I choose not to have one is the day I die. And think how much work I'll save the embalmer, from all the gin I've consumed over the years. I'm sure I'm half embalmed as it is.'

'You are getting more appalling every year.'

Lola gave a happy smile. 'Yes, I know.'

Bett picked up Lola's left hand and started moving her wedding ring around, the way she had done since she was a little girl and she and Lola were talking like this. She knew every twist of gold. 'Do you still miss Edward, Lola?'

'He's been gone sixty years, Bett. You get used to anything after that length of time.'

'What was he like? What were the two of you like together?'

'Why are you interested so suddenly?'

Bett put down Lola's hand and smoothed the bedcover, idly noting a tiny cigarette burn on one corner. Guests always did ignore the sign about no smoking in bed. 'I was thinking about it last night. That we have been coming to you for years with every detail about every little aspect of our lives, moaning and groaning, and maybe it's your turn to talk, and ours to listen. I was thinking about your slide show, those photos you had of Ireland and the early days. I want you to know that if you feel like reminiscing about those days, about Edward, what it was like when you and Dad started running the guesthouses and all of that, or if there is anything else you want to talk about, I'm here, okay?'

Lola burst out laughing. She reached up to touch the curly head beside her. 'Darling, thank you very much. If anything comes up I'll be sure to call you.'

'I mean it, Lola.'

'And I do too.'

In the kitchen of her house, Carrie glanced up at the clock. Nearly ten o'clock. He should be here any moment. She checked her appearance again, smoothed down her dress, straightened the knives and forks on the table. She was nervous, she realised. Of her own husband.

Of her estranged husband, to be accurate.

She went out onto the verandah. The paddocks all around the house were dark for as far as she could see. In the daytime she liked the peace and quiet. In the night time, without Matthew, it gave her the creeps. She jumped at the sound of a bird in the gum trees behind the house, then jumped again at a rustle in the agapanthus lining the driveway. It was a hot evening, but she still shivered.

She longed for a return of the days when the very sight of the house would give her a lift. She and Matthew had spent months searching for their ideal home. They had agreed on everything – they wanted an old-style, stone house, with a full return verandah, preferably with open fireplaces for those cold Clare winter nights. They wanted just a small block of land, perhaps an acre or two. Ideally, they would find a house that already had the major renovations done – all the plumbing and rewiring. And they wanted at least three bedrooms.

'Four,' she'd said.

'You want three children?' he'd laughed.

'At least,' she'd said airily. 'And as soon as possible.'

'Not too soon.'

She should have picked up the hints then, shouldn't she? But no, she'd chosen to ignore him, to go on making plans, picking out nursery colours, before they even had a nursery, let alone a baby . . .

They'd found this house by accident. One weekend Matthew had collected her from the motel after work and for a change they'd gone for a drive rather than head back to the small unit they were renting. They'd taken one of the dirt roads just to the south of the town, winding up between the vineyards. And there it had been. A hand-painted For Sale sign at the end of a track leading up to an old stone house. They'd driven straight up and found the owners inside – a pair of middle-aged hippies, there was no other way to describe them. They'd been living in the Valley for the past two years but had decided to head north to the tropical heat and rainforests of Queensland. They hadn't listed the house with any real estate agents, preferring to let the buyer find them, they'd earnestly explained. Matthew and Carrie had been squeezing each other's hands underneath the table. The house had almost everything they had been looking for – the original stone work, the verandah, the slate floors. It had been rewired and the plumbing was in reasonable condition. The main problem had been the colours the walls had been painted, tangerine and purple, swirls of this and that. 'I think they studied at the Marijuana School of Interior Decoration', Matthew had whispered as they toured around. But it hadn't put them off. They'd made an offer the next day. Two months later they'd moved in.

Carrie forced herself to stay outside now, leaning against the verandah post she'd painted herself, waiting for the sound of his car. He'd been surprised at her call that afternoon, she knew that. No wonder, considering what she had shouted at him last time they had spoken, several weeks ago now. 'It's over, Matthew. We're finished. Can't you see that?'

He'd sounded wary on the phone. Exhausted. But he'd agreed to make the long drive from the station he was working at, to hear what it was she had to say. That counted for something, surely.

The problem was she didn't really know what she wanted to say to him. She jumped as a flicker of light was reflected against the pale bark of the gum trees. Car headlights. Matthew? Her heart started beating faster as the car came closer . . .

Three hours later the peace of the farmhouse was broken by the sound of a long, shuddering snore from the other side of the double bed.

'Shut up, Matthew,' Carrie said crossly into the darkness. She gave him a sharp pinch, which caused a moment's break in his loud snoring, before he settled back into it again. She sat up looking at him. Well, that had gone really well. It had been after midnight by the time he'd finally arrived. She'd worn a track in the verandah from her pacing, had nearly leapt out of her skin each time car headlights appeared down the road. By the time he had rung to say he'd had serious engine trouble and been stuck on the side of the road trying to fix it for the past two hours, she'd been beside herself with worry. She'd also been a little drunk from the red wine she'd been sipping out of nervousness. When he'd finally arrived she'd wanted to fly at him in anger and frustration, but the thought of Anna and Bett laughing at her and her broken marriage had kept her voice low and sweet. She greeted him, offered him a beer.

She had led the way into their living room, smiling as he took a chair – not his usual chair, she noticed – offering him a sandwich, some cheese. It was too late for the dinner she'd prepared. He'd shaken his head, watching her closely, as nervous of her as she was of him, she realised.

'So how was work today?' she asked cheerily, even though the sight of him – dirty, exhausted, his clothes covered in dust – supplied her with the answer.

He ran his fingers through his hair. She knew the gesture well. It meant he was tired and it also meant he was feeling impatient. 'Can we cut to the chase here, Carrie? What did you want to talk about?'

He was angry, too. And she supposed he had every right to be. She'd kicked him out of the house after all. Hung up on him each time he'd called. Returned his letters unopened and unanswered. She felt a dart of shame that, yes, perhaps he had some right to be cross with her. So what did she want to talk to him about? She didn't know any more. 'Us, I suppose.'

'What else have you got to say? I thought you'd made yourself pretty clear.'

She took some heart from the fact he had at least come tonight, long drive, long day and all. She decided to tell him the truth. 'It's about Bett.'

He ran his fingers through his hair again.

'She's staying on in the Valley. She's taken a job at the local paper again.' She debated whether to tell him about Lola's musical, then decided against it. This was about Bett, not Lola.

'Has she? Good on her.'

'So how does it make you feel?'

'About her job? Carrie, it's got nothing to do with me. It's up to Bett where she wants to work.'

'I don't mean about her job. I mean how do you feel about Bett being close by again.'

She saw a flash of something – temper? – cancelling out the exhaustion in his eyes. 'Carrie, I feel what I felt when you asked me about Bett three weeks ago. Six months ago. A year ago. I can't keep telling you.'

'I don't believe you.'

He raised his voice at her then. 'Because you don't want to believe me. And I can't do anything about that. Jesus, Carrie, it's like banging my head against a brick wall, and I'm sick of it –' He stopped there. 'Listen, can I have a shower, have a coffee maybe? Can we talk about it after that?'

She turned her back, shrugged. She saw in the reflection in the window that he stood and looked at her for a few moments, before he went to the bathroom. She took her drink out onto the verandah, waited for him to join her, calming herself, preparing the words again, hoping to make herself understood this time. Twenty minutes later she was still waiting.

She had walked into their bedroom and found him asleep on top of the bed, half undressed. He'd been so exhausted it seemed he hadn't even got to the shower, simply lain down on their bed and fallen asleep. And he was still asleep. No amount of clanging saucepans or poking had stirred him. She had felt a ripple of guilt looking down at him, at the boyish face asleep on the pillow, the light-brown hair tousled, dirty.

Staring at him in the bed beside her now, she was reminded of earlier days, in the first year of their marriage, when he'd arrive home from similar busy, dirty days working out on farms and stations. She'd greet him at the door with a kiss, putting her finger on his mouth to stop him talking, leading him into the bathroom where she'd slowly undress him, and then herself, moving him into the shower, still silent, now kissing him on the lips, on the shoulder, on the brown skin of his arms, on his flat brown belly, lower down until he would be groaning against the side of the shower. And after that it would be into the bedroom, where he would return the favour, no longer tired, stroking and caressing her, until she could hardly bear it and would pull him down into her. The memory stirred her now, and she moved in closer to him.

'Matthew?'

She touched his back through his T-shirt. No response. She ran her hand down his side and he flinched. She waited, tried again, moving lower towards his crotch. He muttered something, moved away, lying on his front, out of reach.

'Forget it, then,' she said loudly, crossly. When had this happened? The two of them who had barely been able to keep their hands off each other since the first night they met. She thumped the pillow in frustration. How had she made such a mess of things?

She fought back tears, fanning angry feelings instead. If it hadn't been for Lola, the way she had started talking incessantly about how much she missed the three of them, how she had dreamt about the Alphabet Sisters again, she'd never have been in this position. Lola had never said it, but Carrie knew what was beneath it all – it was all Carrie's fault, for stealing Matthew from

Bett. If she had never done that, they would all be living happily ever after, wouldn't they? She hadn't been able to get the guilty feelings out of her mind, at the same time that Matthew's work started taking him away for stretches at a time. When he was home, they seemed to fight. And not just about having a baby any more, either. They'd found plenty of other subject matter instead. Finally, in a fit of temper two months earlier, she had said they needed a trial separation.

He'd been shocked. 'Why?'

'Because it's not right. We shouldn't have got together. You should have stayed with Bett.'

'Carrie, we've been through this. I fell in love with you. It would have been wrong for me to stay with her.'

'Maybe it wouldn't have. Maybe that's what you should have done. It was a test of your love for Bett.'

'What?'

'You know, like a temptation. And you failed. And now we're both being punished.'

'What are you talking about? Have you had religious cranks staying at the motel?'

She couldn't explain it any better. And then he'd got angry, and they had rowed about all sorts of other things, until they had both been glad when he had stormed out and she had told him not to come back.

At the back of her mind were Bett and Anna's voices. 'We told you so.' She couldn't bear it. What a horrible, awful, unfair mess, she thought, curling tighter into a ball on the very edge of the bed.

Beside her Matthew gave another loud snore. It was all she could do not to smother him with her pillow.

In her room at the motel, Anna was lying on her bed, with Ellen tucked in beside her fast asleep. Anna's eyes were wide open as she stared into space. Her skin felt clammy, her stomach was churning, she felt exhausted but unable to sleep. She was in the country, the fresh air – wasn't she supposed to feel better? Truth was, she'd never felt so tired or so awful in her life.

She'd had another fight with Glenn on the phone that evening. More guilt, more blaming, more heated words, all in hushed tones so that Ellen, in the bath, couldn't hear. She'd come out wrapped in a towel, and asked, 'Is that Daddy?' At Anna's nod, she'd reached for the phone and settled herself on the bed, chattering away to him, all the solemn little phrases tumbling out of her. 'Is work busy?' 'Is Singapore hot like here?' 'Will you bring me a present when you come home?' As if things were perfectly normal with them all. And then the worst of it. 'Will you say hello to Julie for me too?' Anna had nearly been sick. Ellen was friendly enough with her father's lover to send her messages.

When Ellen had handed back the phone, Anna had barely been able to speak to him, only keeping her voice civil because she knew Ellen was listening to every word. Afterwards, she'd wanted to throw the mobile across the room, hoping to see it smash, the parts fly into all corners. On the verge of doing that, in sight of Ellen or not, it had started ringing again. Not Glenn this time, but her booking agent, Roz. She apologised for ringing so late, but explained that a big job had come up from one of her past clients. Was Anna available?

'They've specifically asked for you. It's a good gig, Anna. You could do it in your sleep.' It was the voice-over for three separate teenage sex-education videos, as well as a series of radio ads directed at parents and teachers. If the response was good, there could even be follow-up commercials. 'Top rates, too. For a few days' work, maximum. Can you do it?'

Anna had massaged her temple with her spare hand. She'd promised Ellen they would have a long break together. God knows they both needed it. But this job would pay well. Which would mean she wouldn't need to take Glenn's money, for a little while at least. The thought made her feel good. 'Of course I can,' she'd said.

Ellen murmured in her sleep. Anna pressed a kiss on her head. Lola's ban on any talk of Matthew came to mind. Was that the key to life? Simply ignoring any difficult subject? Should she have ignored the fact that Glenn had become bored with her? Just kept on smiling, attending social functions with him, perhaps taken a lover or two of her own? Ignored the calls from Julie, the intimacy in her phone conversations with Glenn proof that their relationship had changed from colleagues to lovers? Just kept smiling, smiling, smiling? Until her face hurt and her body ached with the tension?

She'd managed to avoid the subject here beautifully so far. She had skilfully answered her parents' few questions about him, deftly explaining his absences from these home visits, murmuring something about work pressures and promotions and overseas trips. There was no risk of Carrie and Bett asking after him – they'd made their feelings about Glenn clear three years ago. She'd felt Lola's eyes on her, as ever, waiting for the questions, but so far, nothing.

Not that she would answer them anyway. 'Yes, Lola, Bett and Carrie were right that night. I did make a very bad decision years ago and I've lived with it ever since. I did ignore all my own instincts, went ahead with a marriage to someone who I knew only cared about my face and my body, not my heart, definitely not my mind or soul.'

But how did she fix the unfixable? Did she go to Bett and Carrie and admit that they had been right? That the terrible things they had shouted at her, the night of their big fight, had actually turned out to be true? That her marriage was over, that she was exactly what they accused her of becoming – cold, fake, self-obsessed? Would they say it had served her right, that she had made her bed when she married Glenn for his money, his social standing, his contacts?

In her arms, Ellen gave a little wriggle. Anna held her tighter and shut her eyes, tired of thinking, willing sleep to come to her, too.

Matthew was gone by the time Carrie woke up the next morning. She looked for a note, an apology. Nothing.

'That's why!' she shouted out the door, to no one but the birds in the paddocks opposite. 'You don't talk to me, you don't tell me anything any more. It's no wonder it's ruined.' She burst into tears and ran back into their bedroom, grabbing the pillow he had slept on and sobbing until it was wet under her cheek.

CHAPTER TEN

BETT TRIED out her new swivel chair again, giving it a little spin and ending up facing Rebecca's office across the corridor. A stack of newspapers lay on the desk beside her. She'd already skimmed through them, enjoying every article, getting up to date with the ins and outs of Clare Valley life. There were stories about water shortages next to photos of largest-ever pumpkins, schoolchildren's charity efforts alongside politicians handshaking.

She'd had a long meeting with Rebecca that morning. Apart from writing general news and feature stories, Rebecca wanted her to write the editorial for a new project, a twelve-page supplement on the Valley's tourist attractions, sponsored by the tourism commission. 'They've asked for lots of colour, all the sights and smells and tastes, so I want you and the photographer to actually try everything out, so you can write it from the visitor's perspective.'

'You want me to do it? The new girl?' It was a dream assignment.

Rebecca laughed. 'Yes, I know. I'd rather be doing it myself. Let me tell you, being editor's not all it's cracked up to be.'

Bett had returned to her desk, feeling buoyed and enthusiastic about a writing project for the first time in months. She started drawing up a list of subjects: the wine-tasting tours, the gourmet cooking course in one of the Clare Valley's grand country homes, the overnight sleeping under the stars experience at the Valley's oldest sheep station, the guided historical walk along the path of the old railway line . . . This was more like it, she thought. She wrote the lead sentence of an article in her head, as she often did for practice. *Bett Quinlan, 32, announced today that she was very happy to be back working for a real newspaper.*

She had picked up the phone to dial one of the tour operators when a voice behind her made her jump. 'Bett Quinlan, as I live and breathe.' It was Neil, the grey-haired sports reporter who'd been with the paper since it started. 'It's great to see you. Welcome back on board.'

She stood and hugged him. 'Great to see you too, Neil.' It had been good to see lots of her old colleagues. They'd asked after London, after her family, normal things. No one had mentioned Matthew yet.

'I've been hearing all about your grandmother's musical. Don't suppose you've got a part for an old fellow like me?' He burst into the first line of 'The Sound of Music'.

'Auditions are on tomorrow night. Why don't you come along?'

'You know, I just might. I wouldn't mind treading the boards one more time.' He gave a quick little soft-shoe shuffle before he walked away.

Rebecca came out of her office. 'I'm thinking about coming along myself.'

'You're kidding? Do you want to be in it?'

'Of course not. But I wouldn't want to miss the chance of seeing some of the locals auditioning. Much better than watching those reality shows on telly. Now then, Hildie's just come in, the photographer you'll be doing the tourism supplement with.' She poked her head into one of the side rooms and called out. 'Hildie, are you around? Come and meet our new reporter.' Then she lowered her voice. 'You might remember him, actually. It was before my time in the Valley, but he used to work here before he went to Melbourne for a few years. I snapped him up when he came back last year.' She smiled over Bett's head at the new arrival.

'Bett Quinlan, all the way from London, I'd like you to meet Daniel Hilder.'

Bett turned and felt the colour run from her face. Her one-night stand had just walked into the room.

In the gym at the country club, Anna looked up at the clock. She'd only been on the treadmill for ten minutes and she was already breathless, feeling out of shape after just a few days away from exercise. She could almost hear her personal trainer's voice. 'A little every day keeps age and fat away.' Too bad. She could do nothing about her age and it wasn't as if she needed to lose weight at the moment. If anything, she needed to put some on. Irony of ironies – now the pressure was off, now Glenn was gone and she could put on some weight if she wanted, she wasn't hungry. She could let herself go completely if she wanted. It wasn't as if there was another man on the sidelines dying to see her naked body.

'Hello, Anna.'

She turned. It was Richard Lawrence, dressed in shorts and a T-shirt, a towel over his shoulder. It was the first time she'd seen him since the morning after Lola's party. He certainly looked much fresher today. Taller than she remembered. Still wearing his glasses. His hair was cropped very short. He looked quite like an athlete, she thought. Like a marathon runner, in fact. Lean and spare.

'Richard, how are you?' She coolly reached forward and turned off the treadmill, gradually adjusting her steps as the belt slowed. She'd always taken care stepping off this kind of equipment, especially since Bett had rung her in Sydney some years before and recounted her humiliating first and last visit to this gym. She had mistimed stepping off the treadmill and been catapulted backwards onto the rowing machine, landing on another woman and pushing her onto the floor as well. It was one of Anna's favourite Bett stories. She had nearly cried laughing while Bett was telling her.

Richard smiled. 'I'm well, thank you. I didn't realise you liked to work out here too.'

'Occasionally. But I'm not in the mood this morning. I think I'll try the natural air approach and walk back to the motel instead.'

'Do you mind if I join you? I've been hoping to have the chance to talk to you again.'

She stood in front of him, a towel in her hands. Years ago she had decided to get it out into the open when men made approaches to her like this. 'Really, Richard, you're being very forward. Are you trying to pick me up?'

'I don't know yet,' he said calmly. 'You're certainly very beautiful, and I like that spark in your eye, but I like to be able to have a conversation with my lovers, not just look at them. So it's probably too early to tell.'

To both their surprise, she burst out laughing. 'That is the best answer I have ever heard. What about your workout?'

He grinned. 'We could walk the long way back, couldn't we?'

Out at her house, Carrie was feeling sick. A book lay on the wooden boards beside her. She'd come home from the motel for a quick break after lunch, hoping for a message from Matthew, an email, perhaps even a letter. She'd found nothing. Pacing the house, feeling restless, she'd tried the TV, then the radio, before crouching in front of the bookshelf in the hall. It was filled mostly with magazines and textbooks. Neither of them was a great reader. She'd come across one of Matthew's few books, a collection of English vet stories. As she flicked through it, his bookmark had fallen out.

It was an old photograph of Matthew and Bett together, arm in arm.

At six o'clock, Bett came running up the path to the motel and practically burst into Lola's room. 'You knew he was working there, didn't you? That's why you said all those things about me looking as good as I could. I thought you meant the other stuff but you meant Daniel Hilder, didn't you?'

'Hello, darling. Did you have a good day at work?'

'Lola, I mean it. Why didn't you warn me?'

'What was I going to say? "Best of luck at work tomorrow, and by the way that man you had the one-night stand with in Melbourne three years ago is working there now so you might want to make sure you've got your lipstick on straight." Really, Bett, wasn't it better to be surprised? Think of how much you would have been worrying last night if you'd known he'd be there this morning.'

'But have you any idea how embarrassing it was? If it's not bad enough knowing people are talking about me and Carrie and Matthew. Why don't we just put me on the back of a truck and drive up and down the main street, letting people laugh at me for all the mistakes I've made in my life?'

'That's a great idea. I wish I'd thought of it. We could get sponsors, perhaps?'

'It's not funny, Lola.'

'Did Daniel laugh at you?'

'No.'

'Did he call all your colleagues over and tell them what happened between the two of you?'

'No.'

'Perhaps he didn't remember it himself.'

'Of course he remembered it. You don't forget a night like that, do you? Or perhaps he has forgotten it? Oh God, that's even worse.'

'The poor man can't win,' Lola said, laughing. 'You'd be furious with him if he did say something about it and furious with him if he'd forgotten it. He's very nice, you know. And you told me the sex was quite something, once you stopped all the crying and talking and got on with it.'

'Did I really tell you that?' She realised that, yes, she probably had. The state she had been in at that stage she was practically stopping complete strangers and telling them intimate details about her life.

'I just can't bear it,' she wailed, as she relived the brief and stilted conversation she'd had with Daniel that morning, with Rebecca standing between them chatting away unawares. 'I knew I shouldn't have come back here, Lola. Anna and Carrie and I are on eggshells with each other. Mum and Dad are still in their own little world. I'd have been better off staying in London.' She was shocked at the feel of a hand across her cheek. 'Did you just slap me?'

'It wasn't a slap, it was a flick of my fingers. Quite a different thing. I was scared you were about to become hysterical and I didn't have a bucket of water handy.'

Bett stood open-mouthed.

Lola took Bett's face between both hands and looked her right in the eyes. 'Bett, face him. Face every single thing life throws at you.

Daniel was kind to you that night, wasn't he? And everything you told him was the truth? Perhaps it was a good thing for him, too, a crash course in understanding women. Perhaps he's been kinder to his own wife or girlfriend because of some of the things you said to him.'

'Wife? Is he married now?'

'No, although there was a serious girlfriend in Melbourne, from what I could drag out of him the other day when I remembered who he was. A live-in girlfriend, that's the phrase, I believe. Horrible term, makes me think of velvet-covered sofas for some reason.'

'Was he living with her when I slept with him? Oh no, that's even worse.'

'I don't think so. He'd only been with her for a year or two, I think.' Lola laughed. 'Bett, don't look so horrified. You didn't get pregnant, did you? Catch anything from him? He didn't have lice? Scabies? AIDS? Don't look so surprised. I watch TV soaps, remember. I know every disease going.' She looked at her watch. 'Darling, the auditions will be starting soon. Do you want to stand in front of a gathering of people in a state like this? And no, you can't get under the bed, so stop looking over there. Go for a walk. Think about things and remember how lucky you are.'

'Lucky? That my most embarrassing moment has come back to haunt me?'

'That's not your most embarrassing moment. You told me your most embarrassing moment was last year when you walked around the centre of London for an afternoon without realising you had your dress tucked in your knickers.'

Bett howled. 'Apart from that.'

'See, you've had more embarrassing moments than you realise. There's no need to carry on as if this is the one that will tip you over the edge.'

'Can't you be kind to me?'

'I am being kind. Cruel to be kind. Bett, go for a walk. Be glad of your good strong legs and stop worrying about tiny things that don't matter. Do you know, I've just remembered another one. That time you made the speech at school and called the guest of honour by the wrong name the whole way through –'

'No more, Lola, or I swear I'll –'

'You'll do what? Elizabeth Quinlan, are you threatening your feeble eighty-year-old grandmother? Get out now or I'll call the police.'

An hour later, Lola was in a new outfit and full makeup, sitting behind a small table at the function room door, greeting people effusively as they came in. Ellen was sitting beside her, politely handing out registration forms to each person.

'Sandra, marvellous to see you,' Lola beamed. 'And which of your daughters is this? And what will you be singing, dear? Celine Dion? Oh, one of my favourites. Here, fill out this form, would you? We'll get started as soon as we can.'

Anna, Bett and Carrie stood at the other end of the room, watching the people stream in and sit down on the chairs lining the walls.

'I can't believe the turn-out,' Anna said. 'I thought we'd be searching for people to audition.'

Bett had a flicker of nerves. 'Do you actually know how to run one of these things?'

'Of course I do. I've been to a million of them. We'll do the warm-up songs, then get everyone to sing a verse and chorus of their chosen song, ask them to stop midway through if we think they're terrible, or hear them to the end if they're okay. Then if we want them, we call their agents and make an offer.'

Bett's lip twitched. She noticed Carrie was trying not to smile too. 'I don't think Len the butcher or Mrs Gill from the primary school are going to have agents.'

'You know what I mean. We need to run it professionally, set the standard from the start. It's going to be hard enough to pull this off in a few weeks as it is, starting from scratch, without any professional actors or musicians or performers, apart from me.' There was a tiny pause. 'And you two, of course.'

'A lot of the people here have got experience,' Carrie said briskly. 'I think you'll be surprised, Anna.'

'I hope I am.'

'Hello, Carrie.'

Carrie turned. It was Kaylene, one of Len's daughters. She worked in one of the Valley hairdressers, although Carrie didn't go to her any more, since she'd learned what a gossip she was. Carrie smiled a welcome nevertheless. The more the merrier tonight. 'Hi, Kaylene. You know Anna? And Bett?'

Kaylene nodded at the other two. 'God, I didn't ever think I'd see you Quinlans standing in the same room. I heard you had a ferocious row over Matthew.'

'Did you?' Anna said coolly. The three of them were standing close to one another and without realising it inched even closer.

'Mmm. Someone said you hadn't spoken in three years.'

Anna, in the middle, put one arm around Bett and the other around Carrie. 'Then it seems that someone was wrong, Kylie.'

'Kaylene.'

'Sorry, Kaylene. We wouldn't let a silly thing like a row about a man upset us, would we, Bett, Carrie?' Behind their backs, she was pinching them both hard.

'Of course not.'

'No.'

'If anything, it's brought us even closer together,' Anna added.

There was no need to lay it on too thick, Bett thought. She didn't dare look at Carrie.

Kaylene seemed disappointed.

'And you've come to audition, Kaylene, have you?' Anna asked nicely.

Kaylene coloured. 'I thought I'd give it a try. I like dancing and my mother says I'm a good singer.'

Bett took pity on her. 'Thanks for coming, Kaylene. Take a seat, won't you, and we'll get started as soon as we can.'

As she moved away Anna grinned. 'Good thing she left when she did. I was about to tell her I'd slept with Matthew too.'

'Anna!' Carrie and Bett were genuinely shocked.

Anna's eyes were full of mischief. 'Only joking.'

Turning back to the piano, fighting a smile, Bett didn't see Daniel Hilder come into the room behind her. Or see Lola greet him with a kiss on the cheek. Or see him take a seat at the back out of her line of vision.

Twenty minutes later the room was filled to capacity. The plan was for Lola to welcome everyone, briefly sketch the musical, then pass it over to Anna who would run the auditions. 'It's your baby, now,' Lola had told them that afternoon. 'I've done my bit. I want to enjoy it all at the end, when all the hard work has been done.'

'You're not going to sit in on every rehearsal, making comments?' Anna asked.

'Me, make comments? What do you take me for? No, I'm leaving it all to you and spending the time with Ellen instead.'

Lola hadn't been surprised when Ellen had said she didn't want to be in the musical. She'd already noticed how self-conscious the little girl was. 'Excellent news, Ellen,' she'd said cheerfully. 'That means you and I can keep each other company while the others get on with the hard work.'

Lola made her way to the front of the room now. Bett enjoyed some of the group's reactions as they took in her outfit – the blue silk shirt, so shiny it could have been a Barry White cast-off, the flared trousers, the crocheted vest in enough colours to rival Joseph's technicoloured coat. Lola waited dramatically for the chatter to stop, then gave a little bow. 'Thank you all for coming. It's the most wonderful turn-out. You may have heard this is my life's work, something I have been planning for nearly ten years –'

Two months, Bett corrected.

'And I am thrilled that so many of you are here tonight to audition, or to at least be entertained by the others' auditions while planning on sneaking off yourselves before we call you up. Hello there, Rebecca. Yes, I can see you edging out the back there.' There was a ripple of laughter. 'Let me set the scene – *Many Happy Returns* is based on the true story of the American war hero General Douglas MacArthur, and his historic visit to the tiny town of Terowie in 1942, in the middle of World War II. My story begins . . .'

Bett gazed around the room as Lola gave a precis of the storyline. There were several people she remembered from her newspaper days, but many she didn't know. A late arrival coming in the door caught her eye. Richard Lawrence. She wasn't surprised to see him. He'd been curious about the whole musical since Lola's party. She brought her attention back to Lola's speech.

'So you'll see it's the age-old story of family against family, young love thwarted, a town pulling together against the odds, the tyranny and ferociousness of war, all to a soundtrack of lots of marvellous old songs from my favourite – sorry, everyone's favourite – musicals.' There was a burst of applause, then Lola held up her hand again. 'So now, over to my granddaughter Anna.'

Anna moved forward, all glamour and poise. 'Good evening, everyone, and thanks for coming. We'll have a warm-up or two, and then we'll hear you do your individual pieces.'

At the piano, Bett watched as Lola made a poor attempt to slip unnoticed out of the room with Ellen. At Anna's nod, she played the intro, then moved smoothly into the first song, 'Do-Re-Mi' from *The Sound of Music*. There were only a few voices to begin with but as she kept playing, more people joined in. By the end of the third verse everyone was singing, even if not all of them were in tune. Bett ignored what looked like Anna wincing, and moved into the second warm-up song, 'Boogie Woogie Bugle Boy'. Things got a little livelier.

Anna stood up hurriedly at the end of the second verse, stopping them there. 'Terrific, we're off to a good start. Now, then, time for the solo spots.'

'There's not hidden cameras here or anything, is there?' Bett overheard one man ask another. 'This is getting a bit too much like that *Popstars* program for my liking.'

'Just sing any old way. Think of the free beer afterwards.'

Bett grinned. It had been Carrie's idea to add the offer of free drinks to the advertisements. 'Otherwise we won't get any men at all, and we need them for the villagers, and the soldiers, not to mention General MacArthur.'

At the desk, Anna picked out a registration form at random. 'Right, then. We'll start with Louise singing "Bohemian Rhapsody". When you're ready, Louise.'

In room seven, Lola was sitting on the side of Ellen's bed, telling stories about the girls' childhood. 'I called it my Collection of Cries, Ellen. I had a whole row of jars and as soon as I'd hear your mother cry, or Bett, or Carrie, I'd sneak up behind them and capture their cries in the jar, then quickly put the lid on. It was marvellous. They'd stop crying immediately.'

Ellen was giggling. 'And have you still got all the jars?'

Lola sadly shook her head. 'No. Unfortunately three bold little girls opened all the lids one afternoon. You've never heard such a racket. Five years' worth of tears and tantrums released in a moment. It took me some quick talking to convince the police nothing terrible had happened. As for the poor motel guests – they didn't know what had hit them.'

Ellen moved further down in her bed. 'Can you tell me another story?'

'I will, of course. But not tonight. It's past all good great-granddaughters' bedtimes.'

'But wait, Lola. I've got another question.'

Lola waited. She was well used to these delaying tactics. Anna had been exactly the same as a child. 'One more question, then.'

'Why have you got a funny voice?'

'What do you mean a funny voice?'

'You talk differently to other people. You talk like this: "It's past all good great-granddaughters' bedtimes".'

Lola laughed out loud. Ellen had just perfectly mimicked her Irish accent. She was definitely Anna's daughter. 'That, my love, is called an Irish accent, not a funny voice.'

'I like it.'

'Good. I'll keep it, then.' She kissed Ellen's forehead. 'Night night, sweetheart. Sleep well. And I'm three doors down if there's anything you need, okay? And Mummy will be here soon, too, just as soon as she's finished the auditions.'

'Night night, Lola.' Ellen's voice was barely audible. Lola waited at the door for a few minutes until she was sure the little girl was content. After a minute she heard the sound of regular breathing and let herself out. Dear little thing.

Letting herself back into her own room, Lola suddenly felt exhausted. She'd have liked to sit and watch every moment of the auditions. She'd have liked to sit in on every production meeting, too. Painted the sets, helped Bett work out the music, sew the costumes, even. But she didn't have the energy for it any more. The spirit was more than willing, but the flesh was getting weaker all the time. Oh, yes, she was in better nick than most eighty-year-olds, there was no doubt about it, but it was all downhill from here and she didn't like it one bit.

She opened the bar fridge and mixed herself a gin and tonic. She'd have a little read, a little think, a little drink and then a good night's sleep. She was longing for her bed, in fact. They didn't warn you of that in the growing old books, did they? That some days all you would ever want to do is sleep, just like a baby. It was true, the older you became, the more your life went backwards, your hair thinning, your teeth falling out, your bladder getting a life of its own. What would be next to go? Her marbles?

She sat upright in her chair. No, she was damned if that was how she was going to go. She'd made it this far, she was going to keep at it. As soon as she started lolling about, getting lazy, giving in, it would all collapse around her. She hadn't let it happen when she was young and she wouldn't now.

She deliberately moved to the hard chair, and sat there, more awake, remembering Bett asking her if she missed being young.

She'd thought about it since and decided she missed one very simple thing. Running. She missed being able to run, wished, just one more time, that she could run like she used to run as a child in Ireland, across the fields behind the house, through the soft rain or on the mild summer days, with the grass and the chestnut trees lush with new growth all around her, feeling the ground beneath her feet, muddy at times, and the long grass against her bare legs. Her favourite route had been from the front door of the big house, down the drive to the oak tree outside the main gate. She'd touch it once, twice, three times for luck, then run back as fast as she could.

She took a sip of gin and moved to turn on the TV, then changed her mind, preferring her own thoughts. She'd been remembering a lot from her childhood recently, ever since she had gone through the few photos she had, picking them out so Frank from the electrical shop could turn them into slides for her. He'd dropped the originals back that afternoon, and come in for a chat, full of questions. He was off to Ireland himself for a holiday in a few months and was keen to hear tips, asking did she want anything brought back or did she want him to call at her old house and take photos?

She'd patted him on the hand. 'Kind Frank, thank you but no. Bett did that for me when she was there a few years ago.' Not that Lola had ever looked closely at the photos Bett sent back that time. Well, there'd been no need to, had there? It wasn't as if they had meant anything to her. All the same, she'd sent Bett a note, thanking her for going to all the trouble of travelling there, talking to locals, taking the photos. And then she had never raised the subject again. She'd had more than the occasional twinge of guilt. Wanting to tell someone the truth. But too much time had gone past by now for it to matter any more, surely.

She took another sip of her drink and turned to her crossword.

She'd finish the last few clues, then go to bed. As she reached for her pen and reading glasses, there was a crackle and a fizzing sound and the ceiling light went out. The wall light was on, so she could still see, but it wasn't bright enough to work by. She'd been telling Jim for years he ought to improve them. She had a spare light bulb in the wardrobe. She stood up and felt the desk chair. Yes, it was sturdy enough and the ceilings were so low, she'd easily be able to reach. It wouldn't take a moment, and she must have changed hundreds, if not thousands, of light bulbs over the years. And made thousands of beds. And set thousands of breakfast trays. And cleaned a *million* lavatories. She must count them all up one day, it could be amusing.

She took a scarf off the end of her bed to unscrew the hot bulb. Opening the wardrobe door to give herself something to hang on to, she climbed up onto the chair. As she did, the chair shook slightly. She turned to grasp the wardrobe door but misjudged the distance. The chair tilted some more and she felt herself falling. She put out both arms to stop herself but it was too late. Her head knocked sharply against the wardrobe door and she fell to the floor.

The break was nearly over. Everyone was milling back in from the bar next door, complimentary beer and wine in hand. At their table in the corner, the three sisters were flicking through the forms.

Bett glanced down her list. Many of the names had enthusiastic ticks beside them. 'What did you think, Carrie?' She was quite surprised how easy it had been tonight to make conversation with her sisters. Then again, Lola's ban on difficult subjects was still firmly in place.

'I thought there was plenty of talent. And these here, see. What about them for the lead roles? Anna, who have you picked out?'

Anna moved her hand. Her sheet of paper was blank, apart from a few swirling doodles.

Bett bit back a smile. 'Anna, it's an amateur musical, remember. We're raising money for a new ambulance, not going for the Tony Awards.'

'But if we're going to do it, we may as well –'

'Do it well,' the other two chorused. The times they'd heard Lola chant that.

Anna sighed heavily, then flicked through the forms again. 'Have we heard this Daniel Hilder audition? He filled out the form and he'd be the right age for the Jack-the-Lad character, wouldn't he?'

Bett stiffened. 'Daniel Hilder's here?'

'The photographer?' Carrie looked up. 'I didn't see him. Will I go and ask him to audition?'

'No.' Bett spoke louder than she intended.

Anna and Carrie looked surprised. 'You don't want him to audition?' Anna asked.

'No, I mean I'll go and ask him.' Bett stood up, taking her glass of wine with her. What would Lola have said to her? Face your fears. You are thirty-two. What happened was years ago, embarrassing and all as it was. Exactly. Of course she could handle this.

She did a circuit of the room, then spotted him walking in from the bar, a drink in hand.

'Daniel?'

He turned. As she came near him, someone behind her stepped back suddenly, bumping her elbow and sending her glass of red wine flying. She stood there with red wine dripping from her chin to her knees and all down the front of her dark-blue dress.

For a split-second she was tempted to run out of the room. Then she had a brainwave. React as if you are Anna, not Bett, she told herself quickly. It worked. 'I'm going to ignore the fact that even happened,' she said coolly.

'Are you?' He seemed surprised. 'All right, then. So will I.'

She stared straight at him, trying to ignore a glint of amusement in his eye. 'I was wondering whether you wanted to audition, because if you do there's still time.'

He nodded, but didn't answer.

'Well?'

He smiled. 'I'm sorry, Bett. I really am trying to ignore that little accident, but it's a bit hard when you've got red wine dripping down your chin.'

She clung desperately to her new cool persona. 'Well, we can't have that.' She reached for a serviette, and wiped it away. 'Would you like to audition? I noticed you'd put your name down, but we didn't get to hear you.'

'I got called out for an hour,' he said. 'An urgent phone call. I missed my slot.' He gave a surprisingly shy smile. 'I thought it might be something different to do.'

How come he was being so normal? Did he have one-night stands all the time or something? Or had he blanked it out? Bett had been trying to but all day she'd been tormented by memories from that night. She tried to block them out again. He's got a live-in girlfriend, remember that. Possibly even married. Possibly even seven or eight children. A Labrador. Halitosis. Alopecia. Fungal toenails. It wasn't helping. She was noticing only good things about him. The dark eyes. The laughter lines. The kind face. The shaggy dark hair. The faded jeans and casual shirt, hanging loosely, sexily, on him.

She opened her mouth, needing to say something about their night together, trying to find the words for it, when she heard a voice behind her.

'Hi, Daniel. I'm Carrie. I don't think we've met.'

'Hello, Carrie.'

Carrie looked from one to the other. 'So are you two ready to get down to it?'

Bett blushed. She didn't look at Daniel. 'Pardon?'

'The audition?'

Yes, the audition. 'Of course. Ready, Daniel?' Bett discovered you could look just to the right of someone's face and it almost seemed as though you were looking directly at them.

He smiled. 'Ready when you are.'

Bett followed them back to the piano, surprised the candles on the tables weren't melting from the heat coming off her face.

In her room, Ellen woke up. 'Mummy?' No answer. 'Mummy?' Then she remembered. Her mum was doing the musical and Lola was looking after her. She'd told her to come to her room if she wanted anything.

Ellen climbed out of bed.

Anna was businesslike. 'Okay, Bett, Daniel, when you're ready.'

Daniel was standing by the piano, looking down at her, ready to sing. She had to blink away another memory of kissing him. If she was remembering his body, was he remembering hers? She sucked in her stomach.

'Bett?' Anna's voice a little louder.

Concentrate, Bett, she told herself. Easier said than done. How had her life come to this? Sitting at the piano in the Valley View Motel about to play the backing music so that Daniel Hilder could audition for a musical Lola had written. She'd have been less surprised to find herself strapped to the nose cone of a space shuttle. She stared at the sheet music. Hands poised over the piano, she glanced up at him, nodded and played the first note.

A loud shrieking filled the room.

They all turned. Ellen was in the doorway, dressed in her pyjamas, tears pouring down her cheeks.

'Mummy, Lola's dead.'

CHAPTER ELEVEN

BETT PRESSED her cheek against the wall of the hospital corridor, feeling the coolness as she spoke into the public phone. 'No, you don't need to come back, Dad. She's in hospital. It's all under control.'

'Are you sure? We can catch a flight and be there in a few hours.'

'Seriously, you don't need to. She's a bit shocked, but it's just a broken wrist and a bad cut on her forehead. She wasn't even unconscious when Ellen found her. It's just Ellen got such a fright.'

Nothing compared to what Ellen's words had done to the rest of them. The auditions had been forgotten, Daniel Hilder had been forgotten, as Bett, Anna and Carrie ran to Lola's room. The first sight was the worst, seeing Lola sprawled across the floor, the chair upended beside her, her left wrist bent at an awkward angle.

'Lola, no,' Bett heard herself scream. Anna reached for her right wrist to feel the pulse, then nearly leapt out of her skin as Lola spoke. 'Hello, darling.'

'You're not dead?'

'Not unless heaven looks like the motel.'

Bett was on the floor beside her in seconds, gently touching her. 'Are you hurt? What happened?'

'The stupid light bulb. I told your father to buy better-quality ones.'

'Lola, we've told you not to change those bulbs.' Anna said crossly. 'You're eighty, too old to be climbing up on chairs like this.'

Lola rallied. 'One minute you're crying because you think I'm dead, the next minute you're telling me off. Talk about fair-weather friends.'

Crouched on the floor beside her too, Carrie put a hand on her own chest. 'Oh God, Lola, at least you're okay. I nearly died of the fright. My heart is still racing, you should feel it.'

'*Jesus*, Carrie.' Bett was shocked as a surge of fury hit her. 'Do you have to be the centre of attention all the time?'

Carrie's eyes widened. 'I wasn't, I was just –'

'You were so. You always –'

'Stop it, Bett, for God's sake.' Anna snapped. 'You're as bad as each other.'

Bett glared at her. 'Don't you start on –'

'I will start on you. Leave Carrie alone and ring an ambulance, would you?'

'I was about to, before she –'

'Darlings, please.' Lola's voice came from between them. Her head was against Carrie's shoulder, her eyes closed. 'Don't fight over me. And, Bett, please don't blaspheme like that again. You know I don't like it.'

Her words set them into motion, even as they avoided any further eye contact. Bett called for an ambulance. Carrie stayed with Lola while Anna moved to the door, asking the crowd that had gathered to please move back. 'She's fine, she'll be fine. She's not dead at all.'

'Mummy?' A familiar little voice came from the back of the group. Anna turned as Richard Lawrence came into view, holding Ellen by the hand.

He brought her forward. 'I found her crying in the function room.'

Anna pulled the little girl into her arms. 'Ellie, I'm so sorry. I'm so sorry to leave you behind.' In the rush to find Lola after Ellen's announcement they had run straight past her. 'You're such a good girl, you might have saved your great-grandmother's life, do you know that?'

Bett was about to suggest a cup of tea, something warm and sweet for Lola, when she saw headlights approaching. She crouched down beside her grandmother again and gently took her good hand. 'Here we are now. The ambulance is here.'

It wasn't the ambulance but an ordinary station wagon. Daniel Hilder got out and walked over. 'I thought it might be as quick for me to bring Lola in to the hospital. The ambulance could be a while yet.'

'You see how important this musical is?' Lola said, rousing again for a moment. 'I told you this Valley needs another ambulance.'

'Lola, are you sure you're okay to move?' Bett asked. 'You're not hurt anywhere else? Your back or your legs?'

'I'm fine. It's just my sore head and this stupid wrist.' She was shaking violently.

Carrie was on one side of her, Bett on the other. Bett turned to Daniel, businesslike, serious, in no need of an inner-Anna now. 'Daniel, we'll accept, if you don't mind. Carrie, you and I go in with her. Anna, you'd better stay here with Ellen. Lola, can you stand?'

Daniel stepped forward. 'I can carry you to the car, Lola, if you need it.'

'So kind of you, Daniel,' Lola managed to be gracious. 'But I'll walk. Where's my little Ellen first?' Ellen came forward and Lola touched her gently on the cheek. 'Thank you, my little darling, for doing exactly the right thing.'

Bett had felt her eyes well up with tears at the sight of Ellen's face, filled with pride. After that it had been all action, getting Lola to the hospital, into the waiting room. Daniel Hilder had been there, gentle, helping, then he had gone before Bett had a chance to thank him.

On the phone, Jim Quinlan sounded relieved. 'You're absolutely sure you don't need us there, Bett?'

'I'm sure, Dad. She's sleeping now. We're going to go home too. I'll call you first thing in the morning.'

As she hung up, she saw her hands were shaking. Nurses were moving swiftly up and down the hospital corridor. Carrie was in a chair down a little way, making a call on her mobile phone. To Matthew, Bett presumed . . .

'Bett?'

She turned. It was Daniel.

'Is everything okay? Is Lola all right?'

She nodded. 'She's going to be fine, they think. It looked more serious than it was.' She glanced up at the clock. Nearly two hours had passed since they had arrived, the time speeding past in the flurry of doctors' visits and X-rays, before Lola was finally settled into a small ward. 'Have you been waiting all this time?'

'I didn't mind. I had a book with me. I thought you and your sister might need a lift back to the motel.'

She was too tired to be embarrassed or to feel nervous with him. She just gave him a big, grateful smile. 'Thank you.'

Ten metres away, Carrie was talking into her mobile phone. '. . . so they'll keep her in overnight. God knows what would have happened if Ellen hadn't found her. She was so shocked she hadn't been able to get up off the floor.'

'What was she doing up on the chair in the first place?' Matthew said. 'Don't tell me, swinging from the light fittings?'

It was nice to laugh. As soon as she'd heard from the doctors that Lola was going to be all right, she had wanted to ring Matthew. He had been wary when he first answered, but his tone had changed as soon she told him what had happened. Just hearing his voice helped calm her, too. Until he suddenly changed the subject.

'I want to come down, Carrie.' He paused. 'Not just for Lola, but also to see Bett. I think I need to. I've been thinking about her a lot.'

Something chilled in her again. She thought of the photo she'd found. 'No, you can't.'

'Carrie, come on.' He sounded cross, impatient again. 'What do you think will happen? That I'll decide I made a mistake and go back to her?'

So the thought of that had been in his head already. 'I don't know what would happen and I don't want to find out.'

'Carrie, don't hang up. Can't you see –'

She didn't want to see anything else that night. 'The doctor is coming back, Matthew. I have to go. I'll be in touch.'

'Carrie . . .'

'Goodbye.' She hung up first, once again. Composing herself, she walked over to Bett and Daniel.

At the motel, Anna was kneeling beside Ellen's bed. She stroked the hair back from Ellen's face and tucked the sheet in close around her shoulders. The child was nearly asleep, stirring now and again to ask another question. 'Lola will be all right, Mum, won't she? They're not taking her to be put down, are they?'

Anna stopped herself from laughing. Their neighbour's cat in Sydney had been run over and had needed to be taken to the vet to be put down. Anna thought she'd explained the situation to Ellen well when it happened, telling her the truth, that the cat had broken so many bones and was in such terrible pain it was kinder to end its life than try to fix it. She stroked her forehead again. 'Of course not, Ellie. The doctors and nurses know exactly what to do and she'll be back home before we know it.'

Ellen's eyelids fluttered, then closed, and in seconds her breathing was slow, measured. Anna waited a moment longer, then leaned forward and kissed her on the forehead and whispered. 'I'm just going to turn all the lights off in the motel and then I'll be right back.'

As Anna came out of her room, she jumped as a figure appeared in front of her. It was Richard. She noticed the bar and function room were already in darkness.

He came closer. 'I hope you don't mind, I wanted to do something, so I closed up for you. I've been here so long I know where all the light switches are.'

'Thank you,' she said, surprised and touched.

'And Lola will be all right?'

Anna nodded. 'I'm sure she will. It's us who nearly died of the shock.'

Richard looked concerned. 'Anna, can I make you a cup of tea? Or perhaps a hot chocolate? I know my way around the kitchen, I think. Would you like that? You must have had a terrible fright tonight.'

'Yes. Yes, I have. Thanks, Richard. That would be really kind of you.'

Then she burst into tears.

The blue station wagon pulled up in front of the motel.

'Thanks, Daniel,' Carrie said from the front passenger seat beside him.

'Yes. Thanks, Daniel,' Bett said from the back.

'I was happy to do it. You're both okay from here?'

'We're fine, thanks.' Bett managed to get in first.

'And will you tell Lola I was asking after her?'

'Of course.' Bett hesitated for a moment, wondering if this was the opportunity to speak to Daniel. She had to mention something about their night together, or the tension at work would be too much. But she couldn't do it now. Not with Carrie in earshot. Her sister already seemed to be taking what seemed like hours to undo her seatbelt and get out of the front.

They finally got out at the same time, standing side by side to wave as Daniel drove off. There was a long, awkward silence. Bett felt uncomfortable. Did she ask Carrie to stay for a cup of tea? Give her the chance to talk over the night? Surely she was feeling as shocked as Bett was?

Carrie took the decision away from her, reaching into her bag for her car keys. 'Anna's turned off the lights, I see, so I'll leave you to it.' Her voice was very brisk.

'Oh. Okay. Goodnight, then.'

'Yes. See you tomorrow.'

Bett walked to her room. Carrie walked to her car. Neither of them turned around, or noticed that the light was still on in the kitchen.

CHAPTER TWELVE

'FUSSPOT.'

Anna grinned. 'Lola, I'm not a fusspot. I'm doing what the doctor told us to do, checking on you all the time.'

'Much ado about nothing, if you ask me.'

'Taming of the shrew, more like it.'

Anna stood by Lola's bed, looking down at her grandmother, sitting up against the pillows, her arm in a sling made from a wildly patterned silk scarf. Her bed jacket was a bright-yellow satin. There were bunches of flowers all over the room – they'd been arriving all day as word got around that Lola was out of hospital and back at the motel. She was wearing full makeup, the foundation applied around the bandage on her forehead. Anna could see she'd missed her mark slightly, a smear of blusher heavier on one cheek than the other, the lipstick wobbly. Lola had been keeping up a brave front since the accident, although her doctor had called Anna aside and told her to keep an eye out for delayed shock. So far there'd been no sign of it, though. Lola had spent the afternoon reading to Ellen and would still be at it if Anna hadn't prised them apart and put Ellen to bed.

Anna gently tucked the sheet in around her grandmother. 'Are you sure I can't get you anything before I go to rehearsals?'

'I'm fine, darling. Stop looking at me as if I'm some museum specimen.'

Anna sat down beside her and took her hand. 'You frightened us, you know.'

'I frightened myself.'

'Don't die, Lola. We wouldn't like it.'

'All right, darling, I promise I won't. Now, off you go to those rehearsals and make your poor sick grandmother proud of you.'

Anna had been gone only a minute or two before Carrie knocked lightly on the door and came in. 'Is everything all right, Lola? Do you need anything?'

'I couldn't be happier, darling. I should have done this months ago. All this spoiling, it's marvellous.' She patted the bed. 'Now, enough about me. Let me interrogate you for a quick minute. Are you coping with all the motel business while your parents are away? Do you need any extra help?'

'Everything's fine. No problems at all.' Carrie was enjoying it, in fact. It was giving her the opportunity to try out a few of her own ways of doing things.

'And how are things with Matthew?'

'They're fine,' she lied smoothly, picking up one of the Get Well cards on Lola's bedside table, concentrating fiercely on the greeting inside. It was from the ladies in the charity shop, wishing her a speedy recovery. Beside the cards was a large basket filled with fruit, chocolate and crossword puzzle books. Jim and Geraldine had sent it. 'He sends his love. Says he would have brought you a bunch of grapes if he'd been here.'

'If he'd been allowed to be here, you mean. Carrie, I've been thinking about the ban and I've decided it can be lifted. I think it would be all right now if he visited here again. In fact, I think Bett would like to see him.'

Carrie's head shot up. 'Has she said that to you?'

'No, but she doesn't need to. I know her. Has Matthew said anything?'

'He said he'd like to see Bett again too.' The words tasted awful in her mouth.

'Good. I'd hoped as much. I'll leave it up to you to arrange it. The sooner the better, I think.'

Carrie turned away before Lola saw her expression.

Lola had just gone back to her crossword after Carrie's departure when there was another knock. A dark curly head poked around the door. 'Lola? Are you okay?'

Lola smiled at her. 'Bett, darling, shouldn't you be at the rehearsal too?'

'I'm on my way. I got delayed with a late arrival at reception. I just wanted to check if you needed anything or if you wanted to come up and watch.'

'I couldn't bear the pain.'

'Oh, you poor thing. Shall I move one of the big armchairs in from the bar? You could rest your arm on that, if you liked.'

'Not the pain in my arm, the pain of seeing you all massacre my masterpiece.'

Bett relaxed. 'Very funny. You might be surprised. We've actually got a pretty good cast lined up.' Anna had spent the day after Lola's accident on the phone, handing out the parts as well as reporting on Lola's condition.

'Lola couldn't have timed it better if she tried,' she'd confided to Bett. 'People didn't dare say no to any of the parts, not knowing it was Lola's life's work. You don't suppose she did it deliberately?'

For once, Bett was sure she hadn't. She'd seen real pain and shock in Lola's eyes that night.

Anna had gone on. 'I asked that Daniel Hilder if he wanted to come and audition again, but he said no, unfortunately his circumstances had changed. Shame, he'd have been about the right age for that Jack-the-Lad character.'

'Yes, that is a shame,' Bett had said casually, relief flooding through her.

Lola was leaning back against her pillows, content. 'I can hardly wait until opening night. Tell me, Bett, are you ready to see Matthew yet?'

'You're asking me just like that? Haven't you got a little bell you can ring to warn me you're bringing up something personal?'

'Do you want to see him? I think you should. Get it over and done with. It will clear the air between you and Carrie.'

'Carrie and I are fine. All things considered.' They weren't, actually. Things may have been thawing between her and Anna, but they were definitely still covered in snow with Carrie.

'No, you're not. Not yet. Think about it, Bett. Remember my two rules.'

'Face your fears and tell the truth. Yes, I remember.' She leaned and kissed her grandmother. 'You know, you're lucky I love you so much or I'd call you an interfering meddlesome old bag.'

Lola laughed and returned to her crossword.

Anna smiled at everyone in the function room. There were fifteen people sitting in a circle of chairs all around her. Carrie was on one end. Bett sat nearby, at the piano, the sheet music piled beside her.

'So you've all got your scripts now? Good. And you're sure which parts you're playing? Yes? No more confusion over who's playing the General MacArthur role?' Two of the men studiously avoided looking at each other. 'Terrific. To get in the mood, I'd like you all to call each other by your characters' names while we're in rehearsals, okay? So we'll start today with a read through of the opening scene with you, Mrs MacArthur, and your son Arthur beside you.'

Mrs MacArthur, formerly known as Len the butcher's daughter Kaylene, smiled broadly at everyone. The thirteen-year-old boy playing the part of the four-year-old Arthur didn't look quite so happy. But a part was a part and he needed all the experience he could get if he eventually wanted to go to drama school. Or so his mother had told him.

Anna moved her chair to face them. 'As it says in the script, you are with your husband and father, General MacArthur, in a plane flying from the war in the Philippines on your way to Australia. A storm is raging all around you. There'll be the sound of gunfire as well as thunder and lightning, so it will be very dramatic.' She hoped it would be, anyway. Her first meeting with Len about the stage set hadn't filled her with confidence. She'd had to gently explain to him they would need more than clashing saucepan lids and glass jars filled with rice to make the storm effects.

'So, Mrs MacArthur, your young son hasn't been well and is feeling frightened, so to ease his terrors, you start singing "My Favourite Things" to him. Would you like to try that scene?'

Mrs MacArthur cleared her throat and looked down at the page.

'Poor-Arthur-you-must-be-scared-of-that-noise-don't-worry-I-know-how-to-put-a-smile-back-on-your-face.'

Anna had heard more animation from the speaking clock. 'That's a great start. But perhaps it would help if I could talk through some of the motivation with you.' She paused, thinking hard. 'Imagine the scene. You've been travelling with your husband and ill son for weeks, bombarded by war, homesickness, longing for the familiar, feeling cut off from everything you know and love – your home, your family.'

She stood up and started pacing the room, drawing on her own experiences as she'd been taught at drama school, thinking back to the latest angry phone call with Glenn. 'Is this what you wanted when you first got married, you ask yourself? Did you go into it with your eyes wide open? Or were you seduced by the thought of glamour and travel and social standing and allowed that to take over? Has your marriage become a shell? Your friends abandoned you because they are sick of the two of you fighting all the time? Is your child suffering?'

'Anna?'

'Do you cry yourself to sleep some nights through loneliness and fear and the pain of broken hopes and dreams?'

'Anna?'

Anna came to as Bett said her name even louder. The group was looking at her in some alarm. She steadied herself and briskly tapped the script. 'Or another simpler way of looking at it would be a mother singing her scared son to sleep. Bett, when you're ready. "My Favourite Things" from the top.'

At the break, Bett brought a glass of water over to her sister. 'Anna, are you okay?'

'Fine. Couldn't be better.'

Bett hesitated. There had been some uncomfortable echoes in Anna's words about Mrs MacArthur. Echoes from the big fight the night she had found out about Carrie and Matthew, when she had turned on Anna, and said terrible things about Glenn, about Glenn and Anna's marriage. Some of it almost word for word what Anna had said. Ever since Lola's accident she'd had an urge to talk about it all. To bring everything out in the open. To stop all this stepping around each other. 'It's just . . . what you were saying about Mrs MacArthur . . .'

Anna waited.

'Was it only about Mrs MacArthur?'

'Of course.' She gave a light laugh. 'My directors were always telling me off for going overboard with my motivation exercises.'

'Really?'

'Really.' Anna busied herself making notes on her script.

Say it, Bett, say it. 'You weren't talking about you and Glenn? It's just some of what you said . . .' She trailed off as she saw Anna visibly sit up straighter and her chin lift.

Bett backed off immediately. 'Never mind. I'll leave you to it.'

That night, Carrie was in the office when she heard a knock at the door. It was Bett. Carrie was surprised. So far they had done their best to avoid being alone together. 'Is everything all right? Lola's okay?'

'She's fine. Watching TV, complaining that her gin and tonic levels are way down and that she's going to have to get drunk for a week to bring them up again.' Bett hesitated. 'I actually wanted to talk to you about something else.'

'Oh. Okay. Come in.'

Bett took a seat and tried to choose the right words. Perhaps that was where she'd gone wrong with Anna earlier. She'd said it too bluntly. She tried to feel her way now. 'It's about Matthew.'

Carrie stiffened.

Bett couldn't help noticing. 'Carrie, I've been thinking about this a lot. I need to see him.'

'What do you mean "need"?'

'I think the three of us need to get together. Maybe Lola was right at the start to ask you to keep him away, but I'm staying on and, with the musical and everything, I think it's important.'

'You've been talking to Lola, haven't you?'

'Yes. But it's what I want, too.' Couldn't Carrie even meet her halfway on this?

'He's away for work,' Carrie said shortly.

'Then when he's back on the weekend.'

'He doesn't come back every weekend.'

'Well, on the weekend he does come back.'

Carrie was looking down at her paperwork again. 'I'll think about it.'

'I don't get it,' Bett whispered to Anna several minutes later. On the way back to her room, Bett had seen Anna's light on, and on the spur of the moment knocked gently on her door. Anna had seemed surprised, but beckoned her in, her finger on her lips. Ellen was asleep in the single bed. A book lay open on Anna's bed. 'What does she think I'm going to do, hurl myself at him when I see him? Manacle myself to his legs?'

'That would make sheep crutching a little tricky for him. You dragging around in the dust at his feet,' Anna whispered back.

'So much for Lola's advice,' Bett said, her voice still low. 'It's all very well to say face your fears but what if your fears don't want to be faced? I actually thought Carrie would want to get it over and done with too. But it's like she doesn't want me anywhere near him, in case I burst into tears and try and steal him back or something.'

'And you wouldn't, would you?'

'Wouldn't what?'

'Try and steal him back.'

'Sorry?'

'You wouldn't want him back, would you?

Bett tensed. 'I don't know.' A pause. 'I'm not sure how I'll react until I see him.'

'Still avoiding the truth after all these years, Bett?' Anna's tone was joking, but her eyes were serious.

Bett looked away. She didn't want to spoil this new fragile friendship with Anna. 'I mean it. That's why I need to see him.' She rushed to change the subject. 'So how did Ellie enjoy school today?' The little girl had started at the local school that week. They had all gathered to see her go off in her school uniform the first day, waving as if she was their own daughter.

Anna hesitated, then accepted the change of topic. 'Fine. She hasn't said much yet. It takes time to settle in, though. You remember what it's like, arriving at a new school in the middle of term.'

Bett nodded. The tension was definitely back between them. What did she do now? Try and break through it again? Ask about Glenn, when he was one of the main reasons she and Anna hadn't spoken in three years? She imagined Lola in the corner of the room, urging her on. 'How's Glenn, Anna?' The words came out sounding half chewed.

'He's fine,' Anna answered.

Bett knew her well enough to know that was the most Anna would say about it tonight. She watched as Anna went to the fridge, took out a bottle of wine and reached for the corkscrew. She didn't look like the mother of a seven-year-old, Bett thought. She looked amazing, in fact – the sleek straight hair, the perfect makeup, the thin, tanned body, not an ounce of extra flesh on her at all. And that cool poise she had, the keep-your-distance kind of elegance that

Bett knew she could never have, not in a million years. It suddenly seemed important to Bett to compliment Anna, to let her know how great she looked, to be the first to start building bridges. As Anna came over to the bed with the opened bottle and two glasses, she smiled up at her. 'Anna, you really are amazing.'

Anna's brow creased. 'Pardon me?'

'You look incredible. The perfect figure, perfect clothes, perfect hair, perfect skin, the perfect marriage, gorgeous little daughter, all so effortlessly.' Bett laughed, pleased with how it was all sounding. 'I'm sure the day will come when we're reading about the Anna Quinlan range of home and beauty products. Martha Stewart, watch out.'

To Bett's amazement, Anna wasn't amused. And she certainly didn't take it as a compliment. 'You think it comes easily? Effortlessly?' Her voice was still low but her eyes were furious. 'You think I am skinny by accident? No, Bett. It's called discipline and sometimes it's called starvation. Think my hair looks like this naturally? No, it costs a fortune once a month. And my perfect marriage?' Anna took a breath, ready to tell all – wanting to tell all, sick of the charade. 'Oh, yes, Bett, it is so perfect that I am –'

'Mummy?'

They both turned to see Ellen tossing around under her sheet, talking in her sleep or having a nightmare, Bett wasn't sure which. Anna put down the wine and moved swiftly over to her daughter, talking gently, stroking her forehead until she settled again. When all was quiet, she moved silently back.

Bett stood up, her voice almost a whisper. 'I'll go. I'm sorry to interrupt –'

'Bett, stay, please.' Anna looked very tired all of a sudden. 'She'll be fine. Please, don't go yet.'

They sat awkwardly for a moment, neither of them speaking. Bett shifted on the bed, wanting to apologise. She had been silly to assume things would fall into place so quickly. Two steps forward, one step back. She took a breath. 'Anna, I'm sorry for what I said about the way you look. It wasn't a dig, I promise. I know you work hard at it. I meant it as a compliment, really. It just came out wrong.' She seemed to have chosen exactly the right words for once. In front of her eyes, tension slipped out of Anna's body, the tight look around her mouth disappeared.

Anna gave an embarrassed smile. 'I'm sorry for snapping at you, too. I'm just really tired, I think. Ellen had nightmares again last night and I didn't sleep well.'

Bett gladly took up the change in subject. 'Does she have them often?'

'Not as often as she used to, but now and then still. She's reliving the attack, I think. And then she won't sleep until I read to her, or cuddle her or she hops into bed with me. Which means she sleeps like a log but I don't sleep at all. She favours the horizontal approach in bed, rather than the vertical.' She smiled again.

'She's been very brave. It must have been hard for her.'

'It was. It was hard for all of us.'

A shaft of guilt went through Bett. She should have been there to help.

Anna stood up, retrieved the wine and poured two glasses, passing one to Bett. 'If we're going to be whispering in the dark like old times, we may as well be drinking in the dark like old times too.'

Bett took the glass, surprised and pleased. 'Do you remember how furious Lola was that night?'

'We were under-age, I suppose. And it was Dad's best bottle of red.'

They sat in silence for a moment, before Anna spoke. 'So London was good? And Dublin?'

'It was, yes.' There it was, three years summed up in one sentence.

'You were working in a record company?'

Bett nodded. Lola had definitely acted as a conduit of news about each of them. 'And you're the voice behind every second ad on TV these days, I believe.'

Anna shrugged. 'Not exactly the Royal Shakespeare Company, but I enjoy it.' Another pause and then Anna spoke again. 'Bett, can I ask you something personal?'

Bett stiffened.

'Did you meet anyone in Dublin or London? Any men, I mean?'

Bett shook her head. On the plane she'd harboured a wish to invent a fantasy husband, a fantasy family, a whole family life to make this homecoming easier. She'd decided against it, knowing only too well Lola would demand photographic proof and all the intimate details. The sad truth was she hadn't met anyone she liked, or anyone who had liked her, either. She decided to keep her answer light. 'No. Still on the shelf. Destined to stay on the shelf, I suppose.'

'Bett, please don't talk like that. I'm sure you'll meet someone, when the right person comes along. Maybe even a nice country boy.'

Bett laughed softly, suddenly exhilarated by the pleasure of talking to Anna again. It was almost like old times – if she ignored the dozens of subjects they couldn't approach. 'That'd be ironic, wouldn't it? I spend three years in Dublin and London and all the time my dream man is waiting in my home town.' She'd been joking, but someone came to mind. 'Do you know who is nice? Richard, the Englishman here at the motel. I sat next to him at Lola's party and he's good company. Really witty. And have you seen when he smiles? It's like a transformation. His eyes get all sparkly. Anna, should I ask him out for a drink, do you think? Tonight, even?'

'I think he's out.'

'No, he's not. I saw him go into his room earlier. We said hello.' Bett stood up. 'Do you know what? I think I will. I'll ask him if he wants to go into town and have a drink with me.'

'No, Bett.'

'Why not?'

'I think there's a motorbike rally on in town. The pubs are jammed. It'll be terrible.'

'Oh.' Bett sat down again. 'Well, perhaps I'll have an early night.'

'Good idea. You look a bit tired. You look good,' Anna said hastily, 'just a bit tired.'

'I am, actually.' She stood up. 'Maybe I'll ask Richard out for a drink tomorrow night.'

'Go to bed, Bett.'

'All right.' She hesitated, then leaned over and kissed her. 'Thanks. It was very good to talk to you again.'

'I liked talking to you too.'

Bett let herself out, quietly closing the door. Anna sat down on her bed and breathed a slow sigh of relief.

CHAPTER THIRTEEN

IN HIS room, Richard typed one more paragraph, then pressed the save button on his laptop computer. Good, he'd managed to get a lot done and still leave himself time to get ready.

As he stretched he looked with pleasure at the growing pile of paper beside him. It had been a good idea to come here. He was easily imagining his characters in the same landscape more than one hundred and fifty years earlier. The Clare Valley was like a wilder version of Tuscany, he'd decided. Rolling hills, vineyards, olive groves, old stone buildings and that incredible wide blue sky, day after day. He'd explored the towns and villages, and a good few of the wineries. He'd soaked up the scenery – the wooded hills, the gum trees silhouetted against the sky and the willow trees edging the dry creek beds. At sunset he'd watched the pink-chested galahs swoop in great flocks. He'd even started noticing the different smells, the gum leaves, the native flowers and the earth itself, baked hot under months of sunshine. The sounds were distinctive, too, the warbling of the magpies and the loud laughter of the kookaburras. It was all helping him get the details just right.

He had talked about writing a book for years, always expecting when he got down to it that it would be a long dark night of the soul. Instead, he'd discovered an interest – and a talent, if the responses from agents to his early chapters were anything to go by – for rollicking, fiction-based-on-fact adventures. He was basing his story on the life of an English petty criminal who had been shipped to Sydney, then escaped to the Clare Valley, where he'd hitched up with an Irish servant girl. The pair of them had gone on to quite a life of crime, before disappearing, either to new lives under assumed names, or to their deaths in the desert. Not exactly Bonnie and Clyde but not a long way off, either.

He said another silent thanks to his aunt, his father's only – and very wealthy – sister, who had died a year earlier, leaving Richard and his two sisters more than thirty thousand pounds each in her will. The money had come through six weeks after he had split with his long-term girlfriend, a reporter on the same newspaper in London. It had spurred him into making some big decisions – to get out of journalism, get out of London and make a real attempt at writing the novel.

He'd spent a month in Sydney before deciding to base himself in the Clare Valley. Not only would it give him a feel for the novel's other main setting, he'd decided it would be cheaper and have fewer distractions, too. He'd found the Valley View Motel on the Internet, liking the idea of a motel room overlooking a picturesque valley view. The motel hadn't quite lived up to its name, he thought with a grin. More Part of a Hill View than Valley View. But what had been happening as expected recently? He certainly hadn't thought he'd want to stay in the Clare Valley for this long. He hadn't expected to uncover such fascinating research material from the local history group. Or to come across such a character as Lola Quinlan. And he certainly hadn't expected to meet anyone so beautiful, or so fragile, or so entertaining as Lola's granddaughter.

There was a knock at the door. He opened it and smiled. 'Hello.'

'Hello.'

He turned and gestured extravagantly towards the small table set with a bottle of wine and two glasses. 'Please, come in.'

Anna smiled. 'Thank you. I'd love to.'

Out at the farmhouse, Carrie was lying in the middle of the double bed, wide awake. After she'd got back from work, she'd scrubbed the whole house and cleaned out the fridge. But she still wasn't tired and she still couldn't get her conversations with Bett and Matthew out of her head.

She'd taken out the photo of them again and looked at it for a long time. She'd thought about burning it, then told herself off for being childish. It wasn't going to change things if the photo didn't exist, was it? Matthew would still want to see Bett. Bett would still want to see Matthew.

From her position on the bed, she noticed a T-shirt had fallen between the wardrobe and the dressing table in the corner of the room. She hadn't noticed it before. She was over to it in a moment. It was one of Matthew's.

She didn't think twice. She stripped off her nightie and pulled his T-shirt over her head, breathing in his smell, feeling the cotton against her skin, trying to imagine how he felt when she hugged him.

It made her feel a bit better.

Anna let herself quietly back into her room. She went straight over to Ellen and kissed her gently. The little girl was still fast asleep.

She walked into the bathroom and started taking off her makeup. What an unusual night. And what an unusual man. She hadn't felt under any pressure. He hadn't made a pass at her or made her feel at all uncomfortable. They had just enjoyed a glass of wine and talked. The same way they had talked so easily the night of Lola's accident, when he had made her the hot chocolate. He was just so interested in everything, in what she did for a living, in what had happened to Ellen, in how long her parents had owned the motel.

'Are you a detective?' she'd asked him.

'No, I'm not. I'm a journalist trying to become a novelist.'

'That explains the questions. But why are you so nice? Are you gay?'

He laughed. 'No, I'm not gay either. Why are you so suspicious?'

'In my experience, people don't ask so many questions unless they're after something.'

'I'm interested because I'm interested in people. And I'm especially interested in people with such beautiful speaking voices.'

She had actually blushed.

'I've also discovered there's nothing to fuel the imagination like hearing other people's stories,' he said. 'So it's not so much curiosity as cannibalism. I'm feeding off you so I can write my own book.'

'Oh, in that case, that's fine.'

He'd understood completely when she had slipped away several times to check on Ellen, a few rooms away.

'Everything all right?' he'd asked each time.

'She's fast asleep,' she'd been able to answer.

'So you can stay a bit longer?' At her nod, he poured her some more wine. 'Then tell me some stories, Anna Quinlan.'

'About what?'

'Well, let me think. An easy one to start with. Tell me why there is so much tension between you and your sisters.'

'You noticed?'

'It's a little hard to miss. I don't think I've seen the three of you so much as have a cup of coffee together since you all got here. My own two sisters spend their entire time in a huddle whispering, so I was just curious . . .'

She hesitated. 'We had a bit of a fight three years ago.'

'About . . . ?'

She decided she wanted to tell him about it. 'Have you ever heard that song "Sisters" from the film *White Christmas*?'

He started to sing it, note perfect.

She raised an eyebrow. 'You know musicals off the top of your head? Are you sure you're not gay?'

He grinned. 'No, I just like old musicals. I can cook, too. So it was a mister who came between you and your sister?'

'No, not between me and my sister. A mister came between my two sisters. Well, moved from one of my sisters to the other, anyway. If you know what I mean. And married her instead.'

'Ah, I see. So that explains them. But what about you? How did you get caught up in it?'

Anna didn't want to spoil the mood by going into it. She was enjoying this gentle atmosphere too much. 'That's a story for another time. It's your turn to tell me some stories. Are you really writing a book or is that a cover story for something much more sinister?'

'I'm really writing a book. Trying to write a book, at least,' he'd said. 'And this is the perfect place to do it. The scenery is beautiful. The wine is delicious. And all the people I've met seem very interesting too.' He paused. 'One in particular, actually.'

'Really?' A look had passed between them. 'That's good.'

She smiled as she finished taking off her makeup and moved quietly back into the bedroom. She'd been flirting with him, she realised. And not only that, she'd enjoyed every minute of it. She kissed Ellen again and climbed into bed. The room was quiet for a few minutes and then she actually laughed out loud. She'd just caught herself lying there smiling into the dark like a teenager.

In her room next door, Bett couldn't get to sleep. First she'd been too hot, and then when she'd turned on the airconditioning, it had been too cold. All the noises outside seemed too loud – guests arriving back late, doors opening and closing in nearby rooms, the murmurs of night-time conversations.

Her mind was filled with thoughts of her sisters. It was strange to think that Anna was just metres away, Carrie a few miles away, home alone in the farmhouse that Bett still hadn't seen. The three of them were managing to work on a musical together, help run the motel together, yet the tension still hummed away between them. Bett knew that Lola was watching their every move, listening in to all the conversations she could, trying to gauge how things were going between them.

Bett had tried her best tonight. She'd broached the subject of Matthew with Carrie. She'd spoken to Anna about Glenn. But she wasn't feeling any better. She turned in the bed again. What else could she do to get rid of this tension between them? Challenge them to a duel?

She lay back, kicked at the sheets, then tugged at her pillow. She turned it over, feeling the cool side. She paused for a moment, then took the pillow in her hands, lifted her legs into the air and balanced the pillow across her feet. She glanced over at the clock and started timing herself. Less than a minute later her leg twitched and the pillow slid off. A very bad performance. She'd obviously lost her touch.

Perhaps that was the solution, though. She could invite Anna and Carrie into her room for a re-run of the Pillow Balancing

Competitions they'd enjoyed as children. She lifted the pillow onto her feet again, remembering the first time they played it, at a different motel but on a hot summer night just like this one. They'd been forced for space reasons to share a dormitory-style room. The windows had been left wide open and the girls were lying in bed dressed only in T-shirts, trying to keep cool. It had been too hot to sleep, too hot to do much at all.

Bett, fourteen at the time, had turned her pillow first one way, loving the brief feeling of coolness against her face, then turned it back. Before a few minutes had passed, it was warm again. 'It needs a constant supply of air on it,' she said out loud.

'What?' Anna said, engrossed in a book. In the bed between them Carrie was asleep.

'Nothing,' Bett said, preoccupied now. She gave up on turning the pillow and instead wriggled down in the bed and stuck her legs straight up in the air. Then she reached up and balanced the pillow across her feet. A few minutes later she was still like that and very pleased with herself indeed. 'Anna?' she whispered again.

Anna didn't look up. 'Mmm?'

'Bet you I can balance a pillow like this for ages.'

That earned a glance from Anna. 'Well, that's really going to get you a place in the Moscow Circus.'

'It's harder than it looks. You try it. It actually takes great staying power and balancing skills.'

'How long do I have to do it for?' Anna said, grunting a little as she reached up and put her pillow in place. Hers wasn't as firm as Bett's, and hung saggily over her feet. 'Hold on. It's not an even competition yet.' Leaning over, she pulled out Carrie's pillow with a tug.

'Ow, what?' Carrie opened her eyes, face crumpled, as if she was about to cry. 'Anna, give that back.'

'I can't, sorry. I need it for equipment.'

Carrie looked around blearily, noticing Bett with her legs sticking upright, a pillow atop of them, and then Anna, getting into position to do the same thing. 'What are you doing?'

'It's the Annual Quinlan Pillow Balancing Competition. First heats start today,' Bett said matter-of-factly. 'And I am winning by a long shot. I'm miles ahead of you.'

Carrie reached over and snatched the spare pillow off Anna's bed, putting it on her feet.

Anna moved the lamp onto the floor and angled the clock so she could read the time. 'Okay, starting in ten seconds. Pillows in position. Go.'

They lay like that for several minutes before Carrie spoke up. 'It's a bit boring.'

'It is not,' Bett's voice was as indignant as possible in her physical position. 'It's a combination of balance and concentration. You just can't stick it.'

'Can so. It's easy.'

Bett shot her a glance. Carrie was looking remarkably relaxed. 'It's easy for you. Your legs are shorter, so there's less muscle to ache.'

'Yours have got more fat, and fat rises, so it should be easier for you.'

Anna quickly stepped in. 'Carrie's right. It is a bit boring. Let's make it more interesting.'

'I know,' Bett said, trying to take back control of her game. 'You have to do something while you're balancing the pillows.'

'Like what?'

'Like, I don't know, doing something revolting with your face. See, like this.' Bett pulled her eyes down with one hand and grimaced, pushing her nose up with the other hand.

Anna looked at her blankly. 'I thought you were going to do something revolting with your face.'

'I am,' Bett said in a voice muffled by the contortions.

'You look the same to us, doesn't she, Carrie?'

'Just the same,' Carrie agreed happily.

'A little prettier than normal, if anything. Are you wearing makeup, Bett?'

Bett just poked out her tongue. 'Go on, Anna. You do something if you're so smart.'

'Okay, then.' She thought for a second. 'Right, I'll be a bat. Listen.' She started making a high-pitched noise, the noise getting louder and louder, unrelenting, ignoring Bett and Carrie's protests until Bett finally threw a book at her. Anna's pillow toppled, with Carrie's tumbling seconds afterwards.

Bett leapt up, holding her pillow above her head. 'I win. Champion of the Pillow Balancing. Out of my way, vermin, and let me take a victory leap.' She leapt from her bed onto Carrie's, badly misjudging the distance and landing square on Carrie's leg. Carrie set up a terrible wailing.

Anna hissed at her. 'Carrie, shush. You'll get Lola in here.'

Carrie didn't shush. 'I don't care. She's broken my leg, the big fat pig.'

'I have not broken it.'

'You have. It was like a ton of bricks fell on me.'

Stung, Bett turned on her sister. 'It was not. If I'd meant to do it, you would have felt it, believe me. Like this.' With that, she leapt onto Carrie's bed again, this time deliberately and twice as firmly landing on her sister's leg.

Carrie set off a squealing to rival any high-pitched bat noise of Anna's. The door flung open and the light switched on. Lola was standing there. 'For heaven's sake. What is going on here? Your parents could probably hear you from the bar. Carrie, would you shut up? You're behaving like a baby over there.'

'Bett stepped on me,' she said through the tears, her voice shuddering. 'She nearly broke my leg.'

Bett was now in bed, all innocent eyes. 'God, Carrie, stop exaggerating all the time.'

Lola wasn't interested in either side of the story. 'I don't care how it happened. Shut up and go to sleep, all of you. I shouldn't have to remind you you've got a concert tomorrow. You're supposed to be having an early night. Anna, you're the oldest. Try and get them to behave, would you?'

The light snapped off and the three lay still.

'I'll get you for that, Bett,' Carrie hissed, the sobbing miraculously over.

'I'll get you first for dobbing on me, you big baby. I'm going to ask Mum to put the cot back in the room for you. You're obviously too young to sleep in a bed yet.'

'Anna, make Bett stop picking on me.'

'Shut up, the pair of you. I need my beauty sleep.'

'Pig.'

'Baby.'

'Pig.'

'Baby.'

The taunts had gone back and forth in the dark bedroom until one or the other of them had finally fallen asleep.

Bett turned over in bed again. It was a strange thing. She wasn't actually sure whether the memory of those times together made her feel good or bad. In the past few weeks it had been getting harder to tell the difference.

CHAPTER FOURTEEN

SITTING ON a comfortable chair in front of her room the following morning, Lola closed her eyes in the sunshine, feeling like a tired old cat snoring on a windowsill. A tired satisfied old cat, at least. Broken wrist and banged head aside, things were going well. She'd managed to get the musical underway, send Geraldine and Jim off on holiday, and get the girls working together in the motel. There was the little matter of getting Matthew back on the scene, getting the reunion out of the way, but that day was drawing closer, Lola knew.

So now what did she do with herself? The best way to keep the mind alert was to keep it occupied, her doctor had said. She needed another project, something else to do. This morning she'd been reading her new copy of *Ireland's Treasures*, the magazine sent airmail to her each week, hoping that might spark some idea. It had arrived the previous day, along with a postcard from Geraldine and Jim in Alice Springs. The pair of them sounded like they were having the time of their lives.

She winced at a sudden wailing noise of a fire siren coming up the valley from the town. So much for the tranquillity of living in the country. If it wasn't the siren, it was the gas guns keeping the birds away from the vineyards, or the tractors or the tankers rumbling up the roads.

Perhaps this was a false alarm or perhaps some poor devil had gone and set his house on fire. She'd drop into the charity shop that morning, find out what she could. The son of one of her co-workers was one of the fire service volunteers. 'Do they actually respond to the noise of that siren?' Lola had asked once. 'What if they're in the middle of something, a good movie or nice sex, for example? Can they pretend they didn't hear anything?'

'Lola!' The woman had been shocked. 'Of course they can't pretend. It's calling them. They have to answer it.'

Such a good method, Lola thought again now, looking down the road seeing several cars speeding into town, either volunteers or sticky-beaks on their way to the fire station. She'd often wished she had something similar to sound when she had a good idea, or wanted to tell the girls something. Or indeed, wanted them home after too late a night out. Not a screechy wail, though – perhaps a blast of Cole Porter or the opening notes of Glenn Miller's 'In the Mood'.

A shout from Carrie broke into her thoughts. 'Bumper, come here! Come here, you brat.'

Oh dear, Lola remembered. She'd forgotten to tie Bumper up again yesterday. She and Ellen had been leading him around from one new patch of grass to another.

'Bumper, you stupid sheep, come here.'

This sounded entertaining. Lola slowly rose out of her seat and walked around the corner of the building just in time to see Carrie chasing after Bumper. The sheep was well and truly spooked, ramming blindly into the crates of beer bottles and rubbish bins in the back of the motel. Carrie called out as she caught sight of her. 'This is your fault, Lola.'

'No, it's not. I didn't invent sheep.'

'You know what I mean. You know how crazy he goes when he hears loud noises.'

'I didn't know there was going to be a fire.'

'Well, help me tie him up, will you? Before he does any more damage.'

'I'm far too old and frail to be chasing sheep.'

'Can I help, Auntie Carrie?' Ellen had heard the fuss from her room. 'Bumper likes me, doesn't he, Lola?'

'He certainly does, darling.'

Carrie winced at the sound of more crashing bottles. 'Sure, Ellie. Give it a try. God knows I'm sick of chasing the silly animal.'

Ellen moved closer to the bottles and loudly and clearly started calling out to the sheep. 'Bumper, come here to me. Here, Bumper.'

Carrie started laughing. Ellen was not just imitating Lola's calls but also her Irish accent.

Ellen was oblivious. 'Here, Bumper. Everything's all right. Come here to me now, my darling.'

Carrie wasn't sure whether it was Ellen's cooing or the fact that the fire siren had suddenly stopped, but Bumper calmed down enough for Ellen to lay her hand on his back and take hold of his collar. With his hooves making little clacking noises on the concrete, she led him over to Carrie. 'There you are,' she said, a smile lighting up her entire face.

'Ellen, you are a genius.' Carrie shook her head in amazement, before taking Ellen by one hand and holding the sheep firmly in the other.

The fun over, Lola returned to her seat in the sunshine and picked up the magazine again, stopping to read a fascinating article about the Lisdoonvarna Matchmaking Festival in County Clare.

An annual event, when bachelor farmers would come down from the hills and meet young ladies in the genteel surroundings of tea dances and elegant lunches. So civilised. One of the matchmakers spoke proudly of his track record – hundreds of marriages, nearly as many engagements. He didn't mention any separations or divorces. It sounded like good fun, Lola thought. Perhaps she could suggest to Geraldine and Jim that they start up something similar here in the Valley. There were already plenty of connections between the town of Clare and County Clare in Ireland. They already exported wine from Australia to Ireland. Perhaps Ireland could ship over a few dozen bachelors in return?

She put down the magazine as Richard Lawrence walked towards her, dressed in shorts and a T-shirt. Lola waved and beckoned him over. He was quite the fitness fan, it seemed. Back from the gym again. Almost as bad as Anna. No wonder he had been so snake-hipped at the party. It had been good to see him and Bett chatting away too, the couple of times she had looked over. They had a lot in common – journalism, London . . .

'Morning, Richard,' she said as he came closer.

'Good morning, Lola.'

'It does the heart good to see a fit young man like yourself out in the air.'

'Young man?' He grinned. 'Don't make me worry about your eyesight now, will you?'

'Oh, you're just a child in my eyes. Tell me now, will you pop in a little later? I've a bottle of gin that I need help opening. Those caps are very tight these days. Around four? Perfect.'

She waved him off as a blue station wagon came up the drive. Lola watched as Daniel Hilder climbed out with a load of newspapers. Bett had chosen her one-night stand well, she thought with a wicked smile. He certainly wasn't fashion catalogue handsome, but there was something so attractive about him. A pair of laughing eyes took a man a very long way, she'd always thought. She had so enjoyed their little chat the other day. If there was one thing she liked, it was a young man with a bit of wit about him. He'd shown such interest in the photos she'd taken out for him, as well. He'd also done a very efficient job of straightening the shower rose and re-hanging the painting. Too efficient, really, for her purposes. She had a feeling there was a bit more there to discover.

She'd recalled afterwards that she had seen his mother in the charity shop now and then in the early days. Making donations, not shopping, of course. The distinction was important for some people. She remembered Mrs Hilder as a well-to-do woman. Very well-spoken, always elegant, beautifully turned out. One of the matching shade of lipstick, nail polish, bag and shoe women. How they did it, Lola just did not know. She glanced down at that day's outfit, her culottes and tunic ensemble. About fifteen different colours fighting for prominence, none of them winning. What had one of the charity shop women said to her once? 'Lola, you always look so different.' 'I suppose you mean different as in terrible,' she had replied, to the woman's horror. Lola laughed at the memory.

Bett came into view, pushing the cleaning cart loaded with soaps, teabags and fresh linen. Lola watched as she took out the master key and let herself into one of the rooms to do her share of the cleaning. Dear girl, it was so good to have her home again. She had been so rocked by the business with Matthew. In Lola's opinion, it had been a narrow escape. Funnily enough, she had always felt Carrie and Matthew made a much better pair than Bett and Matthew. She had held her tongue on the matter for once, though. She'd held high hopes that Bett would meet someone in Melbourne, or Dublin, or London. Someone with a bit more spark than Matthew. But it hadn't happened. Bett was still single. Madness. What were the men of the world thinking letting a fine woman like her run free?

Moments later Daniel Hilder stepped lightly down the front steps and climbed back into his car. Lola could see him checking something in a folder beside him. In a few minutes he would drive right past her room, on to the next delivery.

She re-read the quote from the matchmaker. 'It's a simple process. We interview all the single men and then we interview all the single women, and then we decide who would be best suited to who. We don't rush into it, either – it's a matter of getting to know people, assessing their suitability before we bring them together.'

She started to smile. The Valley View Motel Matchmaking Festival might not have the same ring as Lisdoonvarna, but the principles were the same, surely? Find a single man who suits your single woman and bring them together. Her smile broadened. She'd already arranged to talk to Richard this afternoon. If she got Daniel now, that would be the two of them done in the same day. Very efficient. As for Bett, well, she didn't need to interview her, did she? She already knew her granddaughter inside out.

Rising as swiftly as her old bones would allow, she moved inside, picked up the cane she used occasionally for walking and knocked the painting off the wall, wincing as it crashed to the floor. Just as well their budget hadn't stretched to glass frames. As the sound of a car started up, she returned to the doorway, waving madly with her good arm.

Daniel slowed the car to a stop beside her, wound down the window and smiled. 'Lola, hello. You're looking very well again.'

'Pulling the devil by the tail, as we say at home. Daniel, you're heaven sent without a doubt. That blasted painting has fallen down again. Could you spare a moment, do you think?'

She smiled to herself as he turned off the engine. This might be even more fun than writing the musical.

The next day, Bett was driving back to the *Valley Times* office with Daniel. They'd spent the afternoon following one of the Valley's young winemakers around his small winery, as he showed them the process from grape to bottle. At the end of the session, Daniel had handed over the digital camera and watched as she flicked through his shots. They were good, a bit quirky, with plenty of action and interest in them. Rebecca would be very pleased.

Bett was pleased with herself, too. So far today she'd managed to stay quite composed in his company. She'd tasted a glass of the new shiraz without spilling it everywhere. Even better, she'd had several conversations with him without turning bright red. Perhaps deep down she actually was a mature grown-up.

The car radio was playing the new single from the country's latest manufactured pop band. He turned it up. 'Great, one of my favourites.'

'You're kidding.'

He had a glint in his eye. 'To tell you the truth, I can't decide between this lot and the all-girl band formed after that supermarket reality show.' He pressed the button to change stations. A screaming punk song filled the car. Bett winced.

Daniel noticed and turned it down. 'I take it you weren't ever a punk?'

She shook her head. 'Why? Were you?'

'For a whole six months. I even changed my name.'

'You didn't.'

'It was written in studs on the back of my best denim jacket. Danger Hilder. I was extremely scary for a twelve-year-old.' He grinned. 'So you were never spiky-haired? Covered in safety pins?'

'No. Unfortunately I reached my teenage years in time for fluorescent socks and sweat bands.'

'Ah yes. I think I may have seen a photo from that time.'

Had he been at Lola's birthday party? No, she was sure he hadn't been. Colour raced up her neck into her face. There was only one other way he could have seen them. 'Has Lola shown you the Alphabet Sisters photos?'

He nodded solemnly. 'Quite a lot of them, actually. She's very proud of you, isn't she?'

'That's it. I'm going to break into her room and burn them.'

'You'll never find them. She had them hidden in books and under boxes all over her room. "I have to hide them or the girls would have them spirited away in seconds."'

She had to laugh at his good impression of Lola. His mobile rang before she could say anything more. He pulled over to take the call and she took the opportunity to have a good look at him. He was probably thirty-five or thirty-six by now, she guessed. She thought she remembered him celebrating his thirtieth birthday just after she'd first joined the *Valley Times*. They had only worked together on a few jobs, but she'd occasionally spoken to him in the pubs, or in restaurants around the Valley. He'd had a girlfriend at the time, hadn't he? One of the high-school teachers, if memory served her right. And she had been going out with Matthew. Engaged to Matthew, even.

Back then, she'd always found him easy to work with. It had been the same today. Bett had interviewed the winemaker while Daniel strolled the property taking photographs, like a normal journalist and photographer team. The only difference being they'd had a night of wild sex three years ago and not mentioned it since. She decided she had to bring it up today. Get it out of the way. Into the open, as Lola would advise.

He finished the call, from one of the other reporters on the paper setting up a photo shoot for the next day. 'Sorry about that,' he said.

'No problem.' She decided to launch straight into it. 'Daniel, before you start the car, I think there's something we need –' She was interrupted by the ringing of his mobile again.

He glanced at the display screen. 'Sorry, Bett. I'll need to get this.'

It was obviously a personal call. He got out of the car and walked a short distance away. Her window was already wound down and snippets floated in. He was soothing someone by the sound of things. Listening a lot and then reassuring the caller. She wasn't close enough to hear any more. 'I'll see you tonight. Okay. Bye.'

He got back into the car. 'Sorry, Bett. You were about to say something?'

She noticed his mood had changed, become more serious. She lost her nerve. 'It doesn't matter.'

'Are you sure?'

'Sure.'

He started the car and they had driven for a little while before he spoke. 'That thing you were about to say. Was it about that night in Melbourne, by any chance?'

'Yes. Yes, it was.' Was that squeak really her voice?

'I wondered which of us would bring it up first.' He was still serious. 'Bett, it's all right. I'm a grown man. I got over it.'

'You got over it?' Had it been that bad? Something that had to be got over?

'Of course,' he said. 'It wasn't the first time and I'm sure it won't be the last time.'

That he had a one-night stand? 'Really?'

'Yes, really. Honestly, don't give it a moment's thought.'

She was feeling worse, not better. 'I thought I had to mention it, at least. You know, now that we were working together. In case you were thinking . . .' she trailed off. In case you were thinking that I was an old slapper who would jump into bed with you at any opportunity. She couldn't say it.

They were coming into the town now. 'Bett, it's okay. I got the message in Melbourne. So please don't feel awkward working with me.'

What message? She hadn't left him a message. She'd been so embarrassed she'd crept out without even waking him.

His phone rang again and he answered it without pulling over. 'Hi, Rebecca. About five minutes away. No worries. I'll drop Bett at the office and head straight out there.' He turned to her. 'Sorry, Bett. Do you mind? That fire out at the old quarry has flared up again. Rebecca wants me to go straight there.'

'Of course.' They were silent as they drove up the main street of Clare. He deftly pulled in behind one of the tall trees sending out splashes of shade onto the hot bitumen.

'See you later, then.'

'Yes, see you.' She got out of the car so quickly she nearly tripped.

The following night the cast was once again gathered in the function room. Bett's hands were folded in her lap. She'd given up playing any of the songs. Carrie was in the middle of the group, looking mutinous. Anna was in front, extremely unhappy.

'General MacArthur, have you actually looked at the script since our last rehearsal?'

'I intended to, Anna, I really did. But I had trouble with the dam at the end of the bottom paddock, and I ran out of time.'

'And what about you, Mrs MacArthur?'

'I looked at it. But the school fair was this week, and I had to choose between making three dozen fairy cakes or learning my lines.'

Anna looked from one cast member to the next.

'The dog ate my script.'

'The cat weed on my script.'

'I got called away to fight a fire at the old quarry.'

Anna sighed, put her hands on her hips, exasperated. 'I bet a million dollars Andrew Lloyd Webber never hears excuses like this.' Everyone laughed. That was the whole problem, she realised. No one was taking it seriously. What would Lola do if she was here? Whatever was necessary, she guessed. She'd have to do the same.

She stood up, composed herself, mentally searched through her voice repertoire until she found the most cajoling one and then coughed politely to get everyone's attention. Speaking persuasively, she started talking about General MacArthur, about what he had meant to people during the war. She reminded them all about Lola's dream, about the need for a new ambulance, about the highs and lows of acting, about pride, belief in your work, determination.

Good heavens, Bett thought. She felt a verse of 'Climb Every Mountain' coming on.

Carrie wasn't listening. She'd learnt her lines days ago. She'd had nothing else to do in the lonely house once she got home from work. She and Matthew had tried to have another conversation on the phone that afternoon. It had ended in disaster again. Another row. More shifting blame. It was getting to the stage where they nearly hung up before they said hello to each other.

She shot a glance at Bett. They'd hardly spoken a word to each other since that night in the office. It was all very well for Bett to say she wanted to see Matthew. What was she supposed to do? Produce him out of a hat? Say, 'Here, Bett, have him back?' She longed to ask Lola's advice, but that would mean telling her the whole story of their separation. She couldn't bear the shame of it. If only there was some way of making things all right between her and Matthew again. She turned away as Bett looked up and caught her eye. She stared rigidly at the script, pretending to be concentrating on Anna's speech.

'So, please, all of you,' Anna said passionately, her voice husky by this stage. 'Please have your lines and the words of your songs learnt before our next rehearsal. We've only got a few weeks to put this together, remember. And I want to say again how much it would mean to my elderly grandmother to see her dream brought to the stage.' She lowered her voice. 'You all know about the accident, and it does worry me how frail she has become, that she is losing her already tenuous grip on life. I think it would give her a real boost and I hope you'll all give it your best shot.'

She gazed around. Was that woman on the left crying? Oh dear, perhaps she'd gone a little too far. 'So, Bett, let's try "Chattanooga Choo Choo", from the top.'

In her room at that moment, Lola took a long sip of her gin and tonic and pointed the remote control at the CD player. She did love singing along with those old show tunes. There was nothing like them to buoy the spirit. But now it was break over and time to get back to work.

Settling herself more comfortably in the armchair, she put on her glasses and studied the two rather wobbly handwritten lists on the page in front of her. She wished she'd thought of doing this years ago. Who'd have thought there could be such entertainment in the little matter of getting two people together?

She had followed the matchmaker's guidelines to the letter. First, draw up a shortlist of available suitors. Hers was short, just the two names. Then draw up a list of their attributes. She'd done that too, based on her interviews, formal and informal, over the past little while. They were similar in some ways. Both seemed very kind, with lovely senses of humour and the necessary glints in their eyes. They both had a bit of life experience behind them, too – always a good thing. They'd both lived in the city, but had chosen to be in the country for the time being – also a good thing.

Now all she had to do was make her final choice. It was hard enough, with both of them having so much going for them. She read the lists again. It was close, certainly, but she was veering towards the one on the left. Yes, she decided firmly. He was the one.

All her project needed now was a name. It finally came to her and she wrote it carefully on the folder.

Operation Richard and Bett.

CHAPTER FIFTEEN

AT HOME in the farmhouse two nights later, Carrie poured a glass of wine and moved from the living room to the bedroom, then back into the kitchen, trying to decide where to do it. It didn't help that there were traces of Matthew everywhere – a pair of boots in the hallway, his Driza-Bone jacket on the back of the door. And memories in each of the rooms too. The painting they had bought in Adelaide not long after they were married. The lamp she had admired in an antique store up north one weekend they'd been away, which Matthew had gone to such trouble to get for her as a surprise, driving three hours there and back. The hall cupboard the two of them had spent weeks sanding back, only to find the wood underneath in such bad condition they'd had to paint it all over again.

She finally settled on the kitchen. She pulled a chair up to the wooden table, reached into her bag and took out the magazine. She'd seen it in the newsagents in town that morning, its glaring coverline talking directly to her – *How To Save Your Marriage*. She'd bought a whole selection of other items to pad all around it – pens and writing pads, even a *Your Garden* magazine – so the woman behind the counter, whose wedding she had helped organise, wouldn't guess.

'You looking for a new man, Carrie?'

She had nearly leapt out of her skin. 'No, Matthew's fine. He's just away for work for a while.'

'Don't want him to catch you looking at that, then.'

'No.' She was flaming red by that stage. It was only when she'd got into the car she realised what the woman was talking about. *Fifty Most Eligible Bachelors. Tasty touch-me-now photos inside!*

She skimmed past the perfume ads, the fashion pages and the eligible bachelors until she reached the *How to Save Your Marriage* article. Please let it be a matter of mixing up a quick potion of pomegranate seeds and vinegar, or chanting over an old photo of the two of them, she thought. She realised a little guiltily that most of their photos were in a bag in the shed where she had thrown them after the last row. Still, at least she hadn't ripped them up. She corrected herself. At least she hadn't ripped all of them up.

She skim-read the introduction to the article. *Do you feel the gloss has gone out of your relationship?* Not just the gloss. The relationship had gone out of the relationship. *Don't know where it went wrong?* She shifted uncomfortably. Next question. *Have things really changed for the worse?* That was easy.

Then try this exercise to get in touch with your feelings. Sit quietly, and recall the early days of your relationship. Think about everything that first attracted you to him, and him to you. Remember your first touch, your first kiss, the first time you made love. Let the memories wash over you. Let go of any anger you may feel now. Let go of any hurts or misunderstandings. Take your mind back to your early days, remembering the wonderful first moments of attraction.

Carrie moved the chair further back from the table, shut her eyes and concentrated. She opened an eye, and read the last line again.

Take your mind back to your early days, remembering the wonderful first moments of attraction. That she could do, at least. It had been the first night she met him, when she got home from her overseas trip. At first, in all the fuss of arriving, her luggage everywhere, the talk and the chat with her parents and Lola, he'd just been Bett's fiancé – medium height, sandy brown curls. Solid looking. But later, in the pub where Bett had insisted on taking her, something had happened between them.

Jetlagged, exhilarated to be home, she remembered being in teasing form. 'Normally, Matt – I can call you Matt, can't I? I mean, we're practically brother and sister. Normally, Matt, I'd have got to know you slowly, vetted you to make sure you were good for my sister, but I'll just have to do a crash course now. You're studying to be a vet, I believe. That's good, a steady job. Now, let me see. What sort of a physical specimen are you? Should I check him out, Bett?'

'Go right ahead,' Bett had said, laughing at her.

She patted him down, commenting all the while. 'Yes, fine shoulders, a lovely broad chest, oh yes, good, a flat stomach too.' Bett was enjoying it, Carrie thought. 'And he's got terrific legs, Bett, hasn't he?' She touched them as well, felt firm muscle under the dark denim. Did her hands brush against his upper thigh deliberately? 'Yes, he's gorgeous, Bett. He'll do very well.'

All laughter and joking, standing there arms around one another, Bett in front of them. But as she sat down, just for a moment there was an exchange of glances between her and Matthew. The laughter had gone out of his eyes and there was a flash of desire. She saw it. She felt the same thing in herself. A tiny spark, the quickest of flickers between them. And then some other friends came up and the night changed, became casual.

Except she remembered it the next day. It was probably jetlag, she told herself. Or the pleasure of touching a man again. She'd gone travelling with a boyfriend through Asia but they had broken up in Vietnam, after fighting in Laos, making up in Cambodia and spending three months rowing as they travelled through Thailand. In Bali she'd had a brief affair with a practised Portuguese man, who had certainly taught her a few bedroom tricks as well as some filthy Portuguese words, but that had been months ago.

In the first few weeks the tension between her and Matthew masqueraded as simple teasing between a brother-in-law- and sister-in-law-to-be, encouraged by the whole family. But it was more serious than that, even from the start. There had been genuine interest in one another, wanting to talk to each other. If Matthew came to collect Bett to go somewhere, he always made a point of seeking Carrie out, just for a few moments of conversation. If she heard his voice, she too would find herself going to him, wandering in almost casually, teasing, joking, on the surface.

Once or twice there was casual physical touch – when Matthew was holding a door open for her, or passing something to her at a family dinner. Just the swiftest whisper of skin against skin. With another person she might not have noticed. With Matthew it was as if all her senses had sprung to attention. Nothing was said, but the contact became something they would engineer. At a family picnic, when Anna, Glenn and Ellen were home one weekend, they all piled into one car. Bett was driving. In the back, Carrie needed to sit on Matthew's knee, Anna, Glenn and Ellen squeezed in beside them, Lola in the passenger seat in front. Had any of them noticed the effect the physical contact had on her and on Matthew? The touch was like exquisite pain to Carrie, feeling his thighs beneath her, the brush of his hand against her bare arm. He slowly moved his left arm so it was almost around her waist. Just as slowly, she lowered her hand so it was on top of his arm. She felt the sunshine on it, her breathing change. Everyone's attention was on Ellen, three years old at the time, and delirious with too much soft drink and attention, squealing each time they turned a corner, their bodies moving from side to side with the momentum. Carrie felt a slow burning between her and Matthew with each motion. When they finally arrived back at the motel, she climbed out quickly. There was just a quick glance between them, loaded with meaning.

He felt the same way, she learned afterwards. It got to the stage that she knew he was in the motel, somewhere nearby, a sort of tingling, humming between them. But he's Bett's fiancé, she told herself.

Remember your first kiss . . .

It happened the day he drove her to the agricultural college with him. She'd been trying to decide whether to do a course, and it was Bett who suggested she make the trip with Matthew. She was aware of dressing more carefully, choosing the pale-blue dress that looked good against her brown skin and blonde hair, the strands even lighter after the long hot summer. Bett waved them off.

They drove for an hour perhaps, not even halfway there, the teasing conversation rippling between them. She felt intensely conscious of her own body, the hem of her dress lifting a little as she moved her legs, crossed them once or twice, knowing Matthew was noticing. She had a bug to thank for the first contact. Feeling hot, she had wound the window down. An insect had blown in, right at her face.

'Oww,' she said. 'Something flew into my eye.'

He pulled over right away, their car the only one on the long straight road. He unbuckled his seatbelt, leaned across. 'Let me see.'

His hand was on her face, his face closer than it had ever been.

There was a moment when all the tension between them seemed to tighten and contract until they were no longer apart but lips on lips, bodies pressed as close as possible.

She pulled back first, reluctantly, eyes wide. 'We can't.'

Matthew didn't answer her, just looked at her in a way she had never been looked at before. Her stomach turned somersaults, and she didn't say anything as he leaned towards her again, the kiss softer, more exploratory, but deeper and sexier than the first one.

A car went past, the driver honking the horn at them. It broke the spell. He pulled away. Looked ahead.

Carrie looked ahead too. 'I'm sorry.'

He made a noise somewhere between a laugh and a sigh. 'I am too.'

They kept looking forward.

'We should keep driving.'

They did, silently for ten minutes, and then his hand came off the steering wheel and crossed the seat, meeting hers. His voice was soft. 'Carrie, I have never felt about anyone the way I feel about you.'

She understood what he meant.

'I don't feel about Bett the way I feel about you.'

'It's wrong. You're Bett's fiancé.' It was hard to say, when the touch of his hand was sending what felt like sparkling explosions into her bloodstream. She placed his hand on her thigh, and heard the little intake of breath. She thought of Bett again, and then consciously, forcibly, blanked her out. This wasn't about Matthew and Bett any more. It was about the two of them and what was happening here.

'You feel it too, don't you?'

She nodded.

'We need to talk about this.'

Ahead there was a sign pointing to a camping ground just off the main road. He turned in. The park was sheltered, too early in the morning, even on a hot day, for anyone to be there. He got out. She got out after him. They stood against the railing, looking down into the dry creek bed, not speaking, the only sounds the crackle of wind through the peeling bark on the gum trees, the warbling of magpies. The sun was hot on her skin.

She touched his arm and he flinched as though it had burnt him. But the movement had set the tension buzzing between them again. She felt her own body respond, felt her breasts strain against her clothes, wanting to touch him again. This had to be right, this had to be real, Bett or no Bett.

He moved first, running a hand gently from the shoulder strap of her dress down her arm. She breathed in deeply. Closed her eyes. He moved his hand, repeating the touch. She felt every nerve-ending in her skin respond. She didn't move, just breathed, as he traced the neckline, his hand brushing against her breasts.

And then she did the same thing to him, ran her hand down the length of his arm, then his other arm, touching the skin, feeling the little hairs. Then her fingers moved from the neckline of his T-shirt, down over his chest, his stomach, and lower, enough to hear a sharp intake of breath.

It became a slow, intense trade of pleasure, taking it in turns, not speaking. He moved towards her, touching her dress, tracing her breasts through the material. It was all she could do not to push herself against him.

Staring into his eyes, she was intensely aware of all the sensations around her, the heat of the sun, the slightest of breezes, the hum of insects. She touched his body again, running her hand over his stomach, over the denim of his jeans, watching the response in his eyes, a darkening of his pupils as she cupped him, stroked him gently.

'We can't. We have to stop this,' she whispered, as he held her hand against his jeans.

'I know,' he said, shutting his eyes in pleasure as she took one of his fingers into her mouth and gently sucked it.

The sound of a car behind them called a halt. Carrie knew she had been seconds from taking off her dress, from undressing Matthew, from making love there, in the open. It was a family, a man and woman with three small children, parking just metres from them, and immediately unloading chairs and barbecue equipment.

'Lovely day for it,' the man called out.

'Sure is,' Matthew answered.

They returned to the car and sat for a few moments, before Matthew started the engine and headed back onto the main road. She wasn't surprised when he pulled into a side road a few kilometres down and turned to her again. Some reason had come into her mind by then – the shock of nearly being caught, the shock of realising she had been about to have sex with Bett's fiancé. And the shock that she still wanted to.

Another hot, deep kiss until she pulled away first. 'What about Bett?' she whispered again, barely able to speak.

'I don't know what to do about Bett,' he answered.

For four weeks they resisted it, trying not to spend time with each other. But it was like a fever, an addiction. The tension between them increased. There were phone calls, three, sometimes four, a day. He wrote her letters. All the while, sexual tension hummed between them.

Lola noticed something, Carrie knew. And perhaps Bett

suspected something. She tried not to spend too much time with her sister, needing to keep the distance. She had one awkward conversation with Matthew about her.

'Are you still sleeping with her?'

Matthew looked uncomfortable. 'I can't. I want it to be you. It wouldn't be fair.'

It made her feel better, for herself, even while she felt sorry for Bett. But it just seemed out of her control, out of their control, as though it was fated, and destined and all the magical things.

Matthew felt the same way, he told her. 'It's different with you, different than it has ever been. With Bett, it seemed easy, like we drifted into it. But with you . . .'

Carrie was torn between wanting to know about his relationship with Bett, and feeling it was best she knew nothing about it. 'We can't talk about her. We have to put her out of our minds when we're together, until we work out whether this is real or not.'

He rang her the night before they were due to go to the agricultural college again. 'I've made a decision, Carrie. I'm going to break it off with Bett. I can't live like this, feeling one thing with you, talking about the wedding with her, feeling like I'm lying.'

'Are you sure?'

'If you are.'

'You know what it will mean.'

'I'm still sure.'

Remember the first time you made love . . .

That conversation had been the turning point. The next morning he collected her from the motel as usual. Bett had left for the newspaper office early. Carrie was glad of it.

They barely spoke as he drove, but she found herself unable to take her eyes off his hands on the steering wheel, feeling the lightness of her own dress against her thighs. He turned into the forest clearing they had first visited five weeks earlier. There was no one else there. The air was as hot and still, the sky as cloudless. They climbed out of the car. He took her by the hand and they started the slow, erotic dance again, his hand tracing her body, her hand tracing his, no words being spoken until they were both nearly faint with desire. 'Are you sure?' he whispered.

She nodded.

From that moment they wouldn't have cared if there had been rows of cars around them. He slowly undid the buttons of her dress, exposing her breasts in the bra she had chosen so carefully that morning. She unbuttoned his shirt, touching the brown skin, the muscles on his arm, then unbuttoned his jeans, moving her hand until she was touching him at last.

He kissed her again. The kiss went on and on, his hands holding her body tight against his. They moved up against a table and had fast, passionate sex, both of them still partly clothed, the sweat covering their skin, their hard, fast breaths and moans the only noise around.

Carrie knew she shouldn't have done it. She knew it the moment they had finished, the moment the tension passed and the two of them were holding each other close, his head against hers. But then he held her even tighter, whispered, 'Thank you,' and she felt that it had been the right thing. And that they would be able to face Bett together. Which was exactly what they did that night. Matthew called her, arranged to meet in the motel. They had both broken the news to her . . .

Remember your wedding day.

Quiet, without fuss, everyone trying to ignore the fact Anna and Bett weren't there.

Think back to the early days of married life.

The first two years they lived in a rented unit in one of the smaller towns in the Valley. Carrie worked in the motel, Matthew finished his study and started working in the vet practice in the town. On weekends they met friends, looked at houses, occasionally went away when her days off allowed them, or he wasn't on call.

It was in the past twelve months it had started changing. She started noticing things about Matthew that either hadn't been there before or had just become apparent. He wasn't exactly mean with money, but he seemed interested in every little thing she spent. 'It would make more sense if we cut down on things like that for the first few years when we're saving for a house,' he said one night, when she arrived home with three bunches of expensive flowers.

'Matt, come on,' she laughed. 'You're running this marriage like it's some kind of business.'

'It is, when we're talking about buying a house. See, Carrie, look at these figures.' She gave them a glance, trying not to stifle a yawn too obviously.

He was the same about the flowering plants she bought for the garden. She'd come home with a car boot full and spent an afternoon planting them, delighted with the effect. He came home late, left early the next morning. It was the weekend before he was able to see them. She blindfolded him and took him outside.

He wasn't impressed at all. 'How much did they cost?'

She gestured vaguely. 'A fair bit, but isn't it worth it? See how brilliant they look.'

'They're all flowering though,' Matthew frowned. 'They won't last. You'd have been better off buying seedlings or seeds. Otherwise it's a waste of money.'

She stood there, debating whether to burst into tears or make a run inside. In the end, she did a combination, stalking to her car and driving off in a temper of showering gravel, making sure he could see her crying face. She drove straight to the motel, looking for sympathy.

Her mother stopped preparing the salad, patted her on the hand, then went back to her lettuces. 'It's part of married life, Carrie. We all have rows.'

Her father asked how much the flowers cost and then laughed when she refused to tell him. 'Too much, then, by the sounds.'

Lola listened to the whole story, then said, 'I see. Now, go home and say sorry.'

'Why should I say sorry? It's his fault I'm upset. He should have been pleased I did the garden.'

'Perhaps he would have been if he'd had a say.'

'He's not my keeper. I won't apologise.'

There was a three-day stand-off, until the night he came to the motel, walked into the kitchen, took her by the hand and practically dragged her out to the car.

Outside, he said just one thing. 'I miss you.'

It was all she needed to hear. 'I miss you too.'

'Will you come home again?'

She nodded. He was driving home when he took a turn off to a park they both knew. Without words, they re-enacted their first time together. In the hot night of a summer, they stood in the open air and made love.

The passion lasted between them for nearly two years. Longer than most, from what Carrie could gather from talking to her friends. One girlfriend said that once their three kids had come along she and her husband had both lost interest. 'Honestly, if he wants to go off and have a mistress, it's fine with me. Between the kids and work, I haven't got time for sex.' Another friend had warned her even before they were married. 'The spice will go out of it now, you know. Now you can actually do it whenever you want. So don't be surprised when a TV program seems more interesting than his crotch.'

Carrie pretended to be shocked. The same friend, a little later that evening and a lot drunker, had gone further. 'Can I ask you a blunt question?' How much blunter could she get? Carrie wondered. 'Has Matthew ever compared you and Bett? You know, said anything about what you were both like in bed? Don't look so outraged, Carrie. He must have thought it. Haven't you ever been curious?'

Of course she had been. But of course she had never asked. She'd told her friend to mind her own business and tried not to think of it again herself. And there had been plenty of consolation in their lovemaking – surely it hadn't been like this for Matthew and Bett, or he would never have left her.

Can you pinpoint when things started going wrong?

Easily. When Lola started obsessing about having Anna and Bett home again. When Carrie started feeling guilty about the marriage. Started wondering whether perhaps it hadn't been a love match written in the stars. Started noticing more things wrong with Matthew. Started picking on him, deliberately wanting him to fight with her, to prove that he loved her. Except it had backfired, hadn't it? She'd picked on him so much he'd been glad to leave.

Are you sure things are as bad as you think?

She realised she was crying, and roughly wiped away a tear. They were, but she wished they weren't. She missed him, really missed him. Their talks at the end of the day. The funny impressions he used to do, especially the ones of Frank Spencer and Basil Fawlty. She loved hearing his plans for the house, going furniture-hunting with him. She loved being in bed with him . . .

Sometimes it can be as simple as sitting down and talking about things. Don't be afraid to be the first person to say sorry.

Sorry? To who, though? Matthew? Bett? Anna? Lola? What was she supposed to do – hire a stadium and make a PA announcement? Get it over in one fell swoop? Stupid magazine. Didn't they realise things were never that simple? She was about to hurl it across the room when the phone rang and her heart leapt. Matthew? She snatched it up. 'Hello?'

'Hello, this is the *Sports Weekly* subscription service calling from Sydney. Is your husband at home please?'

She burst into tears. 'No, he's bloody well not.'

CHAPTER SIXTEEN

IN ANNA'S room the following night, Lola and Ellen sat side by side on the single bed, both wearing dressing-gowns. They had towels wrapped as turbans on their heads and their feet were soaking in basins filled with steaming, fragrant water.

'So, Madame Lola, you'd like which treatment today?' Anna said in an excellent French accent.

'The full works, thank you. I'd like to look twenty years younger by eight p.m.'

'No problem at all, madam, even if it will involve a little plastic surgery. I have a very sharp knife and I enjoy using it. And you, little madam, what would you like done? The full treatment?'

Ellen nodded. 'I would like to look twenty years older, please.'

Lola hooted with laughter. 'We'll meet in the middle yet.'

Anna gently tucked in the turbans around both their faces, giving Ellen a little stroke on the nose for good luck. 'What I shall be doing today is applying my finest products in the most gentle way, giving you both the full pampering treatment. So sit back, relax, and let Anna of the Magic Fingers do her best work.'

She had applied the first of the creams to their faces when there was a knock at the door. Bett poked her head in. 'Anna, message from – Good God, what is this? A cult meeting?'

Lola and Ellen looked out at her through faces covered in thick white cream, their eyes panda-like. 'We're seeking eternal youth and beauty, as supplied by Madame Anna of the Magic Fingers,' Lola said. 'Would you like to join us?'

'I'd need a full construction team, not Anna of the Magic Fingers.' She sat on Anna's bed so she had a full view of the proceedings. 'A message from Len the butcher for you, Anna, to say that the set designs are nearly finished and he'll have the last one done by this weekend.'

'All those years of cutting up chops have finally come into their own,' Lola said.

'Enough talking, thank you, Madame Lola,' Anna said. 'You are supposed to be relaxing.'

'How can I relax when my musical is at such a crucial stage? Tell me again, I know Carrie is Juliet, but who is playing Romeo? And the man playing General MacArthur – are you sure he has the right gravitas?'

'What's gravitas?' Ellen asked, her voice muffled as Anna started wiping away her first layer of cream.

'It's another word for seriousness,' Bett said, as she picked up a magazine from the bedside table.

'Ladies, please,' Anna stepped back. 'I won't be held responsible for the consequences if my attention is diverted.' She pretended to remove Ellen's nose. 'Please, a little quiet.'

'A little gravitas,' Ellen said.

'Exactly. Oh, Anna, I can feel the years slipping away,' Lola purred like a cat as Anna gently stroked the cleansing cream away with soft cotton wool and sure fingers.

There was quiet for a little while and then Ellen spoke up. 'Mum, is it true that Lola was raised by the fairies in Ireland?'

'Of course I was, Ellen,' Lola murmured.

'Lola, tell Ellen the truth.'

Lola crossed her feet in the water bath and gazed across at Ellen, all shiny-faced. 'Once upon a time . . .' Then she stopped. 'I can't tell a story and have a facial at the same time. Bett, can you tell it for me? That way I can hear it too.'

'Of course.' Bett put down the magazine and made herself comfortable on the bed, sitting cross-legged. 'Your great-grandmother was born in Ireland, Ellie, on the other side of the world. Over there they have counties, and she was born in a county called Galway. Her father was a businessman, and her mother was a very elegant lady and they lived in a beautiful big old two-storey house covered in ivy, with a long drive leading up to it, surrounded by fields and streams and black-faced sheep.'

'Did you have a pet sheep there when you were a little girl, Lola?'

'Hundreds of them, Ellie.'

Bett continued. 'Lola went to boarding school, where they taught her to be a fine lady, and how to ride horses and arrange flowers and be gracious and good and kind. And then in the school holidays she would come home and have parties and they would dance and listen to music. At one of these parties she was introduced to a handsome young man called Edward, who was the son of a friend of her father's. Before six months had passed, Lola and Edward were engaged to be married. How am I going so far, Lola?'

Lola's eyes were shut. 'Perfect, darling. Keep going.'

'Edward's father had business interests in Australia, and to Lola's great excitement, he suggested that Lola and Edward spend a year in Australia. Within four months of their wedding the two of them were living in Melbourne.'

'Did you fly in an aeroplane, Lola?'

'Oh no, Ellie. In those days we travelled by ship. It took four weeks to get here, imagine that.'

'Edward's job was to keep an eye on the wool and the wheat and other crops that were being produced on his father's farms, and while he did that, Lola stayed in Melbourne, making the house beautiful.'

Anna stopped applying the second cream, waiting for Bett to tell the next bit of the story.

'Around this time World War II broke out and Edward, your great-grandfather, volunteered to join the Australian Army. He trained to be a soldier, only getting to see Lola once every few months, before he was sent away with the rest of the troops. And then something very sad happened. Edward was killed on the very first day of fighting.'

'He was killed?'

Lola had told the lie so many times the words came easily. 'That's right, Ellie. The soldiers told me afterwards he had been very brave. That I should be proud of him.' Far better than the truth – that her husband had not been a brave soldier but a weak, bullying drunk.

Bett took over again. 'And two days after Lola got word of that, Ellie, she discovered that she was having a baby. And that was James, your grandfather.' She had always found it so heartbreaking that Edward had died without knowing he was going to be a father.

Beside her, Anna was quiet. She always imagined Lola, so young, away from her family and her own country, discovering she was not just a widow, but about to become a mother too.

'Why didn't you go back to Ireland, Lola?' Ellen asked.

'I wasn't well enough to travel and it was wartime. There were no ships available for passengers like me. And by the time the war was over I had started up the guesthouse, and Jim was nearly ready for school. I decided I liked Australia. I loved the sunlight and the birds and the plants. So we decided to stay.'

'Wasn't that brave of her, Ellie?' Bett said. 'All the way across the other side of the world, with a little son to look after?'

'If you had gone back to Ireland, would I be an Irish girl now?'

'I don't know, Ellie. Because if I had gone back to Ireland, your grandfather might not have met your grandmother, and they might not have had three daughters, and you might have been born into another family altogether.'

Ellen seemed to take all that in. 'And have you ever been back to Ireland?'

'No, I haven't. My own family are gone now and it's too far away for a creaking old woman like myself.'

'But I visited Lola's house when I was in Ireland, Ellie,' Bett said.

Anna looked over. She hadn't known that.

'And were there still sheep and ponies and parties?' Ellen asked.

'None that I saw, but there might have been some behind the walls.'

'What did it look like?' Anna asked.

Bett remembered the day she had gone across to Galway on a day trip from Dublin. She had rung Lola the night before to get directions, surprising her. 'Would there be family left that I could speak to?'

'Oh no, Bett. The family would be long gone,' Lola had said.

It had taken Bett a whole morning to find the house, following Lola's directions. It had been different to what Bett had imagined, much smaller, the drive not as curvy as she remembered Lola telling them. The front entrance has been spoiled by a small clump of pine trees, she thought. She had taken a roll of photos and sent them back to Lola. She'd been a little disappointed with her reaction, she remembered. Lola had seemed grateful, but not all that interested. As she described it to Anna and Ellen now, the thought that had been niggling at the back of her mind since the slide show at Lola's party came back. It was about the trees.

'Lola, that slide you showed at the party, that was of your house, wasn't it?'

'It was.'

'And what tree was out the front?'

'A huge oak tree.'

Bett clapped her hand to her forehead. 'I can't believe it. How stupid was I? You know how I got so lost that day I went looking for your house, trying to follow your directions? That weekend I went to Galway to see if I could find anyone who remembered you and Edward? I was sure I'd followed your directions perfectly, but the house I went to had pine trees out the front, rows of them, not an oak tree. No wonder I couldn't find anyone who knew you. I was at the wrong house the whole time, wasn't I?'

'Yes, Bett, you were,' Lola said honestly.

'Oh, Bett, you silly sausage,' Ellen said.

The three of them burst out laughing. Bett turned to Lola. 'Why didn't you tell me when I sent you those photos, Lola?'

'I didn't want to embarrass you, Bett.'

She clapped her hand to her forehead again. 'Idiot. My one chance to uncover the mystery that is Lola Quinlan and what do I do? Go in the wrong direction completely. Sorry, Lola.' No wonder she hadn't been that interested, trying not to hurt Bett's feelings for turning up at the wrong house.

'It doesn't matter at all, Bett.' Time to change the subject, Lola thought. 'So that brings you up to date, Ellie. Time now to concentrate on the beauty treatments.' She leaned back and shut her eyes, glad of the silence. She had always hated lying, even though sometimes it had to be done. She especially hated lying to Bett.

CHAPTER SEVENTEEN

IT WAS Bett's turn to walk Ellen to school the next day. She waited in front of the motel as Ellen ran over to say goodbye to Bumper the sheep. She'd already taken ten minutes to say goodbye to Lola and Carrie. It was probably as well Anna had left early that morning for her voice-over work in Sydney, or they would have been delayed another twenty minutes while she said goodbye to her.

'Ready?' she called as the little girl ran over, her school bag bumping on her back, one sock already down at her shoes. She had been going to the new school for nearly two weeks, and the good-bye routine each morning seemed to take longer every day.

Ellen nodded.

'Sure? You don't want to say goodbye to that magpie over there?'

'Which magpie?'

'Forget it,' Bett said laughing, as she reached and took her hand. It was a beautiful summer morning, the front gardens in the main road lush with growth, the air crisp, the sky already a deep blue. As they walked, Bett started singing 'Oh What a Beautiful Morning'. 'There you are, Ellen. A little taste of the Alphabet Sisters for you.'

'Did you and my mum and Auntie Carrie really travel all around the country singing?'

'We did, indeed. Your mum stood on the left, then me in the middle, then Carrie on the right. And we'd sing songs and sometimes we'd even dance a little bit.'

'Do you still do it now?'

Bett laughed at the mental image. 'No, we're probably a bit old for it, I think.'

'And why did you stop?'

'It's a long story, Ellie. I'll tell you one day.'

'Does that mean you don't want to tell me? Mum says that sometimes, even when we've got plenty of time.'

'It must run in the family.'

'What does that mean?'

'It means that we do things the same way. We might all look a bit the same, or like the same things, or be good at the same sorts of things.'

'So I could be a singer too?'

'Would you like to be up on stage?'

Ellen shook her head. 'No. I don't really like people looking at me.'

'I don't like it all that much either.' They walked on a little way, swinging their hands. Bett pointed out a tall gum tree with a fork in the middle. 'See that tree up there, Ellie? Your mum got stuck up one like that one day when she was a bit older than you, when we were living in a different motel. We had to wait three hours before we could get her down. Dad, that's your grandpa, had to call the fire engine in the end. And even then she'd only get down if they sounded the siren.'

Ellen laughed. 'Tell me another thing about my mum.'

'She borrowed all of Lola's makeup once, and dressed the three of us up thinking that no one would notice. Except we were all even younger than you, covered in lipstick and eye-shadow.'

'I borrowed Mum's lipstick once. And Julie let me use some of hers once too.'

'Julie?'

'Dad's friend. She's really nice to me.'

'Your dad's friend?'

Ellen nodded. 'She keeps his secrets too.'

Bett stopped. 'Sorry, Ellie, who is Julie?'

'She works with Dad. In his office.'

Bett got it then. God, for a minute it had sounded like this Julie was Glenn's girlfriend or something. 'Julie is Glenn's secretary, Ellie, is that what you mean?'

Ellen nodded again. 'He's in Singapore with her at the moment. Mum doesn't like it.'

'Your dad being away? No, I guess she wouldn't. She must be missing him.'

'I miss him too. But he rings me every night.'

'Does he? Oh, that's good,' Bett said, keeping her tone neutral. Ellen didn't need to know what she thought of Glenn. They reached the school gates and Bett knelt down in front of her niece, checking her shoe-laces were tied and the ribbon was straight in her hair.

'There, you're perfect. So, have you made lots of friends already?'

Ellen looked at her feet. 'Not yet.'

Bett reached over and touched her cheek. She knew only too well that feeling of starting in a new school. 'You will, Ellie. Don't worry. These things just take time.'

Ellen nodded.

'Good girl. So have fun and I'll see you after school, okay?' She gave her a big hug and watched as Ellen ran off to her classroom.

It suited Bett to walk her niece to school and then get into work early. To be efficient, she told herself. To be hard at work by the time Daniel Hilder arrived, was the truth. Rebecca had picked up something and challenged her about it the day before.

'We're old friends, aren't we?' Rebecca asked.

'Sure.'

'Can I ask you a favour, then?'

'Of course.'

'Go easy on Daniel Hilder for a while.'

'What do you mean go easy?'

'Be nicer to him.'

'I am nice.'

'Bett, you're not. You go all stiff and weird. And he changes when you're around as well. I don't know what's between the two of you, but he could do with a bit of support.'

'Is something wrong?'

'It's his story not mine, but things are tough for him at home, let me say that.'

'With his girlfriend?'

'His girlfriend?'

'He's living with someone, isn't he? Someone he met in Melbourne?'

'No, they split up months ago, I think. He came back on his own. Bett, for a journalist, you're not very up to date with the facts.' Rebecca was looking intently at her. 'What's going on? Did you and Hildie go out together years back? Before I got here? Have a messy break-up?'

'No.' If she concentrated hard she could keep the blush from rising. 'No, we didn't. I was going out with Matthew when Daniel was here before.'

'Ah yes, you and Matthew. I never did get to the bottom of all of that business either.' Rebecca's phone rang. She grinned. 'Saved by the bell, Bett. I'll keep that interrogation for another time.'

In Sydney that afternoon, Anna was speaking in a low, measured voice. 'Take the condom carefully in one hand and slide it over the erect penis.'

Bob's voice came into her headphones. 'Sorry, Anna. Can you do that last bit again? Problem with the tape there.'

Anna stepped close to the mike again. 'I suppose you think this is funny, Bob? How come we managed to do the entire section about childbirth without any problems but we've had to do this bit how many times now? Three?'

'It's that husky voice of yours. You know it drives me crazy.'

'One more time, Bob. Or I'm reporting you and your faulty recording equipment to Actors' Equity.'

'Okay, tape rolling, vision coming up now.' A picture of a woman fitting a condom onto a model of a penis appeared on the small TV screen in front of her. Just a model, Anna noticed. It seemed these school educational videos weren't that far advanced yet. She matched the script to the visuals, nearly knowing the words by heart she'd read them so many times that day. 'Be sure to tie the end of the condom and ensure there is no spillage of the sperm. Carefully dispose of the used condom. Do not flush it down the toilet.' Do not hurl it out the window of a car, like most teenage boys of her acquaintance had done.

Bob's voice in the headphones again. 'Perfect, thanks. Though, could we try that bit about oral sex one more time?'

'Your mind is a sewer, Bob. One more crack like that and I'm ringing your wife and claiming sexual harassment.' She knew Bob's wife well.

He grinned through the glass at her. 'Okay, half-hour break, I think. You're starting to sound a bit breathless, or perhaps that's wishful thinking on my part.'

'Very funny.'

'See you back here at three for the joys of teenage pregnancy. How about that? I'm a poet and I didn't know it.'

Outside the sound booth, Anna made a coffee and took it onto the little balcony. She leaned her head against the warm brick wall and shut her eyes, surprised by a sudden longing for a cigarette. She'd given up eight years before, when she was trying to get pregnant, but even now she had the occasional urge. More so recently. She blamed it on all the tension at home. Once upon a time she would have dismissed anyone who said emotional problems had an effect on a person's health. Now she wasn't so sure. She was either tired all the time and wanting to sleep, or so wired she couldn't sleep at all. And she was getting short of breath now and again. She'd been noticing it more in the past week or two.

On her way to the airport in Adelaide the previous day she'd seen a sign for a medical clinic. No appointments necessary. On the spur of the moment she'd gone in. The surgery had been busy, four or five different doctors coming in and out. She'd almost convinced herself she was over-reacting and had been about to leave when her name was called.

The doctor was in his mid-sixties, she guessed. Red-faced, cheerful. She'd run through her symptoms. Feeling tired. Feeling short of breath. Loss of appetite.

'Could you be pregnant?'

She and Glenn hadn't had sex in months. 'No, no chance.'

'I see your home address is Sydney? But you're living here? Can you tell me a little of what's going on in your life?'

The doctor started smiling sympathetically midway through Anna's reply. 'I think we've found our answer. Your daughter's accident alone could be the cause of this. You would have unleashed enough adrenalin that day to fuel you for a year. Do you get a tight feeling across your chest, as if it's hard to breathe. Yes? And any nausea?'

She nodded. 'All of those things.'

'It sounds to me like you are having panic attacks. Also known as anxiety attacks. It happens when a person is especially stressed. You subconsciously hold your breath, so then your lungs have to work twice as hard, and your heart as well, which explains the breathlessness. And loss of appetite is often another sign of stress.' He glanced at Anna. 'You're very thin already. You really do need to keep an eye on that, make time to eat.'

He checked her blood pressure, her eyes, her tongue. All fine. 'And your age is on your side, too. Thirty-four? Prime of life. Tell me, can you take life a bit easier? Slow down a little?'

Anna laughed and decided not to mention the fact she was in the middle of producing a full-scale amateur musical. 'Not really. Not at the moment.'

'Then can you spoil yourself a bit? Is there something you enjoy doing that you haven't had time to do recently? Someone you like being with? A place you like going to? Somewhere that makes you feel good and relaxed and happy? Often that's as good as any tablets or meditation exercises I could give you.'

She made a follow-up appointment for a few weeks' time. But the doctor was reassuring. 'Slow down, Anna,' he said. 'Don't forget to enjoy life while you're rushing through it.'

Her booking agent, Roz, a calm, older woman, had been just as reassuring when they'd had lunch that day. 'So let me get this straight, Anna. You've been feeling tired? A bit anxious? Breathless now and again? Now, why would that be, I wonder. It's not as if you've got any stress in your life, is it? A daughter in and out of hospital for the past year. A husband in and out of his secretary's bed, the dirty old dog. Don't look so shocked. You know I've never liked Glenn. And now you're back home with your two estranged sisters for the first time in years and directing an amateur musical at short notice. No, from my expert reading, I'd say you should be feeling light as a feather with all that going on.'

Anna started to laugh. 'Well, when you put it like that.'

'I do put it like that. Anna, don't worry. Of course you're stressed. That doctor's right. You just need a break and I hereby give you one. Once you get this school health project out of the way, of course. I want to get my commission out of you first.'

Anna had laughed, feeling more relaxed immediately. She was enjoying the work, too. The only difficulty was the voice-overs weren't being recorded in order, which was making things a little confusing. The young actors in the documentary had met at a disco, then swiftly had a child together, then had sex and now the girl was about to have her first period. No wonder the poor things were so upset.

A memory came to Anna out of the blue, of the day her own first period arrived. It was one afternoon in the summer school holidays, when she was thirteen, before they'd moved to the Clare Valley. She knew exactly what it was. She had been keeping a lookout for months, reading up on it all, supplementing the slap-dash school sex education program. She went to her mother in the kitchen, whispered the news in her ear and was rewarded with five glorious minutes of her full attention. 'Are you okay?' 'Do you know what to do?' 'Have you got any cramps?' There was even a brief hug, before the phone rang and something on the stove boiled, and her mother left her to it.

Feeling on top of the world, she walked over to the manager's house and into the bedroom she shared with both sisters.

'I'm a woman now,' she said to Bett, who was lying on the bed reading.

'What were you before, an iguana?' Bett answered, not looking up.

'No, I mean I've got my first period, which means I am physically officially a woman.'

'You're disgusting. I don't want to know about it.'

'What's disgusting? It's perfectly natural. You'll be next.'

'I'm not interested.'

'What? You're going to stop it happening, are you? Take boy pills? Start playing football perhaps? Hang upside down . . .' Anna poked Bett with her foot.

Bett swiped at her. 'I mean it. I'm not interested. Bleuch.' She gave a shiver of disgust.

Anna looked at herself in the mirror, staring at her face, convinced that, yes, she even looked different. Not exactly more mature, but more knowing. As one of the books had said, she was now privy to one of the great female secrets of the universe. She smoothed her hair, and looked at Bett in the reflection. 'Apparently once you and Carrie get your periods there's every chance we will all start having them at the same time.'

Bett was now lying on her stomach, face buried in her pillow. 'Shut up, shut up.'

Anna hadn't realised it was going to be this much fun. 'It's to do with the moon,' she said, coming over to her, leaning in close. 'All of our wombs are linked, with the sky and the sea, in tune with nature. The three of us will be able to dance naked, creatures of fertility and womanhood. Once a month under the moon.'

'Shut up. I'm not listening. You're disgusting.'

'You're just jealous.'

'Jealous of what?' Carrie came into the room.

'Of me. Because, young Caroline, I, Anna Mary Quinlan, officially became a woman today. I'm having my first period.'

'Really? Cool. I can't wait. Are you using tampons or those pad things?'

Bett had groaned and covered her face with her pillow. 'You're both disgusting.'

Twenty years later, the memory still made Anna laugh. Bett had always been so funny about anything to do with becoming a woman, much to her and Carrie's entertainment. So easy to tease, too, about boys or sex or relationships. She guiltily remembered the time she and Carrie had been asked to the school social, but Bett hadn't. She should have sympathised more, Anna thought now, been supportive. But she'd been so excited at her own date, getting ready, applying makeup, that she hadn't noticed how forlorn Bett was. She and Carrie went off in one car, bright, dressed-up, not even worrying about Bett, who had chosen to stay home with Lola. Anna felt a ripple of shame, thinking of how she would feel if Ellen wasn't asked out. It must have been hard for Bett sometimes – the two of them fighting off attention from boys, but not Bett. She remembered another time she and Carrie were getting ready to go out. Bett had been reading, pretending not to be watching, not to be interested. Carrie, with the know-all confidence of a thirteen-year-old, had taken it upon herself to give Bett some advice. 'You could look quite nice if you did something with your hair. And I can teach you how to put on makeup if you want me to.'

Anna had seen the flash of anger, just before Bett lifted up her book. 'I don't want your help.'

'Well, don't blame me if you never get asked out,' Carrie said before flouncing out.

How could they have been so cruel? Anna wondered. That hadn't been the only time, either. Was it too late to apologise now? Surely it was never too late. She had a sudden urge to ring Bett, to say sorry for everything, not just those awful teenage years, but for all they had said to each other that night of the fight. She took out her mobile and switched it on. She'd had it turned off during the recording. It beeped, telling her she had two messages. The apology to Bett was forgotten as she listened to the first one.

'Anna, hello, this is Mrs Harold from Ellen's school. Would you please be able to come and collect Ellen? She's very upset and I think it's best if she goes home for the rest of the day. Can you call me as soon as possible?'

The second message was also from her. 'Anna, Mrs Harold again. Can you call me as soon as you get this message?'

Anna checked the time. Both calls had been left in the last fifteen minutes. She pressed the speed dial on her mobile and didn't bother with greetings when Mrs Harold answered.

'It's Anna, Ellen Green's mother, Mrs Harold. Is she sick? Hurt? What happened?'

'Hello, Anna. No, it's just there's been a bit of an incident in the playground.'

A rush of panic up her back again. 'Not another dog?'

'Nothing like that,' the voice soothed. 'But it would be better if we talk about it face to face. Ellen is here in the office with us. Could you come in as soon as possible?'

'I'm sorry, I can't. I'm in Sydney. For work.' Anna waited for the disapproval, the change in tone, and was amazed when it didn't come.

'Is there anyone else who could collect her? One of your sisters? Lola?'

Anna gave a little prayer of thanks for small towns. Of course they all knew the set-up. 'I'm sure one of them can. I'll give them a call now. Can I talk to Ellen first?'

The woman's voice was lowered. 'She's fallen asleep. It might be best not to wake her for the moment.'

'Of course. Right. I'll call home straight away.'

Ten minutes later it was all sorted. Bett had been back at the motel for lunch and had answered the phone, listening closely as Anna explained the situation. 'Of course, I'll go and get her now. I'll ring you as soon as I get back.'

Hanging up, Anna realised that the back of her neck was damp with sweat and the churning feeling in her stomach had returned. Ellen in trouble and here she was hundreds of kilometres away. Thank God for families. What did people do when they didn't have sisters they could call on to help? Then she remembered. Exactly what she'd done for the past three years. Felt desperately alone.

Anna felt the phone vibrate against her leg just as she was voicing the segment about the different methods of pregnancy testing. It was her turn to stop the tape. 'Sorry, Bob. I'll be right back.'

She answered it outside. 'Bett? Is she all right?'

Bett's voice was low. 'No, she's really upset. Crying a lot. She's with Lola at the moment. She's trying to put her back to sleep.'

'What happened?'

'The kids were picking on her. A gang of them.'

'What were they doing?'

Bett paused. 'Calling her scarface.'

Anna had never felt such rage. 'The little fuckers. The mean little fuckers. That's it, I'm taking her out of school. Can you tell her I'll be home tonight, as soon as I can get a flight, but she's not to worry, she'll never have to go back there again.'

'Lola said –'

'I don't care what Lola said. She's my child, Bett, and she's not going back to that school again. Put Lola on.'

A minute went past, then Lola's Irish voice came on the line. 'She's sleeping now, Anna. Poor little mite. She was very upset.'

'Of course she was. And she's not going back there again, Lola. I'm getting a flight tonight, and she'll stay home with me tomorrow. I'll teach her from now on myself if I have to.'

'I thought you'd say that. But what about your work? Didn't you say it was three days' worth? You don't have to rush back. We're all here. She's fine with us. We'll spoil her rotten tonight and then tomorrow I'll take her to school myself.'

'Lola, didn't you hear me? She's not going back to that school.'

'It's the best thing to do. She has to face her fears.'

Anna lost her temper. 'Don't you tell me about facing fears, Lola. I have seen that child face more fears than you and I ever had to face. I've seen her face nearly ripped away by a dog's teeth, and those little, those little fuckheads at the school dare to tease her about it.'

'They are seven-year-old children, Anna. They don't know they're being cruel. It's just the way kids are. And that's why she needs to go back, to show them they haven't won.'

'It's not a matter of winning or losing. I just don't want her to be hurt any more. She's not going back, Lola. I'll be home as soon as I can, no matter what you say.'

'Anna, I know you're upset but please don't talk to me in that way. Stay there. Bett and I are here with Ellen. She'll be fine tonight. I think you're wrong but if you don't want her to go to school tomorrow, then that's fine, she won't. I'll keep her here with me. But don't cancel your trip, or rush home yet. You said this job was an important one.'

The tension was draining from her. 'It is.'

'Then finish it. And I will watch over Ellen like she has never been watched over before, I promise. I'll get her to ring you when she wakes up. And you can ring her again tomorrow. All day long if you want.'

Anna realised she was right. 'I'm sorry, Lola. Sorry for swearing.'

'That's all right, darling.'

Lola let Ellen sleep for an hour or so, gave her a sandwich, then decided it was time for a little walk and a little talk. 'You and me and Bumper need to spend some time together, I think.'

Hand in hand, with Ellen holding Bumper by his lead, they set off slowly along the perimeter of the motel. Lola pointed out different trees, a galah on a branch, curling bark, even a lizard sun-baking on a rock, before heading over to the bench Jim had set up especially for her. Halfway up the hill, it had a wonderful view over the vineyards. The bench looked almost golden with the late afternoon light streaming onto it. Lola sat down with Ellen beside her, Bumper in front of them, safely tethered, slowly pulling on shoots of grass from under the bench, making little tugging sounds. Lola had always found sheep one of the world's most relaxing creatures to be near. She gave him an affectionate scratch on the head. 'If he was your sheep, what would you call him, Ellie?'

'Mike,' she said without hesitation.

'Mike the Sheep. Well, that's an interesting one. Now, my dear little Ellie, I've been thinking about what happened this morning and there's some things I'd like to say to you. Would you like to hear them?'

A tiny nod.

'Ellie, do you know why the kids at school were teasing you?'

'Because I'm horrible. Because I'm ugly, and I've got a horrible scar.' The tears started coming again.

Lola pulled her close with her good arm, held her tight and waited for the tears to quell again. 'No, that's not the reason. They teased you because they're scared of you. Because you look a bit different. And people have always been scared of people who look different. Do you know what a scar actually is, Ellie?'

'It's what happened when the dog –' The rest of her words were lost in a shuddering sob.

Lola waited a moment again, and then turned Ellen around so they were face to face. 'A scar is a sign that you've survived something, Ellie. That something happened to you but your body was so strong and clever it joined itself up again. Have you told the kids at school what happened?'

A shake of the head. 'Mum says to just ignore them.'

'Well, most times Mum is right but sometimes it's good for people to know the whole story.'

Ellen twisted away. 'I don't want them to know the whole story. I don't want them to know anything. I never want to see them again.'

'Good idea. We'll run away together, will we?'

Ellen went still. 'What do you mean?'

'If those children are being mean to my beautiful great-grand-daughter, then I never want to see them again either. We'll run away together. Where shall we go?'

A shrug.

Lola continued. 'Good. I'll decide, then. We're going to go to a land where everyone is a little bit different, and that way we won't stand out. What do you say to that?'

She had Ellen's complete attention now. 'What land?'

'Well, let's think about it. I'm really old and I get called things like "dear" and "poor old thing" and spoken to in a strange voice and I don't like it much. Do you know what I heard a young man in the charity shop call me last month? An old wrinklehead. Isn't that rude? So I want there to be lots of wrinkled old people there so I don't stand out. And I think we should have lots of really tall people there too, because they get called names too, don't they? And over-weight people, because they get called Fatty and Chubster, don't they? And people with red hair get called names. And people with no hair. And people with glasses.'

'And people with big noses,' Ellen said in a little voice.

'Yes. And tiny chins. And big bottoms. And bad teeth. Or no teeth. Or teeth that are too big. Or people with broken bones like me. People in wheelchairs. Heavens, it's getting pretty crowded in that land, isn't it?'

'No one with scars like me, though.'

'Of course there will be. There'll be lots of people with scars. Don't you think you're going to be the Scar Queen there, young lady. You can be the Princess of Scars perhaps. So let's see. We'll start with Harry Potter, will we? He's got a terrific scar across his forehead.'

'He's not real.'

'It's our land so we can have whoever we like, whether they're real or not. I've got a scar, you know. On my leg, from when I was kicked by a horse when I was a little girl.'

'I didn't know that.'

'I'll show you one day, when I'm not all trussed up in support tights. I'll probably have a scar on my head, too, when this silly thing heals.' She touched the small bandage on her forehead. 'Your mum has got a scar too. Did you know that?'

'Has she?'

Was Ellen too young to learn that she'd been born by Caesarean section? Perhaps. 'That's a very special scar, and you should ask her about it one day, get her to show you. Your grandfather's got a scar, too. I'll get him to show you when he comes home. On his knee. He took a terrible tumble down some stairs once when he was a little fellow. Auntie Bett probably has one, too, from when she fell off her bike once. I think Carrie's got one as well. We'll have to form a scar club in this land we all live in.'

Ellen was giggling now. 'When do we get to go there?'

'We're already here.'

'At the motel? This is it?' She sounded very disappointed.

'Not just here, Ellie,' Lola said matter-of-factly. 'It's here in the Valley, here in Australia, here in the whole world, with all sorts of different people who look different in all sorts of ways. Because no one is perfect, darling, not a single one of us. We all have something a bit different about us, scars or big noses or small feet or crooked teeth. And that's not going to change no matter where we go to live. What we have to do, you and I, is work out the best way for you to get by here, as happily as you can.'

'But not at that school.'

'Not for a day or two perhaps. Not yet, anyway.' Lola had had another idea, but it was probably too soon to mention it to Ellen. 'But I hereby promise that we'll do all we can to make things as good for you as they can be. And that is enough about that for now.' She stood up with an exaggerated groan. 'Come on then, Princess Scar. Will we go in and see what they're planning for dinner?'

A little sparkle was back in Ellen's eyes. 'Yes, Granny Wrinklehead.'

Lola squeezed her hand. 'It's Great-Granny Wrinklehead, you scallywag.'

The following morning Lola let Ellen sleep in. If she had been her child, the little girl would definitely have been back in school the next day. But Anna had insisted. So a day off it was.

They spent the morning together. She and Ellen had their breakfast in the motel kitchen, then Ellen helped the cleaners do a couple of the rooms, carrying in fresh linen and new packets of biscuits. Ellen seemed bright enough, Lola thought, watching her playing, but there was a tight quality about her. Tension, imminent tears.

Anna arrived home late that afternoon, driving at great speed into the carpark. Ellen had been listening out for her. Lola watched with interest as she changed moods in an instant. One moment she had been playing very happily with her dolls – some complicated scenario involving one set of dolls trying to book into a motel the other set of dolls were running, but not liking the rooms. Lola had started to lose track. Then, at the sound of Anna's car, she started crying and ran out to her mother, wailing at the top of her voice. 'Mummy, Mummy.'

Anna pulled her tight and held her close, the two of them staying like that for some time. They ate dinner together, Ellen still teary, needing to be fed like a toddler. The evening before she had used a knife and fork without any problem, Lola recalled. She nearly needed to tape her mouth shut to keep the comments in. Ellen was Anna's daughter. It was up to Anna to raise her as she saw fit, she told herself. But what if there is another, possibly better, way to approach this? she also asked herself.

Once Ellen was in bed, a tortuous enough exercise, with more tears and tantrums, Lola made a pot of tea and took it into the bar, where Anna was alone, curled up in one of the big chairs, looking at the TV, but in a dazed way. She was still a picture, Lola thought, but so slender these days, fragile even. 'Anna, darling, some tea?'

Anna smiled gratefully. 'You've come to lecture me, haven't you? Tell me where I'm going wrong with Ellen. What a bad mother I am. That I've made the wrong decision taking her out of school.'

'I think you're a wonderful mother. I think Ellen is a wonderful child. But there might be other ways to approach this situation.' She told Anna about her conversation with Ellen the previous day. As she expected, Anna wasn't happy.

'Lola, I don't want you to call her Princess Scar. It's not funny.'

'It's not meant to be funny. It's a new psychological treatment. The more you expose someone to something, the less frightened they are of it. I read about it in the paper. They do it with spiders, slowly expose someone to –'

'I don't care if you have the backing of the Harvard Medical School. I don't like you calling my daughter Princess Scar.'

'What about Scar?'

'Fine. You call her Scar and I'll tell her to call you Great-Grandmother. Old Grandma. The Old Bag.'

Lola smiled. 'All right. I'll stop calling her Princess Scar. But I mean it, Anna. You can't keep taking her out of situations each time they get tricky for her. So you take her out of this school, move her to a new one and the same thing happens there. Then what? You take her out of there as well? Try another school? What will that do to the poor little girl, being moved in and out of schools like that?'

'You and Dad did it to the three of us all our lives.'

'Touché,' Lola smiled. 'But every few years is not the same as every few weeks. And Ellen is facing different things than you three had to put up with. You need to make her stronger, braver, not more cowardly.'

'My daughter is not a coward.'

Lola held up her hand. 'No, she is most definitely not. But she knows how to cry when it suits her, and she knows how to upset you.'

Anna was silent.

'She'll get through this, Anna, she will. But you need to help her, make her brave. You can't protect her all the time.'

Anna opened her mouth, wanting to tell Lola everything – about Glenn, about their marriage being over, about the hundreds of things she wanted to protect Ellen from. But it was too much and the words stuck in her throat.

Lola was watching, waiting, then moved over to her. 'I am an interfering old woman, Anna, but I think I am right. I think Ellen has to go back to school, face them again. It'll be for the best, you wait and see.'

'All right,' Anna's voice was low.

'Are you sure you're up to the rehearsals tonight? I can cancel them if you want.'

Anna smiled, a little shakily. 'You know yourself. The show must go on.'

Anna walked Ellen to school the following day. She was called back before eleven a.m. to collect Ellen once more. The other children had been teasing her again.

After she'd put Ellen to bed, Anna confronted Lola. 'Oh, that really made her brave. Not just Scarface today, but Chicken as well, because she hadn't been to school yesterday. And then they finished it with Crybaby, when she started crying. Shall we send her back again this afternoon so they can really finish her off, Lola? I'll kill them. Little bastards.'

'Do they actually know what happened to her? Know why she has that scar?'

'Oh, yes. I went in and sat every single one of them down and explained that Ellen had been attacked by a dog and that things had been very rough for her and that they should be admiring her, not attacking her. Of course they don't. Do you think I wanted to draw any more attention to her than she needed?'

'I think that's exactly what you should do. I think you should go in and sit down and tell everyone of those little bastards, as you call them, what happened to Ellen. Show them the photos. Let them ask Ellen questions. And then see what happens.'

'What good will that do?'

'I think it will help them understand.' Lola could see Anna's hurt, and could also see her desperation. 'Trust me, Anna.'

Lola rang her friend the principal that afternoon. They had a long discussion and set a time and date. She found a letter and some photos she had received from Anna several months after Ellen was attacked, showing what good progress she had made. Lola rang Frank in the electrical shop and asked him to make up several more slides as quickly as he could. Then she sat down with Anna and Ellen and put her suggestion to them.

Three mornings later, Anna stood in front of a classroom of seven-year-olds, more nervous than she had ever been on stage or in a recording studio. The teacher hushed the children then introduced her.

'This is Anna, Ellen Green's mother. She wants to talk to you about what happened to Ellen and I'd like you all to listen and watch closely.'

Anna told the story simply. She showed a slide of Ellen before the attack, then explained what had happened with the dog on the day in the park. She showed slides of Ellen in the hospital, straight after the attack. Several of the children gasped. She showed another slide of a close-up of the wound. The dog's toothmarks were obvious. She didn't need to point them out. She showed slides from the next month or two, as Ellen went through surgery, stitches, plastic surgery, in and out of hospital.

'That's why Ellen has the scar on her face. It's a sign that she survived a horrible attack from a very large dog, and I am so glad she did, because she is very precious to me, and to her father, and to her aunties, and grandparents and great-grandmother. I wanted to tell you this today so that you will understand and I hope you will be kind to her. She is a very nice little girl.' Anna's voice cracked slightly and she coughed to cover it.

The teacher went outside and fetched Ellen, who had been waiting there with Lola. They had explained to her exactly what Anna would tell them, and that she would come in afterwards and rejoin her class. She was very pale as she took a seat next to Anna in front of the students, nestling close, her hair in front of her face.

The teacher smiled at her, then turned to the class. 'So then, children, any questions for Ellen or her mother?'

A little boy held up his hand. 'What happened to the dog?'

Anna answered truthfully. 'It had to be put down. That means the vet had to give it an injection to make it die, in case it did something to another child, something even worse.'

That satisfied the little boy. Another boy put up his hand. 'Was there a lot of blood when it bit Ellen?'

Ellen nodded.

'There was,' Anna said. 'Ellen lost so much blood that the hospital had to give her some more.'

'Did Ellen get to go in an ambulance?'

Ellen nodded again, still silent.

'Cool.'

All the questions were now being directed to Anna. 'Will she always have that scar on her face?'

'We're doing laser treatment on it at the moment.'

'Laser? Like in *Star Wars*?'

'Not quite, but they shine a special light, a laser beam, onto Ellen's face to break down the scar tissue bit by bit. So when she's older hopefully it won't be so obvious.'

'Is Ellen scared of dogs now?'

To Anna's surprise, Ellen answered. 'Not all dogs. Just big dogs.'

'So you can't have pets, then?'

'I've got a sheep called Bumper Baa. My Really-Great-Gran gave it to me. It's got something called lanolin in its wool which makes your hands soft.'

The teacher was trying not to smile. 'Bumper Baa? That's a very good name for a sheep, Ellen.'

'It's my Really-Great-Gran's idea. She's outside, but she told me she'd have her ear pressed against the door so she could hear everything we're saying. She's very old, but I heard my grandfather say she still has hearing like a bat. And my grandmother said, "Yes, an old bat".'

They all clearly heard Lola's laughter through the door.

Anna was waiting at the school gates at the end of the day. She stood back a little from the other school mums, though she knew they were watching her and probably knew who she was. The principal had sent out a note to all the parents, explaining that Anna would be giving the talk, and why, asking for their help in stopping the children calling Ellen names.

The bell went and the children came streaming out. Anna recognised a couple from the class, but there was no sign of Ellen. She finally appeared, on her own. Around her there were little groups of girls and boys, in pairs and trios. Anna searched her face for tears. Nothing. 'Hi, Ellie. How was the rest of the day?' She kept her tone breezy and light.

'Good, thanks.'

'Lunch was good? And recess?'

Ellen nodded. 'But I'm still hungry. Can I please have an ice-cream when we get home?'

'I think you can today.' No mention of the talk that morning. Anna decided not to push it either, not to ask if any of the other children had talked to her afterwards, or if they had picked on her during the breaks, even though the words were burning a hole on her tongue.

They were nearly at the car when a little girl ran over, her mother a few metres behind. 'Ellen, can you ask your mum now?'

Anna stopped. 'Ask me what?'

The little girl spoke before Ellen. 'Ellen and I were wondering if I could come and play at the motel and see the sheep one night?'

Ellen looked up at her. 'I can show Hannah round, Mum, can't I? Patrick and Samuel wanted to come too, but I said I thought they would have to wait their turn. That was the right thing to say, wasn't it?'

Anna leant down and tucked Ellen's hair behind her ears, smiling at her. 'That was the perfect thing to say.'

Hand in hand they walked over to talk to Hannah's mother.

Chapter Eighteen

'So how are rehearsals going?' Daniel asked.

Bett and Daniel were in the car on their way back from Martindale Hall, a nineteenth-century Georgian-style house near the small town of Mintaro. Bett had spent the morning roaming through the lavish rooms, imagining herself living in such glory and grandeur.

'Good,' she lied. No, they weren't. The way things were going there was more chance of Lola appearing on the cover of *Vogue* than her musical being ready for its gala premiere in mid-March. 'Actually, no they're not. You might have had a lucky escape.'

'I don't know. I'd like to have got up on stage again, as it happens.'

'Again?'

'You're not the only child performer in this car, you know.'

'You were a child performer?'

He nodded. 'Briefly. As a twelve-year-old. In my Danger Hilder days. But I wasn't a common-or-garden variety street punk rocker. I had my own band.'

She saw that glint in his eye again. 'Really? What were you called?'

'Promise you won't laugh?'

'No.'

'We were called Dangerous.'

She smiled. 'Talk about scary. Did you get many gigs?'

'One.'

'Oh. Well, I suppose kindergartens don't have big budgets for live bands at their end-of-year shows.'

'It was on a TV show, actually. A talent quest.'

She turned fully in her seat. This was getting better and better. 'Did you do a cover or an original?'

'Bett, I was an alternative artist. An original, of course.'

'Would you sing it for me now?'

'No.'

'It's a shame videos weren't invented back then.'

'They were, actually.'

'You've got a tape of it?'

He nodded.

'Can I see it?'

He laughed. 'Of course not.'

'Daniel, please.'

'No.'

'I beg you to let me see it.'

He raised an eyebrow. 'You beg me?'

'You're going to tell me you've lost it, aren't you?'

'No, it's at home.'

'In Melbourne?'

'No, home here. In my mother's house. I'm staying there at the moment.'

'I really would like to see it.'

He hesitated, then grinned. 'All right. Have we got time now?'

'Now?'

They were a few kilometres south of the Valley town of Sevenhill. 'My mother's house is over there.'

It was a big old stone house, with a verandah running around all four sides, the roof clad in corrugated iron, painted red. They walked up a path of flagstones, well-cut grass to the left, a well-tended vegetable patch on the right. Bett noticed corn, tomatoes, watermelon, the leaves lush and green, the fruit hanging heavy. 'Your mother's a good gardener.'

'She used to be. That's my patch these days. Six months of back-breaking work in that. To think I could go and buy it in the shop in less than five minutes.'

He opened the door and she followed him inside to the living room. It was a bright cheery area, full of feminine touches – bright cushions, light curtains, women's magazines, and family photos on lots of the cupboards. He switched on the overhead fans, sending a cool breeze through the warm room.

'You're sure you want to see this?'

'If you're sure you want to share it.'

'I bet I'll regret it, but yes.' He smiled. 'I'll get the tape.'

While he was gone she studied a photo on the TV, an old black and white shot of a man and a woman with a baby. Daniel's parents, she guessed. His mother was very elegant. The house was obviously her work as well. Looking around, she noticed several unusual touches. There were coloured lines on the floor, and locks on the cupboards. Like a kindergarten crossed with a *Home Beautiful* centrespread.

He returned with the tape. 'Unfortunately I was able to land my hands on it straight away.'

She put down the photo, hoping he hadn't minded her looking. 'Are you an only child?'

'No, I've got a younger sister. Christine. She's away studying in New Zealand at the moment.'

'Oh, right. And has she got children?'

'No.'

She didn't think he had children, either. She was puzzled. The house looked like it had been well and truly childproofed. Maybe his mother did child-minding. She'd liked to have asked more questions, but he was now crouched in front of the television and video recorder. She looked at his long back, lean under the T-shirt, and had to blink away a clear memory of kissing it.

He pressed play and then pause so that a shimmery stilled image appeared on the screen. 'You realise I'm only doing this in the interests of fairness. After me seeing those photos of you and the Alphabet Sisters.'

She took a seat on the sofa and nodded. 'I understand. The "I show you mine and you show me yours" principle.' In light of their Melbourne meeting, it suddenly felt like the wrong thing to have said.

His lip twitched. 'That's right.' He leaned against the door frame behind her and pointed the remote control.

She was laughing out loud in just moments. It was a low-budget TV talent show from the early 1980s. The set appeared to be made of tinfoil and plastic cartons. Dangerous were on third, after a woman singing a fast and off-key version of 'Love Me Do' and a dreamy-looking harpist playing a Scottish air, also very fast. The host introduced Dangerous with mock fear, warning viewers that the following scenes might disturb.

She recognised Daniel immediately, a smaller version of himself, with black kohl around his eyes, black lipstick, spiky hair and ripped clothes. Skinny white arms poked out of his torn T-shirt and he'd perfected a good snarl that obviously amused the director. There were at least six close-ups of Daniel pulling a face at the camera. The lyrics were straightforward, about being tormented with nightmares about rats and spiders and snakes.

She was still laughing by the time Daniel pressed pause. She had to wipe her eyes, sure there was mascara all over her face. 'So did you win?'

'No, and to this day, I don't know why. I think we were much better than the harpist. Did you like the lyrics? I can write them down for you if you want.'

'No, thanks anyway. What was that rhyme in the chorus again, snake with awake? Very inflammatory.'

'Don't mock a twelve-year-old. It was hard to talk about bringing down the government when you couldn't spell the word. I stuck to what I knew. The girls at school were terrified of me.'

'You're lucky Lola hasn't seen this. She'd have written a part in the musical especially for you. You beat the Alphabet Sisters hands down.'

'Oh, I don't know. What was it you won? Third prize in the Miss Indooroopilly Talent Quest of 1978? Even though you were the only entrants?'

'Lola told you about that as well?'

'No, you told me. That night in Melbourne.'

'I did?'

'Don't you remember? When we left the party and went to that little Italian bar. You told me all about the Alphabet Sisters. I hadn't laughed so much in a long time.'

'I did? You hadn't?'

He gave her a long, thoughtful look. 'Bett, do you actually remember much of that night?'

She'd spent three years trying to forget it. 'Um, yes, some of it.'

A pause. 'Do you mind telling me which parts?'

'I remember meeting you at the club.'

'Yes.'

'And I remember . . . going to the bar. And then to your flat, talking, and then, um, going to bed with you . . .'

A glimmer of a smile. 'Good.'

Something about the way he was looking at her made her want to tell him the truth. 'But mostly I remember waking up and being so embarrassed at my behaviour I crept away as quickly as I could.'

'Embarrassed? Why?'

'You know,' she said feebly. She couldn't say the rest of it. Because I seemed to have got it into my head I was a sex goddess. Because I didn't so much throw myself at you as hurl myself at you . . .

'Bett, don't be embarrassed. I enjoyed it. All of it.' He gave a slight shrug. 'That's why I was disappointed that you'd gone when I woke up. Before we'd had a chance to swap numbers. I went back to the bar we met at a couple of times, but I didn't see you there again.'

'You did?' She hadn't gone within a two-mile radius of the place after that night.

'I was going to ring the motel here, to see if they had a number. But I thought because of all the problems with your sister and your fiancé that might be a bit awkward.'

She cringed inside. Had she shut up for a single moment all night?

'And then I figured if you'd wanted to see me again, you would have left a note. Look, as I said the other day, I was disappointed you didn't want to see me again, but I got over it. I don't want you to feel awkward about this.'

'That's what you meant last week when you said you'd got over it?'

He looked puzzled. 'What did you think I meant?'

'That you'd got over the night. Got over how terrible it was. And then you said that it wasn't the first time and it wouldn't be the last time. I thought you were talking about having one-night stands.'

He threw back his head and laughed. 'Oh, yes. Danger Hilder rides again. No, Bett. I actually don't make a habit of one-night stands. Not that we were a real one-night stand, anyway, were we? Don't one-night stands have to be between strangers?'

'I'm not too sure of the official definition. I haven't made a habit of them either.'

'No?' There was a sparkle in his eye. 'You're very good at them, for a novice.'

'You're one to talk.' She could hardly believe they were joking about this.

His phone beeped and he checked the text message. 'I don't know why I thought country papers would be quieter than city ones. We'd better get back.'

They were pulling into the carpark behind the *Valley Times* office when she felt she had to mention it one more time.

'Daniel, thank you for being so nice about it today.' She hesitated. 'And three years ago.'

'It was my pleasure, Bett.'

Bett knew he was remembering exactly what she was remembering. 'Good. Great. Well, see you later, then.' Once again, she nearly tripped as she climbed out of the car.

CHAPTER NINETEEN

'WELCOME, GENERAL MacArthur. Can I offer you one of our finest lamingtons?'

Anna sighed. Still no good. So much for her pep talk the previous week. Yes, some of them had learned their lines, and yes, some of the songs sounded a bit better, but the acting was still atrocious. There was no other word for it. This was the fifth run-through of the scene featuring the CWA president, Mrs Smith, greeting the newly arrived General MacArthur at the Terowie Station and it was getting worse, not better.

'One more time? With perhaps a little bit of enthusiasm?' The woman sounded as though she was offering him a plate of snake heads instead of cakes.

Mrs Smith put her hands on her hips. 'I can't help it if I don't like lamingtons. Have you ever tried to make them? You get chocolate icing and coconut all over the place and the cake always crumbles.'

'Well, could you pretend you like lamingtons? Just for this scene?'

'Can't I offer him a cheese sandwich or something simple like that?'

Anna kept her voice calm. 'An American General has survived

days of fierce battles, has travelled on a train for hours and hours to your tiny town in the middle of nowhere and you want to offer him a cheese sandwich?'

'He might like cheese sandwiches. We might have heard from one of his people that he likes cheese sandwiches. Sometimes the simple things are what people want. I read in a magazine once that Princess Diana used to get sick of all that fancy food and would long for a night in front of the TV eating cheese on toast.'

Anna tried counting to ten. Then to twenty. It didn't help. What had got into them all tonight? She looked around the room. Romeo and the American GI were playing an improvised game of table tennis in a corner of the room. The musicians from the high school were reading pop magazines instead of rehearsing their songs with Bett. General MacArthur was sending text messages. The plumber playing Jack-the-Lad had disappeared, muttering something about a burst pipe in one of the pubs in town.

Things had been as bad earlier, too. Kaylene had at least learnt her lines, but was insisting on speaking them in an English accent.

'Kaylene, you can't,' Anna had said. 'She's American.'

'But she doesn't sound posh enough. Can't she be English? I love doing English accents.'

'If we were doing *My Fair Lady*, yes. But you're Mrs MacArthur. Mrs Married-to-the-American-General-and-an-American-herself MacArthur. So will you please speak in an American accent?'

Kaylene folded her arms. 'There's no need to get huffy about it.'

Things had gone no better with Kaylene's father, either. Len had arrived with the first of the set panels that evening. His painting of the railway station at Terowie looked more like the interior of a submarine. He had been telling her for days how well the train was going and then had produced it in a shoebox. It was five inches long.

'Len, I don't know if this is going to work on the stage. It's a bit small, don't you think?'

'This is the model, Anna.' He roared laughing. 'As if this would be the real one.'

'It's just you've spent days making it and I'm a bit worried we're running out of time.'

'It's the detail that takes time. See, Anna, take a look. I've even painted tiny people in the carriages. Have a look.'

Anna looked. Yes, so he had. A row of faces grinned wildly out of one of the little carriages. Marvellous. Splendid. Especially if she was planning on staging this musical in an ant farm. What was she supposed to do – give everyone in the audience a pair of binoculars?

'So can it be a cheese sandwich, Anna?' the CWA woman asked stubbornly now. 'Maybe even a cheese and tomato sandwich?'

Anna stared at her. 'Can you please excuse me?'

She marched out the door, across the carpark and knocked politely on Lola's door.

'Come in.'

Lola was in bed, a folder of papers on her lap. 'Anna, darling, how are things going?'

Anna opened her mouth, screamed, then shut her mouth again. Feeling much better, she turned on her heel and returned to the rehearsals.

The next morning in his room, Richard Lawrence took a break from his writing and picked up the latest edition of the *Valley Times*. As he flicked through the pages, an article on page five caught his eye.

Auditions Unearth Valley's Hidden Talent

Auditions for the forthcoming fund-raiser musical *Many Happy Returns* unearthed a surprising amount of local talent, musical director Anna Quinlan said this week.

All seven lead roles have been cast, with a large chorus also assembled for the 1940s-style musical, written by Anna's grandmother, Lola Quinlan (80).

The musical is loosely based on the true story of General Douglas MacArthur's wartime visit to the small town of Terowie.

It will be staged at the Clare Town Hall on March 20, the anniversary of General MacArthur's visit to Terowie. All proceeds will go to the Buy a New Ambulance Fund. Tickets are available from the Valley View Motel.

Richard smiled. Anna had told him she'd given a diplomatic interview to the local paper. She had called over for another drink after rehearsals the evening before. She was such good company, full of stories about plays she'd been in, voice-overs she'd done, but filled with questions for him as well, about London, about his work. She'd also been keeping him hugely entertained with stories of the rehearsals, five-inch trains, stubborn actors and all.

'It's not too late for you to join in, you know,' she'd said. 'I'm sure I could find you a part. General MacArthur even.'

'No thanks. I'm happy to save myself up for the opening-night audience.' He'd already extended his stay for another fortnight so he could be there.

His mobile rang, and he hoped briefly it was Anna calling from Adelaide. She'd told him she was going there early that morning to hunt down some costumes for the musical. She'd thought it was safely in Len's hands and then discovered his idea of an army uniform was a spray-painted ice-cream container helmet and a broom stick as a gun – with the bristles still attached.

The name Charlie came up on the phone display. Charlie Wentworth, a university friend currently travelling around Australia producing an offbeat cable TV travel series. 'Charlie, hello.'

'Mr Lawrence, how are things with you? That book of yours still coming along?'

'Couldn't be better. How about you? Still headed this way?' He settled back, preparing to be entertained as his friend filled him in on the latest batch of items he'd been filming. The program specialised in quirky 'Did you know?' stories. Last time they'd spoken Charlie had just finished a segment on Australia's oversized tourist attractions – the giant fibreglass pineapples, koalas, lobsters and oranges dotted around the countryside.

Charlie had just as many stories this time. Richard laughed as he heard of a filming disaster in the Flinders Ranges the previous week. Charlie had tracked down a camel that made a sound uncannily like the tune of 'Jingle Bells' when it brayed. The animal had upped and died the morning they arrived.

'How very inconsiderate, leaving a hole in your schedule like that.'

'Who are you telling? Keep an ear out for stories for me, would you? I'm desperate, to tell you the truth. Any sort of Australiana you can lay your hands on.'

Richard picked up the newspaper beside him. 'All right, then. Did you know that in 1942 General Douglas MacArthur, yes, as in the song "MacArthur Park", caught a train from Alice Springs, stopped at a tiny outback town and made one of the most famous speeches of the war?'

'Is there a plaque marking the spot? A MacArthur plaque?'

'Very funny.'

'What's the place? I've never heard of it.'

'Terowie,' Richard read from the newspaper. 'I think that's how you pronounce it. It's not far from where I am. Less than an hour, anyway. You could drive through it on your way here, check it out.'

'Rich, you might have saved my bacon. Are there any locals who'd remember it? Anybody I can get to talk about it?'

'I don't know. The only expert on the subject I know is an eighty-year-old Irishwoman here in Clare who's written a musical based on it.'

'An eighty-year-old Irishwoman who's done what?'

Richard filled him in. He could nearly hear Charlie thinking it through. 'Could we film a bit of it, do you think? Just enough to add a bit of colour and movement to the station footage?'

'Let me check and I'll call you right back.'

He dialled the number of a phone just two rooms away. 'Lola, hello, it's Richard. Something very interesting has come up. Would you have a moment to talk about it?'

Ten minutes later, Lola hung up the phone and beamed from ear to ear. God had been smiling on them the day Richard Lawrence came to stay at their motel.

'Would I like to be interviewed on a TV program? Would I like my musical to be filmed? Richard, has Elizabeth Taylor got any jewellery? Was Fred Astaire light on his feet? When? Now? All I need is five minutes to pop on a bit of makeup.'

Richard had laughed down the phone. 'It won't be for a couple of weeks, Lola, if it happens at all. They're still working out their filming schedules. It's just a possibility, an idea, but I wanted to check with you first, to see if you minded.'

'Such manners, Richard. You're one of the world's gentlemen.

Let me say loudly and clearly, we would love to appear on the program. Just say the word and I'll have them all primed and ready.'

'I'll call my friend back, then. He'll probably want to talk to you himself as well, if that's okay?'

'Oh, darling, it would be my pleasure.' She was thinking quickly. 'But it might be best to keep it a secret from everyone else for the time being, from my granddaughters as well as the cast, don't you think? Just in case it doesn't come off. I'd hate to disappoint anyone.'

'That's probably good advice,' he'd said.

Which Lola had no intention of following herself. She ran her eye down the cast phone list in the folder beside her, trying to decide who would be the best one to tell. Who had the biggest mouth, to put it bluntly. Of course, Len the butcher. Plant a little seed with him and before long it would have turned into a big oak tree. And if Lola knew human nature as well as she thought she did, Anna might find her problems at rehearsals magically disappearing.

She dialled the number. 'Len, it's Lola Quinlan, up at the motel. Oh, I'm absolutely grand again, not a bother on me. I've had a bit of news about the musical, and I'm bursting to tell someone and I know how involved you are in it, but will you promise me you'll keep it to yourself?' She lowered her voice to a whisper. 'It looks like a British TV company is going to come and film a documentary about us. I'm not sure when, soon. Yes, isn't it wonderful? The only thing that's worrying me is everyone might not have learnt their lines by then, or the set won't be ready and we'll be the laughing stock of the United Kingdom. Or of the world, if they end up showing it on all the cable channels. Oh, I'm absolutely serious. The producer is a mad fanatic about General MacArthur, apparently. He couldn't believe his luck when he heard about it. Don't tell anyone, though, will you? And it's especially important that you don't tell my granddaughters. Even if you happen to let it slip to someone else, as long as they don't find out. I want it to be a real surprise for them.'

She hung up, pleased with herself. She waited and then tested her hunch, ringing Len's number. It was engaged. Good. She had a feeling it would be engaged for the rest of the night.

At the rehearsals three nights later, Bett turned away from the piano, amazed. Anna and Carrie came over.

'Has someone put something into the town water?' Anna asked.

'It's bizarre, isn't it?' Carrie whispered.

Every single cast member knew their lines, and the words to the songs. They had all arrived on time. There was an air of excitement about them as well, faces made up, clothes a little more flash. Kaylene looked like she was on her way to a nightclub.

'That pep talk you gave them really had an impact,' Bett said.

Anna smiled proudly. 'It must have. Whatever it was, I'm not questioning it. If this keeps up, we might get there yet.' She clapped her hands to end the break. 'All right, everyone, from the top once again.'

CHAPTER TWENTY

IT WAS one week later. Lola lay back further against her pillow and yawned delicately. 'It's a terrible thing, but since I've turned eighty I seem to be feeling tired earlier each night.'

'Is it your arm? Do you need any pain-killers?' Bett turned from the wardrobe where she was hanging up Lola's clothes. The three of them had been taking turns dressing and minding Lola since she had broken her wrist. Tonight Bett was on duty. Carrie was on a night off. Anna had gone to Adelaide again to collect the last of the costumes. Ellen was already tucked up in Bett's room for the night.

'Not at all. It's not giving me any bother at all. You're the ones it's bothering, having to come in here every morning and night to dress me. And don't think I'm not noticing that you're trying to change the clothes I wear, because I am.'

Bett smiled innocently.

'What do you think of that Richard Lawrence, Bett?'

Bett didn't blink at the change in subject. 'He seems nice.' He seemed very nice, actually. But she still hadn't invited him out for that drink. Life seemed to have suddenly got too busy, between the musical, and work in the motel, and the assignments with Daniel around the Valley . . .

'He has an excellent sense of humour, you know.'

'He seems to have, yes.'

'I wish I'd known at your age that a sense of humour is worth far more than a bulging wallet or a bulging –'

'Stop it, Lola.'

'Truly, a shared sense of humour is all you need to get you through.'

'Was Edward funny?'

'No.'

'He didn't make you laugh?'

'He might have once, that time he tripped over the fence wire. Yes, that was very funny.'

'Why did you marry him, then?'

'Things were different in my day. And especially with my family.'

'It was an arranged marriage, do you mean?' Lola had never been so forthcoming.

'A suitable marriage would probably be the correct term.' Lola wasn't in the mood to talk any more about that right now. She yawned widely, covering her mouth in a mannerly way. 'As a matter of fact, Richard was asking about you today.'

'Was he?'

Actually, he hadn't been. Lola hadn't seen him today. 'Yes, he asked me if you were single. He also said he thought you had the most beautiful eyes he'd seen.'

'What?'

'And the creamiest skin. Is that how he put it? No, sorry, he said milky-white skin.'

'Richard said that? He's hardly spent any time with me. How would he know what my skin is like?'

'He mentioned how much he enjoyed your company the night of my party. How entertaining you were.'

'Did he?'

In Lola's experience, nothing made someone more attractive than to think they found you attractive. And Richard may well have thought all those things about Bett. Perhaps he was too shy to mention them.

A knock at the door. Richard poked his head around. 'I'm ready when you are, Lola. Oh, good evening, Bett.'

'Hello, Richard.' Her smile was very broad.

Lola yawned extravagantly. 'I'm so sorry, Richard, but I just seem to be overcome with tiredness this evening. And so suddenly.' She turned to Bett. 'Richard was saying today how curious he was about the whole MacArthur story and kindly invited me out for a meal so he could pick my brains.' Another yawn. 'Richard, my dear Bett knows the story as well as I do, if not better, and she'll have that journalist's way of giving you the concise story, whereas I would be inclined to ramble all over the place. Or nod off mid-sentence, the way I'm feeling tonight. Bett, would you mind at all taking my place as Richard's dinner guest tonight? Richard, I promise she's sparkling company.'

Richard handled it all very smoothly. 'It would be my pleasure, of course. But I wouldn't like to deprive you of a night out, Lola. We can reschedule for another night when you're not so tired if you like.'

'I seem to be tired every night these days.'

Bett glared at her. It was only tonight she'd been complaining of this sudden tiredness. 'I can't go out, Lola. I'm minding Ellen tonight.'

'Is she asleep yet?'

Bett shook her head.

'Then bring her in to me and I'll mind her myself. We'll both be asleep before eight o'clock, I should think.'

Five minutes later Ellen had been transferred into the double bed beside Lola. Bett had hurried back to her room, changed into a new skirt, run a brush through her curls and applied mascara and lip gloss.

She poked her head into Lola's room. 'You're not up to anything, are you?'

'How could I be? I'm too tired. I look tired, don't I, Ellen?'

Ellen was propped up with several pillows, in imitation of Lola. 'Yes, you look very, very tired.'

That sounded suspiciously rehearsed to Bett. 'Goodnight, then.'

'Have fun,' Lola called.

'Have fun,' Ellen echoed.

Lola waited until Bett had definitely gone, then brought out a packet of chocolate éclairs from under her pillow, pointed the remote control at the TV and grinned at her great-granddaughter. 'Make yourself comfy, Ellen. You're going to love this.'

As the opening credits of *Mary Poppins* came up, Lola smiled to herself. *Operation Richard and Bett*, we have lift off.

Richard had made the dinner booking at Lorikeet Hill, a small winery-restaurant south of the town. The food was delicious, the Irish music playing in the background soothing. The wine relaxed Bett's mood and loosened her tongue. Richard seemed genuinely interested in so many things. Not just the General MacArthur story, but in Lola, Anna, Carrie, herself – all of them.

He refilled her glass. 'So you went to journalism college a couple of years after you left high school?'

'That's right.'

'And Anna went to drama school around the same time?'

She nodded. 'She always said that the Alphabet Sisters had given her the edge. Not many people have spent six years touring the country by the time they're nineteen.'

'And she met her husband in Sydney?'

'That's right.' She pulled a face. 'Unfortunately.'

'You don't like him?'

'Sorry, that was very childish.' And alcohol-induced, she realised. Bett tried to find the words. 'If Glenn was an animal, he'd be a bear. If he was a vehicle, he'd be a bulldozer. But he adores Anna, and I suppose that's all that matters at the end of the day.'

'He adores Anna?'

'He idolises her. Worships the ground she walks on.' It had given herself and Carrie the creeps, in fact. Glenn had a way of looking at Anna, of talking about her, as if she was his latest acquisition. 'This is my new car, this is my big house on the harbour and this is my beautiful actress wife.'

Richard was looking at her closely. 'And how long since you've seen Glenn and Anna together?'

'It's been a while, actually.'

'A while?'

'More than three years,' she admitted.

As the waiter came up and removed their plates, Bett realised how much she'd been talking. He must have been a skilled journalist, she guessed. She should be taking tips from him, not spilling her soul. She waited until the waiter left before she spoke again. 'You're not about to write an unauthorised biography of the Alphabet Sisters, are you? I don't know if there's enough scandal for a book.'

'Oh, I don't know about that.'

She caught something in his tone and narrowed her eyes. 'You know, don't you?'

He gave a slightly sheepish smile. 'A little.'

Bett cursed Lola inside. Of course she would have told Richard all about it. 'Can I ask exactly what you were told?'

'That you had been engaged to a man here in Clare but then he met your younger sister and fell in love with her instead. And that there was a row between you and Anna and Carrie, and that you hadn't spoken or seen each other from then until Lola's party.'

'Well, that's it in a nutshell, I suppose.'

'That must have been terrible for you.'

She took a sip of wine. 'Yes, it was. It's been hard. I've missed them a lot.'

'Them?'

'Anna and Carrie.'

'I actually meant it must have been terrible when your fiancé left you for your sister.'

Bett blinked. 'Yes. Yes, it was.'

The waiter came then with their main courses. Bett was glad of the interruption, taking the opportunity to steer the conversation back to safer ground. They spoke about the musical, about Lola, and then Richard moved on to the Alphabet Sisters again.

'Do you miss those days? All that adulation? The tours? The motel rooms?'

'Well, we'd grown up in motel rooms, so that was never a luxury for us.'

He laughed. 'No, I suppose not. What did you demand? That the promoters give you a three-bedroomed suburban house to stay in?'

'Exactly. And you should have seen our backstage requests. Bottles of lemonade. Comics. Barbie dolls.'

'Now we're getting down to the nitty-gritty.' He grinned. 'I think I always wanted to be a showbiz journalist. You know, sniffing out the stories behind the stories, the truth behind the public image.'

'Oh, we were squeaky clean, I promise. Except for the time Anna and I stole a bottle of Dad's wine. And Lola told Carrie off for swearing a few times, but I think she apologised afterwards.'

'So why did it come to an end?'

Bett thought about it. She could wave it away. Or she could tell the truth. 'Because of me.'

'You?'

'I finished it. I refused to do it any more.'

'Why?'

Because of their awful final performance at the local music society Christmas show. The real number one on her embarrassing stories hit parade. 'It's a long story.'

'Tell me,' he said.

She took a sip of her wine, gathered her thoughts, then started to talk.

They'd been too old for it, really – Anna eighteen, Bett sixteen, Carrie nearly fourteen. The three of them had stood in age order, as always. Lola had gone all out on their outfits, dressing each of them in red satin, with a green tinsel hat. In the mirror, Bett had been aware that her dress was tighter on her than Carrie's and Anna's were, but Lola had just hugged her, told her she was gorgeous and sent the three of them out onto the stage.

Midway through 'Sisters', their opening number, she looked out into the audience and noticed the three cool boys of the town. Her heart gave a leap, as she veered from self-consciousness to excitement. She looked away, then looked back. The three of them were actually looking at her, concentrating on her for once, not Anna, not Carrie. She had a rush of confidence, stood straighter, sang louder, smiled wider.

Then one of them shouted, 'Piggy in the Middle.'

The people in the front of the hall heard. She noticed neighbours leaning and asking what he'd said and then stifling a laugh themselves. The three boys kept it up as a sort of chant, under their breaths. She tried to keep singing, knowing her cheeks were fiery red, feeling as though her skin was about to burst. They nudged a few of their other friends into it as well then, a row of them mouthing the chant 'Piggy in the Middle'. Anna hadn't noticed or, if she had, hadn't cared – too busy striking an aloof pose, always the lady. Carrie had probably been too busy revelling in the fact she was attracting most of the admiring glances, people nudging each other and whispering, 'Isn't that little one cute?'

Somehow she got through the other three songs. But she was in tears when they came off stage. Lola was waiting. She had noticed everything. 'They're just stupid, silly boys, Bett. Ignore them, do you hear me?'

In Lola's arms, Bett was almost comforted. Then from behind her came Carrie's voice. 'Maybe you could lose a bit of weight, Bett, if you don't mind me saying. We probably would look better if we were all the same sort of size.'

Her tears stopped abruptly. She felt as though iced water had been flung over her. 'What do you mean by that? I spoil the look?'

'Not spoil it. But if we are going to do this thing seriously, keep up the Alphabet Sisters, then maybe you do need to think about losing some weight.'

Bett turned to her other sister. 'And what do you think, Anna? Do you think I should lose weight?'

Anna gave a shrug. 'Carrie's got a point, yes. But it's your choice how you look.'

Bett refused to sing with the Alphabet Sisters from that moment on. There had been three more performances booked after the Christmas one, but she point blank refused to do them. Lola tried talking sense. Anna tried to apologise. Carrie was sent in, pleading, eyes filling with tears. But it was too late for Bett. The Piggy in the Middle taunt had lodged itself firmly in her brain. She was never going to perform with her sisters again.

Anna didn't mind too much. She'd already set her heart on getting into drama school and treated the Alphabet Sisters as a joke by this stage. But Carrie was very upset. One of the performances was going to be televised on the local TV network. She'd been looking forward to it for weeks. She kept trying to talk Bett around.

'Please. You have to do it, Bett.'

'No, I don't. I told you, I'm never singing with you again.'

'But I apologised.'

'Only because Lola told you to.'

'But I really am sorry.'

'You should have thought before you spoke.'

'You're spoiling it for everyone else. Not just me. For Lola. For the TV people.'

'I would have thought you and Anna would love to have the stage to yourself, without me spoiling the perfect look.'

Carrie had lost her temper. 'I didn't call you Piggy in the Middle, it was those boys. But you are behaving like a pig now. A selfish pig. And I'll get you back for this, I promise.'

Bett didn't tell Richard this, but the truth was that her sisters' lack of support had hurt far more than the taunts. It had been the start of a horrible period of her life. From that moment on it seemed as though Anna and Carrie had been set adrift from her, into a world of romance, dates, boys and confidence. Bett had felt like Cinderella and Bessie Bunter rolled into one – overweight, unhappy, finding pleasure only in food and books and her piano.

'And that was the end of it,' she said to Richard. 'We just stopped.'

He had been listening closely. 'They always say it's the people closest to you who know how to hurt you the most.'

'I suppose so.' She tried to lighten the mood. 'That'll teach you to ask me a question when I've had half a bottle of wine. You should have shut me up.'

'I didn't want to. I was very interested. And I'm sorry, Bett. Being a teenager's not much fun for anyone, but that must have been hard on you.'

'Yes. Yes it was, actually.'

'And is that why you think Carrie made a play for Matthew? To get you back for something that had happened years before?'

'I'm sorry?'

'You said that Carrie told you she was going to get you back for it one day. And then years later she broke up your engagement and married your fiancé. Do you think it was connected?'

Was he mad? Carrie and Matthew had genuinely fallen in love. Bett had always known that. She'd seen how they were with each other. It had been an almost instant attraction.

She stared at him as she realised what she'd just admitted to herself. Behind his glasses, Richard was assessing her closely. Kindly, but still closely. She decided then she'd definitely had enough of talking about herself.

'No, I don't think it was connected at all. In fact, I'm sure it wasn't.' She made a point of picking up the water jug and refilling his glass until it was nearly overflowing. 'So, enough about me.' She was pleased with how firm her voice sounded. 'This book of yours, Richard. It's set in the 1850s, did you say?'

CHAPTER TWENTY-ONE

ANNA GLANCED at the dashboard clock as she drove through Auburn, the town that marked the start of the Clare Valley. She was making good time. She noticed her hands on the steering wheel. They were actually quite relaxed, not gripping it like it was a lifeline. In Sydney she'd often caught herself driving like that. Then again, in Sydney lots of things had been different. Up there her thinking time had been filled with jagged thoughts of Glenn, memories of rows past and premonitions of arguments they were sure to have in the future, a constant barrage of angry voices and disagreements. But since she'd been in the Valley there had been softer images in her mind. Nicer things to think about.

The musical, for one. It had surprised her how much she was enjoying it. Not just the rehearsals, but all the production side as well. She'd had a very productive trip to Adelaide today, collecting the final props and costumes from different fancy-dress shops around the city. Everything was slowly coming together.

She was even feeling a bit better. Not quite so tense. She'd tried to explain exactly that to the doctor that morning, when she'd called in to the surgery for her follow-up appointment. She'd expected to get the cheerful red-faced older man again, not this serious-faced woman, who looked less than twenty-five and seemed determined to find out the cause of every scratch or bump she'd ever had in her life.

'Look, I'm sure it's probably just stress,' Anna had said to her. 'As your colleague said a few weeks ago, I needed to slow down a bit.'

'I don't like the sound of that breathlessness. How many weeks now?'

'A month, maybe two.'

'And it's getting worse?'

'I've been stressed,' she repeated. 'It's probably just panic attacks. And things are getting much better at home.' Not just with her sisters, either. She'd even managed to have a normal phone conversation with Glenn in Singapore. Short, but at least neither of them had hung up.

'You've never had asthma?'

'No, I haven't.'

'Anna, I'd like you to have a scan. Just to ease all our minds.'

'Is that necessary? It's just I've a lot on, and it means coming down to the city again. I live two hours away.' She gave the young doctor the look which usually stopped other people in their tracks. Not this time.

'I think it's very necessary, to put my mind at rest as much as yours. That's why we have all this technology, to show us what's not there as well as what might be there.' She made several phone calls, while Anna sat fidgeting.

The doctor put down the phone and smiled. 'We can get you in at the end of next week. They've had a cancellation.'

Anna scribbled the date and the address in her diary. It was two days after the musical. She'd be down in Adelaide anyway returning the costumes. 'Fine, thanks.'

As she walked back out to the car she'd taken her mobile from her bag and checked her messages. There was just one, from Lola, asking her to call. There'd been a little incident with Ellen at school today, but it was nothing to worry about.

Anna had called the number immediately, her heart beating faster. 'What is it, Lola? Not more trouble?'

'Hello, darling. No, I wouldn't say it's trouble exactly.'

How could Lola sound so calm? Amused even? 'More bullying? Or no, not another dog?'

'No, a sheep. Bumper the sheep, to be precise.'

'Bumper?'

'Ellen took Bumper to school today. For show-and-tell. I had a phone call half an hour ago from her teacher to ask if I could come and collect him.'

Anna had felt a bubble of laughter start deep inside her. 'How did she get him there without anyone seeing? I thought Bett walked her to school this morning.'

'She did, bright and early. Then it seems Ellen walked back to the motel, untied Bumper and headed back to school. Along the back roads, you'll be pleased to know.'

'And her teacher didn't mind?'

'The teacher didn't know until it was Ellen's turn to stand up in front of the class. She apparently said, and I quote, that she had to "slip outside for a moment and fetch something". She'd tethered him to a tree at the end of the playground.' Lola was laughing now too. 'You probably also should know that she's invited everyone in her class back to the motel for her birthday party. And they've all accepted.'

'But it's not her birthday for months.'

'I don't think she specified a date. She seemed more interested in outlining what the food and entertainment would be. Prawn cocktails, hide-and-seek in the motel rooms and rides on Bumper's back featured quite prominently, I believe.'

Anna had been laughing properly by then. 'Oh, Lola, I'm sorry. Can you sort it out for me or do you want me to drive back right now?'

'Sort it out? What's there to sort out? I'm going to take lessons from her.'

Anna grinned again at the thought of it. Being in the Valley had been so good for Ellen. She had noticed her daughter growing more confident every day. Happier. More relaxed. The way a child should be.

As she drove past more vineyards, getting closer to Clare, Anna started thinking of someone who made *her* feel good and happy and relaxed. Richard. She thought of the late-night glasses of wine and conversations they'd shared. He was so curious, courteous. He had a way of resting his head slightly on one side, like an owl, she'd thought at first, but then it became more endearing than that. He wore glasses, which he adjusted a lot, especially when he was talking passionately about something. He liked cricket, and didn't like it when she told him how bad the English team were these days. He also disagreed with her opinions on Harold Pinter, Neil Simon and David Hare, but completely agreed with her in regard to Shakespeare, Beckett and O'Casey. That had led to her telling him all about her unsuccessful acting career and how it had led to her new very successful voice-over career.

He had turned on the small TV in the room and made her sit with him until one of her ads came on. They hadn't had to wait long. He sat in silence as the ad played. Afterwards he took her hands and kissed her on each cheek. 'You were marvellous, darling.

Such a combination of pathos and urgency. It was a truly bravura performance.'

The ad was for brake fluid and she had been the voice of the car. She'd inclined her head, accepting the praise, trying not to laugh. 'I do actually think that was one of my best moments.'

'Can I get a video? I'd love to see it again. I'm sure there were some subtleties of your performance I missed.'

She smiled now, remembering the teasing. Fun teasing, not the sneering way Glenn had often spoken about her work. They'd talked for hours that night. He'd told her more about his life in London. He'd talked about the three-year relationship he'd had with a fellow reporter, until she had ended it the year before. It was another reason why he had decided to leave London. And so she had told him about Glenn, and Glenn and Julie, and Glenn and Julie and Singapore.

She felt warm, good, thinking about him. And the more time she spent with him, the sexier she was finding him, too. Not in the confident, macho way she had found Glenn sexy. Richard was more quietly confident, slow burning rather than white heat. She found it even more attractive that he hadn't made a pass at her. He just listened. Seemed so interested. When it was time to leave he walked her to her own room, five doors down. 'Sleep tight,' he'd said, before kissing her on the cheek, gently touching her arm at the same time. She had never felt quite so cared for in her life.

They'd arranged to meet for a glass of wine when she got home tonight. He was taking Lola out to dinner, he'd told her the night before, but expected to be home by eleven. It was half past ten. She couldn't wait to see him.

Bett and Richard stood in the motel carpark.

'Thanks, Richard. That was a lovely night.'

'You're welcome, Bett. I enjoyed it too.'

She wondered whether she should invite him in for a glass of wine. Or would he invite her in for a glass of wine? But there was no spark between them, she'd realised. She liked him, enjoyed talking to him, even if she had told him too much. But that was all.

'Well, goodnight.'

'Goodnight.'

Inside her room, she sat on the bed and pulled her knees under her chin. Her conversation over dinner kept echoing in her mind.

'It's been hard. I've missed them a lot.'

'Them?'

'Anna and Carrie.'

'I actually meant it must have been terrible when your fiancé left you for your sister.'

She went into the bathroom and stared at herself in the mirror, not liking what she saw. She wiped her hand across her lips, smearing her lip gloss. She leaned in closer and saw her mascara was already smudged. How many years had she stared at that face, felt cross, felt angry, felt powerless? When was maturity going to kick in? When would she get the ability to deal confidently with everything life sent to her?

She decided to have a shower, needing to stand under the stream of water, wash away some of the troubling thoughts. She turned the shower tap on full blast, wanting to fill the room with steam before she got in. As she went back out to the bedroom area to get her dressing-gown, she heard a car pull up next door, the headlights momentarily coming through the thin fabric of the motel curtains. Anna arriving home from her trip to Adelaide, she guessed. Five to eleven, a late enough night for her. Bett undressed, stepped under the streaming water and shut her eyes.

After carrying the costumes into her room, Anna simply turned off the light again, shut the door after her and walked five doors down. She knocked lightly, two little taps.

He answered immediately. 'Anna, welcome back.' His smile was as warm as his voice.

'Hello, Richard.' She took in every detail of him.

'Anna? Are you all right?'

'I'm fine.' She was more than fine. She was happy, she realised. She was home at the motel. She knew Ellen was safe in Lola's room. There had been a note on Anna's bed in Ellen's best handwriting. 'I love you Mummy', with a picture of Bumper the sheep and the two of them in bright colours. Anna felt light after months of heaviness. She spoke softly, but surely. 'Richard, I know I should be coy. And that we should spend more time together first. And have dinner, and go for walks, and get to know each other better. But I don't want to wait that long. I want to go to bed with you.'

'Now?'

'Yes.'

'Right now?'

'Yes.' She faltered slightly.

'Will you at least give me time to make the bed?'

She smiled. 'No, I won't.'

'Never mind, then. We'll have to manage.' He took her by the hand and drew her inside his room.

Bett sat on the edge of her bed, wrapped in a towel. Her mind was leaping all over the place. From the dinner with Richard tonight to her conversation with Anna the other night. '*Still avoiding the truth after all these years, Bett?*'

She hadn't been avoiding it. She'd known for years, in fact. It's just she had chosen not to tell anyone, to let the rift go unhealed between them, for three long years. But why? Because she wanted to keep the rift going? Because she was glad to be away from her sisters?

Yes.

That night of their fight she'd felt a hot high flame of anger that she'd never felt before. In the days and months that followed she had easily found other fuel to keep it burning. Some of it had surprised her. Memories of Anna doing things first – learning to ride a bike, wearing a bra, wearing makeup – and feeling jealous, that she always had to wait her turn. Being equally jealous of Carrie, who had been born with all the right accessories for life success – a mop of blonde curls, a small frame, even a slight lisp as a child, like some modern version of Shirley Temple, without the saccharine sweetness.

She had a sudden urge to talk to Anna about it all. About everything. To apologise for the terrible things she had said about Glenn. She'd had no right. Anna loved him and Glenn loved Anna. Their marriage was their business. The remorse lasted for a moment, then she started remembering things about Glenn. His arrogance. The way he could be so condescending. It was no good. She couldn't pretend she liked Glenn. But she could still apologise for saying such mean things about him.

Bett pulled on her dressing-gown, slipped outside and headed to Anna's door. The lights were out. She knocked gently.

'Anna?' she said softly.

No answer. She must have gone straight to sleep.

Bett looked down the row of rooms and saw a light on in Richard

Lawrence's window. Perhaps she could start with him instead, use him as a trial run. She imagined it. 'Hello, Richard. You don't know me that well, but I need to make another confession, if you don't mind.'

As she watched, his light went out. She felt a sudden frustration. Why had everyone decided to have an early night? She waited a moment, then turned and went back into her own room, pulled back the sheets of her bed and climbed in.

In his room, Richard traced a finger across Anna's face in the light from the moon coming through the curtains. 'Do you know, I'm not sure if we got that quite right.'

'I'm not too sure either,' Anna answered, just as solemnly. 'Perhaps we could try it again?'

'What a great idea.' He leaned down to kiss her again.

CHAPTER TWENTY-TWO

By the time dawn came, Bett still wasn't asleep. It was a combination of the wine she'd drunk and the conversation with Richard, she decided. It seemed to have unleashed memories she'd kept well locked away for more than three years. Uncomfortable memories.

The motel room felt very claustrophobic. She needed to feel her limbs moving, hoped that would calm her mind. She pulled on tracksuit pants, a light windcheater, laced on her sneakers and crept out of her room as the sun was coming up over the gum trees on the hill across the road. She started walking out of the town, headed north past the vineyards, the early autumn colours of red and yellow appearing on the edges of the leaves, still heavy with fruit.

Walking usually soothed her. She'd been walking for an hour a day most days, since the year after she first started working on the newspaper. Lola had got her started, in her usual blunt way. She had come into Bett's room one afternoon, pulled a chair beside the bed Bett was lying on and looked very serious. 'Bett, we need to talk.'

'About what?'

'Do you remember that Piggy in the Middle jibe that upset you so much all those years ago?'

Bett had put down the bag of chips she was eating. 'Yes.'

'You might want to be careful or someone will call you that again.' She ignored Bett's shocked expression. 'I'm not the body police, but I don't like to see someone letting themself go, and that's what you're doing.'

'I've got every right to be as fat or as thin as I like. And you can hardly talk about clothes.' Stung by Lola's remarks, she'd wanted to hurt her back.

'I'm happy with what I wear, Bett. And if it makes you happy, you can be as big as you like and wear shapeless clothes for the rest of your life. But you're not happy, are you?'

For a moment her temper had flared. She had started to deny it. And then she had let the defences down, confessed all to Lola. No, she wasn't happy. She was extremely unhappy. Everything had been getting on top of her and the only comfort had been food. Sitting for hours studying or working at her desk, she'd consoled herself by eating biscuits and cakes and chips. And she was wearing baggy clothes because that was all that fitted her these days.

Lola had listened and then waited for the tears to pass. 'You have two choices, Bett. You can do something about your weight. Or you can stay as you are and decide not to let it bother you.'

'It does bother me. Of course it does. But what do I do? I'm useless in a gym or those aerobics classes. And I really love food. I don't want to live off cabbage soup for the rest of my life.'

'What are those two things hanging off your waist there?'

'They're my legs.'

'And what can they do?'

'Hold me up. Walk.'

'Walk. Exactly. From today I want you walking an hour a day, in rain or shine, fog or mist. Or, more likely, seeing as it's summer, in blazing sunshine day after day.'

'Walk?'

'Walk. The world's best exercise. The world's best calmer. No one ever regrets a walk, Bett. I'll be your trainer. I'll make you do it.'

'You'll walk with me?'

'On these old legs? I'd collapse in a moment. No, I'll drop you off somewhere and then I'll drive to the end of the walking trail and pick you up an hour later. And that way I'll know how far you've gone, and if you get to me any quicker I'll also know you've hitched a lift. And I can sit in the car and listen to classical music, which will calm me down at the same time the walk is calming you down. Is it a deal?'

Bett shook her grandmother's hand. 'It's a deal.'

So she had started it, walking for an hour every day, along the dusty roads at the back of the valley. Lola would drop her off and then head off in her small white car, driving past her, sitting upright in the car like a meerkat as she went past. The girls had always laughed at Lola's style of driving. Bett walked until she met Lola waiting some miles away, reading the paper, doing a crossword or sometimes dozing, classical music or a tape of musical highlights playing loudly from the car. Three months later Bett had summoned up the courage to go clothes shopping. She'd dropped only a size, but her body shape was different, firmer. She wasn't skinny – she'd never be skinny – but she was fitter and had definitely found a figure that she was comfortable with.

She'd met Matthew not long afterwards. He had moved to the Valley as a junior vet, while he was studying at the nearby agricultural college. She had interviewed him on his second day for a feature on new arrivals in the town. As an interview subject, he hadn't seemed eligible, so she hadn't been as nervous of him as she would have been if she met him in a bar or somewhere social. When he mentioned he didn't know anyone locally yet, she'd invited him for a drink up at the motel bar. Her father had poured him beers and asked him lots of questions, while Bett sat beside him, joining in, enjoying the fact it was her, not Anna or Carrie for once, sitting beside a good-looking man on these bar stools. Carrie had been on her overseas trip at the time. Anna was in Sydney.

The next weekend she and Matthew met again, this time in one of the three pubs in town. Again, she'd had no nerves. She felt relaxed with him. They met the weekend after that. It had become a regular thing, so stress-free, so easy that people in the town had started calling them a couple before they had thought too much about it themselves.

He'd kissed her on their fifth date. By the seventh date it had progressed to his hands touching her body. She'd decided six weeks into the relationship that she was going to sleep with him. She had gathered early on that he was more experienced than her. He'd had a number of girlfriends in Perth, he'd told her. On a weekend away, two months after they'd met, they'd had sex for the first time. It had been nice. Not earth-shattering, not painful, not even especially passionate, but comfortable. Easy. Gentle. It had continued that way, too. She was still self-conscious, not liking to make love in full light, feeling a bit awkward in the sexy underwear he started buying her. But the relief she felt outweighed any of that.

Because the truth was she had been a virgin when she started going out with Matthew. At twenty-eight years old. There had been several near misses, one or two very close encounters, but something had stopped her each time. She hadn't told Matthew. He hadn't guessed either. And she'd certainly never told Anna or Carrie. To the two of them, losing their virginity had been straightforward, pleasant. Just a matter of them getting it out of the way, was how it had seemed to Bett.

After five months she and Matthew had fallen into an easygoing relationship – meeting for drinks once or twice a week, dinner one night a week, after which she would usually go back to the house he was sharing in town. Sometimes they would make love, sometimes they wouldn't. Then one night, out of the blue, he asked her to marry him. They were on their way back from a friend's wedding. All night long the two of them had been teased, been asked when their big day would be. 'A wedding begets a wedding, you two, remember.' The speeches had been very moving, the couple talking of their love for each other, the importance of their families, how they couldn't wait to set up home together, start their own family.

On the way back to Clare, Matthew told her more about his own childhood, how his parents had separated when he was young, and how he'd shifted around a lot. 'I don't want the rest of my life to be like that, Bett. I want to stay in one place. Have children. Make them feel safe.'

It had moved her almost to tears at the time, thinking of him being so lonely as a child, wanting to make sure that his own kids didn't go through what he'd been through.

'You understand, Bett, don't you? You know exactly what I mean.'

At the back of her mind, Bett wanted to disagree. She'd quite liked all the shifting they had done as children. But that night the champagne had taken over her emotions. 'Of course I understand. And I think you'd be a great dad, make a great husband and father.'

He stopped the car, took her hands. 'Bett, do you want to get married? You and me?'

She felt a warm, comforting feeling. Even a sort of relief again. She wasn't a failure, someone loved her enough to want to marry her. They drove straight to the motel to tell her parents and Lola. That night, Carrie happened to ring from her travels and they told her the news too. Word whipped around the town. Rebecca came into work with a bottle of champagne. It was a very happy time.

But had it felt like it was something they both were destined to do, couldn't live without doing? No. If anything, the pressure came from people around them, their friends, who were all busily planning their weddings and buying their first houses.

They didn't rush into any wedding planning. They set a date, booked the church for a year's time, to be sure of a place more than anything. Bett started thinking about her wedding dress. But, mostly, life settled down – Bett with her work at the newspaper, Matthew with his work and his study, both living separately. The fact that they were engaged was a nice link between them, but nothing momentous, life-changing. Again, that thought – comforting. Which had started to feel like boring.

Bett recalled coming at the subject in a roundabout way during a phone conversation with Anna. 'Did you ever have doubts about Glenn before you married him, Anna?'

Anna got to the point immediately. 'Why, are you having second thoughts about Matthew?'

'No.' A pause. 'But it stands to reason, doesn't it, that you'd start to see faults in someone, especially after you've been going out with each other for a while?'

'You and Matthew, you mean? You've only been together for less than a year, though, haven't you? I think that's still officially known as the honeymoon period. What sort of things are you talking about?'

'Well, with Glenn, for example, do you ever, um, I don't know, run out of things to talk about? Find yourself sitting there wondering what to say next?'

'No, I don't think so.' Anna laughed. 'If we're not talking, we're usually fighting about something, so communication isn't usually the issue. Have you run out of things to say to Matthew?'

Bett had, but she'd hedged around it. 'Maybe we've just been too tired to talk. Things have been pretty busy work-wise for both of us.'

'But you must have things in common you can talk about, even if you are tired. Do you like the same things? The same sort of books or music?'

Bett grimaced. She and Matthew couldn't be further apart in their musical tastes. He was strictly John Cougar Mellencamp. He listened to the rock stations, she preferred the alternative ones. He liked listening to her play piano, but now she thought about it, only when she was playing the sing-a-long Top 40 ones, not the musical numbers or classical pieces Lola had taught her. Matthew didn't read much, either, apart from veterinary magazines, whereas Bett always had two or three books on the go.

'Um, no, not really.'

'Does he make you laugh?'

She had to think. Occasionally he did. But his main party piece was his impressions of Basil Fawlty, Frank Spencer and Elvis Presley, and the truth was she'd never found them funny. A bit embarrassing, if anything. 'Sometimes,' she said to Anna.

'What about his work?'

It had been interesting enough to begin with. But she had never been that keen on animals – well, she liked cats, but she wasn't that keen on their inner workings, not to the extent of talking about intestinal worms over dinner most nights. Carrie was the animal fiend in their house, the one who collected photos of dogs and horses and stuck them on her schoolbooks and on the wall above her bed. She'd even had an imaginary horse for a few years, called Plink for some reason, on which she would gallop around the motel carpark, to the amusement of their guests.

Bett remembered thinking that the music Matthew listened to was the same sort of music Carrie had liked. That she wasn't a reader either. That even the way he looked was more to Carrie's taste than Bett's. Carrie had always liked the rugged outdoor type.

She and Anna had talked about it some more, before Bett deliberately moved the conversation on to other matters. Four days later, she got a letter from Sydney.

Dear Bett,

> *I've been thinking a lot about our phone call last night, and rather than ring again, I decided to write this to you. First up, it's none of my business, so there's the disclaimer out of the way – if you take my advice, I won't be held responsible for the consequences. But what seemed to be coming loud and clear through everything you were saying is that you have serious doubts about marrying Matthew. You kept asking whether I'd had the same sorts of doubts about marrying Glenn, but as I said last night, Glenn and I are completely different to you and Matthew. It's a different combination, a different situation. The problems we have are not the problems you and Matthew might be having or would have.*

> *Can I ask you a very blunt question? Why are you marrying him? I'm not too sure you love him, as you're not too sure yourself, but do you even like him all that much? It worried*

*me when you said that you and he don't have all that much
in common. It worried me even more when you said that you
weren't getting any younger, and besides all your friends were
getting married. As Lola would say, if all your friends jumped
off the roof, would you do that too?*

*While I'm on the subject, why does Matthew want to
marry you? He sounds like the world's greatest romantic,
but has he got a sense of you? Is he interested in you, as Bett,
rather than as a woman he can marry? It just sounds to me as
though the pair of you have drifted into something and don't
know how to drift out of it again.*

*If you are still reading this, then you are probably think-
ing I should mind my own business. But you are my sister and
I love you dearly and what you do is my business. I worry
about you, worry that sometimes you stick your head in the
sand, pretend everything's okay when it patently isn't, just to
avoid confrontations. But it would be a lot less messy to get
out of this engagement than it would be to get out of a marriage. It sounds like the two of you get on okay, and maybe
you would make better friends than lovers, or better acquain-
tances than husband and wife. You said a telling thing last
night, that because Matthew was your first serious relationship, you had nothing to compare him to, so you were just
assuming that being bored, being annoyed, was normal. I
don't think that's a normal comment for someone a few
months away from tripping up the aisle.*

*I'll shut up now, I promise. I just wanted to say that I'm
worried about you and I hope you'll think about this carefully.
Everyone makes mistakes. It wouldn't be the end of the world
if you called it off.*

Never forget how much I love you, even when you are driving me up the wall.

Anna xxx

Anna had come back to the Valley not long after to see Carrie, but Bett hadn't mentioned the letter or her doubts to her again. There'd been so much fuss about Carrie's return that it had been easy to avoid the subject. Bett had loved the novelty of having a boyfriend to show to Carrie. She'd enjoyed the feeling of going to the pub with them that first night, watching as Carrie jokingly road-tested him for her, patting him down. She hadn't minded at all when the two of them often became the three of them, Carrie joining them for dinner, drinks in the pub. When Carrie was around, Matthew seemed to have lots more to talk about. It had been easier to have the three of them. There were none of the long silences there had often been between her and Matthew. Carrie bubbled into the space, brought out a different side of Matthew. They had kept finding things in common – music, antique shopping, even clothes shopping. It was Bett who had suggested Carrie go to the agricultural college with Matthew and sit in on some lectures, when she'd seemed so interested in his vet stories. Bett had a clear memory of that day. 'Matthew and Carrie should be together, not Matthew and me.' She had actually thought that.

She stopped walking, alone on the path, the early-morning air crisp around her, cool against her skin. Her memory jumped to the night Matthew had told her about Carrie. He had called her at the office, his voice sounding strange, asking if he could meet her after work. He said he had something very important he needed to tell her . . .

Fury, hurt and anger had propelled her through the next few months. Then the ticket overseas had turned out to be a lifeline. A chance to start afresh, leave the mess that was her life in the Clare Valley, her relationship with her sisters, far behind her.

It had been frightening but it had been a chance to be herself, to stop measuring herself against Anna and Carrie. Except she hadn't been able to leave them behind, had she? All the memories had come with her.

And they were still there.

CHAPTER TWENTY-THREE

SEVERAL DAYS later, out at the farmhouse, Carrie pointed the remote control at the TV and turned down the volume. Lola had insisted she take the night off from the motel. 'You've been working too hard, darling. Have a break. Prepare yourself for the musical, with lots of relaxing, lots of good food, lots of snuggling up to Matthew.'

Some chance of that. She was too stressed to relax, there was no food in the house and the only snuggling she'd been doing was with the sofa cushions. She'd spent all afternoon watching imported American confrontational chat shows on TV. It was so much easier for Americans, Carrie thought. They were so good at that 'come on TV and let it all hang out' approach. She didn't think her own Irish-Australian heritage stretched to the same candidness. The program credits came up, with a contact number if you needed a family matter sorted out. Would the producer's budget stretch to flying the entire Quinlan family over to America? she wondered. They could start small and work their way up, she supposed. Just fly her and Matthew over for a start.

If only it were that easy. What would the producers do? Make them talk about their true feelings? Insist they were honest? Carrie could almost hear herself telling Matthew how sorry she was for all the fighting. How much she missed him. How she wanted to give it another go.

She sat upright.

She did. That was exactly how she felt. But what would Matthew say if she told him all that? If she asked him to come home again?

She realised there was only one way to find out.

Anna ran her hands down Richard's body, stretching herself so she was full length against him, skin against skin. He smiled into her eyes, leaned forward, kissed her on the lips again. There was just a white cotton sheet covering them, the one lamp throwing a soft light into the room. There had barely been time to draw the curtains when she had called to his room that evening before they had undressed one another and started kissing for a very long time. Luxurious, gentle lovemaking had given way to more conversation, whispered confidences, shy offerings of what they thought of one another, which had led to more lovemaking.

Anna felt wrapped in warmth, in compliments, in his admiration. She loved the touch of his fingers on her body, his lips on hers, the sound of his voice telling her stories, asking her questions, showing interest in her like she hadn't felt in years. She'd felt the same intense curiosity about him, wanting to hear all about him as well. She had never had this with Glenn, simple lying under the sheet together, talking, their bodies entangled, the memory of lovemaking fresh on their skin and in their minds, the promise of more to come in the stroking of fingers on bodies, the look in each other's eyes. She felt reckless, like a naughty teenager again, staying out late, comforted by the thought of Ellen safe with Lola.

He had just told her some of the conversation from his dinner with Bett several nights before. She was struck equally by his gentleness and his curiosity, as if he was trying to understand her, and her sisters, and the feud between them.

'I can understand why Carrie and Bett might have fought, but why did you and Bett fight about it all?'

'Oh, not just me and Bett. Me and Carrie too.' She smiled. 'We were never a family to do things by halves. I fought with her straight after I'd fought with Bett, actually.'

'Tell me about it.'

'You really want to hear?'

'I do. I love hearing you talk.'

Anna had been in Clare on a quick weekend visit, while Glenn had taken Ellen to visit his parents in Queensland. She was in her room when Bett burst in, wild-eyed, her mop of curls more unruly than usual. She spilled out the story in moments, before Anna sat her down and made her go through it again, slowly and in detail.

Bett took a deep breath. 'Matthew had some news, he told me. Something urgent he needed to talk to me about. So we met here, in the bar. I thought it would be about a job move or something about work, but no . . .' A pause, as Anna could see Bett was trying not to lose control. 'No, he said he needed to call off our wedding.' Bett told Anna that she had scarcely mouthed the word 'Why?' before Matthew had delivered the answer. 'He said: "Because I've fallen in love with Carrie."'

And then into the bar walked Carrie. A glance between her and Matthew, Bett said, and she had known. Carrie felt the same way about Matthew.

'You should have seen them, Anna. The two of them sitting there, holding hands, telling me how hard it was for them, for *them*, but that they'd thought it best if they broke the news to me together.'

Anna winced. 'They were holding hands in front of you? Being that open about it? So they've been lovers? Already?'

'I don't know. They must have been. Of course they have.' Bett was very distressed. 'Carrie kept going on about how they had tried to fight it, but it had been too strong, too *passionate*, between them to ignore.'

'I can't believe Carrie would do this. And what is Matthew playing at? Creeping from your bed to Carrie's? What has he got, some kind of sister fetish?'

Bett shifted uncomfortably. 'Matthew and I . . . hadn't actually been . . . well, not for a while.'

'Since before Carrie got back or after?'

'Before. I don't know, between everything, all the wedding plans, and my work and his work, there hadn't been time.'

Hadn't been time? Anna was puzzled. Wasn't sex something you made time for – especially when you were in the first flush of love? 'Bett, things really hadn't been okay with you and Matthew before this, had they?'

'Of course they had,' Bett said quickly. 'Things were perfectly fine, until this. That's why I just can't believe it.'

Anna frowned. 'Really? You don't remember calling me about Matthew, saying that you were worried you weren't suited? That you didn't think he had enough get up and go in him?'

'I didn't think he'd get up and go to my sister, though, did I?' For a moment they both nearly started to laugh, then Bett started pacing the room again. 'I can't believe it.'

'Bettsie,' Anna used the pet name, 'come on. Remember our phone call? The letter I wrote that you never acknowledged? You know you weren't feeling sure about Matthew. You told me as much. Maybe this was the chance to have told him. To bring it all into the open.'

There was no answer.

'Oh, Bett, please.' Anna gave a quick laugh. 'Don't deny it. You must be the only journalist in the world who makes a habit of changing the facts to suit yourself.'

'You're one to talk. You're hardly broadcasting from the Palace of Truth yourself.'

Anna abruptly stopped laughing. 'And what is that supposed to mean?'

'Forget it.'

'Bett . . .'

Bett lifted her chin. 'You and Glenn.'

'What about me and Glenn?'

'Why do you stick with him? Are you happy together? Do you really love him? Does he love you? Or is it because of Ellen? Or your social standing?'

'Don't do this. Don't try and change the subject.'

'I'm not changing the subject. I'm saying that people in glass houses shouldn't throw stones.'

'And sisters who come seeking help shouldn't turn into complete and utter bitches.'

'Bitch? Excuse me? I have been completely humiliated and you turn on me.' She stood up, her eyes blazing. 'Fine. Brilliant. Off you go to Carrie, then. Tell her how delighted you are. Tell her what a wonderful success she has made of her life. The two of you again, Miss Perfect and Miss Even More Bloody Perfect. No need to worry about me cluttering up your perfect space again. Just as you've always wanted it.'

'What the hell are you talking about?'

Bett gave a rough laugh. 'It's the same old story again, isn't it? You and Carrie together, doing it properly, like you always said. Not making a mess of things, not spoiling the look – that's how you both put it, isn't it?'

'For God's sake, that was years ago, we shouldn't have said –'

'Yes, you should have. If you've both always thought that I lowered the tone, ruined the perfect picture, then of course you should have said it. Let's bring everything out into the open, shall we? Carrie's done it again tonight. You both did it years ago, so it's my turn now.'

'Bett, calm down.'

Her eyes were glittering. 'No, I won't. Enjoying life up there in the ivory tower, are you, Anna? Good. Great. You're welcome to it, though I'm sure Carrie and Matthew will enjoy popping in for a visit now and again, if they pass muster, don't spoil your décor.'

Anna only just held her temper in check. 'Stop it, Bett. You're upset. You're not seeing things clearly.'

'Oh I am, Anna. I'm seeing things more clearly than I have ever seen them before. What was it you and Carrie said to me that day? That I spoiled the look? Well, not any more. I should thank Carrie and Matthew. They've given me the exit I always wanted. Goodbye, Anna. I wish I could say it's been a pleasure being your sister but quite frankly it hasn't.'

Anna was now furious herself. 'Taken an overdose of your melo-dramatic pills, have you? Calm down, for God's sake. I told you I'm on your side.'

'You are not. You never have been. It's only ever been about you. We saw through it, though, you know that. No one likes Glenn. I mean, all right, marry for money if you have to, but couldn't you have picked someone who was a little more like a human being?'

'That's enough.'

'Good thing Ellen is so pretty, I suppose, though God help the poor girl if she ever puts on a gram of excess weight. I can see it, you'll have her down at the Kiddy Gym, in at the beauty parlour, applying layers and layers of fakeness. Like mummy, like daughter.'

'You bitch, Bett.' Her own fury rose like a geyser. 'I wanted to help but you're beyond it. Forget it. Go. Good riddance. You're on your own now.'

Bett stared at her coldly. 'Maybe I have been for years, Anna.' She walked out, slamming the door behind her.

Anna barely had time to catch her breath when the phone on the bedside cabinet rang. It was Carrie.

'Annie?' She only called her Annie when she was upset. 'I need to talk to you. Are you alone?'

Anna noticed then that her hands were shaking. 'Yes. Bett's just left me.'

'Can we talk to you? Will you come to my room?'

So 'they' had become 'we' already. A united team. Quelling her angry feelings towards Bett, trying to be calm – someone had to be the voice of reason in this situation, surely – Anna went straight to Carrie's room. Inside, Carrie and Matthew were sitting side by side on the bed. Carrie was crying. Beside her Matthew had his arm around her shoulder, awkwardly stroking her, looking embarrassed, stopping, then stroking again. Anna found it very distracting.

'So it's true,' she said, looking at them both.

Two nods, Matthew a little shame-faced, Carrie more defiant. 'Is Bett okay?'

Anna gave an almost laugh. 'Okay? Well, no, I wouldn't say she's okay.'

'We couldn't help it, could we, Matthew? It just happened.'

Anna looked from one to the other. 'And you're sure?'

Matthew nodded.

Carrie looked at him and nodded too. 'We are. Hurting Bett was the last thing, the very last thing, I ever wanted to do. She's my sister, but this became bigger than both of us. As if all the choice was taken from us.'

Between Bett's histrionics and now Carrie's mea culpa act, Anna had suddenly had enough. 'All right, Carrie. You don't have to lay it on too thick.'

The crying stopped. 'What do you mean by that?'

Anna put it to her straight. 'You know you and Bett have circled each other for years. I'm not saying you deliberately made Matthew fall in love with you, but be honest with me if not with yourself. At the start was there not a bit of playing with fire, flirting, to annoy Bett?'

'Are you saying I deliberately made this happen?'

'Subconsciously, maybe. I don't think you thought it would come to this though, no.'

Carrie's lower lip was quivering. 'Yes, you are. That's exactly what you're saying. That I made this happen to hurt Bett.'

Anna laughed. She couldn't help herself. Carrie looked like a sulking five-year-old. How could she have a proper fight with her sisters when the pair of them carried on like this?

Carrie turned stony-faced. 'It's not funny. You've always taken Bett's side. It's always been the two of you, ganging up on me.'

'What?'

'You know it has been. You both always hated me tagging along behind you, getting in the way.'

'Carrie, what are you talking about? Stop behaving like a child.'

'That's it exactly. You've been saying that to me for years. Well,

I've had enough. Enough of you and Bett telling me what to do and lording it all over the place. It's always been like this, since the school fair that time.'

'What school fair?'

'That one before we moved to the Valley and Mum and Dad said you and Bett had to take me and you didn't. You paid that girl to look after me.'

'Carrie, that was twenty years ago. You were eight years old. We didn't want you hanging around.'

'Exactly. You didn't want me hanging around. How did you think that made me feel?'

'Like an eight-year-old who had been left behind by her older sisters. Like every single eight-year-old with older sisters in history, I expect. Carrie, are you actually listening to what you're saying? You are linking the fact you have broken Bett's heart by running off with her fiancé with something that happened when you were eight?'

'It's symptomatic.'

'What the hell does that mean?'

'Patterns. Recurring events. Here it is again. Matthew and I have made an adult decision. We love one another and yet here you are sticking your nose in and meddling when it's none of your business.'

Anna's hackles hadn't just risen, they were now practically visible, sticking out in sharp points from her shirt. 'Caroline, you need a slap. You're the one who has made all this happen.'

'I'll tell you something, then. I'm glad it has.'

'You're glad?'

Carrie looked uncomfortable for only a brief moment. 'If this is what it took for you and Bett to see I'm not a child any more, then, yes, I'm glad.'

'Sorry, Carrie, can I get this clear – you're glad you've broken up Bett's engagement? I hope to God you're joking because if you're not you are a much sadder case than I already thought.'

Matthew leaned forward then. 'I have to step in here, Anna.'

Anna didn't look at him. 'Shut up, Matthew. Mind your own business. This isn't about you any more.'

Carrie gasped. 'Don't you dare talk to him like that.'

Anna was beyond reason now. 'What? I should keep it sweet with him in case he gets sick of you and wants to make a play for me? He's going for the hat-trick, is he?'

Now Matthew and Carrie looked outraged. 'That was uncalled for, Anna.'

Inside, Anna knew it was exactly that. But the pair of them, sitting there, all smug and wound around each other, had suddenly annoyed the hell out of her. Carrie with her hand on his thigh, Matthew stroking Carrie's arm, the physical attraction between them so obvious. When was the last time Glenn had stroked her in public like that? In private, even? She blocked the thought and concentrated on the two angry faces glaring at her.

'I apologise for that remark. But I don't apologise for anything else I said. It's time you grew up, Carrie.'

'I grew up? At least I'm being honest with myself, going into a relationship for love, not gain.'

'How dare you! First Bett and now you. How dare you both cast judgement on me like this.'

'Bett told you what she thought of Glenn as well? Good. Isn't it time we said something? Rather than keep up any pretence that we like him? Well, we don't. And I don't like you when you're with him. You changed when you went to Sydney, Anna. Got airs and graces. Too good for us any more.'

'Shut up, Carrie.'

'It's true. How come it's all right for you to march in here and tell me off, but you won't listen to a few home truths about yourself?'

'You self-centred, selfish little –'

'I don't care what you think of me, actually.' Carrie's lip quivered again. 'Come on, Matthew. This is pointless. Let's go.'

'You can't go,' Anna had said, suddenly exhausted. 'You're in your room. I'm the one who has to go. And I'm happy to, believe me. Goodbye, Carrie. Goodbye, Matthew. Good luck whatever happens to you both in the future, but I'll tell you something – I don't want anything to do with it. '

'Good. Because I don't want you to have anything to do with us either.'

And with that Anna had slammed the door.

Richard shook his head in amazement. 'And where was Lola in all this? I can't imagine her sitting back and letting it happen.'

'No, she didn't.'

There had been a family conference, Geraldine and Jim, Anna and Lola, with a number of phone calls made to Carrie on her mobile phone. She had left the motel and gone to stay with Matthew in his house on the other side of the town. Bett had left too. Got in her car the next morning and just driven away. She had phoned Lola to tell her she was safe, that she was in Melbourne, and had then turned off her mobile.

Jim Quinlan had been sure it would all blow over. Lola had put him right on that. 'Darling, you haven't noticed any of this going on, have you?'

'Noticed what?'

Lola had shaken her head. 'Geraldine, what about you?'

Anna remembered her mother looking a little uncomfortable. 'It's been so busy here, Lola, I thought they were all getting on so well.'

'They were indeed,' Lola had laughed. 'Just in the wrong combination.'

They'd all agreed what to do next. The wedding would have to be called off, the church booking cancelled, any engagement presents returned and word carefully put around a few key information-brokers in the town. Lola volunteered to do it all.

Anna had left the Valley the following day, still furious with Bett and Carrie. 'They've shown their true colours, Lola – Bett lives in fantasy land and Carrie is a selfish little cow, and I don't care how long it is till I see them again.'

'Now you're being childish.'

'Don't you start with the insults. I had enough from those two. I don't care if I never speak to either of them again.'

'Ah, so that's it. Not just disgust at their behaviour, you didn't like what they had to say either? And what's all this dramatic nonsense about never speaking to each other again? Of course you will. This situation will all blow over soon.'

'It won't, Lola. I saw a side to Bett and Carrie that I didn't like one bit. I'm not running to them, I'll tell you that. If they find it in themselves to apologise, well, we'll see, but I'm not making the first move.'

'When did you get so haughty? It must have happened when you were in Sydney because I certainly would have put a stop to it if I'd seen it happening here.'

'I am not haughty. That's a terrible thing to –' She'd stopped there at the sight of Lola laughing.

'Don't fight with me as well, darling, or you'll have no relatives left at all. All right, you're not haughty and you're not too proud either.'

Anna coloured, hating being caught out. 'I need to calm down, like the whole situation needs to calm down. And then I'll see how I feel.'

One month later she was still cross, and she'd heard nothing from Carrie or from Bett, who had now decided to stay in Melbourne. Well, if they weren't going to apologise for their behaviour, she wasn't either. The one-month silence between them grew to two, then to twelve.

Anna heard via Lola that Bett had gone travelling overseas. Carrie married Matthew, a very small affair in Adelaide – neither Anna nor Bett was invited. Lola attended with Geraldine and Jim, and sent a photo and a report to each of them, with a note of disgust at the end: 'This should have been a fun, happy day for the whole family. I am still ashamed of the three of you. It will only take one apology to get the ball rolling, you know . . .'

Anna put the photo away and turned all her attention to Glenn, Ellen and work, returning home to the motel just once a year, timing it to coincide with Matthew and Carrie's annual holiday away. One year became two, became three years, when the attack on Ellen happened, and took precedence over everything else.

'And that's how things were between us,' she said to Richard. 'Until Lola's party.'

'You've been through a lot lately, haven't you?' he said.

She lay looking into his eyes. 'Yes. Yes, I have, I think.'

She felt the touch of his fingers on her arm, on her bare skin. 'Too much to go through on your own. I wish I'd known you then. I'd like to have helped.'

She moved closer, moulding her body against his, feeling an

answering reaction from him, his fingers tracing her body. 'You're helping now,' she said. His lips met hers once again.

At that moment, in the vet's quarters of the Red Hills sheep station, Carrie was kissing Matthew's lips, then his chest, going lower and lower.

'Carrie . . .' he murmured.

'Shh,' she said. 'I told you, I'm tired of talking. We're not to say a word.'

'We have to talk.'

'Matthew, if you say another word I'm getting back in my car and driving straight back home.' Once she'd made her decision it had been simple. She loved Matthew and she was going to fight for him. She'd changed her clothes, packed a bag, and driven for two hours without stopping. He'd been in his quarters when she knocked on the door. She'd given him no chance to protest, no explanations, just moved into his arms and started kissing him. It had taken him only a second to respond.

She unbuttoned his jeans, lowered his boxer shorts, did exactly what she knew he loved and was rewarded with his groans of pleasure above her. She stopped abruptly, slowly took off her clothes and stood before him in her transparent pale-pink lace underwear.

'I've missed you so badly.' His voice was nearly hoarse.

She held herself a little away from him. 'And you don't regret marrying me?'

'No, I don't.'

'You don't want to go back to Bett?'

'No.'

'Are you sure?'

He pulled her close. 'Carrie, can you shut up about Bett for one minute and come here so I can . . .' He finished what he was going to do in a whisper in her ear.

Carrie shut up.

CHAPTER TWENTY-FOUR

THE PHONE rang as Bett was passing reception. It was her turn to mind the bar and the phone. Carrie was on a night off and Anna had said she wanted an early night. Ellen was in with Lola again. She'd decided her favourite sleeping place was her great-grandmother's double bed. Bett had checked on the pair of them a little while before. They'd both been asleep, books strewn on the bed around them.

Bett picked up the phone. 'Valley View Motel.'

'Hello, could I speak to one of your guests please.' The caller had a well-bred English accent. 'Mr Richard Lawrence.'

'Certainly, sir. I'll put you through to his room.'

She tried it and got the engaged tone. 'Can I take a message? I'm afraid I can't get through at the moment.'

'I've been trying for the past two hours and it's been constantly engaged. And his mobile is turned off too. Is that a small motel?'

'Reasonably small, yes. But it's a good motel.'

He laughed. 'I'm sorry. I'm not asking for economic reasons. It's just it's urgent I speak to Richard this evening. Would it be possible for someone to knock on his door in case he's accidentally left the phone off the hook? I need to check something with him urgently.'

'Of course. Who can I tell him is calling?'

'Please tell him it's Charlie. It's about the filming.'

Bett walked over to Richard's room. The curtains were drawn but she could see the faint outline of a bedside lamp. She knocked softly at the door. 'Richard, I'm sorry to disturb you. There's an urgent phone call.'

She heard moaning.

'Richard?'

Another kind of deep sigh.

Good God, was he all right? 'Richard?' She tried the handle.

The door swung open just as Richard and Anna reached orgasm together.

Bett was back at the reception desk in record time. 'Hello? Um, Richard is a bit tied up at the moment. Can I take your number and get him to call you back?'

'Are you sure he didn't want to be disturbed?'

'Pretty sure.' She didn't know who had looked the more startled, them or her.

'Could I speak to Lola, then?'

How did he know Lola? 'She's asleep, I'm afraid.'

'Damn.' He sighed. 'I'll just have to leave a message, then. Can you tell him we need to change the filming arrangements? Can he have everything set up for the day after tomorrow rather than next week? He'll know what I mean. And could he ring me as soon as possible to confirm?'

She took his details, and tucked the note in her pocket. There was no way she was going to go back to Richard's room with the message. Not yet, anyway. She was completely shocked. How long had this been going on between them? What about Glenn? What about Ellen?

She was in the kitchen making up the breakfast trays for the morning when she heard the door open behind her.

'Bett?' It was Anna. 'I think we need to talk.'

Bett didn't turn around. 'Anna, you don't have to explain anything. Seriously. What you do is your own business.' Bett picked up the next order form – one cereal, bacon and eggs, eggs hard not runny, underlined five times. And honey, not marmalade please. Also underlined.

'Bett, I want to explain.'

Bett picked through the box of preserves, searching for a little sachet of honey. 'You don't need to.'

'I still want to explain. I don't want this to cause another rift between us.' She hesitated. 'I know you were a bit interested in Richard.'

Bett kept busy with the tray. 'It's hardly the same situation, is it? I mean, I was engaged to Matthew when Carrie slept with him. All I'd done with Richard was tell you I might like to have a drink with him.' An awful thought occurred to her. 'Were you laughing at me? You and Richard? Laughing that I was going to invite him out?'

'No, Bett, we weren't. I promise we weren't. Richard doesn't even know you were going to ask him out. Please, Bett. Please put down that bloody honey and listen to me.'

Bett turned. Anna was dressed in a silk dressing-gown. Bett was struck by how tired and fragile she looked. 'So how long has this been going on between you?'

'Not long. A week or two.'

'And what about Glenn?'

'Glenn and I have been over for a long time, Bett. He's having an affair.'

'He's *what*?'

Anna walked over, shut the kitchen door and started talking.

Forty minutes later, Bett was holding her crying sister close against her. 'Oh, Anna, I'm so sorry for you. I didn't realise it had been so bad. Why didn't you tell us?'

'When? How? We weren't talking.'

'But what about telling Lola? I can't believe you've been through all this on your own.'

'It was pride. I knew if I told Lola, she'd tell you and Carrie. And I decided I could bear the life, the silences with him, more than I could bear the two of you telling me you'd been right. That he wasn't right for me. That I shouldn't have married him. All the things you both said that night.'

'Does Ellen understand what's going on?'

'Some of it. She's picked up the tension, and the fact he's away so much. Even though he'd try and get back in time to take Ellie to school most mornings.' Glenn would come in, freshly showered from Julie's bathroom, to be sitting there in the kitchen when Ellen woke up, for all the world the perfect father. 'That's the only good thing. He adores her at least. And she adores him. And he's wonderful with her.' It was a simple fact. 'It's the two of us . . .' She stopped, started crying again. 'It's been a mess, Bett. A horrible, awful, lonely mess . . .'

Bett held her close until the tears stopped again. 'And this thing with Richard?' she asked softly.

'I don't know. All I know is that he is kind and he listens to me and he makes me laugh. It might last a day or a week but it's what I need now. Do you understand?'

Bett thought of her night with Daniel three years ago. 'Yes, I do.'

'I'm sorry. I should have told you the night you were going to ask Richard for a drink. Told you that he and I were becoming friends.'

'I don't mind at all. Really, I don't.' She smiled. 'But you might want to think about locking the door from now on.'

Anna hugged Bett close again. 'We needed to talk. Years before this. Why has it taken this long?' She took a step back. 'Bett, I'm so sick of having secrets from each other. Please, can't you and Carrie sort things out too? Have you talked to her about Matthew yet?'

Bett shook her head, wary again.

'Please, Bett. You have to. She thinks you're still in love with him, I'm sure of it. You need to –'

The door opened behind them. It was Richard. 'I'm sorry to interrupt. I'll come back –'

Bett was relieved. She moved away from Anna. 'It's fine, really.'

He looked uncomfortable. 'Bett, I must apologise. I'm sorry if that put you in an embarrassing position.'

Her lip twitched. Actually it had been him in the embarrassing position. 'It's fine, Richard. And I'm very sorry for barging in on you like that.' She took out the note from her pocket. 'I had a message for you. Someone called Charlie rang to tell you the filming will have to take place the day after tomorrow not next week. That you'd know what he meant but could you call him back.'

'The day after tomorrow?'

Bett nodded.

'Is something wrong?' Anna asked him.

He gave a slightly awkward smile. 'I think there's something I'd better tell you both.'

As she drove into the Clare Valley that night, Carrie knew that everything had changed for the better. She loved Matthew and she knew he loved her. He had actually cried in her arms.

'Carrie, I stopped loving Bett when I met you. I don't know any more if that was what I felt for Bett. We got on well, but –'

'But she loved you so much. She was so upset when you split up.'

'I know. I'm so sorry, but I couldn't do anything about it. I had to be with you.'

They talked about the past few months, about the fighting and the separation. 'You changed when Lola started talking about Bett coming back.'

'I got so worried that you'd decide you'd chosen the wrong girl.'

'Of course I wouldn't. But it felt like you were trying to push me away. So I went. But I missed you, really missed you.'

'It was other things too. You started talking about money all the time.' She paused, then forged ahead. 'You stopped talking about having a baby.'

He had held her close. 'Carrie, I didn't think we could afford to have a baby yet. I want one as much as you do, but I want us to have some security first. I'm not qualified yet. The house isn't finished. I want it to be all ready when the baby comes.'

'So you do want one?'

'Of course I do. I tried to explain that's how I felt, but I couldn't get through to you.'

Carrie recalled heated conversations, flaring into rows, which generally ended in her storming out, back to the motel or over to a friend's house. That was what he had been trying to tell her, she realised guiltily. She'd heard 'I don't want a baby', when what he had been saying was 'I don't want a baby yet'.

That morning over breakfast he had agreed to come back to the Valley to meet Bett. He would come the day after tomorrow, in fact. Carrie kept driving, straight to the motel. It was after ten but she was determined to speak to Bett that night, to arrange a time and place for the meeting.

All the motel lights were on. She was surprised to find both her sisters in the office. Anna was on the land line, Bett on the mobile phone. Bett was finishing a call just as Carrie walked in.

'Carrie, you're back early. That's great. Can you –'

'In a moment, Bett.' She couldn't let herself be distracted. 'I'm sorry to get right to the point but we need to talk about something.'

'In a minute, Carrie. Something's come up. We need to ring –'

'It's important.' Her tone surprised them both. 'Matthew is coming back to the Valley and he wants to see you. And I want him to see you. Do you still want to see him?'

Bett blinked at her. 'Sure. Yes. Fine. Can we worry about him later, though?' She thrust a list of phone numbers at her sister. 'We've got a musical emergency on our hands.'

By eleven o'clock the following morning the cast and a hastily assembled crew were in the Clare Town Hall. Len was directing a small group of men, who were moving paint pots, set panels and ladders noisily across the wooden floor. The piano had been transported from the motel in the back of a refrigerated truck, sandwiched between twenty boxes of ice-cream. They were just waiting on the arrival of the forklift from the local supermarket to help lift it onto the stage.

Richard was worried. 'It's not a full-scale documentary, Anna. It's just a short segment. Maybe only a few minutes long. I'm worried you're going to too much trouble.'

Anna lowered her voice. 'I think your friend Charlie is doing me a favour, actually. We'd never have got this done on time otherwise.'

Bett had phoned her editor, Rebecca, to see if she could come and lend a hand too.

'Are you going to ring Daniel?' Rebecca asked. 'Can you tell him if he needs someone to look after his mother, I'll do it. He'd probably be more use to you than me.'

'What do you mean look after his mother?'

'Well, not look after. Sit with. Listen, I'll save you the bother and ring him myself and you can get onto the others. Should I tell him to come straight to the town hall? Okay, see you.'

Lola, her arm still in its sling, was watching all the activity from a chair to the side of the stage. It was an excellent vantage point. In a corner of the hall, three of the ladies from the charity shop were organising the costumes onto racks. Bett was at the piano, frowning a lot but otherwise looking in control of her little band of musicians, who had been summoned straight from the high school, still in their uniforms. Len was moving set panels. As Lola watched, Daniel Hilder arrived and started helping him. Up on the stage, Carrie was practising her solo dance scene, striking quite an elegant pose. One thing puzzled Lola. Anna's behaviour with Richard Lawrence. Were eyes deceiving her or was there a lot of flirting going on there? More than flirting, in fact. Little hand touches. Glances. Quick conversations.

She made her way over to Bett and sat down on the piano stool beside her. 'Hello, darling.'

'Hello, Lola,' Bett smiled distractedly. Some of the songs weren't working, now that she had seen them performed on stage. The tempo or the length was wrong. She was going to have to cut a verse out of 'Oh What a Beautiful Morning' and quicken the tempo of

'I Could Have Danced All Night'.

'Bett, can we have a word about Richard Lawrence?'

'Mmm?' Bett had her pen in her mouth, sheet music in one hand and was trying out a chord with the other.

Lola lowered her voice. 'Have you and he had another dinner or a drink or anything since the night I was so tired?'

'Me and Richard?' Bett took the pen out of her mouth. 'Oh no, Lola. Richard's having an affair with Anna. Anna and Glenn's marriage has broken up, too, by the way. Months ago. He's been having an affair with his PA. I only found out last night. Sorry. I know Anna would have told you too but all this took over.'

Lola didn't even blink. 'Oh. I see. Well, I'll leave you to it, then.' She returned to her chair and sat for a moment taking all that in. Anna and Richard. Who would have thought? She turned slightly so she could see them, standing on the edge of the stage. Anna was smiling at something he was saying. His expression was courteous. Mindful. And very affectionate. Still waters ran deep, as the saying went. As for the break-up with Glenn – was she surprised? Not particularly, she realised. She actually quite liked Glenn, with his bristling energy and booming voice. He'd always been so good with Ellen, too. But possibly hell to be married to. No, perhaps Anna was better off with a gentle man for a while. Yes, she quite approved, she decided.

Len's voice sounded through the hall. 'That's it, Daniel. No, sorry, a bit to the left. Now right. Forward. Forward. No, back again. To tell you the truth, I think it might be upside down.'

Lola watched as Daniel Hilder and Len stood in front of one of the Terowie Railway Station set panels and determined that, yes, it was indeed upside down. They carefully lowered it to the floor again. Lola put on her glasses and took the opportunity to assess Daniel one more time. He was good-humoured, that much was obvious. Anyone who could work with Len for more than ten minutes without throwing up their arms and running shrieking from the room was definitely good-humoured. And patient. He could do with a haircut, though. And he would look a bit neater if he tucked his shirt in every now and again. But that casual, unstructured look was quite the fashion, according to a TV show she'd seen the night before. Yes, he'd do fine. A worthy second choice.

Operation Bett and Daniel sounded so much better, anyway.

CHAPTER TWENTY-FIVE

CHARLIE ARRIVED at half past nine in the morning, sweeping into the town hall with his film crew. He was as flamboyant as Richard was quiet, long hair tied back in a ponytail, hugely amused by everything and everyone. 'Anna, it's a pleasure. I've heard great things about you. And Bett, I'm charmed. And you must be Caroline, is that right? But where is the magnificent Lola, whose phone calls have been entertaining me so hugely these past few days?'

'I'm right here.' They turned around. Lola was dressed in a brightly coloured combination of a long red satin overshirt, wide-legged paisley trousers, glittering costume jewellery, teased white hair and bright-red lipstick. Her sling was of gold lamé. She had wound a coloured ribbon around her walking cane.

Charlie bowed deeply. 'Lola, it's an honour. I don't suppose you could do that entrance for me again? On film this time?'

She gave him her most dazzling smile. 'Darling, I'll come somersaulting in if you want me to.'

An hour later Anna had nearly chewed her bottom lip to pieces. It had taken three takes to get 'My Favourite Things' right. The train stalled midway across the stage in the first verse of 'Chattanooga

Choo Choo'. General MacArthur forgot his lines and said 'I might return' instead of 'I shall return'. Mrs MacArthur defied Anna and started speaking in her English accent as soon as the camera was rolling. Carrie's solo version of 'I Could Have Danced All Night' was beautiful until two of the dancers gave a yelp behind her. They'd trodden on each other's toes.

But Charlie was delighted. Not just plenty of material for his own program, he'd whispered to Richard, but some perfect footage to sell on to one of those video blooper shows. Especially when the front of the train took off, leaving the engine driver standing behind on an empty stage. And the marching scene when the two soldiers missed their step and clashed, forehead to forehead, into each other.

Charlie strode into the centre of the hall and clapped his hands. 'Wonderful job, everyone, just wonderful. If we can have the three granddaughters up here singing "Sisters" together, we're done for the day.'

Bett turned from the piano. Carrie stopped in the middle of the stage. On the hall floor Anna stepped forward. 'Sorry, Charlie, that's not part of the show.'

'But it's in the script.' He waved his copy.

Anna noticed he had a copy of Lola's original version. 'No, we took it out.'

He frowned. 'But that's the charm of the whole story. I had the whole thing edited in my head. Shots of Terowie, the MacArthur plaque at the railway station, snippets from the musical, an interview with Lola, the three of you singing, finishing up with Lola coming in proudly behind you.'

Lola stepped forward. 'Would you want me to be smiling, Charlie, or would you prefer I had a tear in my eye?'

'We'll try both, Lola, I think. So you'll do it, girls? Terrific.' He didn't give them a chance to protest, turning to call to the cast and his crew. 'All right, everyone. Thanks for a great morning's work. We'll have a break and be back in twenty minutes with the three sisters on stage together.'

Bett sat at the piano, fighting a rush of memory and self-consciousness. Back with the three sisters on stage together? Oh no, they wouldn't be. She couldn't do it. Not in front of all those people. In front of Richard. In front of Daniel. All of them thinking the same thing that boy in the audience had thought all those years ago . . .

'Bett?'

She turned. Anna and Carrie had come up to the piano. Anna seemed exhilarated after the filming. 'What do you think? Will we do it?'

'No,' Bett said automatically. She said it to Anna, trying not to look at Carrie.

'Come on. It'll be fun.'

'I really don't want to, Anna. Thanks anyway.'

Anna noticed then that Kaylene was standing nearby and blatantly eavesdropping. Anna spoke loudly and deliberately. 'Let's go backstage, then, will we? See if we can remember all the words.'

They followed her into the long dressing-room behind the stage, past rows of stacked chairs, trestle tables, coat racks and a makeup mirror covered in fly spots. Anna checked that they had it to themselves, then turned to Bett again. 'This isn't because of that Piggy in the Middle business, is it? Bett, that was more than fifteen years ago, for God's sake. Carrie apologised to you. I apologised to you. Can't you leave it all behind?'

Bett felt a ripple of temper start inside her. 'It's not always that simple, Anna.'

'Of course it is. Is it really going to kill you to get up on stage again? You know how much it would mean to Lola. And it would mean a lot to me, too. We can talk about it all again now if we have to. Apologise again if we have to. Can't we, Carrie?'

There was only silence from Bett and Carrie.

Anna lost her temper. 'Fine. Brilliant. More silences. Well, I've had enough of it, do you hear me? All this tiptoeing around each other. All the things we won't talk about. Well, not any longer. I'm going to start talking about all the things the three of us have managed to avoid so beautifully the past month. How long is this going to go on otherwise? Another three years?' She was having trouble getting her breath, and had to pause for a moment. 'I hereby put it on the record that I hated that stupid fight we had. I hated getting caught up in it. I hated the fact you both came running to me to try and fix it and I ruined it. Do you think I liked not talking to you both? Liked having my marriage crumble around my ears and not having anyone to talk about it with, or –'

'Marriage crumble?' Carrie was shocked into speech. 'But Glenn worships you.'

'No, he doesn't, Carrie. Glenn and I are getting divorced. And in the new spirit of openness, here's another piece of news. I'm having an affair with Richard Lawrence and loving every minute of it.'

Carrie turned to Bett. 'Did you know about all this?' At Bett's nod, she lost her temper too. 'Of course you did. Fine. Perfect. The two of you, ganging up on me again, like you always have.'

'What? What are you talking about?' Bett was furious now as well. 'It was never me and Anna. It was always the two of you, doing it all so well, managing everything so perfectly. I was always the one who was left behind.'

'Stop it, Bett,' Anna snapped. 'Stop changing the facts to suit yourself. You did it with Matthew three years ago but I'm not going to let you do it again now.'

Carrie tensed. 'What do you mean she did it with Matthew? Did what with Matthew?'

'Changed the facts. Didn't you, Bett? And I still don't understand why.'

'Anna, stop it –'

'No, Bett. I've been trying to talk to you about this since we got here. You know exactly what I'm talking about and it's time Carrie knew too. Time we brought all of this business out in the open so we can get on with our lives and –'

'I've been trying,' Carrie interrupted. 'I've asked Matthew to come and see Bett. I know I should have done it before now, but it's been very difficult –'

'It's not just about seeing Matthew again, Carrie. Is it, Bett? It goes back further than that.'

Bett's face was burning. 'This is wrong, Anna. This is the wrong way to do it.'

'Then what is the right way? Because I don't know any more. All I know is I've had enough of secrets and rows and the three of us not talking about things. We were lucky to have each other and now it's all ruined.'

'It's not ruined.' Bett stared at Anna, remembering all her sister had been through with Glenn and Ellen. On her own, because Bett had been too proud to admit the truth to Carrie, to try to heal the rift between them.

'It is ruined.' Anna seemed defeated. 'Okay, then, forget it. I tried, but I can't make you do it. I'll go and tell Charlie we won't be singing together because we're never going to be friends again, so there's no point.' She was nearly at the door when Bett spoke.

'Anna, wait. Please.' She took a breath. 'I'll tell her.'

Carrie was looking back and forth between the two of them. 'What? Tell me what?'

'About Matthew and me. About what happened three years ago.' Bett could feel Anna's eyes on her, willing her to tell the truth. 'I was going to split up with Matthew, Carrie. I didn't want to marry him.'

Carrie went still. 'I don't believe you. You're just saying this now.'

'It's the truth. I'd been talking to Anna about it. Telling her things weren't going well with us.'

Carrie looked at Anna. Anna nodded. 'What do you mean not going well?'

Bett wavered. How honest could she be about the man who was now her sister's husband? 'I'd realised we weren't suited to one another. I don't know if we ever had been.'

Carrie seemed genuinely shocked. 'Then why did you get engaged?'

Bett told the truth. 'Because I thought he would make me feel better. Stop me making mistakes. Help me to fit in. I thought that once I had a boyfriend everything would be all right.'

'So were you ever in love with him?'

She paused. 'No, I don't think I was.'

'But I don't understand. You were so upset when . . . when he fell in love with me.'

'I was hurt. Of course I was. And shocked. But I was just as upset with you. And then with Anna as well. It was the way you both reacted. You, Carrie, as if it was your right. You didn't even seem surprised that Mathew would have fallen in love with you. It was as if you expected it to happen. All this dreamy talk, that it was

357

written in the stars, that it had swept you both off your feet. And it was the way you told me, as if I could never hope to understand, that it was something way out of my reach. The way it had always been.' The words were pouring out of Bett now. 'And you, Anna. When I came to you after Matthew and Carrie told me, all I wanted was your sympathy. And you just stood there, all cool and collected, making me feel like I had made a mess of everything yet again.'

'I didn't, Bett. I just wanted you to admit that you'd been having doubts about him. Because you had been. But you just lost your temper and started attacking me instead.'

'I couldn't help it. It just seemed that you were criticising me, judging me again. And I couldn't bear it.' She felt tears in her eyes and roughly wiped them away. 'It just seemed like the final proof, that I was stuck in the middle, that I'd never be as good as either of you.'

'But how did you think it was for me?' Carrie said passionately. 'I fell in love with him, and you wouldn't stay long enough to let me tell you that it was genuine. You wouldn't listen to us, even though we wanted to try and explain. And when I went to you, Anna, you just attacked me too, asked me was I sure that it wasn't just infatuation. You just spoke to me as if I was a child, like you always had.'

'I couldn't win, could I?' Anna said. 'Caught in the middle, yet again. I told Bett she should admit the truth, to you and to Matthew, and she just flew off the handle. And then you flew off the handle too, Carrie. You told me to mind my own business, told me that you were an adult, that you could do what you wanted. And I thought, well, to hell with the pair of you.'

'So did I,' Carrie said. 'That's exactly what I thought. To hell with the pair of you. I wanted to live my own life.'

'Me too,' Bett said. 'That's exactly what I wanted to do. As far away as I could.'

Carrie turned to her. 'That's why you went away? Not because of me and Matthew?'

'It was about you and Matthew at the start. I couldn't stay here, with everyone talking and whispering about us.'

'So why didn't you come back, though? Why did you stay away?'

Bett hesitated. 'Because once I'd got over the shock and got through the first few months in Melbourne, I realised I liked being away from you both. I liked the freedom. I liked being just me, not Bett, sister of Anna, or Bett, sister of Carrie. I had to get away from you both. I couldn't take it any longer.'

The words came haltingly as she tried to explain further. How sometimes it had been the best thing in the world to have a sister on either side, protected, surrounded. But how other times it had felt like she was being suffocated and squeezed. The oldest did it first, the youngest did it sweetest. What had been left for the one in the middle? She'd had to go away, hadn't she? Or she'd never have found herself, found what she was capable of . . . She slowly came to a halt. To her surprise, Anna and Carrie didn't look hurt. They looked – what? Relieved? As if they understood?

'I felt like that too,' Anna said suddenly. 'To begin with, anyway.'

Bett stared at her. 'What was there for you not to like? You always ruled the roost with us.'

'But I was so tired of it, Bett. Tired of sorting out your fights, tired of giving you both advice when I had my own life to live, tired of the two of you passing remarks about Glenn. Not just the night of our fight, but ever since I'd met him. It was getting to the stage I didn't know what I thought of him myself. I kept getting confused with what you both thought about him.'

'I was glad at the start, too.' Carrie said in a low voice. 'It had always been the two of you ahead of me, getting all the grown-up attention, while I was just the silly little sister. And it was the same that night we fought about Matthew, Anna. You made me feel like I'd been sneaky and devious. And I hadn't been, really I hadn't. We both hated the fact it was going to hurt you, Bett. If there had been any other way of telling you –'

'Why didn't you say that to me, then?'

'You wouldn't listen. You just went running off as soon as Matthew told you. And then we were all fighting and . . . and it was just a mess. And the next morning you were gone before we had a chance to talk to you again.'

'I had to go. I had to get away from everything, from all of you. I wanted to be me for a while. Just me. Not one of the Alphabet Sisters or even one of the Quinlan sisters any more.'

'And do you still feel like that? Now?' Anna looked very serious.

Bett shook her head. 'I haven't felt like that for a long time. I got so lonely without you both. Once the novelty wore off. Once I'd proved to myself I could live away from you, that I could do things on my own, even live overseas. That I wasn't a disaster area. I wanted the freedom, I loved the freedom, but –' her voice wavered. 'I missed you both so much. And then Ellen was attacked, and, Anna, this is a terrible thing to say, but one part of me was glad, because it was a reason to write to you. So I did. I sent that letter. But then I didn't hear back so I thought, well, you didn't want contact again.'

'Me too,' Carrie said. 'I wanted to go to Sydney, but Lola and Mum got in first. I rang and talked to Glenn, left a message. But then I didn't hear anything back either.'

Anna remembered receiving Bett's letter, reading it once, then putting it away. She remembered Glenn passing on Carrie's message and then doing nothing about it. 'I couldn't contact either of you. I'm sorry. I didn't have any room for anyone but Ellen. I was so angry with everyone at that time, at myself for letting it happen, at Glenn for blaming me. I couldn't handle anyone else. I'm sorry.'

There was silence and then Carrie spoke. 'Do we all have to tell the truth now?'

'It might help,' Anna said.

'I think you both should know that Matthew and I have been separated for a while.'

'*What*?' Anna and Bett spoke in unison.

'We've been separated for a few months. We only decided to get back together yesterday.'

'So we were fighting about the two of you and you weren't even together?' Bett said.

'We were at the start. But everything went bad for a while.'

'Oh, Carrie, why?' Anna asked.

'Misunderstandings about all sorts of things. And I got guilty. I thought it was because of the way we got together. That I was being punished for taking Matthew away from Bett.' She wasn't looking at either of them. 'And I wasn't sure if Matthew was over Bett.'

'Carrie, he was. I'm sure he was.' Bett had seen the wedding photo. She knew Matthew had never looked at her the way he looked at Carrie in the photo. 'I'm sorry. I'm sorry for not telling you before, Carrie. And I'm sorry that you had to go through everything on your own, Anna. It had just gone on for so long, and even though I wanted to I just didn't know how to fix it.' She was embarrassed to feel her eyes filling with tears. 'It was easier to keep away, to keep blaming the two of you, rather than myself.'

'It doesn't matter now, does it?' Anna asked. 'We're talking again, aren't we?'

They both nodded.

'And we'll keep talking, won't we? No matter what?'

Another nod.

There was a warm silence for a moment and then Carrie turned. 'Bett, am I allowed to ask you something personal?'

She tensed again. 'I might not answer it, but ask, sure.'

'Is there something going on with you and Daniel Hilder?'

Bett looked up in surprise.

'It's just I noticed he looks at you all the time in a particular way. Doesn't he, Anna?'

Anna nodded enthusiastically. 'Like this.' She put on a pantomime adoring glance, all big eyes and amused smile.

'He does not.'

'He does, Bett. But it's more like this.' Carrie put on an even more exaggerated look, soft smile and indulgent expression.

'Stop it. You're imagining it.'

Carrie grinned, then turned her attention to Anna. 'And you and Richard are really an item?'

Anna nodded.

'Wow. So I should give him a discount on his room, then? Or will he be moving in with you?' She laughed. 'Just joking.'

Anna smiled. 'And you and Matthew, Carrie?'

Carrie's expression softened. 'It's okay. It's very good again, actually.' She hesitated. 'You really don't mind, Bett?'

'I don't mind at all, Carrie. I honestly don't mind one bit.'

They moved unselfconsciously towards each other, into a long, warm hug. Then Carrie stepped back.

'Do you want to meet him again, Bett? Now?'

'Now?'

'Matthew's here. He came down this morning. He's outside. Will I get him?'

Bett hesitated, then nodded.

Carrie was nearly at the door before she turned and came back. 'This is a bit awkward, but . . . well, do we need to tell Matthew that you were going to break up with him? It's just I'd hate to hurt his feelings.'

Bett nearly laughed out loud. But of course Carrie wanted to protect Matthew. 'Perhaps he doesn't need to hear it right now.'

Carrie nodded, relieved. 'I'll be back in a moment.'

Anna waited until she was gone before she spoke. 'Do you want me to go, to leave the three of you alone?'

Bett shook her head. 'No, all for one, one for all, don't you think?'

'I'm glad you told her, Bett. I'm sorry I had to force it.'

'I'm glad you did.'

They heard noises from the hall, as the camera crew finished its break. Set panels were being dragged across the stage again. They heard a faint hum of traffic from the main street. A car door shutting. Footsteps and the glass door opening. Bett turned and there he was, with Carrie a few feet behind.

'Hello, Bett. Hello, Anna.'

'Hello, Matthew,' they said in unison.

Bett took in every detail of his appearance. The sandy hair, the curls now cropped short. The square, kind face. The work clothes. The stocky body. It was like looking at someone she had been at school with years before.

He looked uncomfortable. 'How are things, Bett?'

'They're fine. It's good to see you again.' And it was. Nothing more and nothing less.

'You too.' Matthew gave an embarrassed laugh, looking from one to the other. 'Bett, I'm sorry for what happened. With me and Carrie. For hurting you like that.'

For one moment she was tempted to tell him the truth. That she should never have gone out with him in the first place. That it had been for all the wrong reasons. Then she looked at Carrie, standing proudly beside him, and realised that this definitely wasn't the time for the truth. 'It's fine, Matthew.'

He didn't seem convinced. 'If Lola was here she would probably use her truth stick, I suppose. Make us all say how we're really feeling.'

'You know about the truth stick?' Anna asked.

Matthew nodded. 'And the Alphabet Sisters stories. Lola used to like telling us them, didn't she, Carrie?' He gave another self-conscious laugh. 'Not that Lola ever used the truth stick on me. It was more a family thing, wasn't it? Very handy sometimes, though, she said.'

'It was, yes,' Anna said. She turned to Bett. There was challenge in her voice, even though she was smiling. 'If Lola was pointing the truth stick at you now, what would you say, Bett?'

Bett answered honestly. 'I would probably say I'm feeling a bit uncomfortable but I'm also very relieved to finally see Carrie and Matthew together. And I think they make a good pair. And I'm so sorry it's taken this long for me to tell you both how I felt. And you, Anna?'

'I'd probably say I've been feeling sick about all of this for weeks – no, years – too. And I'm glad it's over and I hope we won't ever have a fight like this again.'

Carrie was gripping Matthew's hand. 'And I would say I'm sorry for any hurt we caused you, Bett. And you, Anna. And I hope you forgive us.'

'And I would say about bloody time.'

It was Lola, standing in the doorway. 'That's the thing about swear words,' she said, smiling broadly. 'Use them sparingly and they always have much more impact, don't you think? So, all set to do the "Sisters" song for Charlie?'

Oh hell, Bett thought. She'd forgotten all about that. 'I'm sorry, Lola, but I can't do it.'

'Why ever not?'

'I've forgotten the words.'

'If she has, then so have I,' Anna said.

'Me too,' Carrie added.

'Oh, I'm sure it'll come back to you once you get started. It's that one about the mister coming between the sisters. No? Then it's just as well I brought these.'

She passed over three sheets of lyrics. They were cornered. 'Come on, then. Charlie and his cameraman are waiting. He was just saying again how this is going to be the centrepiece of his segment.' Complete lies, of course. Charlie had no interest or intention of using any of this footage of the Alphabet Sisters. He had staged that little scene earlier purely as a favour to Lola. She had explained the whole situation to him on the phone the day before and he had been highly amused and happy to oblige. And, by the looks of things, it had worked.

'Come on then, girls. Time's money and I'm short of both.' She started shooing them in front of her, one by one. Then she stopped. 'And you too, Matthew. I've had the very amusing idea of using you as well.'

Half an hour later, Charlie strolled over to where Lola was sitting, watching all the action. She took his hand and smiled up at him. 'Thank you, Charles darling. You're quite an actor yourself.'

He bowed deeply. 'A pleasure to be of service. You never know,

I may end up using the footage yet. They were rather good, weren't they? Some wonderful harmonies.'

'Once they stopped laughing, yes, they were. That was always their problem. They didn't take it seriously enough.'

'Matthew was a good sport, to stand there like that while they sang that "Sisters" song around him.'

Not so much a good sport as terrified of what might happen if he didn't do as he was told, more like it. 'Wasn't he just?'

'I'll send you a tape of it all anyway. For your records.'

'My records. What a marvellous phrase. Thank you, I'd love that.'

Lola gazed around. Anna, Bett, Matthew and Carrie were in a corner of the room with Richard and Daniel, the group of them laughing. Well, thank God. If the feud had gone on one day longer she was going to go simply and utterly mad.

'So what's your next project going to be?' Charlie asked.

'Well, I have the little matter of our gala world premiere, of course. But after that?' She smiled up at him. 'A musical adaptation of *One Flew Over the Cuckoo's Nest*, I think.'

Their parents arrived home that night. There was an hour debriefing about their holiday, an hour hearing about the musical, ten minutes on Lola's accident and then Jim Quinlan was back behind his bar, sorting bottles, and Geraldine was in the kitchen organising the freezer.

Lola watched the three girls vying for their mother's attention and had to stop herself from shaking Geraldine. She'd managed to restrain herself for many years. She could manage for another few, she decided.

In bed that night, Jim and Geraldine were talking about their holiday and homecoming.

Geraldine took off her glasses and reached out to turn off the bedside light. 'The girls seem to be getting on very well again, don't they?'

'Remarkably well. I was sure there would have been at least one row or something while we were away, but it seems not. Perhaps that's all it ever needed, just getting them back under the same roof again.' He chuckled. 'I take my hat off to Lola.'

Jim didn't see Geraldine's expression. 'They're grown girls. I knew they'd sort it out eventually themselves.'

'Of course they would. Goodnight, darling.'

'Goodnight, Jim.'

He put his arm around his wife and shut his eyes.

CHAPTER TWENTY-SIX

BETT WOKE up with just the slightest hint of a hangover. She and Anna and Carrie had stayed up talking and drinking red wine until very late. Richard and Matthew and Lola had joined in at first, before stealing away one by one, leaving the three girls on their own. They had taken over the small motel bar, shamelessly helping themselves to glasses of wine from their father's fine cellar of local reds, leaving increasingly scrawled notes to him.

'He won't mind, I know he won't,' Carrie had said as she opened one of the oldest bottles of shiraz. 'Anyway, it's not as if he can sack us, is it?'

Another time, after that much wine, Bett might have woken with a headache, a sense of the dreads. But not this morning. There was nothing to cringe about. She didn't feel that she had said anything stupid, or talked too much. She could remember every word, every joke, every laugh they had shared, even though it had been nearly two a.m. by the time they went to bed, practically pouring a giggling Carrie into the taxi they had called.

Bett stretched, enjoying the feel in her muscles, the look of the sunlight streaming in through the thin curtains, the sound of the birds outside. She had a glorious, light feeling inside her, that things were going to be okay again. That things were okay with Anna and Carrie again. She hadn't felt so good in years.

She checked the time. Eight o'clock. She'd better get up and get ready. She had two more assignments with Daniel that day, and they'd arranged to meet at the office at nine thirty.

There had been more teasing about him from Anna and Carrie the night before.

'You must have noticed something, Bett,' Anna had insisted.

'Picked up the *vibes* from him,' Carrie had added, in a bad American accent.

'You're reading too much into it,' Bett protested. 'We just get on really well. It's nothing more than that.'

'No?'

'No. Stop it, you two.'

'You really, genuinely, sincerely don't have any romantic feelings towards him?'

'No, I don't,' she said, fighting a little voice in her head that was suggesting something quite different.

'Then let me ask you a few simple questions.' Anna winked over at Carrie. The two of them were really enjoying this. 'Does Daniel make you laugh?'

'Yes. A lot.'

Anna was ticking them off on her fingers. 'Do you think he's good-looking?'

'Yes.'

'A-ha!' Carrie said. 'The giveaway.'

'I'm just stating a fact,' Bett said quickly. 'He is.'

'In what way is he good-looking?'

Bett took a sip of wine and thought about it. 'He's got gorgeous eyes, all kind of crinkly, and that lovely sort of dark shaggy hair, and he wears great clothes, I reckon.' She stopped. 'What? What are you both laughing at?'

'Nothing,' Anna said, quite straight-faced. 'So you've noticed all these things about him. You admit that you get on really well. He doesn't take his eyes off you. But you still don't think anything's going on between you?'

'It's not.'

Anna turned to Carrie. 'It's sweet that she's managed to keep her innocence for so long, Carrie, don't you think?'

'Remarkable really, in this day and age.'

'Stop it, you two. Leave me alone.' Bett had been laughing too by this stage. She was also thanking her lucky stars that she had stopped herself just in time from telling them all about her one-night stand with Daniel. God only knows what they would have made of that . . .

She hadn't minded the teasing one bit, though. It had been good fun. Not like old times all over again, either. Much better than that. It had been the start of new times between them.

Getting ready that morning, she chose her favourite dark-green shirt, her favourite vintage skirt and the Italian shoes that people always remarked on. She applied a bit of mascara. And while she was at it, she popped on a bit of lip gloss, too. She was going to be out and about doing these two interviews, so she may as well look presentable, she told herself.

'You look smart, Bett,' her father said as she walked into the kitchen for a coffee. 'Have you got something special on today?'

'No. Just doing a couple of stories for that tourism project.'

'With Daniel?' Lola piped up from her chair.

'Yes, actually.'

'Marvellous!' Lola beamed.

Lola didn't have to have looked quite so delighted, Bett thought as she walked into the newspaper office a half hour later. Her grandmother's face had lit up as if Bett had said she was heading off to elope to Gretna Green. What had got into everybody suddenly? She and Daniel were becoming good friends, that's all. Men and women could be friends, couldn't they? She and Daniel just got on well. They worked well together. They made each other laugh. Quite a bit, in fact. And yes, perhaps they'd had a night of pretty terrific sex three years before, but that was in the past. All it meant was . . . She stopped there. All it meant was if they were to have sex again, it would probably be just as great.

'Morning, Bett. Ready to get going again?'

It was Daniel.

The colour whooshed into her face.

She was a little awkward with him to begin with, she knew she was. As they spent the morning at an art gallery tucked away in the hills south of Clare, she was more businesslike than she'd been on any of the previous assignments. Brisk even. She noticed him glance at her once or twice.

'Everything okay with you, Bett?'

'Fine,' she said cheerily, cursing Anna and Carrie for putting the idea into her head.

After the art gallery their next stop was Sevenhill Cellars, the Valley's oldest winery.

'We've a few minutes before they're expecting us,' Daniel said, glancing at his watch. 'Do you mind if we take the scenic route? The light's good today for a shot I want to take over the hills.'

'No, I don't mind at all.'

Daniel smiled his thanks and then turned the car off the main road onto the bumpy dirt road.

Her reply echoed in her mind as she watched him stop and start the car at different spots along the road, choosing scenes where the sunlight filtered through clumps of gum trees, sending dappled light onto the rows of vines, or near the dry creek beds, lined with water-smoothed pebbles of different shapes and sizes. No, she didn't mind at all if she got to sit on the bonnet of the car in the sunshine and watch him at work. She didn't mind at all seeing him concentrate on finding the best picture, walking along the road looking for the right angle, sending her a grin when he took a shot he was happy with. She didn't mind at all if they got to spend a bit more time in the car together. She didn't mind, in fact, if they spent the rest of the day in the car together, talking and laughing.

The realisation came on slowly and surely throughout the day. She found herself watching him more closely, being more conscious of him than she ever had before. She was acutely aware of him walking close behind her as they were taken on a tour of the cool stone winery building, breathing in the rich smells of the wooden barrels of wine around them. As she interviewed the winemaker and spoke to the people at the cellar door, she knew Daniel was nearby. She watched him deftly take the cameras out of the bag, check settings and switch lenses. She noticed the casual, assured way he put light meters into his pockets, the way his body moved so lithely as he walked around, looking for good angles, trying for unusual shots. She noticed his manner with the people he was photographing, how quickly he put them at ease.

They drove back into Clare in the early afternoon. The sight of his lean, brown hands on the steering wheel was beginning to have quite an effect on her. The way he tapped his long fingers gently in time to the music on the radio. The way he changed the gears so skilfully. She dragged her eyes away from his hands, then found herself noticing his thighs instead, how good they looked in the jeans he was wearing. As they stopped at an intersection, he pushed back the rolled-up sleeve of his shirt to check the time. She noticed every detail in an instant. The brown skin of his arm, the golden hairs, the muscles. She nearly leapt out of her seat when he reached over suddenly to catch a brochure that kept sliding back and forth along the dashboard.

He sent her a puzzled look. 'Bett, are you sure you're okay today? You seem a bit distracted. Jumpy.'

'Do I? Am I? Sorry. I must be coming down with something.'

They started talking about the work they'd done that morning, and then the dress rehearsal for the musical. He casually referred to the fact that Matthew had been there and they were all getting on just fine, and she just as casually remarked that it was good to see Carrie and Matthew so happy together.

'I'll be able to die a happy man now too. I actually got to see the Alphabet Sisters perform.'

She pulled a face. 'I did warn you. We weren't exactly The Supremes.'

'Oh, I don't know. I just wish I'd seen you in your heyday. When you were really at the height of your powers.'

'Count your blessings that you didn't.'

He was laughing as he pulled into a shady spot in the main street, a hundred metres or so down from the *Valley Times* office. 'So did you have a triumphant last performance? The audience in tears, waving cigarette lighters at the three of you?'

'Not quite.' She hesitated for only a second. 'It was awful actually. Three boys shouted Piggy in the Middle at me when we were on stage one day and it ruined it for me from then on.'

'They called you Piggy in the Middle?'

She nodded.

'How ridiculous.'

'Ridiculous?' She didn't understand.

'Well, Pretty Girl in the Middle I could understand.'

She went still.

'Or Bright-eyed Girl in the Middle.'

She held her breath.

'Or Great Fun To Be With in the Middle.'

She was smiling now.

'But Piggy? No. They were three blind boys, obviously,' he said, very matter-of-fact. 'Three blind stupid boys. Three blind stupid boys who wouldn't know a world-class singer and performer if she came up and –' he foundered for a moment.

'Grunted in their faces?' she helped him.

He grinned. 'Well, I was thinking more along the lines of yodelled.'

Later that day Rebecca called her into her office. 'Everything go well today?'

'It did, thanks. Just the Drover's Experience story to go next week and that tourism project is all done.'

'You and Daniel getting along okay?'

'Yes, thanks.' She couldn't read the expression on Rebecca's face. 'I have been going easy on him, I promise. Like you asked me to.' She was still puzzled by what Rebecca had meant by that. Daniel hadn't let on that anything was wrong at all.

Rebecca was trying not to smile. 'I know. I suppose I was wondering what your definition of going easy on him might be.'

'Why?'

'It's just I had two calls today from people wondering why my reporter and my photographer were sitting in the company car in the main street for nearly an hour talking and laughing their heads off. Was it a stake-out, they wondered? Were we on to a hot story?'

Bett gave a strange-sounding laugh. 'God, this town. They just make up gossip if they can't find any, don't they?'

'Do they?' Rebecca smiled mischievously. 'You tell me. You've lived here longer than I have.'

CHAPTER TWENTY-SEVEN

OPENING NIGHT arrived. The last tickets had been sold that morning. It was a full house.

Lola had pulled out all the stops, raiding not just her own wardrobe, but Carrie's, Anna's and Bett's as well. It had taken everyone some discipline not to gasp or laugh too loudly when she first stepped out of her room, ready to be driven to the town hall by Jim. After seeing her, Geraldine had decided to drive down a little later.

Lola now stood, dressed in full splendour, at the front door of the town hall. Her floor-length orange taffeta skirt clashed with the purple tunic, which clashed with the gold wrap. It all clashed with her makeup. She had a rose and a fabric butterfly pinned in her hair, and nearly rattled as she walked from all the jewellery. Beside her, in a much more low-key outfit but just as bright a smile, was Ellen. She'd been put in charge of handing out programs as people came in.

Lola was shining, accepting compliments and handing them out just as enthusiastically. 'Mrs Gillespie, you look marvellous.' 'Yes, I am as proud as punch. It's a wonderful night for all of us.'

Ellen greeted every one who passed her with the same message. 'Good evening. Enjoy the show, won't you?'

Backstage, Anna was moving back and forth, checking on

costumes, makeup and sets. She was glad and relieved to feel the adrenalin coursing through her, giving her the energy and buzz she had always loved before a performance. She'd had a very bad night's sleep, tired but unable to sleep, feeling the tightness across her chest again. Perhaps that scan the young doctor had mentioned was a good thing, she'd thought as she lay there in the dark, thinking the worst. She'd confided in Richard, and been comforted by his matter-of-factness.

'It's probably asthma, by the sound of things. But the doctor's right. You're just as well to get it checked out. When is the test?'

In Adelaide, two days after the musical, she'd told him. She was going to return the costumes at the same time. She'd been surprised by his next words.

'Would you like me to come with you? I can help you carry things, wait while you do the tests and then take you somewhere really splendid for lunch. To celebrate the musical. And to celebrate you and –' he had stopped there. 'Well, just to celebrate.'

She had been very touched. 'I'd love that,' she'd said.

'Anna! Anna!' She turned as Len ran in, a panicked expression on his face. 'One of the wheels of the train has jammed. Has anyone got any oil?'

Anna swiftly produced a bottle from a basket by the window. She'd brought oil, nails, sticking plasters, double-sided tape, needle and thread, ready for any eventuality. There was even an industrial-sized upholstery stapler that Lola had produced from somewhere.

'Deep breath, now, Len. Everything's all right. Everything's going to be fine.'

'Damn right it is,' he said loudly, cheery again. 'Thanks, Anna. Break a leg, everyone.'

At the edge of the room, leafing through her music for the tenth time, Bett overheard and grinned. Probably not the best thing for Len to say, even if it was a theatrical tradition. Knowing his ability to create chaos, the entire cast breaking a leg each was entirely possible. She was loving this part of the evening, all the excitement before the show began. Carrie was beside the mirror, applying makeup to all the cast members, who were lined up in a row like laughing clowns at a fair. Lola's ladies from the charity shop were making last-minute adjustments to the costumes. In the middle of it all was Anna, calm, in control. As Bett caught her eye, Anna smiled then mouthed something.

'What?' Bett called.

Anna's voice came over clearly. 'Break an egg, Bett.'

Bett laughed. She'd completely forgotten the Alphabet Sisters' own version. 'Break an egg, Anna,' she called back. Carrie looked up and grinned too.

Bett tucked the music under her arm and went up onto the stage, nervous and excited. She peered through a gap in the curtains into the hall. It was now nearly filled. There was a warm, bubbling noise of conversation, mixed with the sounds of chairs scraping, people finding their seats and greeting friends. It was fifteen minutes to curtain up.

Bett made her way down the side stairs out into the little musical pit they had set up at the foot of the stage, the area marked out by trestle tables standing on their side. One wobbled as she went past. Len's work again, unfortunately. Such enthusiasm, but he had a mind like a dragonfly, jumping from one project to another before the first was finished.

The other members of her small band were already seated: a sax player, a guitarist and a drummer, each of them dressed in dark trousers and white shirt. She greeted them warmly, noticing their flushed cheeks, their bright eyes. From their excitement, it could have been Carnegie Hall, not the Clare Town Hall. She took her seat and nodded, and they began playing the first of the introductory tunes, Glenn Miller's 'In the Mood'. Looking up from the keyboard, her fingers so familiar with the notes, she spied Rebecca in the audience, with a gang of people from the newspaper. Daniel was at the end of the row. He winked at her as she caught his eye. She grinned and winked back.

The noise in the hall changed as Lola started making her way to the stage through the centre aisle. She climbed the stairs, then paused dramatically in the middle of the stage, just as Bett finished the last notes of Vera Lynn's 'We'll Meet Again'.

'Ladies and gentlemen, boys and girls, thank you all very much for coming tonight. My name is Lola Quinlan.' She gestured flamboyantly. 'Welcome to the world premiere of *Many Happy Returns*!'

At interval, Anna went out to the hall to say a quick hello to Richard and Lola. She couldn't get near her grandmother. Lola was standing in the middle of an admiring crowd, holding court. 'The idea first came to me in the middle of the night about twenty-five years ago . . .'

Anna smiled as Richard came up to her. 'So? What do you think?'

'It's wonderful.'

'Wonderful?' Anna pulled a face. 'I don't know about that.' She lowered her voice, started ticking things off on her fingers. 'General MacArthur forgot his lines again. The train got stuck. The dancing wasn't in formation. Some of the singing was flat . . .'

He caught her hand and squeezed it in his. 'And it's still wonderful. Look at the mood. Everyone's having a great time.'

She grinned. 'They are, aren't they?' The audience had cheered

Lola when she got up at the start. There had been some singing along with 'My Favourite Things' and 'Oh What a Beautiful Morning'. Len's trick with the corn – where the sheaves suddenly came up through the stage – had almost worked. They'd risen about three inches, at least, which was better than nothing. Kaylene had veered between her English and American accents, sounding vaguely South African by the final scene of the first act, but she had put across the right emotion.

Back at the piano, five minutes before the end of interval, Bett felt a touch on her arm. It was Daniel. 'Congratulations. It's hilarious.'

'Hilarious? It's supposed to be serious drama, not great fun.'

'Sorry. Of course it is. That's what I meant to say. It's hugely dramatic. The whole gamut of human emotions.'

'Careful. We have an audience participation spot, and I have connections with the director.' The bell sounded to indicate the end of the interval. 'Are you staying on for the party?'

'If that's okay. Len invited me, but I wasn't sure.'

'You were last-minute crew and nearly cast. Of course you should be there.' She wanted him to be there.

He smiled. 'Great. I'll see you later, then.'

'See you.' Bett was smiling too as she turned back to the piano. Lola was right. There was something very attractive about a man with a glint in his eye.

In the middle of the next act she heard a faint crying from the audience, like a child, but rising louder and louder. She turned her head slightly, to see Daniel help an elderly woman out of her seat and towards the back of the hall. The crying faded to a little whimpering sound. Were the war songs reviving sad memories? Bett brought her attention back to the stage as Kaylene did her best to reach a high note but unfortunately failed. Bett played extra loud to try and cover up for it.

They all crowded into the backstage area afterwards. The noise was deafening.

'We got five curtain calls! Five!' Carrie exclaimed. Not only that, she'd been applauded wildly after her rendition of 'I Could Have Danced All Night'. Lola had received another huge cheer and then called the three of them up beside her to receive enormous bouquets of flowers. Backstage it was all excitement, backslapping, relief, re-enactments of moments when scenes hadn't worked, overlaid with compliments and praise. Some of the cast took their makeup off and changed into normal clothes. But as the after-show party got underway, Bett noticed many of them were still in their costumes and stage makeup. They looked happy to stay in them forever, in fact. Lola was beaming as though lit from within, brighter even than the night of her party.

Bett was surprised by a sudden big hug. It was Rebecca. 'Congratulations, Bett. It was fantastic. I don't know how you all did it. What next, the West End?'

A face popped in between them before she had a chance to answer. Len the butcher. He kissed each of them on both cheeks, nearly spilling a glass of champagne. 'Bett, Rebecca, a night for celebration, don't you think?'

Bett clinked glasses with him. 'It was fantastic, Len. Thank you so much for all the hard work.'

'Well, I think we all contributed.' He leaned forward conspiratorially. 'You weren't put off by poor old Mrs Hilder's crying, I hope? Daniel was very good to bring her out, though, don't you think? His sister's the same, takes her out everywhere. Can't imagine my girls bringing me out if I lost my marbles like that. They'd have me locked in a home before I knew what had hit me.' He gave a loud roar of laughter, then raised his glass to them again. 'See you later, then, ladies. On the dance floor, perhaps?' He gave a little twist of his hips, then moved away.

Rebecca shook her head after him. 'And the prize for the most sensitive man in the Clare Valley goes to Len once again. Daniel would hate it if he heard his mother being talked about like that.'

'Is that the trouble at home you spoke about?'

Rebecca nodded. 'Seeing as Len has introduced the subject so delicately, yes, it is. Daniel's mother has Alzheimer's. That's why he came back to Clare, to look after her. He and his sister have been taking it in turns staying with her. But it got to the point that Mrs Hilder was beyond staying at home. They had to move her into Lilac House a week or two ago. You know it? The care house next to the hospital?'

Bett nodded.

'He only told me about it because there were times he'd need to leave work to go to her.'

'Why was it such a secret?'

'I don't think it was out of secrecy. It was more loyalty, a way of protecting their mother. You don't remember her?'

Bett shook her head.

'It's so sad. She was the most elegant, proper woman. You know the sort? Everything perfect, under control. And she just had a complete personality change the worse her condition became. She started swearing, going down the street in unsuitable clothing. The one good thing was she wasn't aware of what she was doing, but it was heartbreaking for Daniel and his sister, Christine. I think that's why they tried to look after her at home for as long as they could.

You know, getting carers, installing all sorts of things to stop her from hurting herself and to keep her occupied.'

Bett thought of the coloured lines, the signs on drawers and the locks on the cupboards she'd seen the day Daniel showed her his Dangerous video. They weren't for any grandchildren but for Mrs Hilder herself.

'Oh, the poor things. That must have been so hard for them all.'

'It has been, I think.'

'You wouldn't know it from Daniel, though, would you?' Bett said. 'He's so good-natured, so lovely all the time.'

Rebecca gave her a knowing look. 'Yes, he is, isn't he? He just gets on with it, I think.' She glanced around. 'I thought he might have come back after he took her back to Lilac House, but no sign of him. His poor mum must have got quite upset.'

Bett had already noticed he hadn't come back. She'd been keeping an eye out for him.

Rebecca hugged her again. 'Enough of such serious talk on your night of triumph. Come on, musical director, help me find a fresh bottle of champagne.'

Midway through the party, there was a sudden, loud clapping of hands. Someone was trying to get everyone's attention. Slowly the talk died down, and the music playing from the stereo was lowered. Lola stood in the middle of the room, with a glass of champagne in one hand. 'Thank you all. I promise I'll only be a minute. We've all got a lot of celebrating to do tonight and far be it from me to put a halt to your gallop.' There was laughter. 'Some weeks ago, when my three granddaughters reunited for my eightieth birthday, I said something to them that I meant from the heart. And I'd like to say it to all of you tonight as well. I never dreamed this would happen in the way it did. Thank you, each and every one of you. You've made an old lady very happy.'

There were cheers, and more applause. Then from the back someone shouted. 'Give us a song, Lola.'

She gave an imperious wave. 'Oh no, I'm far too old for that. I'm an observer these days, not a performer.'

'Oh come on, Lola. We all did it. Now it's your turn,' General MacArthur called.

At different spots around the room, Anna, Bett and Carrie started smiling. Anna wished Ellen was here to see this, but her daughter, so tired she had been drooping, had just been taken back to the motel by Geraldine and Jim.

'Yes, come on now, Lola. You can't let everyone down,' Carrie called out, egged on by Matthew beside her.

'You're only as old as you feel, remember,' Anna added.

'She taught us everything we know, you know,' Bett said to Rebecca.

'Really? In that case you can be her backing singers.'

Someone overheard. 'Yes, bring on the Alphabet Sisters as well!'

This time there was no hesitation. There was a tumble of movement and laughter, as Lola was lured into the middle of the room, and the three girls made to line up behind her, like an old-fashioned backing group, standing sideways. Everyone was laughing.

'So what do we sing?' Bett said. She wished again that Daniel was there. She knew he would have enjoyed this.

'It has to be Lola's choice,' Anna said.

'One of your favourites, Lola,' Carrie added.

Lola was thinking hard. Then she beckoned the girls in, told them her choice. There was more laughter, and a huddle of heads as they all checked they knew at least some of the words. Then Lola stepped forward and bowed dramatically. 'Ladies and gentlemen, boys and girls. It gives me great pleasure to introduce myself, and my three granddaughters, for your listening pleasure tonight.'

And in a voice that threatened to shatter every piece of glass in the building, Lola – backed very badly by a laughing Anna, Bett and Carrie – warbled her way through her own unique, high-kicking version of 'There's No Business Like Show Business'.

In bed that night Lola stretched one leg, then the other, did her facial exercises, then gave up. She didn't want to do exercises. She wanted to just lie there and grin all night long. She wanted to savour every minute, rewind it all, relive it second by second, from Bett's music, to Anna's direction, to Carrie's singing and dancing. Had she ever felt as proud as in the Alphabet Sisters days as she had that evening, standing there on stage with her three girls, her son, Jim, and grand-daughter, Ellen, smiling up from the audience at her? Even Geraldine had been smiling, had actually hugged her afterwards.

And had she ever felt as good as she had at the party afterwards? All those people coming up, showering her with praise, firing questions. Were they going to stage it again? What about a tour? Had she thought about sending the script to a professional company? What about next year's project? She had laughed them all away, insisting tonight was no night for future plans, it was for savour-ing a triumph.

But lying there, she did have a thought. Richard had put it in her mind, with all his research into English convicts and Irish servant girls coming to the Clare Valley in the 1850s. What a marvellous storyline that would make. She could follow just one of them, or no, perhaps two, even three sisters, on their journey from Ireland to

South Australia. It could involve one or two scenes on a ship. After Len's triumph with General MacArthur's train, surely building a ship would be no bother to him. And all those lively Irish jigs and reels. Such scope for a plot, too. One of the servant girls could fall in love with her cruel, handsome master . . .

Lola sat up and reached for the notebook she kept on her bedside table.

CHAPTER TWENTY-EIGHT

FORTY-EIGHT hours later Bett was sitting beside a campfire near a clutch of gum trees, watching the flickering fire, experiencing first hand the Drover's Experience. This would be the final article for the tourism supplement. This time next week she'd be back on court reports and police articles.

She had a notebook filled with quotes from the drover himself, craggy-faced, brown-skinned, laconic. The perfect face for a man with his job. 'Straight out of Central Casting,' Daniel had whispered earlier as he set up shots of Fergie with his sheep and the blue sky behind him.

They'd eaten dinner by the campfire – damper bread, billy tea, stew in a pot, exactly as the tourist groups would enjoy it in the months ahead. Their tents would be pitched in a circle around the campfire too, logs of wood acting as seats, under the huge night sky. Tonight there were just the three tents, one for Fergie, a long way back from the main camp site – 'I snore,' he'd explained succinctly – and one each for Bett and Daniel.

Fergie had told Bett some of the tales he'd be sharing with the tourists. He knew the whole story of the area, from its Aboriginal history to the early pioneer days. He'd spent most of his life working in shearing sheds and had plenty of stories about them as well.

Bett took down the final details and then put her notebook away. 'This isn't for the article, but tell me, do you ever get sick of sheep?'

Fergie laughed. 'No. If I do, I get a whole fresh bunch every spring, remember. That's the wonder of nature.'

Daniel came back to the campfire. He'd been taking photos from a distance as the final light faded around them. 'We'll take a few more in the morning, Fergie, if that's okay.'

'I'll be up at five, Dan, with my best smile on.' He pulled an exaggerated face and they both laughed. 'Early to bed for me, anyway. Dan, you'll sort out the fire, won't you? Goodnight to you both.'

Bett stretched out her legs towards the fire, alone for a moment while Daniel went to his tent to put away the camera equipment. Her mobile rang, the noise incongruous in the surroundings. She read the name on the display. 'Lola? Is everything all right?'

'Everything's fine, darling. Your parents are in the bar with a couple of guests, swapping stories about train journeys. Carrie is home with Matthew, and little Ellen is staying over with them for the night. Anna is in Adelaide returning the costumes. Richard's gone with her for the trip. Do you suppose they'll be staying in separate rooms tonight?'

'You're too old to be thinking things like that.'

'What is the tent situation like there, darling?'

'We have one each, Lola.'

'Really?' A pause. 'You know that if it gets cold, the best way to warm up is through body heat?'

'I'll tell Fergie that, will I?' She had discovered earlier that Lola and Fergie knew each other from some years back. 'That will be a surprise for him in the middle of the night. A little visit from me.'

Lola laughed. 'Goodnight, darling. Have a nice night.'

Bett glanced up as Daniel came back to the fire. He nodded to the phone. 'Everything all right at home?'

'Everything's fine. And you?' She had seen him talking on his mobile phone too.

He took a seat on the other log next to her and stretched out his legs. 'Not so bad.'

Bett hesitated. 'Rebecca told me about your mother, Daniel. I'm sorry. It must be very hard on you and your sister.'

'It has been. But worse for Mum, of course.' He picked up a long stick and broke it in pieces, throwing the bits into the fire. 'I'm sorry about the night of the musical, Bett. One of the songs distressed her. That's the sad thing about it, it's so unpredictable. It could have been a voice that sparked a memory, as easily as a song. But we don't want her to never go out. She's very healthy apart from that. It's her mind not her body that's been affected.'

'You and Christine have been very good to give up your lives for her like that.'

'We don't see it like that. You just do it for family. You'd do it for Lola, wouldn't you?'

'In a shot.'

'You just need her to slow down enough so you can look after her, I guess?'

She smiled, then was serious again. 'If there's ever anything I can do for you or for your mother, just ask, Daniel, won't you?'

'Thanks, Bett.'

There was a long pause before he spoke again. 'So are you going to stay on in the Valley, now the musical is over?'

'I don't know yet. I'll see what happens.' She took up a stick too and poked at the embers, watching sparks fly into the air. 'So did you get some good shots today?'

'I think so. A good subject always helps.'

'It's not just that. You're a very good photographer.'

'Thank you.'

'So is that what you always wanted to do? When you were growing up?'

'Always. I had a box brownie as a teenager. Before that one of those homemade ones from cardboard.' He grinned. 'I had to draw my own photographs, but it was a start.' He threw another bit of wood into the fire. 'And what about you? Did you always want to be a journalist?'

'Not always. It was a choice between something to do with music and something to do with writing, and writing won. And now I really love being a journalist.'

'You do, don't you? What about it, exactly?'

She realised he was genuinely interested. She thought about it for a moment. 'I like watching something happen and turning it into a sentence, or a story. Capturing it, I suppose.'

'And you don't miss the music? You can't do both?'

'I tried. When I was in London, I wrote about music and bands but it wasn't for me in the end.'

'No? What happened?'

She told him stories from her time in the record company, encouraged by his laughter. It did seem ridiculous from this distance, coaching teenage pop stars, telling them what they thought. She laughed too. 'You see what a mess the music industry is in? Where were you, Danger Hilder, when we needed you most?'

He smiled and reached down to the bottle of wine. 'More?'

'Yes, please.'

The sounds around them became distinct. The slow glug of the wine into her glass. A quiet crackle from the flames in front of them. A bird far off in the trees. Faint rustling noises and low bleats from the sheep in the distance.

'So was it hard to leave London?'

She shook her head, remembering the day she'd decided to resign. 'Once I'd decided, it was the simplest thing in the world. I knew this was where I wanted to be.'

'It's easier for women in lots of ways, don't you think?'

'What's easier?'

'Life. Decisions, everything.' He waved an arm. 'Women seem to know how to do it. You always seem so confident, assured. You know what you want, how to make things happen.'

'Women generally? Or me? Because I haven't a clue.'

'What are you talking about? That was one of the first things I noticed about you, how confident and alive you are, how comfortable you are in your own skin.'

'No, I'm not.' Bett was astonished. 'I'm a walking disaster area.'

'You are not. I used to see you in Clare, when I was first here. You'd be talking away to people, interviewing them. And I'd see you in pubs and restaurants with Matthew, telling stories, always so confident.'

'You should have looked closer, then.'

He gave a soft laugh. 'I was probably too busy worrying about my own appearance.'

'But men don't think like that, do they? Get worried about what people think of them? I mean, I haven't got any brothers, but I thought you all knew exactly what you wanted, how to act, how to –'

'Of course we don't. I can't speak for the entire male population, but I get scared and worried about things. That I'll make a mess of something, choose the wrong moment, misread a situation . . .'

She was speechless.

'I'm scared now, for example.'

'Of what?'

'You.'

'Scared of me?'

He hesitated. 'Of what you'd do if I asked you if I could kiss you.'

She blinked. 'You want to kiss me?'

'I've wanted to kiss you for weeks.'

'Why haven't you?'

'In case you slapped me. Told me to go away. Told me you didn't like me in that way.'

'Oh,' she said. A warm glow had started deep inside her. 'And how were you planning on going about it?'

'I was thinking of coming over and sitting beside you, and perhaps putting one hand on your cheek. And then if that went okay, I was probably going to lean down and kiss you. That was when I was worried that you might slap me.'

'I see.' She thought about it for a moment. 'I don't think I would.'

'No?'

'I don't think so.'

'Should I check?'

She nodded.

He moved towards her. She sat, her face turned up at him, nervous but also excited. She'd had one glass of wine, not the quantities she'd drunk last time they'd kissed. She'd had a good, busy, interesting day, not weeks of frenzy and turmoil. Her breath caught at the touch of his lips against hers, soft, exploring. She felt the touch of his hand on her face.

'Aphrodisiac qualities, those campfires, I've always found.'

They both jumped at the voice. It was Fergie, coming out of his tent. They separated, embarrassed, and stared into the fire again until Fergie returned from the tree he was visiting. He gave them a cheery wave from the opening of his tent.

A moment passed, and then they turned back to one another. This time she met his lips halfway. They kissed, long, slow kisses that tasted like red wine. He kissed her eyelids and the lobes of her ears and the side of her neck. She kissed the side of his face, the corners of his lips. Did she put his hand on her breast or did he do it himself? Bett wondered. She touched the side of his body, his back, their lips soft against one another all the while, the kiss continuing. They both stood up. He pulled her in against his body and she could feel his arousal, feel herself pressing against his body, her breasts full, aching to be touched.

A huge sneeze from Fergie's tent resounded in the air. She could feel Daniel laughing, even as she laughed herself.

'The cry of the wildebeest,' he whispered, kissing her again. He moved his hand down her body. Without realising it she started to tense.

He pulled away. 'Do you want me to stop?'

She shook her head. Tell the truth, she heard a voice inside her say. 'I'm just a bit nervous.'

'Of me?'

She shook her head. 'Maybe not nervous. Maybe self-conscious.'

'But you're perfect. And I should know. I've been staring at every inch of you for weeks. I could draw you from memory, you know.

This curve here,' he brushed her thigh. 'The curve of your arm.' He touched her arm. 'Your breast.' Her breathing faltered as he slowly stroked her breast. 'These curves here.'

He laughed at the expression on her face. She laughed too, relaxing, feeling his hands on her, not minding at all now. She touched his back, feeling the skin under his shirt. There was another long, luxurious kiss. She pulled back again, needing to say something. 'I'm sorry about last time. That time in Melbourne. I don't know what got into me. I was very drunk.'

'You needed to be drunk that night?'

She nodded.

'Can I get you a glass of wine now? A bottle?'

She laughed, then it became serious. 'I don't think I need to be drunk tonight.'

He touched her cheek. 'Are you sure?'

She reached up, kissed his lips, felt his body against hers. Then they stopped talking and started kissing again, different, deeper, sexier kissing. Somehow they moved from the campfire to his tent, to the sleeping bag on the ground, as warm flickering shadows from the fire played against the canvas. She loved the feeling of his hands on her body, her breasts, between her legs. And she loved the feel of his body, lean and silky to touch. Was there touch memory, she wondered. Did her body remember what it had felt like to have Daniel against her that night? Because it was responding now as though it couldn't wait to repeat itself . . .

Bett woke up as sunlight was coming into the tent. She felt stirring beside her and turned towards Daniel.

'Good morning.' His voice was soft.

She smiled. 'Hello.'

'Did you have a good night's sleep?'

He knew full well she hadn't. Nor had he. They had been making love most of the night. 'Not really. To be honest, I'm a bit worried.'

She felt him tense. 'What about?'

'My article. Do you suppose I can promise this experience for every woman doing this camping trip?'

He relaxed. 'I could have a word with Fergie. It could be a handy sideline if I lose interest in the photography.'

She laughed, closing her eyes as she felt his fingertips brush her bare skin. His voice was quiet. 'So if you were writing an article about what happened last night, what would you write?'

She thought for a moment. '"Local reporter Bett Quinlan announced today that she was a little bit embarrassed to be waking up naked in a tent with Daniel Hilder but said she didn't regret a second of the previous evening's shenanigans."'

'Shenanigans?'

'Shenanigans. Your turn.'

'"Photographer Daniel Hilder today admitted that he had fancied local reporter Bett Quinlan for some time." Have I got the tone right?'

'Yes. Yes, that's very good.'

'"When questioned, he said that he had always been a sucker for a shock of brown hair and a pair of cheeky eyes, and Ms Quinlan fortunately was endowed with both." Am I still getting it right?'

Bett's head was on his chest, her eyes closed as he stroked her skin. 'It's very good.'

'"When asked about Ms Quinlan's murky past, Mr Hilder gave an insouciant" – I'd have an asterisk there and at the bottom of the page the translation – relaxed, okay? Anyway, "gave an insouciant shrug and said, 'The murkier the better, as far as I'm concerned. The more dirt there is the more we have to talk about.'" I think I've got the hang of this now. Can I go on?'

She nodded.

'"When asked about his future plans, Mr Hilder gave another insouciant shrug, clearly being short of gestures that day, and said, 'It's up to Ms Quinlan, really. Loath as I am to resort to clichés, in this case the ball is in her court.' The press corp then gathered around Ms Quinlan seeking her reaction."'

She could feel his fingers all the way down her back now. '"Ms Quinlan responded to reporters' questions by first checking what the time was –"'

Daniel lifted his wrist. 'Six thirty.'

'"And then wondering aloud if it would be possible for Daniel Hilder to make love to her so beautifully one more time before they left the tent that morning."'

He moved closer, then kissed her lips. His fingers caressed her body again. It seemed it was a yes.

Bett deliberately didn't turn on her mobile for the journey home later that morning. It was a one-hour drive along curving roads, the yellow stubbled paddocks stretching out on either side. They talked and laughed, easily, eagerly. He stopped the car once, didn't speak, just reached over to kiss her. She met him halfway again.

It was early afternoon by the time they arrived at the Valley View Motel. They had taken the slow way home. He pulled into the drive in front of the reception area and turned off the ignition. Bett smiled at him. She felt like just sitting here and smiling at him all day.

'Can I see you tonight?' he asked.

'Again?'

'It's fine if you don't want to.'

'I'd love to. Let me just check in with everyone, make sure nothing's happened while I've been gone.' She'd only been away one night, she laughed to herself. Back here motel life would have gone on as normal, yet it felt like her life had changed completely overnight.

'I'll call in and see my mother too. But I'll ring you afterwards? About six?'

'Perfect.' She waited on the steps of the motel until he had driven away, then turned. She felt like she was radiating happiness. 'Hello?' she called as she came into reception. There was no answer. She checked the bar. It was empty too. She'd already noticed Anna's car wasn't in its usual place. She and Richard must still be in Adelaide. There was no one in the function room either. Or in the kitchen. 'Hello? Where is everybody?' She went outside and heard her name being called.

'Bett?' It was Carrie, coming from Lola's room. She was crying.

'Cancer?'

Bett looked at the faces in front of her. Lola was ashen. Carrie's eyes were swollen. Her mother and father were tightly holding hands.

Jim Quinlan repeated what Anna had phoned and told them. She had called from the hospital. 'She had an MRI scan this morning. There's a tumour in her lungs. A very large tumour. They admitted her straight away.'

Bett stared at him. 'But I don't understand it. She hasn't had any symptoms.'

'She has. It's just they were mistaken for other things. Stress. Exhaustion. Anxiety attacks. And she's always been so thin, so even the weight loss wasn't too out of the ordinary.'

'But what made her have the scan? Why didn't she tell us?'

'A young doctor in Adelaide arranged it.' Jim's voice was dull. 'She didn't want to worry anyone, she said. Not with so much else going on.'

Bett tried to take in everything as her father kept talking. The doctors had told Anna she may have had the tumour for months, even years. It was only now that it had grown so large that it had started causing her problems.

It was as if the world was slightly off kilter. As if voices were not in tune, the colours not right, as if she was several steps behind. She wanted to blink, to start this again, to get out of Daniel's car, come in the door and see Lola reading in the bar, her parents working, Carrie in the office, Anna and Ellen playing Scrabble. Not this gathering.

Someone was missing. 'Where's Ellen?'

'She's in her room playing. Anna spoke to her on the phone but she's asked us not to tell her too much yet. Not until we all know more ourselves.'

'So can we go to Anna? Ellen, all of us? Now?'

Geraldine shook her head. 'She said there was no need to come down tonight. They're giving her sleeping tablets. She'd be asleep before we got there. Richard's with her in the hospital. They're starting radiation treatment first thing in the morning.'

'So it's treatable? So she's going to be all right?' Bett looked around again, knowing she hadn't been the first to ask that question in that room tonight.

No one would answer her.

CHAPTER TWENTY-NINE

TIME STARTED moving at a different pace, as though they were in slow motion, in a bubble of their own, while outside things continued as normal. Anna's treatment started immediately, a team of people working with her – a specialist, a doctor, nurses. Bett felt she was always two steps behind what was happening, barely taking in the news that Anna had cancer in the first place, before they were talking about doing a biopsy, operating or not operating, chemotherapy or no chemotherapy.

Geraldine and Bett were the first to go to Adelaide to be with Anna. Richard returned to Clare. They took it in turns talking to Anna's doctors, getting reports, phoning back to the motel. Everyone had questions and no one was satisfied with the answers they were getting. 'What do they mean it's an aggressive tumour?' 'If they hadn't found it now, what would have happened?' 'Will she lose all her hair when they start the treatment?'

There was test after test. Anna spent most of every day in bed, already exhausted from the X-rays, the scans, the drugs, the shock. Bett and her mother sat beside her, reading, talking a little, watching her while she slept. Bett couldn't reconcile that this already more frail-looking Anna was the same woman who had been smiling up on stage just a few days before. She was still bright and cheerful at first. But the mask dropped when the two of them were alone for the first time. Geraldine had left the room to get coffee.

Anna reached for Bett's hand. 'I'm scared, Bettsie. I'm really scared.'

'We all are, sweetheart. But we'll know more soon, won't we?'

'I don't know. The specialist said I could be in here for weeks. What about Ellen? Who'll look after her if I'm in here for that long?'

Bett squeezed Anna's hand. 'All of us. We're fighting over who gets to look after her. Don't worry about Ellen.'

'Will you ring Glenn?'

None of them had even thought of telling Glenn.

Bett called him in Singapore that night. She could hear the shock in his voice. 'I'll come back as soon as I can, to help look after Ellen. I can be there by the end of the week. She's going to be all right, isn't she? What about the hospital? Is it the best one? Money's no problem, Bett.'

She could tell he was truly concerned. It made it easier to talk to him, to put her anger towards him aside. Did some love survive at the bottom of all failed marriages? she wondered. 'It's a very good hospital. They're doing every test, every scan. We can't get near her for doctors and nurses.'

'What does Ellen know?'

'We don't know what to tell her yet. She knows Anna is in hospital, but we just said it was for a day or two, that she'd be home soon.' Lola had sat with Ellen and explained that Anna wasn't feeling very well, that there was a germ in her body the doctors were trying to get rid of and that fighting the germ sometimes made Anna very tired. They would bring her down to visit Anna very soon. In the meantime, Ellen was talking to Anna twice, sometimes three times a day on the phone.

'And will Anna be home soon?'

Bett had told him the truth. 'We don't know.'

'And you're sure there's nothing I can do, Bett? Nothing you need brought down to Adelaide? Nothing I can do at the motel?'

'I'm sure, Daniel, honestly. But thank you anyway.' She'd called him from the public phone in the hospital corridor. It was the first time she'd spoken to him at length since they'd spent the night together. They had spoken briefly when he had phoned her, the night they had learnt about Anna. She'd been barely able to talk, in deep shock. She had asked him to tell Rebecca the news. Rebecca had rung the next day, offering help as well, with everything from making beds to driving the family to and from Adelaide. 'Don't even think about work, Bett,' she'd said. 'Just stay close to your family. Will you ring me if there's anything any of us can do? It doesn't matter how small.'

There was someone waiting to use the phone. 'I'd better go, Daniel.'

'Of course.' He hesitated. 'I'm thinking of you, Bett.'

'I'm thinking of you too.' She hung up and went back into Anna's room.

Lola and Carrie came down several days later. They brought Ellen with them. They'd told her the truth – that Anna needed to stay in hospital for longer than they expected, while the doctors did more tests on her. Ellen seemed to take it all quite calmly. As Lola said, she was used to hospitals.

Bett drove her mother back to the motel, lost in her own thoughts as she passed the car yards and housing developments of the city's outer suburbs, the scenery gradually changing to open countryside, farms and small towns the further north she drove. Her mother made calls on her mobile throughout the journey, speaking to cancer support agencies, arranging for information to be sent to them, returning phone calls from friends in the Valley enquiring about Anna, offering their help. Her manner was direct, matter-of-fact. Things to be done, practical issues to be organised. Geraldine specialised in those, Bett thought.

She had seen her mother walking down the corridor with Anna the previous night. All around them were other families, some of them in even worse situations, one or two older women in distressed tears. Geraldine had held herself erect, composed. She'd helped Anna get back into bed, hadn't flinched when Anna's gown had lifted slightly and they had seen just how thin she was. She had been almost businesslike when the nurse had come in and expressed concern about how little Anna had eaten of her evening meal.

But an hour later Bett had gone in search of a cup of tea. She had been about to turn on the light in one of the side sitting rooms when she'd heard a noise. Standing still, she had seen a figure in one of the armchairs in the corner of the room. It was her mother, staring out of the window, softly crying.

Bett had hesitated, about to go in and comfort her, when her mother had noticed her first. Geraldine had stood up immediately, briskly wiped away the tears. 'A cup of tea, Bett? Let me get one for you. And Anna too?'

Neither of them mentioned her tears.

Anna and Lola were alone in her room. Lola had been reading to her, picking out bits of ten-year-old gossip from a magazine she had found in the waiting room. Midway through an article about the cast of some since-axed soap opera, Anna put her hand on Lola's arm. 'Lola, I'm so scared.'

The magazine was put away. Lola took both her hands in hers. 'Darling, of course you are. You don't know what's going to happen. That's always scary.'

'Come with me. I want you to come with me and help me.'

'I would if I could, darling.'

'What's going to happen to Ellen if I don't get better? How is she going to cope without a mother? It's not fair, she's suffered too much already.'

'Anna, you mustn't think like that. And you must never worry about Ellen. She'll never be on her own, Anna, I promise you that.'

There was a knock at the door. It was Glenn, in his suit, straight from the airport.

Lola stood up and moved aside immediately. As she shut the door she saw him reach down and hold Anna tight.

Carrie refused to talk to Glenn. She ignored the concern he was showing, the offers of financial help, the offer – gently declined by Anna – to move her to a private hospital in Sydney. Outside, in the waiting room, Carrie railed at Lola.

'It's his fault. This wouldn't have happened if it wasn't for him. I read all about it on the Internet. Stress can cause cancer and that –' she searched for the insult, 'that bastard caused her so much stress and pain. How dare he come here like this? How can you even let him stay here, Lola?'

'It's not Glenn's fault. It's no one's fault, Carrie. It's just happened.

We can't waste time blaming someone, fighting amongst ourselves. We have to think of Anna.'

Carrie was in tears. 'I know. I'm trying to, but I'm so mad, Lola. And I feel useless and I feel like there's nothing I can do. It's all happening too quickly.'

Their lives started revolving around visits to Adelaide, taking it in turns to sit with her, talk to the nurses, listen to the doctor, wait for the specialist. They spent a lot of time in Anna's room, talking, reading, or sitting quietly while she slept, exhausted from the latest round of treatment.

Her room was on the second floor of the hospital, looking out over the parklands. A glass office block stood to the left. The day-to-day movements of the workers, dressed in suits, behind desks, drinking coffee or talking on their phones seemed more and more ridiculous to Bett as each day passed. The hospital waiting room seemed more real, with its scuffed plastic seats, misspelled signs about canteen opening hours, even the empty drink can lying underneath the soft-drink dispenser.

Carrie was with Anna when the specialist came to talk to her, two weeks after she'd been admitted to the hospital. Coolly, succinctly, he explained the situation. It was a very aggressive tumour. They had discovered some secondaries, but so far they were confined. Surgery wasn't an option at this stage. The tumour was too large. There was more treatment to try – more radiation, some new drugs.

'And if the new drugs don't work?' Anna's voice was as calm as his. Beside her, Carrie was tightly holding her hand.

His tone softened. 'Then we're looking at a palliative care situation.'

Bett arrived back at the hospital several days later with more cards and letters from people in the Valley. Word had quickly got around. Each day at the motel there had been calls from people offering to help mind Ellen, to cook for the motel guests if Geraldine needed to be in Adelaide. Prayers were being said for Anna. Len the butcher had dropped off a folder of information he had gathered from the Internet on miracle cures. Bett had left that behind in Clare.

She was shocked at the change in Anna. Her sister was sitting up in the bed, pillows propped all around her, like a tiny bird in a white nest. She was even thinner and her skin seemed to be changing in texture and colour. Her breathing was changing too, becoming more laboured.

She managed a big smile, though. 'Hello, my darling. You've come to admire my new nose jewellery?' Anna had two plastic clips in her nostrils, carrying oxygen into her system. She wasn't able to breathe fully without it any more.

Bett managed a grin too. 'It's very fetching. Does it come in a range of colours?'

'Horrible clear and even more horrible white, I think. I did tell them white wasn't my colour but they can be very obstinate in here. It'll be all the rage next year, you mark my words.'

Bett sat in the chair beside the bed and took Anna's hand. They were touching her constantly now. Whoever was sitting beside her would be stroking her arm, or holding her hand, or just resting their fingers on her. 'Can I get you anything? Do you want the radio on? Any tapes?'

Anna shook her head. 'Tell me about Ellen this week.' Ellen came down to the hospital three days every week, but stayed in the Valley, going to school the rest of the week. The doctors had advised them to keep things as normal as possible for her.

Bett told her the latest stories. Ellen had invited two of her friends over to play after school. Lola had caught them tying hats to Bumper's head. They had been rehearsing their own mini musical, for when Mum came home.

'She'd better hurry it up, then.'

'What do you mean?'

'I've made a decision, Bett.' Her voice became serious as she explained what the specialist had told her that afternoon. That there was still another course of treatment ahead of her. More radiation. Another course of tablets. Still in the experimental stages. 'I agreed, Bett. What did I have to lose?'

'But isn't it dangerous?'

'What? Might it kill me?' She laughed softly at the expression on Bett's face. 'I can joke about it, Bett. It's me who's dying of cancer.'

'You're not dying of cancer. There's still lots of things they can try.'

'I'm too tired. That's the worst thing about it. If I wasn't feeling so sick I'd be interested in thinking about it and talking about it. But if I wasn't so sick I wouldn't be dying, would I?'

Bett was shocked by a sudden flare of temper. 'That's not what I meant. How can you joke about it? Why aren't you angry? Why am I the cross one? Why aren't you raging against the light and the night or whatever it is you're supposed to be raging about?'

Anna was calm. 'I am, Bett. I don't want to die yet. I've no intention of dying yet.'

'Then don't be so bloody passive about it. Fight it.'

'You don't think I am? You really think I want to bow out here and now, slip off, leave all this? Bett, I hate this. I hate every tiny thing of it. Lying here like this, being pumped full of this drug and that drug, getting X-rayed, feeling my lungs trying so hard. All my life I was never conscious of what my body was doing to keep me alive, and now it's as if I can hear every cog turning, every cell doing its job. Of course I hate this. I see a sunrise, or a bird or the smallest beautiful thing and I treasure it and I want it forever and I can't have it. I might not have any of it for much longer.'

'What would you like? If we could get you anything, make anything happen for you before you went,' Bett stumbled on the word. 'What would you want?'

'It's not the obvious things. It's not seeing Ellen walk up the aisle, or holding my first granddaughter. It's the ordinary things. I want mornings in a coffee shop with her when she's about twenty-five. I want her rushed, saying, "I can't stay long, Mum, I have to go and meet someone."'

'What else?'

'I want more drunken nights with you and Carrie and a call from you the next morning to tell me I was all right, that I hadn't been badly behaved. I want you to ring and not introduce yourself – you know, you never do that, you always launch straight into a conversation. And I want to hear all those stories again about your misadventures. Please, Bett, tell me the one about you falling off the treadmill again? I love that story.'

'You're very cruel.'

A smile, vivid in the pale, thin face. 'I know. Shall I start you off? Once upon a time, you were in a gym and . . .'

'The new drugs haven't worked. It's spread even further.' Geraldine spoke as soon as she walked into the kitchen two weeks later.

Jim, Lola and Bett stopped what they were doing. They had known Geraldine was ringing Adelaide and talking to Carrie, who'd been in with Anna for the previous two days. They had known that crucial X-rays were taking place that morning, to check on the growth of the tumours. All day each of them had kept busy, filling the hours. The bar was cleaner than it had ever been. The kitchen had been completely reorganised. Bett had got down on her hands and knees and scrubbed the showers in all fifteen rooms, playing the bedside radio at top volume in each, blasting sound into the air to keep her thoughts from pummelling her.

Geraldine spoke as if she was reading from a list, her voice expressionless, her eyes distant. 'The radiation hasn't worked either. It's spread into her lymph nodes. And her spine.'

A few weeks ago Bett hadn't known what a lymph node was. 'Did Carrie talk to Anna's specialist? About what Anna's decided to do?'

A nod. 'He said that if that was Anna's decision, he fully supported it. He told Carrie afterwards that he felt it was the right option.'

Anna had made her decision three days before. If the latest, more intrusive attempts to stop the cancer hadn't worked, she was going to stop all the radiation, the scans, the invasive procedures.

Jim spoke. 'So she's coming home?'

Geraldine nodded. She didn't need to spell it out. Anna was coming home to die.

CHAPTER THIRTY

HER FAVOURITE room in the motel was prepared. They hung bright curtains in the windows. Lola chose a colourful bedspread and a new rug for the floor. Ellen picked fresh flowers and put them in vases. Lola had tried to explain to her that Anna was still very sick, but Ellen hadn't seemed to take it in. She'd been too excited by the fact that her mother was actually coming home. Jim went to the garden centre and bought plants and trees in pots, arranging them outside the room, to give Anna something green and restful to look at from bed. Bett scoured every surface, washed the windows, wiped down the walls, until she had touched every inch of the room.

She smiled at Richard as he carried a box of Anna's favourite books into the room. She was helping him arrange them on a shelf when he spoke, his voice low.

'I should leave, Bett. This is a time for close family.'

She was struck by the deep sadness in his expression. 'No it's not, Richard. It's a time for anyone who loves Anna to be close to her.' She touched his arm. 'I know it's been very hard on you. When things had only just started between you. But you make her very happy.'

'I'd like to have made her happier. For longer.'

Bett blinked away tears which had suddenly come into her eyes. 'So would we,' she answered softly.

Anna arrived home the next day in the car with Carrie and Geraldine. She'd travelled in a nest of pillows, fragile from the treatment and the illness, but refusing to make the trip in an ambulance. She was even thinner, her hair a dark little cap around her face, now even more gaunt. 'I know my hair's a mess, but at least I've still got it. You should have seen some of the bald heads in that ward,' she tried to joke.

She had to be helped into the room. The oxygen came everywhere with her, pushed on a small trolley beside her. Her voice was changing, becoming weaker, but she was still bright, interested. 'Ellie, did you do those drawings for me? They're gorgeous.' She leaned and kissed her daughter, who was clinging tightly to her hand. 'And all the flowers. And look at that bedspread. It's beautiful, everyone. Thank you very much.'

As Anna was settled, Ellen skipped around, unable to stay in one place, running up to her mother, hugging her, then running away again. She sidled up to Bett, as she stood outside Anna's room, arranging a chair and table for the times Anna felt able to sit up, outside in the morning sunshine. It had been Richard's idea.

'My mum is very sick, isn't she?'

Bett stroked her hair. 'She is, Ellie. She's very sick.'

'When she gets better, Daddy and Mum and I are going to go on a holiday.'

'Did he say that?'

She nodded. 'He said he would take me on a long trip, maybe even to Disneyland.'

'That'll be fun,' Bett said, keeping her voice bright. She knew what Glenn had been trying to do. She also knew Anna wouldn't be going with them.

The days fell into a pattern. Anna had more energy in the mornings. She could sit and talk with one or other of them, eat a little, before needing to go back to bed again. Now and then she managed to go for a short walk, or would let them push her in a wheelchair, in the cool of the morning, or after dusk, when the heat of the day had passed. The palliative care nurses visited twice a day and monitored her pain. They showed Bett, Carrie and their mother how to measure the morphine, answered their questions, calmed and soothed them.

Anna slept a great deal. When she was feeling strong enough, she came into the kitchen in a brightly coloured silk dressing-gown and sat in a corner, watching all the activity around her. Ellen continued going to school, but ran in each afternoon, with a new drawing, or a love note, which Anna would exclaim over and put into her pocket.

When Anna was too tired to get up, they all took turns spending time with her in her room. Geraldine was there the most, tidying the room, counting the tablets, straightening the curtains or just sitting quietly by Anna's bed. She seemed to know when Anna was feeling any pain, when she needed more oxygen, what she might like to drink or eat, almost by instinct. No one remarked on it, but everyone noticed.

'Can I get you anything, love?'

Anna looked up from the bed. Ellen was tucked in beside her, asleep. The two of them had been watching cartoons together. 'No thanks, Dad.'

'A cola? A squash? A rainbow drink?'

'A rainbow drink? Now you're talking. Not for me, but for Ellie when she wakes up.'

'You're not thirsty at all? Or hungry?'

She shook her head. Her appetite had almost gone now.

He had turned to go to the bar to make Ellen's drink when she called after him. 'Dad, can you make Ellie's drink later?'

'Yes, of course. Is there something else you want done instead?'

'Would you just sit here with me for a while?'

He sat down in the chair beside her bed, taking her hand in both of his. 'Of course, sweetheart. For as long as you like.'

Lola carefully draped the scarf over Anna's bedspread, then stepped back and looked critically at it. 'It will do for the moment. I've got my eye on a rather nice pink one down at the charity shop. I think I'll put in a bid for that and bring that home for you as well.'

Anna smiled up at her. 'I love you, Lola.'

Lola stopped still. She gazed down at Anna, then gently, slowly, lifted her hand and stroked the soft cheek. 'Not as much as I love you.'

'Do you believe in heaven, Bett?'

'I want to. I want to know that you are going somewhere special, somewhere that you'll love, and that you'll get a good spot ready for us when we arrive.'

'I will, I promise. Sun or shade?' She was trying hard to sound bright.

'A bit of both, I think.'

'Bett, will you do something for me?'

Her voice was getting weaker. Bett had to lean in to hear her. 'Anything.'

Anna reached under her pillow and took something out. 'Would you look after these for me?'

It was an envelope, filled with small pieces of paper, each neatly folded. 'What are they?'

'They're birthday cards for Ellen. Little notes. Until she turns twenty-one. I was going to ask Glenn to give them to her, but I'd love you to do it instead. If you don't mind.'

'If I don't mind? I'd love to give these to her.' She realised she had a lump in her throat. 'I'd be honoured.'

'And you'll help him look after her, won't you? Even if it's hard sometimes. I know you and him haven't always –'

'Of course I will. We love her dearly, Anna. You know that. I love her dearly.'

'And, Bett, will you tell her about me? Please? I don't know how much she'll remember.'

Bett blinked away tears, so used to them now she barely noticed them. 'Of course I will. I'll tell her how beautiful and how kind and how brave –'

Anna's smile was frail but full of mischief. 'Well, you don't have to get too carried away.'

Richard moved the chair in close to Anna's bedside and reached into the box beside him. 'I've Jane Austen or Seamus Heaney or even a bit of Ian Fleming.'

'Don't read to me. Talk to me instead.'

'What about?'

'Anything you like.'

'Anything? Then in that case I want to talk about you.'

Anna didn't speak, just kept looking at him.

He started, haltingly. 'I want to talk about how unfair this is.

And how much I wish this wasn't happening. But that would all be about me, not about you.' His face was very sad.

'I'd liked to have made you so happy, Anna. I'd liked to have gone travelling with you. I'd liked to have made you laugh, and heard more of your stories. I'd liked to have got to know Ellen. For the three of us to have got to know each other.' He paused. 'I'm sorry, it's about me again, not you. What I would have liked. But it's the truth. All I would have wanted was to be with you. Making love, on orange bedspreads in motels all around the world. Drinking wine and talking all night. Telling you how much I loved you, every day, until you got tired of hearing it.'

Tears formed in her eyes. 'I wouldn't have got tired of hearing that. I'd have liked that.'

He gently wiped away the tears. 'I'd also liked to have spent one entire week doing nothing but lying in bed and listening to your voice.'

'You wouldn't have let me sleep?'

'Not a wink.'

'I'd have liked all of that,' she said softly.

He didn't say anything more then, just picked up her hand and pressed a kiss against her palm. Then, still holding her hand, he quietly started reading to her.

Carrie learned she was pregnant a week after Anna was brought home from Adelaide. Bett was in the room with her when she told Anna. 'It's still early, only a few weeks. But I wanted to tell you.'

'Carrie, that's fantastic news.' Anna's smile was almost luminous now in her thin face. 'That lucky little baby. I've so many clothes and toys of Ellen's in storage in Sydney. I'll make sure to ask Glenn to send them down to you.' Because she wouldn't be needing them.

All the things that didn't need saying any more. 'And you're feeling okay? Not too sick? Oh, you're lucky. I was sick every morning. I actually lost weight in the first few months. The first time I wasn't dieting in years. The freedom of it. Enjoy every minute of it, Carrie, won't you?'

Carrie kept the smile fixed on her face. Anna was now virtually skin and bone, her face gaunt, her eyes large, yet managing to laugh about not having to go on a diet.

'If you get morning sickness, dry bread is supposed to be good, but only if someone brings it to you. Is Matthew being good? Obeying your every command?'

'He's great. It's apparently not even the size of a clothes peg yet, but he keeps telling me he can feel the baby moving.'

'Oh, that's sweet.' She shut her eyes.

Bett moved closer to her. 'Anna? Are you in pain?' They had given her morphine an hour before, but they could give her more if she needed it.

Anna opened her eyes. 'No, I was just remembering when I was pregnant with Ellen. It's a wonderful time, Carrie. Write it all down, so you'll remember it. You'll tell yourself there's plenty of time to do that, because there's no way you'll forget something like this, it's so amazing. But then an even more amazing thing will happen, and then another, layer on layer of them. When you first see them, and when they look at you, and when you're feeding.'

It was the most she had spoken in some days. 'Ellen used to go cross-eyed when she was feeding sometimes, just from the concentration. We used to laugh and laugh at her. And when she first started walking, one of her feet would turn in a little, like a rolling gait. And do you remember, when she first started talking, she'd always repeat the last two words you said to her? I remember Glenn saying it was like having a performing parrot in the house.'

She looked from one to the other. 'You'll make sure Ellen gets to see her cousin a lot, won't you? You'll go up to Sydney or ask Glenn to fly Ellen down here?'

Carrie hadn't dared ask. 'She'll stay with Glenn after . . .'

'After I'm not here.' The smile again. 'I'm lucky in a way. He loves her so dearly and she loves him just as much. It will be hard at first, I know. I've asked him to make sure Ellen spends as much time as she likes here with all of you.'

'She can live with us if she wants to. I'll adopt her.'

'I will too,' Bett said.

Anna gave another gentle laugh. 'Glenn loves her and she loves him. But will you both help him look after her for me?'

Carrie's eyes filled with tears. Anna was talking about Ellen more and more. 'We will, Anna, we promise. She'll come here to us as often as she wants, and we'll go and see her in Sydney or Singapore or wherever she is. We'll do everything we can for her.'

Bett reached for their hands and held them tightly. 'I'm so sorry. I'm sorry for taking three years away from all of us. For taking so long to tell the truth about Matthew. If I had done it earlier –'

'It wasn't just you, Bett. It was just as much my fault.' Carrie was as upset. 'I should have rung, should have tried to –'

'Stop it.' Anna sat up a little, her voice surprisingly strong. 'Don't. Don't do this. Don't waste all this time wishing that you'd done this or done that. Please. It's not worth it. It's what happened. And maybe we're better with each other now, because of that.'

'But I'm sorry –'

'Stop it. I mean it, Bett. I don't want to waste time talking about it.'

Carrie managed a smile. 'You were always so bossy, you know that.'

Anna's head was back on her pillow. 'I'm the oldest. I'm allowed to be. And soon Bett will be the oldest so you have to let her boss you.'

She didn't get any further. Bett and Carrie were crying too hard.

Bett was bringing a new jug of water into Anna's room the next day when she heard voices inside. Anna and Ellen together. She stopped, not wanting to interrupt and also needing to hear.

'Ellie, do you know how much I love you?'

Ellen's voice was as melodic as her mother's. 'One hundred times?'

'More.'

'One thousand times?'

'More.'

'A million times?'

'Even more than that.'

Ellen started to giggle. 'A million billion trillion hundred thousand times.'

'Not even close.'

'More than that? Is there a number bigger than that?'

'Well, there'd better be. Because that's how much I love you.'

Bett walked away as silently as she could. She couldn't bear to hear any more.

'All right, everyone, smile!'

It was Richard who had suggested they take some photos. It hadn't occurred to any of them, too busy caring for Anna day to day.

'I have a decent camera with me,' he had said to Bett that morning. 'It just might be good for Ellen, especially . . .'

She had been too overcome to speak for a moment. 'We hadn't even thought. Thank you.'

It became a joyous afternoon. Lola brought in all her scarves and beads. Geraldine filled vases with flowers and autumn leaves. They took it in turns, sitting on the bed beside Anna, in different combinations. Anna's voice was stronger than it had been for some time, directing them.

'If she makes us start singing, I'm out of here,' Matthew said. 'She's very bossy, isn't she?'

'Always has been,' Bett and Carrie said at the same time.

They took photo after photo. Anna with Lola. No one commented that it was Anna who somehow looked older. Yet her eyes were still bright.

Anna with Bett. She gently got on the bed beside her sister and held her hand. Ellen was put in charge of decorations and darted forward with a flower for Anna's hair.

Jim and Geraldine sat on either side of Anna. Geraldine's eyes were over-bright. Bett saw that she was holding Anna's hand as tightly as she was holding Jim's.

Carrie and Matthew stood on one side of the bed. Anna reached up and put her hand on Carrie's stomach.

The next one was Bett, Carrie and Anna together. 'Give us a song, Alphabet Sisters,' Matthew called, trying to be cheery. They shook their heads, without needing to even look at one another. They couldn't have done it.

Richard took about ten shots of Anna and Ellen together, pulling faces at each other, hugging one another. He took one of the two of them with their faces pressed cheek to cheek, looking directly at the camera, solemn-faced. Everyone in the room held their breath, until Ellen moved, and the moment passed.

Then Ellen became over-excited, insisting on being in every photograph from then on, bursting into tears and having to be soothed. 'She's my mummy who's sick in bed, so I have to be in every photo.'

'Of course, Ellie.' Anna patted the bed beside her. She was exhausted from the activity, her eyelids starting to flutter. 'Hop up here, sweetheart. Will we have one big family one to finish? All of us together?'

'I'll take it,' Matthew and Richard said as one.

Carrie looked over at Matthew, beckoning him over. He shook his head. She understood. This one was for immediate family only. They moved in around Anna's bed, surrounding her. Lola on a chair beside her, Ellen tucked in next to her, Jim and Geraldine on either side. Bett and Carrie sat where they could.

Bett was struck with a memory of people at airports, crowding around the person who was heading away on a long journey, wishing them well, sending them love.

'Smile, everyone.'

They did their best.

A week later, Bett and Daniel walked down the tree-lined road behind the motel. There were vineyards on one side and paddocks of grazing sheep on the other. Sunlight flickered through the trees, sending shadows, then flashes of light in front of them. Since Anna had come home Daniel had called by every few days, dropping in just for a few minutes with flowers for Anna or a bottle of wine for the rest of them. Each time he had invited Bett to go for a walk or a drive with him, or for a meal in one of the local restaurants. The first few times she had said no.

'Go, Bett,' Lola had finally insisted. 'You have to have some time for yourself. Otherwise you'll have nothing left to give her.'

'But what if . . .'

'Take the mobile and I will ring you if there is any change. But there won't be. You heard the doctor as clearly as I did. He said weeks not days.'

As if that made a difference, Bett thought. Oh, we've got weeks with her and there was me thinking it was only days, silly old me. She was so angry and so sad, all at once, and it was massing in her, settling inside her.

From then on she started walking with Daniel several times a week, out on the quiet back roads behind the motel, or along the walking track that followed the path of the old railway line through the Valley. The walks began to mean a great deal to her, brief breaks from the slow heartbreak of seeing Anna fade away a little more each day, seeing the weight disappearing from her, the alertness dulling bit by bit, as she ate less, slept more. Daniel visited Anna briefly and was able to nod in understanding when Bett spoke of the light in Anna's eyes, the warmth of her smile. They spoke about his mother too, both of them painfully conscious of the difference in their situations. Mrs Hilder was physically healthy but fading mentally, already long gone from Daniel and Christine. Anna was still herself, the personality still strong in the failing body.

That morning had been particularly bad for Anna. She hadn't been able to eat anything at all and they'd managed to get her to sip only tiny amounts of water. The morning dose of morphine had finally eased her. She had been sleeping, with Geraldine and Lola by her bedside, when Daniel had come to collect Bett.

They walked for some distance before Bett was able to talk, to find the words for what she was thinking. 'I always thought it was good to know lots of things, Daniel. To experience lots of things. But I don't know if that's true any more.' She stopped and looked up at him. 'I know words I don't want to know. Like palliative care.

Metastases. I know how to give Anna morphine. I know that when her breathing changes it's because the tumour is pressing on her lungs. I know that oxygen comes in tanks not just in the air. And I don't want to know any of those things.'

As they started walking again he put his arm tighter around her.

'She's not even dead yet, and I miss her, Dan. And sometimes I go into the room and she's asleep and I think, oh she's died, as if it will be some simple thing like that. But I know it won't be. And I can't bear that she's suffering. But the thing is I just don't want her to leave us.'

Her tears came in a flood. He took her in his arms and held her close for a long time.

Glenn came to stay at the motel full time. He and Richard circled each other for a day or two, before there was a silent acceptance of each other. They took their turns at Anna's bedside.

Walking past the kitchen one afternoon, Bett heard Glenn's low tones, followed by her parents'. She walked in. It looked like a legal meeting. She excused herself and was about to walk away, when Glenn beckoned her in.

'Bett, please, it's all right. We're talking about Ellen.'

Bett waited.

'I was just explaining to your parents that Ellen's going to come to Singapore with me to begin with, after . . .' his voice seemed to catch. 'Afterwards. But you'll always be her family as well. I want you to know that. I want her to come here as often as she can, I want you to feel you can all come and see her as much as possible. No matter what the situation might be, or where we are.'

Bett needed to bring everything out into the open. This was no time for secrets. 'Will your girlfriend be all right with her?'

She saw her parents' heads shoot up. She would have to

explain it to them later.

'She and Ellen get on very well,' he said simply. 'And she knows Ellen will always come first to me.'

Bett knew he meant it. He was trying as hard as he could. 'Thank you, Glenn.'

Then Geraldine spoke, her voice very soft. 'Ellen needs to know that it's not going to be long now. We need to tell her. Prepare her.'

There was a pause before Glenn spoke again. 'Anna and I talked about it last night. She's asked me not to tell Ellen in front of her. She said that it would –' that break in his voice again. 'It would be too hard for them both.'

Bett had never seen Glenn look so vulnerable. 'Can I help, Glenn? Do you want me to be with her when you tell her?'

He nodded. She could see he was now fighting tears too. 'Yes please.'

She knew he was thinking what she was thinking. How on earth did they do it?

The moment came the following afternoon. Ellen had spent the morning lying on the bed beside Anna, chatting away as normal. When the palliative care nurses arrived, she'd only gone a little way away, sitting outside Anna's room, drawing with chalk on the footpath. She was still there when Glenn and Bett went to find her.

Hand in hand the three of them walked over to Lola's seat overlooking the vineyards. Ellen clambered up onto her father's knee, waiting, as if she knew something important was happening. Glenn cleared his throat. 'Ellie, we have to tell you something very sad about your mum.'

'I already know.'

'You know?'

'She's not going to get better, is she?' Her voice was very matter-of-fact.

Glenn and Bett exchanged glances. 'How did you know that?'

'I heard the ladies talking about her. They said they thought she might not have more than a few weeks to live.'

Bett took her niece's hand then. 'Ellie, do you know what that means?'

Ellen nodded. 'It means she's going to die.'

Another shared glance. Bett could see Glenn was struggling.

'And do you know what that means?'

Ellen shook her head.

Bett tried to find the right words. 'It means that this time we have with her now is very special, Ellie, because after your mum dies –' She lost her way for a moment. 'Ellie, after she dies that means we won't be able to see her any more.'

Ellen looked puzzled. 'But she doesn't go anywhere, does she? Doesn't she just stay in the bed even after she dies? And we keep on visiting her?'

'No, Ellie. It means she's going to go away from us.'

'But where is she going to go? Why can't I keep seeing her?'

Bett couldn't speak any more. It was left to Glenn to try and answer. He held Ellen tight against him, pressed his face against her hair, tried to hide his tears. 'I don't know, Ellie. I don't know.'

Anna started sleeping most of the time, so thin now there seemed almost nothing of her beneath the cotton sheet. The days revolved around the visits from the doctor and the nurses, or coaxing her to eat a spoonful or take a sip of water.

Somehow, around all this, the motel kept running. Geraldine and Jim worked like automatons, spending every spare moment with

Anna. Guests were dealt with efficiently, briskly, checked in and checked out in record time. Lola spent hours in Anna's room, reading snatches of poetry, arranging tiny bouquets of autumn leaves, late flowers, or coloured pieces of silk for Anna to look at. Richard read to her, or just sat with her. Glenn kept close to Ellen. Carrie started to show her pregnancy but didn't mention the nausea, or the tiredness, her own discomfort nothing compared to Anna's. Ellen moved from confusion to understanding, then back to confusion. Bett cleaned the motel rooms in the morning, spent all afternoon with Anna, then waitressed in the evening, a forced smile fixed on her face. Daniel called by every day, but they had stopped going for their walks. She needed to stay close to her sister.

They all took turns sitting with her, watching her sleep, the sound of her breathing more ragged each day, the effort of getting air into her lungs racking her body. She spoke rarely, but her eyes were bright, her smile still her own.

Four weeks after Anna had come home from the hospital, Bett was woken by a knocking at her door. She hadn't been in bed long. All of them had been around Anna's bed until after midnight, talking a little, praying a little, mostly just quiet in their own thoughts. They were now keeping a vigil at her bedside. Bett was due to be back with her in just three hours' time.

At first she confused the sound of the knocking with the sound of the rain that had been pelting down on the roof when she had gone to bed. It had been wet for five days running. Then she heard a voice and was out of bed before Lola opened her door. She knew by the expression on her grandmother's face before Lola had a chance to tell her.

Anna was dead.

CHAPTER THIRTY-ONE

ANNA'S FUNERAL took place on a perfect autumn day. The sky was blue. The air was crisp and clear. The rows of vines around the church and the cemetery were vivid reds, browns and oranges.

They all dressed up. Lola, Carrie, Geraldine and Bett put on makeup, did their hair, getting ready quietly and calmly, moving from room to room at the motel. The men shaved carefully, polished their shoes, wore good suits. Ellen wore her favourite clothes, the pink dress and matching hat she had worn the night of Lola's party.

They took up the entire front pew of the church. Lola. Jim. Geraldine. Bett. Daniel. Carrie. Matthew. Glenn. Ellen. Richard. There wasn't quite enough room, but they couldn't be separated, needing the touch of another each time they sat down. Ellen had hardly let go of her father's hand since Anna had died.

Several feet away from them, in the middle of the aisle, was Anna's coffin.

The church was crowded. The service was simple, the readings and music beautiful. Lola had produced a sheet of paper the day after Anna died. It was a list of the songs she wanted played, the readings she loved. She had dictated it to her grandmother several weeks before.

They had all been sitting around the kitchen table in the motel when Lola had shown it to them. Numb with shock, Carrie and Bett had found it irrationally funny, nearly falling into each other's arms in hysterics, a raw mixture of laughter and tears. 'She's still telling us what to do? Even now?'

After the funeral mass, after the time in the cemetery, everyone came back to the motel.

'I'm so sorry.' 'We're so sorry for you all.' 'Please accept our sympathies.'

The mood was dull, subdued. There was talk, but not a great deal. Cups of tea. Sandwiches. Bett felt removed from everything. She kept expecting to turn and see Anna in a corner of the room. The old Anna, not sick Anna. She kept expecting to see that glossy dark hair, that tall, straight back. She wanted to hear her voice.

She saw her father in the corner. He was pouring tea, his head bent low to hear what an elderly lady was saying to him. He looked ten years older. Her mother was on the other side of the room. Her face was like a mask. Carrie was standing with Matthew. He had his arm tightly across her back. Richard was in a corner, in conversation with the local priest. He seemed dazed, as though he wasn't taking any of it in. Glenn was holding Ellen, so tightly it was as if he never wanted to let her go.

'Bett?'

She turned. It was Daniel. 'Is there anything I can do?'

In that moment it seemed to hit her. There was nothing he could do. There was nothing anyone could do. He opened his arms and she moved soundlessly into them.

Glenn and Ellen left a week later. The departure was heartbreaking for all of them. Ellen kept going to Anna's room, as if expecting her to be there. An hour before they were due to leave, she disappeared. It took them nearly thirty minutes to find her. Bett reached her first. Ellen was tucked up behind the shed at the back of the motel, holding tightly to Bumper by his lead.

'Ellie, you need to go, sweetheart. Daddy's nearly ready.'

Ellen wouldn't look at her. 'I don't want to. I want to stay here.'

'You can come back here whenever you like.'

'I want to be here now.'

Glenn came up behind her and took in the situation. He got down to Ellen's level. 'Ellie, I promise you can come back very soon. I want you to come home with me for a while first, though. I need your help.'

She shook her head.

Bett realised this was a moment for father and daughter. She silently slipped away, back to where Lola and her parents and Carrie and Matthew were waiting. There was still the jolt at Anna's absence. The gap where she should be. The terrible reality of all of them gathered without her.

Ten minutes later Glenn and Ellen came towards them, hand in hand. Ellen was subdued. She said goodbye to each of them very solemnly, hugging them around the neck. Each one of them had the same farewell message. 'See you soon.' 'We'll see you soon, Ellie.'

Then each of them hugged Glenn goodbye as well.

Richard left three days later. Bett had gone for a drink with him the evening before. He was as sad these days as they were.

He was going back to London again. For a few months anyway. He'd been offered work at his old newspaper. 'I'll be back, I hope. In a while. I just can't seem to finish anything here at the moment.'

'Will you keep in touch with us?'

'If you'd like me to.'

'We'd like it very much.'

They all hugged him goodbye as well.

Carrie and Matthew came for dinner at the motel most nights. They were trying to fix up one of the rooms of their house as a nursery, but Carrie was finding it very difficult. 'I'm so scared something will happen to the baby, that it's bad luck. I keep thinking about everyone dying. We'll have to go through this again and again, with Lola, with Mum and Dad, with you, with . . .' She was crying. 'I want her back, Bett.'

'I want her here so she can tell me off. I wouldn't even mind if she yelled at me for a week.'

There was a kind of laughter those nights, but it was fragile, like glass.

Two weeks after Anna died, a videotape arrived addressed to Lola from Richard's friend Charlie Wentworth. It was the complete version of the program he had been making, as well as all the rough footage he had shot the day he was in the Clare Valley with them.

He had enclosed a note. Richard had told him about Anna. He explained that the program had gone to air in the UK and Ireland a fortnight before, but that he thought they might like the extra footage just as much. 'I am thinking of you all at this time of great sadness,' he'd signed.

They watched it together, on the video in Lola's room, in virtual silence. Another time the scenes would have caused much hilarity. They would have set the video up on the bar TV, ordered drinks for everyone, watched the tape over and over, laughing at everyone's expressions. Not this time.

The segment about General MacArthur's visit to Terowie took up just a few minutes of the program. There were shots of the MacArthur plaque at Terowie Railway Station, then a shot of the Valley View Motel, followed by Lola sweeping in and pretending to work at her desk. The voice-over explained she had emigrated from Ireland sixty years previously and considered this musical her life's work. There were several scenes from the musical itself. It was fun, snappy.

The extra footage Charlie mentioned contained image after image of Anna, up on stage with Carrie and Bett, attempting to sing 'Sisters', first accompanied on stage by Matthew, then on their own. There was a kind of joyousness, laughter, a lightness between the three of them. It had taken four attempts, but they had finally got their harmonies right, standing in a row with their arms around each other, singing and laughing. The camera kept rolling afterwards, long enough to capture Anna firstly hug Bett and then Carrie, giving them flamboyant two-cheek kisses, actor-style.

It was like watching something from another century.

Bett went back to work at the newspaper three weeks after Anna's death. At first it was as if she was sick. People kept a distance from her, wary, in case she burst into tears. Only Rebecca was normal, and Daniel.

She went to his house for dinner the weekend after that. It was the first time she'd been out at night in the weeks since Anna died. She hadn't been able to go too far from any of her family. He made a simple meal of pasta and salad, opened a bottle of wine for her. Afterwards, she sat in his arms on the sofa, watching TV.

She tried to concentrate on the program, but the dialogue didn't make any sense and the people looked ridiculous, all made up, wearing glamorous clothes. As if any of that really mattered in the end.

She felt Daniel kiss the top of her head. Another kiss on the side of her face. She turned, met his lips, a soft, gentle kiss. His hand went lower, skimmed her arm, touched the side of her breast. She felt the stirring of feeling, a slow melting feeling begin and then the sadness roared in at her again. She couldn't do this. Not with Anna dead.

She sat up abruptly, and moved away from him. 'I'm sorry, Daniel, but I can't.'

'It's okay, Bett.'

It wasn't okay. 'I'm sorry. It's not you, I promise. It's me.'

'Bett, it's fine. I understand.'

It suddenly seemed urgent to explain it to him. To tell him exactly how she felt. 'I need you to know that I love it with you. I love being with you.' She meant every word. She did love him. 'It's just –' she was struggling now, 'something is different at the moment. Lola keeps telling me it will get better eventually, that it won't always hurt as much as this. But I'll understand if you can't wait. If you want to stop seeing me.'

'Bett, please, come here. Come closer to me.' She moved and he met her halfway, holding her tightly in his arms. 'I'm not going anywhere. And I don't want you to go anywhere either.'

One night in the motel bar, Jim, Geraldine and Bett were shocked into silence by the sound of Anna's voice. It took them a moment to realise it was coming from the TV.

They sat staring at it, hearing her voice warmly extolling the virtues of a new range of baking products.

Geraldine started crying. Jim turned off the TV.

Bett went to Lola's room each night to say goodnight, to check she was okay, to make sure she had everything she needed. Lola had changed too. She seemed older. When Bett hugged her now or when she curled up beside her on the bed like now, she felt that the spirit that had driven Lola had dimmed somehow. Nothing felt quite the same.

'It hurts so much, doesn't it, Lola?'

'It does, darling.'

'Was it as bad as this for you when Edward died?'

There was a long pause. 'It was different.'

'Does it really get better?'

'You get used to it, Bett. It becomes a part of you, like everything that happens to you in life becomes a part of you.'

Lola stopped talking then, just stroked the head on the pillow beside her until Bett fell asleep.

CHAPTER THIRTY-TWO

'ENJOY YOUR stay, won't you?'

It was six weeks after Anna's death. Bett was at reception, checking in some late-night guests. Carrie had gone home for the night. Bett had handed them their room key, explained how to order breakfast, where the dining room was and the opening hours for the bar. She'd felt like a liar, a fake, the entire time, as she smiled and tried to talk normally to them. She wondered if any of the guests noticed there was something not quite right with the family in charge of this motel. Could they see that their smiles weren't real? That they seemed to move more slowly than usual? That the life had gone out of all of them?

She had never expected it to hurt this much. She'd never expected to feel grief like a physical pain. But it was. She would be walking along and she'd feel the reminder of Anna's death like a punch, a blow from nowhere. She felt exposed to the world, over-sensitive, anxious, as if she had lost several layers of protective skin. She wanted to stop complete strangers, tell them that her sister was dead. That her beautiful thirty-four-year-old sister had died and that they had been given only weeks to say goodbye to her. Her heart ached for anyone who had lost someone suddenly, in a car accident or from a heart attack. She at least had had some time to say goodbye, to tell Anna how much she loved her. How much worse would it be if they hadn't had that chance?

She hadn't ever thought it was possible to have so many tears. To wake up every day with the same feeling in her chest. But she was a different person now, Bett realised. They all were. Her parents had changed, too. They worked as hard and the motel kept running, but there was a different rhythm to their movements. The same heaviness that Bett felt in herself.

Bett closed the registration book and found the day's mail lying underneath it on the desk. She started opening it: bills, circulars and several cards in pale cream envelopes. Word of Anna's death had filtered through to her acting friends, advertisers she'd worked for in Sydney, clients, neighbours and mothers of Ellen's friends. The cards had come in a rush the first few weeks. Even now, weeks after, they were still arriving in twos and threes each day, some addressed simply to the Quinlan Family, some to her parents, some to Lola, or Carrie, or her. She opened them automatically, reading the messages, simple and heartfelt. 'We are thinking of you in your great sorrow.' 'She was a beautiful woman, we loved her and will miss her very much.'

Bett noticed the airmail sticker on the final envelope as she slit it open. There had been quite a few cards from Anna's overseas friends, actors working in Los Angeles or New York, or in different parts of Europe. This one had an Irish postmark. She opened the card and read the message. Then she sat down and read it one more time, trying to make sense of it.

Dear Lola,

I write this tentatively, hoping that you are the same Lola Quinlan, originally from Leixcraig House, Kildare, Ireland, whom I knew more than sixty years ago.

I saw a program called 'Did You Know?' on the Discovery channel last week, featuring you and a musical you had written on General MacArthur. Would you be the same woman who married my brother Edward and then emigrated to Australia with him just before the war?

I am sad to write that Edward died five years ago, leaving behind no family. After he left Australia he continued to travel, spending some years in America, before returning to Ireland and the family home in Kildare. He died at home, aged 78. May he rest in peace.

Edward never explained the whole story of your separation but I wish you no ill will, Lola. If you find it in yourself to contact me, I would be pleased to hear from you.

> *Yours truly,*
> *Margaret Hegarty (née Quinlan)*

Bett walked as if she was in a dream, through the motel, out to the yard, along the row of rooms until she reached Lola's door. She knocked once, twice. A soft voice called her in.

Lola was at her writing desk. 'Bett? More cards? People are very kind.'

Bett couldn't speak.

Lola was puzzled. 'Bett? Are you all right?'

She handed the letter over to Lola without a word. She watched as Lola started to read, watched Lola's hand creep up to her neck. Heard as if from a long way away Lola say softly, 'Oh, dear God.'

Bett found her voice. 'So Edward didn't die during the war.'

Lola looked up. Her hand was still at her neck. 'No, Bett, he didn't.'

Bett wasn't angry or upset. Not yet. She just needed to understand. 'So who was Dad's father?'

'It was Edward. He just didn't know that I was pregnant when I left him.'

'You left him?'

'I had to. If I had stayed with him I –'

'You would have given Dad a father.' Bett was stunned. Confused. 'Lola, I don't understand. We had a grandfather all this time, and we didn't meet him. He didn't meet us. Me, or Carrie, or –' her voice faltered, 'or Anna or Ellen.'

'I'm sorry, Bett.'

'Sorry for what? For leaving him? Or for not telling us the truth?'

'Only for not telling the truth. I couldn't stay with him. He was not a good man. We shouldn't ever have been together. And I didn't realise it until too late. Until we were married and here in Australia.'

'But why the lies? Why say he was dead? Why not say you had left him?'

'Because this was the 1940s, Bett. Because a month after I left him I discovered I was pregnant with your father. I was a young woman in a new country at wartime. What choice did I have? It was better if people thought I was a tragic widow. A widow was respectable.'

'But I can't understand why you didn't ever tell us the truth.'

'How could I? Tell Jim that the father he thought was long dead was in fact very much alive? And then what? Try to find him? Trawl every bar in the country? The truth is, Bett, I didn't ever want to see him again. I didn't know what would happen if he found out he had a son and I didn't want him to find out. He hit me once, one night

435

he returned from a drinking binge, and that was enough for me. I didn't want his family or mine getting their hands on Jim.'

Bett took back the letter, trying to make sense of everything she was hearing. She read the address. 'She's writing from Kildare. Is that where Edward was from? Where you were from?'

Lola nodded.

'That day I went to take photos. You sent me to completely the wrong place, didn't you? Not just the wrong house, but the wrong side of the country.'

Lola was very calm. 'I had to.'

'Why? Because you thought I'd find out the truth? Find him?'

'I panicked, I admit it. I was worried that you would go to the right house and possibly even find Edward living there. And I didn't want you to have that shock. You might never have come back home, then.' Lola glanced down at the letter again. 'But it seems he was dead by then. You wouldn't have met him then either.'

'This will devastate Dad, you know that.'

'Only if he finds out.'

'You're not going to tell him? Show him that letter?'

'No. There's no point now. What he knows is enough. It was my decision years ago and it's one I've stuck with, even if it has been difficult.'

'But how can I keep a secret like that from my own father? From Mum? And Carrie? Ellen? Don't you see they have to know?'

'No, I don't.'

'You'd let the lie continue? You, who spent your entire life telling us to face our fears and tell the truth?'

'This is different.'

'No, it's not. Lola, can't you see this changes everything? It's like everything you've ever told us has been a lie.'

'It changes nothing, Bett. I am the same person, you are the same person, all the things we have ever done or said to each other are the same.'

Bett stared at her. 'I think you're wrong. This changes everything.'

She left the room, shutting the door behind her. She ignored Lola's call to come back.

Bett returned to the reception desk. She updated the booking register. Set out the last of the breakfast trays. She sent her parents to bed, and closed down the rest of the motel herself, switching off the lights one after the other.

She walked across the carpark to her room, pausing for a moment to look up at the clear sky, the Milky Way and the Southern Cross easily visible. She opened the door quietly and then nearly leapt out of her skin as she saw Lola, sitting in the armchair in the middle of the room.

'You won't do this to me, Bett. I won't have it.'

Bett was speechless.

'I won't have you walk out on me like that, or ignore me, or stop talking to me because of this. Do you hear me?'

Bett had never seen Lola so angry. 'I'm not ignoring you. I'm trying to take it all in. I can't hear something like that, and just let it wash over me.'

'Of course you can. That's exactly what you have to do with it. With any news. Let it wash over you, let it soak into you, and then get on with it. Nothing has changed, Bett. I still want you to face your fears and tell the truth. Even if your fear is that the family is ruined and that you hate and despise me forever. But at least you would have been courageous enough to say it.'

'I was trying to work out what I thought about it.'

'So tell me now. How do you feel?'

Lola didn't need to mention a truth stick. Bett could feel it being pointed at her without being told. 'I'm shocked.'

'Why?'

'Because I discovered my grandfather was alive all the time I thought he was dead.'

'Yes, that would be a shock. What else?'

Bett hesitated. 'I'm disappointed.'

'Why?'

'Because the grandmother I idolised for years was lying to me for years.'

'A little melodramatic, perhaps, but all right, accepted. What else?'

'I'm sad, Lola.' The truth burst out of her. 'Sad, sad, sad. And I can't take any more of it. Any more bad things. Any more shocks.'

'Yes, you can. And you'll take a lot more before you're dead yourself. There'll be more deaths, more disappointments, more people will let you down.'

'I can't, Lola. I can't take any more hurt.'

'You can and you will. Because there won't just be hurt, Bett. There'll be great happiness and moments of joy and lighthearted-ness and pleasure. Because that's what life is like. Multicoloured, not black and white. Stop judging people. Stop judging me. Step outside of yourself for one moment and think why I would have done what I did. Why I chose not to tell you.'

'I don't know.'

'Then try harder.' A long pause. 'Perhaps I was wrong. But I thought I was right. I had to believe I was right, to go on. There was a time, when your father was small, when things were very hard, when it would have been easier to go back to Edward, to Ireland, to take that life, take back the security. But I couldn't do it. I wanted more, for me, for Jim, for my life. I wanted freedom and I wanted adventure and I wanted a life. I was trapped in my family, Bett. You can't know how that feels, having all the freedom that you and your sisters had. I had none of that. It was rules and regulations and expectations and it was suffocating me. And marrying Edward and going to Australia seemed like a lifeline. But I knew within weeks that I'd made an even bigger mistake. He wasn't what I thought he was. I wasn't what he thought I was.'

'I can understand that. What I can't understand is why you didn't tell us the truth.'

'I've wanted to. For years. But there just never seemed the right time. I wasn't sure who to tell. Even how to tell it. And these were lies out of necessity, not out of malice, or trickery. There is a difference. And the lies became real to me. I began to think of Edward as dead. Began to think fondly of him in a certain way. Because when life puts you in those situations you have to go on, you have to make something of yourself. I started living life pretending I was a brave young widow and so I had to become a brave young widow.'

'But it wasn't true.'

'No, it wasn't. And I can't force you to forgive me. But I can ask you to use your imagination, the imagination I have done my best to feed over the years. I want you to imagine yourself in my place, to see how it might have been for me. You know me. And I know you. Don't disappoint me.'

'You've disappointed me.'

'No. What I've done is show you one more bit of truth about me. And that is something you would rather not see. In fact, you've disappointed me.'

'What?'

'I would prefer you were the perfect understanding granddaughter just as you would prefer me to be the perfect faultless grandmother. But I'm not perfect. I never have been. I never will be.'

'You were perfect. You were the most wonderful grandmother.' Bett started to cry. 'You still are the most wonderful grandmother.' She found herself in Lola's arms. 'I'm sorry, I'm so sorry. It was your life. You had to do what you had to do. Of course I know that. But it's one more hurt, Lola. One more person gone, one more thing changing.'

'You wouldn't have liked him.'

'That's not the point. I might have liked him.'

'Really, you wouldn't have.'

Bett was suddenly crying and laughing. 'But I wanted the choice.'

'We don't always get a choice. We don't always get what we want. I wanted a good husband, not an awful drunken old bully. I wanted lots of things I didn't get.' She held Bett close. 'I also got things that I never wanted or expected.'

'Like Anna dying.'

'Anna dying. But also the life I've had with all of you. Because the real truth is that I have never loved anyone in my life like I love your father and the three of you, and now Ellen too. And if I had to do it all over again to give you a better life, I would. Do you understand that? Because you have all been the most wonderful thing that ever came to me. More than I ever imagined I would have. We don't get a list that we can tick off, Bett. I've learned that. Some things we can make happen, other things happen to us, other things surprise us, other things sneak up. We just have to keep going, whatever happens.'

'I can't. I just hurt too much.'

'It will all become a part of you. I promise you that. This news. Even Anna's death. You might think I am just a mad old woman, but I've seen a few things in my day.'

'I just want her back, Lola.'

'We all want her back, darling. All of us.'

Bett cried then as if it was the first time since Anna died, until her body hurt from it. Lola held her tight until it passed, until Bett's breathing calmed, the shaking stopped. She spoke again, her head buried against Lola's chest, her face wet with tears. 'I'm so sorry, Lola.'

'It's all right.' She kissed Bett's forehead, tucked a lock of hair behind one of her ears.

'I would never have stopped talking to you.'

'I know. I wouldn't have let you.'

'And I won't tell Dad or Mum or Carrie. It's not for me to tell them any of this.'

'You can if you want to. It's up to you. I can't stop you.'

'What good would it do?' Bett hesitated. 'Are you going to write back to Edward's sister?'

Lola shook her head. 'There's no point. I think it's best that I don't.'

'But is it wrong for me to have a secret from the rest of my family? That you and I know, and the others don't?'

'A family without secrets is a very boring family. And I don't think we want to be a boring family, do we?'

Bett shook her head.

'Come here to me.' She took Bett's face between her two hands. 'I'm sorry I hurt you, too. Because you are very precious to me. I want you to know that. And I'm glad you know. I'm glad it's you who found out.'

Bett mirrored the action, her hands against Lola's soft, powdered skin. 'I'm glad it was me, too.' She stared at the older woman's face, the blush, the lipstick. 'But you've been very bold, you know that.'

'Very bold, yes. But what else am I?'

'You're my darling.'

'That's right. Now go to bed, Bett.'

'No.'

'You're disobeying me?'

'Yes. I want you to talk to me about it. I want to hear everything. About what it was like for you. How you found the first guesthouse to manage.'

'It was an ad in the newspaper.'

'How you managed to buy that first one.'

'I saved. I saved and scrimped until I had enough.'

'And were you ever frightened? Did you ever think you'd done the wrong thing?'

'Many times. I cried myself to sleep many nights. But I kept telling myself that it could only get better. That it was better than what I'd had before. And that I would get through, for Jim's sake and for my sake too.'

'But even though you were scared and it was hard and there were bad times, it worked out in the end for you, didn't it?'

'In most ways, yes.'

'I need to hear that, Lola. I need to hear that things can be bad but they can also get better.'

'I promise you.'

'You never saw your parents again, did you?'

'I didn't, no. I wrote for a while but then it got harder to make it up, to explain why I never mentioned Edward. So I wrote less often, until –'

'You lost contact.'

'It wasn't unusual in those days. Letters took a long time to arrive. People didn't expect to see their sons or daughters again after they went to Australia.'

'Did you miss them?'

'To begin with. But things were different back then. We didn't expect to be close to our parents.' They exchanged a look.

Bett sat on the bed beside Lola's armchair, picked up her hand and started turning the ring. 'This isn't from Edward, either, is it?'

'No. I bought it for myself.'

'I want to hear where. I want to know why you bought that particular one.'

'Why do you want to know all that?'

'I just do. I want to hear all your stories. The real ones.'

Lola smiled. 'You sounded just like your niece then, do you know that? Can I get my gin and tonic first?'

'Will you get me one as well?'

'At last. A drinking partner. I've been waiting for the day. Would you like ice? Lemon?'

'Yes, please.'

Lola was nearly at the door when she turned. 'It's going to be a long night, isn't it?'

'I hope so,' Bett said.

'Shall I fetch the whole bottle?'

Bett smiled at her grandmother. 'I think you may as well.'

443

Epilogue

ANNA'S GRAVE was on the high side of the cemetery, overlooking a sweep of vineyards curving in lines along the contours of the hills, tracing the edge of the dam. It was a cool, crisp May day, the sky blue and grey, the air fresh. They parked their cars at the bottom of the hill, walked up past the other graves, gravel and fallen gum leaves crunching under their feet. They had been preparing for two days, working from the detailed list. Everything they needed was now packed neatly into two baskets.

Glenn, Matthew and Jim carried the chairs, arranging them around the gravestone, looking out over the hills. Geraldine and Bett laid the fold-up table with a linen tablecloth, champagne glasses and the plates of food. 'And orange juice for Ellen. Did we bring the orange juice?'

Ellen held it up. 'It's here, Lola.'

'Good girl.'

Once everything was organised, Lola stood up. 'Now, we have to do exactly as she says. Just a moment, I can't read my own writing. Oh, well done, Anna. What a perfect way to begin.' Leaning on her stick, she started reading aloud from a piece of paper, written in her own hand. Anna had dictated the words to her three weeks before she died.

'"First of all, pour champagne and orange juice and drink a toast to each other and to me." The champagne is a gift from Richard, by the way. The finest French, he told me.' Richard wrote to Lola every month or so. He was still at the newspaper in London, but he'd started working on the novel again, he'd told her. Lola shook her head, laughing softly. 'Do you know Anna even dictated stage directions? "You are all to lift your glasses into the air – joyfully." Not too joyfully, everyone, or you'll spill it.'

Anna had left exact instructions on how they were to mark the first anniversary of her death. Carrie had laughed as she read through it several days before. It was like a mini play, filled with stage directions, a cast list ('my family'), what props they'd need, and the setting: her graveside at lunchtime.

'Is this joyful?' Ellen asked, moving her glass of juice vigorously from side to side.

'I'd say that's more enthusiastic than joyful,' Bett said, stepping out of the way as drops of juice flew through the air. 'Slow it down a little. That's it, Ellie, perfect.' She turned in time to see Carrie juggling her baby daughter on one hip, a bottle in one hand, a glass in the other. 'Carrie, are you okay there? Do you want me to take her?'

She pulled a face. 'Would you, Bett? Just for a second? Until I grow another arm?'

Bett took her five-month-old niece, moving her head back as a little hand made a grab for one of her earrings. She'd been christened Delia Anna three months earlier. 'Her name had to start with the letter D, didn't it?' Carrie had said. 'We had A for Anna, B for Bett, C for Carrie and then a jump to E for Ellen. This way she's a bridge between us. She joins us all up again.'

'Ready, everyone? You all have your glasses?' Lola called out the toast. 'To us and to Anna.'

'To us and to Anna,' they echoed. The clinking of glasses was loud in the clear air.

'And now to the food,' Lola said gloomily. They all stared down at the array of dishes on the table. No one moved.

'It's a bit hard to know where to start, isn't it?' Jim said.

'I just wish I hadn't been pregnant when Anna asked me what my favourite food was,' Carrie said, looking balefully at her plate piled high with sardines.

'I certainly wouldn't have said mashed potatoes if I'd known what she was up to,' Geraldine said, looking just as bleakly at the large bowl. 'Bett, will you share your chocolate pudding?'

'Only when you've finished your potatoes. You know the rules, Mum. No dessert until your plate is clean.'

Jim squeezed Geraldine's hand. 'You can have some of my cake, love.'

Glenn took a tiny spoonful of Beluga caviar and said nothing. Ellen was also perfectly happy with her plate of donuts. Matthew was already halfway through his ham and pineapple pizza.

'Are we allowed to top up the glasses, Lola?' Glenn asked. Lola checked Anna's instructions. 'She didn't say, but as the matriarch, I'll make the decision. Of course you can. Have as much as you like.'

'Will I give Mum a glass of champagne?' Ellen asked. 'She liked champagne, Dad, didn't she?'

'She sure did.' He poured a glass and they watched as Ellen balanced it on the gravestone.

'I was talking to her last night,' Ellen said as she came back and settled herself on her father's knee. 'I asked her how things were and told her about the flight from Singapore and how Dad and I are going to Disneyland next week.'

'And did she say anything back?' Bett asked, keeping her tone light.

Ellen gave her a pitying look. 'No, of course not. I say her bits for her. Like when we do plays at school, and I play more than one part. So I told Mum that we were going to Disneyland and she said, "That's wonderful, Ellen."' Ellen lowered her voice and for a minute sounded very like Anna. '"Have lots of fun, won't you? But don't eat too much ice-cream before you go on the rides or you'll be sick."'

Lola peered up into the sky. The blue was nearly gone, darker clouds coming in their direction. 'I think we should move on to the entertainment section of the afternoon. You've all been rehearsing, I hope? Bett, we'll start with you.'

Bett stood up and took a sheet of lyrics from her bag, remembering the moment she had unknowingly chosen her song. She had been sitting beside Anna's bed, answering her soft-voiced questions about her days in London, when, midway, Anna had stopped her and said, 'Name a song, Bett, quick. The first one that comes to mind.'

'"London Calling" by The Clash,' Bett had answered, surprised. 'Why?'

'Just wondering. Go on, you were telling me about your boss Karl and the punk bands . . .'

Bett finished her song and took a bow. Carrie was next, with a stirring version of U2's 'I Still Haven't Found What I'm Looking For'. Anna had asked her to name a song while she was searching through the pile of magazines on Anna's bedside. Ellen sang 'Don't Sit Under the Apple Tree'. Lola, Bett and Carrie joined in on the chorus. Geraldine followed her with 'Sadie the Cleaning Lady'. She'd been washing the windows in Anna's room. Glenn had been at the airport when Anna phoned and asked him. He did a very enthusiastic version of 'Leaving on a Jet Plane'. They all laughed as Jim sang 'Bob the Builder'. He had been looking out at the house being built on the hill opposite the motel when Anna asked him. Lola sang 'Lola' – she and Anna had been reminiscing about the eightieth birthday party. Matthew sang 'Baa Baa Black Sheep', doing his best through everyone's teasing. 'I'd just come from work when I visited her. What did you expect me to say? Nellie the Elephant?'

Lola applauded. 'Beautiful, everyone. You should be proud of yourselves. And now, another message for all of us.' She unfolded the last piece of paper and started reading, her voice strong and clear in the afternoon air.

To my darling family,

If it is possible for me to be watching you today, I promise you I will be. If you notice some champagne missing from your glasses, that will be me who has taken it, too. This note won't be the Gettysburg Address, and I can't think of anything as memorable as General MacArthur's 'I shall return'. All I want to say is that I love you all very much, and thank you for all you did for me and for my beautiful Ellen, during my life. I have been very, very lucky. Thank you for being so obedient today and don't worry, I'm not going to make you come back here year after year. It's up to each of you how you remember me from now on, but please keep eating your favourite things, drinking champagne, talking to each other and singing good and bad songs, even if I'm not there to boss you around.

With all my love,
Anna

Lola held up her glass. 'Another toast, I think. Just to Anna.'

'Just to Anna,' they all echoed.

Everything was packed up into the baskets again and the chairs folded by the time the first spatters of rain started falling. Geraldine, Jim, Glenn, Carrie and Matthew walked ahead, Delia in Matthew's arms. Behind them, a little more slowly, came Lola, Bett and Ellen.

'I miss my mum every single day,' Ellen said.

Bett squeezed her hand. 'I do too, Ellie.'

They reached the bottom of the hill and started walking to the wrought-iron gate at the entrance.

'What would Mum have done if we hadn't been obedient today?' Ellen asked as they reached it.

'Haunt us, probably,' Lola said.

'What's haunt?'

'It's when someone keeps appearing all the time to keep an eye on you, making sure you're okay,' Lola explained.

'Like Daniel does with Bett, you mean?' Ellen said.

Lola smiled at Bett. 'A bit like that.'

Arm in arm, the three of them walked back to the carpark where Daniel was waiting for them.

One year later

Bett looked up as the screen door snapped shut. 'Is everything all right?'

'It's fine,' Daniel said. 'She just rang to say they're running a bit late. Mum's insisting on wearing something pink, apparently, and

Christine said she couldn't decide between the dark pink or the light pink. They'll be here soon, though.'

'That's great. There's no rush, anyway.' It wasn't a formal lunch, just a barbecue and some salads. Everything was ready to go, the barbecue coals heating, the table already set in the garden. They'd been lucky with the weather, blue and clear, with no sign of the rain they'd had the previous year. It was just as well. It would have been very crowded in their small living room. Bett checked the time. There was still an hour before Ellen was going to ring from Singapore. Everyone was sure to be there by then. Bett had promised Ellen, and Glenn, that she would be able to say hello to them all, even if she wasn't with them on the actual date of Anna's second anniversary.

Two years on, Bett had realised that it wasn't the date that made them think of Anna, in any case. Thoughts of her flowed freely between all of them, no matter where they were or when it was. There were memories and conversations that made them sad, memories that made them laugh. It helped them all when Ellen came to stay, or when they went to visit her and Glenn in Singapore. Ellen was so like Anna physically it still surprised them to see her each time, yet they could see her own personality getting stronger. Sometimes they would share their thoughts of Anna with her or with each other. Other times the memories were more personal, private. It was as Lola had said. Anna's life and Anna's death had become a part of them all.

Bett shifted up a little so Daniel could sit on the high-backed swing seat beside her. They both put their feet up on the verandah rail. Daniel went back to the book he'd been reading when the phone had rung. She returned to the last few pages of hers.

They had moved into this house together nearly a year before.

It was a stone cottage in the hills behind the motel, right on the northern edge of Clare. The town was on one side, gum trees, bare paddocks and vineyards on the other. The intention had been to renovate the house themselves, but they'd been rapidly losing interest. Reading was much more fun than scraping paint, they'd discovered.

'Bett?'

'Mmm.'

'What about Fred?'

Bett gave it some thought. 'No, I don't think so.'

'Florence?'

'No.'

'Flossy?'

'If we have a pony instead of a baby, sure.' She turned. 'Daniel, the name doesn't really have to start with an F.'

'Yes, it does. I love the idea of it.' He put down the battered copy of *1001 Names for Your Baby*. 'And we have to get in quick, before Carrie and Matthew have another one, and we get stuck with G.'

Bett laughed. 'Can we get the wedding out of the way before we worry about the baby's name? I'm not even pregnant.'

'Not for want of trying. Have we got a few minutes now to give it another go, before the others arrive?'

'No, we haven't. Anyway, what if we can't have children?'

'Then we'll get lots of pets and treat them like our children.'

She smiled and went back to her book. She was on the second to last page when he spoke again.

'Bett, how do you feel about having eleven children? Or eleven pets?'

'Pardon?'

'I've just worked it out mathematically. If you and Carrie

spend the next eleven years having a baby a year, you and I will end up with Z. Isn't that great? I've always liked the name Zelda, or Zephaniah if it's a boy. Or we could try for quadruplets. That would speed it up a bit. But maybe that's asking a bit much. What about going as far as Yvonne?'

'That's a lovely offer, Dan, but no, I don't think so.' Bett stood up as Carrie and Matthew's car turned off the main road and started up the dirt road to their cottage. She could already see Lola waving majestically from the back seat. Not far behind them she saw her parents' car.

Daniel stood beside her, his arm across her back. He leaned down and brushed his lips against her ear. 'Xanthes?'

She shook her head.

He lowered his voice even more. 'Wilhelmina?'

She started to laugh. 'No, Dan.'

'Violet? Ursula? Thomasina? Please, Bett, can't we have a Thomasina? You'd grow to love her, I know you would. And Saxon. And Rhiannon. As for Quincy, and Peony . . .'

She turned in his arms. 'All this time we've known each other and I never realised you knew your alphabet backwards.'

'I can juggle a bit too. I could teach the children. We could go on the road, pick up where the Alphabet Sisters left off. All of us juggling together. Little Olaf, and Nero and Magenta. Leopold. Klaus . . .'

Carrie and Matthew's car came to a halt at the end of their garden.

Bett looked up at Daniel and smiled. 'Have you finished?'

'Nearly,' he said, a sparkle in his eye. 'Jefferson. Indigo . . .'

She was laughing again as she walked down the steps to greet her family.

Visit **www.panmacmillan.com** to read more about all our books and to buy them. You will also find features, author interviews and news of any author events, and you can sign up for e-newsletters so that you're always first to hear about our new releases.

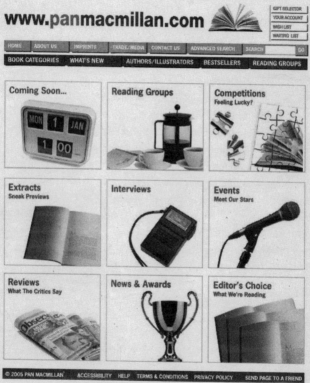